D0349932

Churchill County Library
553 S. Main Street
Fallon, Nevada 89406
(775) 423-7581

OCT 12

City

of

Saints

Also by Andrew Hunt

The Turning: A History of Vietnam Veterans Against the War

*David Dellinger: The Life and Times of a
Nonviolent Revolutionary*

The 1980s (coauthor)

City

of

Saints

Andrew Hunt

Minotaur Books

A Thomas Dunne Book
New York

This is a work of fiction. All of the characters, organizations, and events portrayed in this novel are either products of the author's imagination or are used fictitiously.

A THOMAS DUNNE BOOK FOR MINOTAUR BOOKS.
An imprint of St. Martin's Publishing Group.

CITY OF SAINTS. Copyright © 2012 by Andrew Hunt. All rights reserved. Printed in the United States of America. For information, address St. Martin's Press, 175 Fifth Avenue, New York, N.Y. 10010.

www.thomasdunnebooks.com
www.minotaurbooks.com

Library of Congress Cataloging-in-Publication Data

Hunt, Andrew E., 1968–
    City of saints / Andrew Hunt.—1st ed.
      p. cm.
    "A Thomas Dunne Book."
    ISBN 978-1-250-01579-2 (hardcover)
    ISBN 978-1-250-01580-8 (e-book)
    1. Socialites—Crimes against—Fiction.   2. Corruption—Fiction.
3. Murder—Investigation—Fiction.   4. Salt Lake City (Utah)—Fiction.
I. Title.
    PR9199.4.H858C58 2012
    813'.6—dc22

2012030078

First Edition: November 2012

10 9 8 7 6 5 4 3 2 1

For my parents.
And for my brother.

Acknowledgments

I owe a lot of people thanks for this book.

I would like to thank my agent, Steve Ross, at Abrams Artist Agency. What a rewarding experience it has been to get to know Steve over the past many months. He has been a tireless advocate, a quick responder to e-mails (often getting back to me before I even hit the send button), and a reassuring voice of support and sage advice through this process.

I reserve a special thank-you for Peter Joseph at St. Martin's Press. From the day in October 2011 that Peter e-mailed me to let me know *City of Saints* won the Tony Hillerman Prize, working with him has been one of the most rewarding experiences I've ever had. He walked me through several edits of the book with a level of skill, kindness, patience, and intelligence that left me inspired to keep improving the finished product. I will forever be grateful for his meticulous eye for detail, superb editing suggestions, and for simply believing in this book.

Thank you to everyone at St. Martin's Press, especially to India Cooper, who invested a level of care of professionalism in the copy editing of this book that deeply touched me, and to Margaret Sutherland Brown, who was always extremely helpful in assisting in the different stages of preparing the manuscript for publication.

Thank you to E. L. Doctorow and Mary Louise Oates for convincing a confused teenager back in the 1980s that he could pull it off. Thank you to Michael Miner, the best writing mentor I've ever had, for those unforgettable days in Vancouver at the Praxis Screenwriting Centre, when he taught me how to tell a good story.

Thank you to Anne Hillerman, Don Strel, and Jean Schaumberg for a great weekend in Santa Fe and for keeping the beautiful spirit of Tony Hillerman alive.

Thank you to my family. Madeline and Aidan: You're the best daughter and son a father could ever ask for. Thank you for putting up with my many shortcomings and for bringing so much joy and love to my life. Luisa: Words cannot express how fortunate I am to have you for a companion. Our long walks and wonderful vegan meals, our laughter, and our many magical moments together, sustained me from page one to the very end of the novel.

Ruth and Tony: You have both enriched my life greatly and I'm proud to call you family. You will both always have a place in my home and my heart.

Finally, this book is dedicated to my parents, Emery Kay Hunt and Linda Hunt, and my brother Jeff. I love each of you with all my heart. I know I live far away, but your love reaches across the vast distances and always reminds me that my home is with you, in Utah.

This was the country the Mormons settled, the country which, as Brigham Young with some reason hoped, no one else wanted. Its destiny was plain on its face, its contempt of man and his history and his theological immortality, his Millennium, his Heaven on Earth, was monumentally obvious. Its distances were terrifying, its cloudbursts catastrophic, its beauty flamboyant and bizarre and allied with death.

—WALLACE STEGNER

City

of

Saints

One

"It is enough. This is the right place."

Brigham Young uttered those words when his wagon reached the mouth of Emigration Canyon and he gazed out at this valley. That was almost eighty-three years ago. July 24, 1847. We celebrate that date in Utah—Pioneer Day—with picnics, fireworks shipped in from China, and, to the extent that it can be called "revelry," revelry. On this bitter cold winter's morning, at half past seven, I stood on the opposite side of the valley and to the south of the vantage point the prophet enjoyed all those years ago. Maybe "enjoy" is the wrong word. When he first laid eyes on the Salt Lake Valley, Young was recovering from a bout of Rocky Mountain spotted fever, or—as doctors now call it—tick typhus.

Closing my eyes to the icy wind cutting my face, I pictured Young, wasting away in the back of his covered wagon, arms and face splotched with rashes, plagued by headaches and muscle pain. If he came out of that canyon now, on this cold February morning in 1930, he'd see a different place than he saw in '47: a city with wide roads, clanging streetcar bells, ten-story buildings, and a huge granite temple with a gold-plated angel on top, blowing his horn triumphantly.

That's the north side of town. Out here, where I stood in snow up to my shins, the valley hadn't changed much since the prophet's arrival. Meadows everywhere, with a farm here and there, but mostly these were unused fields, home to clusters of box elders and pines. Deputy Lund and I drove to this spot following an early-morning call to my home from the weekend dispatcher. I asked her to contact the coroner before heading out. It had snowed the night before, so our Model A county car struggled to get out here.

The gangly deputy pacing in the snowy clearing—auburn hair, high cheekbones, long neck—that was me, dressed in regulation cream felt Stetson, leather jacket with green deputy's shirt underneath, khakis, and black patent leather shoes that do a bad job of keeping snow out.

My confusion came from being green. I had been doing this a mere eight months up till that morning. Despite that, dead bodies were nothing new to me. I had encountered my share since starting this job. I had hauled corpses out of collapsed mines, dislodged them from the interior of crunched automobiles, and served as a stretcher-bearer for a body found at the bottom of a canyon. He was eighteen—poor lad—and not sufficiently experienced to take on such a steep climb.

But murder victims? This lady was my first, and a baptism by fire she was. The fabric of her dress—torn to shreds—still hung on her battered body. Her skin was split open in at least thirty places, and broken bones jutted out of some of them. Splattered blood in the snow resembled rose petals sprinkled on a white wedding cake. Squatting near her, I lifted her skull high enough to see it was smashed and one of her eyes was missing.

Not even a seasoned lawman should have to behold such a sight, I thought.

More questions galloped circles in my mind. *How old was she? Was she from around here or passing through? Why did the last person she ever encountered in her life hate her enough to do this?*

Such questions would drive me crazy if I let them. My attention shifted to lesser concerns, like feeling irked for having to work on a Saturday. No choice, though—I was the low man on the totem pole. So it stood to reason I would have to be there, shivering and spotting those little details: bits of brain in her hair; bone jutting out of her thigh covered with snow; her torn stockings, light brown, held up by garters.

I didn't need a professional with a degree from Johns Hopkins to tell me this was no accident. The killer had it in for this woman. Her mangled remains spoke volumes, and I'd grown weary of standing in that place, trying to make sense out of something senseless in that bitter cold. My hands had gone numb from the cold, and I exhaled steam. Despite the freezing weather, the seagulls circled in full force, crying and diving.

"ID'd the stiff yet?" asked Roscoe Lund, my partner.

He said it in a taunting way, as only he could, as if to rub it in that I hadn't identified her yet. He sat on the Ford's running board, dressed in a deputy's outfit that matched mine. No taller than me, Roscoe was twice as thick, owing primarily to muscle. He kept his Stetson tilted far back on his bristly head, and his perpetual five o'clock shadow hardened his appearance. He had a bulbous nose, not as bad as W. C. Fields, but getting there, and the indentations on it gave me reason to believe it had been broken. His deep voice, wide shoulders, cleft chin, and short neck gave him a giantlike quality—as if he had climbed down the beanstalk and, instead of chasing Jack on the ground, run straight to the sheriff's office to apply for the deputy vacancy.

I continued squatting by the woman's remains, turning halfway so I could see him out of the corner of my eye. "I'll let the coroner have at it."

Roscoe picked odd times to smile. Like now, for instance. "Not so much as a driver's license, huh?"

"Nope, but I don't want to move her before Livsey gets here. I'm sure he'll give her a good going-over." Livsey was Tom Livsey, deputy county coroner.

"Who do you suppose she is?"

"I don't know." I reached out and hooked my index finger over a string of pearls wrapped around her busted neck and gave them a wiggle. A few were spotted with blood. "I'm guessing she's loaded. Or she's married to someone who is."

Roscoe popped a lid off a can of smoking tobacco and sprinkled a line on cigarette paper. He licked the edge and rolled it, put the end between his lips, flipped open a lighter. The flame danced, and the cigarette tip crackled orange as he inhaled. *He doesn't care about this dead woman. He just wants to wrap this up and go home and go back to sleep,* I thought as I eyed him puffing.

Roscoe had never told me where he lived. He had complained about having to get up at 6:00 A.M. on a Saturday but did not mention a wife or any other family. The only fragments I knew came from rare hints he dropped. He offered no clues about his age. I guessed him to be in his late thirties. He once let it slip that he served in the American Expeditionary Force and fought in the Battle of Belleau Wood near the Marne back in June of '18. That was the most he ever said about himself, and even then, he was spare with the details. He also made a fleeting reference to almost dying of influenza after returning to the States, but he obviously recovered.

That was all I knew about Roscoe Lund. Oh, and one other thing: He made it a point to say, often, "Goddamn Mormons" or "Mormon sonsabitches—hate 'em all." He would glare at me each time, knowing full well that I had been a lifelong member of the Church of Jesus Christ of Latter-day Saints.

He didn't go on the warpath today, though. He stayed focused.

In this case, focused for him meant saying—over and over—how much he hated being out here so early on a Saturday morning. I went over to the car, to where he sat smoking, opened the back door, and snatched a folding plate camera off the backseat, expanding it like an accordion.

"Got a yen for snappin' pretty scenery, have we?"

I glanced at the overcast sky. "It's supposed to snow more."

I went back to the spot and began snapping photos of tire tracks. They were everywhere—crisscrossing north, south, east, west, and all points in between—and they all led to the same place: the corpse.

"How many times you figure she was hit?"

"I count at least five separate sweeps in this direction."

"Five?" echoed Roscoe, flipping his cigarette into the snow.

"Yep," I said, holding the camera to one side and gesturing to each pair of tracks. "One . . . two . . . three . . . four . . . five . . . possibly a sixth set over here. Maybe a seventh. I can't be sure." I pointed to a piece of bloody white fur near the victim. "I'm guessing that's her ermine, and there's a high-heel shoe over there in the snow."

"Christ almighty," he said, shaking his head. "Who'd wanna hit a broad that many times? Once probably would've done the trick."

"Do you mind?" I asked, not looking up from the viewfinder. "Lady or woman. *Not* broad."

Roscoe laughed. "I don't think she cares."

"Yeah? Well, *I* care."

"Oh yeah, I forgot. The choirboy has a thing for damsels."

More viewfinder scenes: tire tracks heading from northeast, crossing over the body, and continuing southwest toward the road. *Snap.* Turn crank, advance film.

"I could use some help," I said, lowering the camera.

"Hey, I won't lift a pinky to do Cannon's shit work—not while that fucker is out glad-handing and kissing babies to get reelected. Hell, he's not even doing that right now; he's getting his beauty sleep while we're out here working our asses off in the freezing cold."

Now I was the one laughing, prompting a glare from Roscoe. "I don't see what's so goddamn funny."

I checked the camera to see how many snapshots remained. "Something tells me when your time comes to keel over, the cause of death won't be listed as work-related exhaustion."

"Keep it up, choirboy. You'll be writing gags for Amos and Andy in no time flat."

I walked to the corpse and tapped the small of her back with the tip of my shoe. "Just a vessel."

"What'd you say?" asked Roscoe.

The wind whistled through the pines. Snow started falling.

"Speak up!" he said. "What'd you say?"

"Nothing."

"Bullshit. You're talking to yourself again."

A Pontiac pulled up and parked at the bottom of the hill, and deputy county coroner Tom Livsey got out of the car and started up the icy path, dressed in a bowler and topcoat, carrying a briefcase full of equipment. I watched him approaching while I returned the camera to the trunk of the car. Tom grew up a stretch down the road from my childhood house in American Fork, so a certain familiarity existed between us. He had a reputation for professionalism and an eye for detail, and he did most of the hard work behind the scenes while his boss, coroner Laird Nash, merrily took all the credit. When Tom reached the murder scene, we shook hands and exchanged pleasantries, but he and Roscoe didn't acknowledge each other.

Tom crouched near the body and lifted a torn piece of her dress with the tip of his pencil. "Who called it in?"

"Virgil Porter," I said. "He lives in that shack over there." I pointed to the top of the hill, at a whitewashed box with a steep-sloped roof. A smoke column curled up from the chimney, and a flatbed truck was parked out front. "He found her body when he got home from work this morning. That was about five, uh, five fifteen or so."

Livsey squinted at the house. "I'm surprised his wife didn't hear anything."

"He lives alone."

"Oh. I see. Did you get a statement from him?"

"Yep," I said, plucking a spiral notebook out of my pocket. "It's all right here. Says he saw a dark object in the snow at the base of the hill, along with some kind of animal—maybe a coyote. He lit a kerosene lantern and came down here, and this is what he found."

"What was his demeanor like, Art?"

"He was visibly upset. Hands shaking."

"I think he shit his skivvies," said Roscoe.

Roscoe's foul language offended Livsey's Mormon sensibilities. He couldn't help making an angry face at my partner. "Find any identification on her?"

"Nope."

Livsey stayed low, examining the body for another minute before standing up straight. "Jane Doe. We don't get enough of those." He looked at us. "I can take it from here, fellas. The morgue wagon is on its way. Thanks for your hard work, Art."

Heading back to the county car, I overheard Roscoe mumble—under his breath, but still audible—"Fuckin' prick." I opened the driver's side door and raised my foot to the running board when I spotted a familiar black sedan with gold stars painted on white front doors. The car halted about twenty yards away, and two men in fedoras and suits got out and began walking toward us. I recognized them instantly as plainclothes Salt Lake City police homicide detectives. The Salt Lake City law enforcement community is small. Most of us know each other by name. Sometimes, thanks to an active gossip mill, we know more about each other than that.

Detective Buddy Hawkins, a redhead, likely in his midthirties (though I'd never asked him his exact age), with fair skin and a prominent chin, had style, no two ways about that. This morning, he had dressed up in one of his fancy double-breasted worsted suits, with a crisp white shirt and red-and-blue-striped tie, and a dark fedora pushed far back on his head. He and I attended the same church, and from time to time we'd strike up a chat after priesthood meetings. Behind him tailed his hatchet-faced partner, Detective DeWitt "Wit" Dunaway, a frumpier dresser, big-eared, hat pulled low. His tie was crooked and poorly tied, and I never knew his disposition to be anything other than sour. They stepped through snow in our direction, and Roscoe muttered something about "those sonsabitches." Unlike Hawkins, who was born and raised in small-town Heber, Utah, Wit hailed from out of state. His previous job had been in Boston, where—according to rumors—he was one of the ringleaders in the big 1919 police strike out there. He lost his job because of it and somehow ended up here, on the other side of the country, investigating homicides, pushing pencils, and cursing his fate.

I lowered my foot off the running board and faced the police detectives.

"Morning, gents," I said.

"Where's the body?" asked Wit. He didn't say it so much as he snarled it.

"In that clearing over there," I said, pointing where we'd been. "Tom Livsey is having a look at her before the morgue wagon—"

Roscoe cut me off. "You boys are outside the city limits. Which means you're outside of your jurisdiction."

"We've reason to believe the victim's from Salt Lake," said Buddy. "So, technically, this case falls under our jurisdiction."

"We couldn't find any ID on her," I said. "Do you know who she is?"

Buddy removed his hat and held it by the brim. "We're not at liberty to say, until our information has been confirmed by the coroner and the next of kin has been notified. Leaving so soon?"

"We've been here a while," I said. "I've got to write a report before I head home."

He tipped his head back to see the sky, and snowflakes dabbed his face. "Lonely place to meet one's end, the Pole Line Road. Experience has taught me that in most cases, the more isolated the spot, the more heinous the crime." He leveled his head at me. "Is that so here?"

"She's mangled, something terrible," I said. "She got hit by a car. Repeatedly."

Buddy nodded. "Do you mind sending me a photostat of your report?"

Roscoe winced. "Dig up your own shit, lazy bastards."

He grinned at Roscoe, then at me, and put his hat back on. "Don't let us hold you up any longer, fellows. See you at church tomorrow, Art."

"Sure thing, Buddy."

Two

In 1904, Dad built a homestead near a stream in American Fork, a stretch of fertile farmland in Utah Valley, south of Salt Lake City. He purchased fifty acres in the shadow of the snow-capped Wasatch Mountains and, just days before my birth, moved the family into the white wood-frame structure that had green shutters on the windows and a long porch. The rail fence Dad put up ran the length of the land, and he was real particular about keeping the tall grass trimmed around the posts. I was weeks away from turning thirteen when an unknown assailant shot and killed him in the line of duty in 1914.

We buried Dad in the southwest corner of the land, beneath some shade trees. Toward the end of his life, he had obtained a permit from the county to create a family cemetery on the property. He built a white picket fence around the chosen spot and planted a flower garden in the center. A year later, this would become his final resting place.

Ever since Dad's death, my family had maintained the tradition of sitting down to Sunday dinners together at the homestead. At first, the ritual simply involved Mom and us four Oveson brothers. In time, the family expanded as we each married, and the weekly gatherings evolved into a huge affair. Automobiles would begin arriving at half past four, and little kids leaped out of the backseats to scramble inside the house and greet Grandma. Each wife prepared a dish, and Mom insisted we start dinner promptly at six o'clock.

Clara, my wife, had bobbed hair the color of honey and bee-stung lips. She was renowned for her baked beans and homemade frosted sugar cookies, but she could also put together a mean casserole if the occasion called for it. Whatever she made, she had to make it big. By 1930, the house was packed with children running in all directions, wives sharing housekeeping pointers, and the four of us brothers, making small talk.

Dad had been assistant chief of the Salt Lake City Police Department, and everyone who knew him thought the top spot on the force was his for the taking. Our maternal grandfather had served as Provo's chief of police, and our great-grandfather had gained notoriety locally as Utah's earliest territorial sheriff. My brothers and I gravitated to law enforcement.

One by one, we followed in the footsteps of our forebears. My eldest brother, Frank, became an agent with the Bureau of Investigation and rose to the position of special agent in charge in the Denver field office and lived there four years. Director J. Edgar Hoover admired and respected Frank and knew my brother wanted to go back to Utah, so he personally promoted Frank to SAC/Salt Lake City in the summer of 1928. Frank never forgot this gesture of kindness, and he named his son John Edgar Hoover Oveson.

The next Oveson brother, John, was elected sheriff of Price, a mining town in central Utah. Before John's tenure, Price had been a rough-and-tumble place, full of hard drinkers and impulsive shooters. John swiftly achieved a reputation as a stern disciplinarian who reined in the bad element, and the people of Price rewarded him with reelection to a second term.

Then there was Grant. His rise to captain of detectives in the Provo Police Department was nothing short of meteoric. Unlike Price, Provo—a city forty-three miles south of Salt Lake—did not have much of a bad element to speak of. From time to time, Grant would get a call to investigate a homicide or assault case, but such incidents were rare.

Grant and I were born rivals. We seldom agreed on the issues of the day, from politics to weather, and our frequent verbal sparring dated back to our childhood. Years of butting heads had taken a toll on our relationship.

I was the youngest of the Oveson boys, and no question, I was the runt of the litter, the frail one of the bunch. I suffered from everything you could imagine: asthma, fallen arches, dyspepsia, heart murmur, rheumatism, a mild case of polio, and a deathly pallor. I almost passed away in the epidemic of '18; in fact, Mom drove to Loftus Mortuary in Orem and ordered a pine casket for me. I vaguely recall coming down with it in the fall, feeling the first symptoms while seated in the back row of the one-room schoolhouse I attended. As I gazed out the window at snow-covered Mount Timpanogos, my vision blurred. Then everything went black.

I regained consciousness in the spring of '19 with a tube in my arm to keep nutrients flowing into my body. My hair had grown long, and my rib cage protruded. Mom wept with joy to see me alert again, and she told me I had been in pain for months, flailing, sweating, and ripping off my pajamas. I could not remember any of it. All I knew was that fall had transformed into spring in the snap of a finger.

That was eleven years ago. So much has changed.

My brothers and I grew into manhood and each served an LDS mission—Frank to London, England; John to Montreal, Canada;

Grant to Frankfurt, Germany; and I landed the warm spot, Los Angeles, probably due to my poor health.

We all looked alike—prominent chins, tousled reddish hair, blue eyes, big smiles. The Oveson boys had something else in common: We married young, after coming home from our missions. We all had temple marriages (meaning we were married inside of the Salt Lake Temple, the LDS Church's main temple). All of us except John married women we'd been sweet on since grammar school. John, the exception, met a lady named Eliza Nichols after he returned from Montreal and, like the rest of us, wasted no time in racing to the altar.

Despite the overlap in our careers and lives, I couldn't relate to my brothers on any level. Their competitiveness never let up. Even idle banter escalated into quests to outjoke each other. Without fail, I would excuse myself and wander off in search of solitude. My walks often took me outside, where I leaned against a fence post and scanned the valley and mountains beyond.

On that particular Sunday, the day after I found the woman's body lying in the snow, I returned to work as soon as church let out so I could finish writing the crime scene report I'd started the previous morning. Truth be known, I'd more or less finished the report on Saturday, but I wanted to find out more about the murdered woman. What was her name? Where was she from? Were there any suspects? The sheriff's office was deserted, with a skeletal crew of deputies out on patrol. Coroner Nash told me there wouldn't be any autopsy information released until Monday at the earliest. So I drove home, preoccupied with that gruesome crime scene. The instant I walked in the front door, Clara steered me to the garage, with Hyrum in my arms and Sarah Jane skipping joyfully. "Hurry," Clara said, herding us into the car. "We can still make it on time to family dinner." Once at my mother's house, I could not sit around the living room and listen to my brothers discussing the challenges of building detached garages and cursing the slowness of mail order catalogs. I had to get away to a solitary place where I could gather my thoughts.

Over time, the faded tractor seat in the barn had become my favorite place to be alone. I sought that place out to get away from my brothers, to preserve my sanity and to calm my nerves. The icy air on that late Sunday afternoon soothed my slightly asthmatic lungs.

"I thought I might find you out here."

Her voice startled me. Clara huddled in the doorway, shivering in the wind.

"Sorry," I said. "I was starting to feel cooped up, with all those kids running around, and my brothers babbling on and on. I needed to get away."

She approached, squeezed my hand, and pecked my cheek. "I understand. I just wanted to make sure you were alright."

I saw her arms were empty and wondered where my son, Hyrum, was. She read my mind. "He's inside. Sleeping. He's almost too big for that bassinet now."

"I know. What about Sarah Jane?"

"She's playing with her cousins. I was hoping I'd find you out here. I can only take so much before I need a break, too."

"Are the ladies getting on your nerves?"

She laughed and shook her head. "They don't get why in the world I'd ever want to go back to teaching high school English instead of staying home. Bess told me I was being selfish."

My eyebrows dipped down. "You're kidding. Bess called you selfish?"

"Well, not exactly. She didn't say I *was* selfish. She said I was *being* selfish."

I hopped off the tractor and threw my arms around her. She wrapped hers around my waist. We smiled at each other, rubbed noses and kissed, the way married people do when they're still deeply in love. I was so smitten I even loved her few freckles. "Always the English teacher," I said, "making the distinction between 'was' and 'being.' Did you tell her to go jump in a lake? Utah Lake is just down the road, you know. I'll be happy to give her a ride if she needs one."

"I'll let you do the honors." We both laughed. "Are you going to tell me?"

"Tell you what?"

"What's eating you? Something's been on your mind since yesterday. You've been preoccupied. I want to know why."

"Is it that obvious?"

She nodded.

"It's a homicide I'm thinking about. It was the reason I left the house so early yesterday morning. And why I went back to work this afternoon."

We were both quiet for a moment.

"I figured as much," she said. "Care to talk about it?"

We loosened our embrace, letting our arms fall to our sides, and I leaned against the tractor, watching the snow fall outside. I had no intention of telling her about the homicide, but the image of the mangled body flashed in my mind whenever I blinked, and I had a hard time concealing my pain when I gazed into Clara's beckoning eyes.

"A car ran over her," I said, "and not just once. It happened several times. I knew if I tried to pick her up, her entire body would've gone floppy. My guess is every bone in her body was broken."

"What was her name?"

"She didn't have any ID. She had a fur and a nice string of pearls, though, so she must've had money."

"Maybe the pearls were fake," she said. "You can get some decent-looking ones at the costume store for two bits."

"I don't think they were fake. I think she's somebody important, somebody with connections."

"It's getting to you, isn't it?"

"It was *the way* she was killed," I said. "It was the ugliness of it, the indignity." I shrugged my shoulders and shook my head. "It makes me wonder about people, about the depths they're capable of sinking to."

"Why don't you talk to the bishop about it?"

"I know what he's going to say." I imitated his deep voice. *"Doubts are a normal part of life. Everybody has them."*

"And you don't want to hear that?"

"Just once, I would like to hear him say it's OK to act on those doubts."

"What do you mean?"

I took a deep breath and rolled my eyes as I searched for the words. "I don't know if I have the stomach for this line of work."

"Nobody says you have to be a lawman, Art. You've got a fine head on your shoulders." Her face lit up, and she squeezed my hand. "Become a teacher! Like me!"

I laughed.

"I'm being quite serious," she said, flashing a smile. "It would be splendid. We could have lunch together every day! And you're a natural. Kids love you. Your mind is always ticking, like a clock. Remember when you read *Scarlet Letter* because my class was reading it?"

I nodded.

She said, "Or you can get a loan from the bank and start your own business. I know the banks aren't giving out loans the way they did before the crash, but the radio says the tough times won't last forever. You'd make a fine entrepreneur."

I appreciated what she was doing, trying to cheer me up, but I actually wanted to wallow in my pessimism. Besides, I thought it was only right that I remain shaken up by what I saw yesterday.

"Look, I'm freezing, Art," she said with a shiver. "Why don't you come inside? Have some dinner."

"I'll be along in a minute."

"Suit yourself, but don't stay out here too long." She smiled and pointed her thumb over her shoulder. "I need reinforcement in there."

She walked out into a blizzard, and her silhouette faded into the blowing whiteness. Moments later, I trudged up the same path, closing my eyes as snow fell sideways into my face, heading in the direction of my childhood home.

Three

The Salt Lake County Jail, a four-story monstrosity topped with a smokestack almost as tall as the building itself, was the grimmest-looking thing in town. This heap of dark bricks and barred windows stood on Second East and Fourth South, across the street from the more elegant City and County Building, an impressive example of Romanesque Revival that could've passed for a fancy university building. To my regret, the county sheriff's department wasn't housed in the City and County Building. Our offices were attached to the county jail, and out back was a gravel parking lot full of county Model A's.

The blizzard that had moved in over the valley the previous night was still dropping snow. Enough had fallen to close all schools for the day, sending joyous throngs of kids to Liberty Park with sleds in tow.

Deputies never got the day off. We were actually doing pretty well when our paychecks arrived on time and were for the full amount. Hard times made everybody feel uneasy about the future, and at that point in my life, I was just happy to be employed. Most of the other deputies felt the same way, but there were plenty who disliked Sheriff Fred Cannon, and that morning you could see it in their grim expressions as they filed into the basement briefing room.

We waited for Cannon to deliver the big announcement. Maybe this morning I'd finally be able to attach a name to the dead woman. I sat on the back row, next to Roscoe Lund, who smelled of cheap aftershave and had refused to put on a tie yet again.

Into the room walked Cannon, followed by Assistant Sheriff A. M. Sykes. Cannon was a stocky man with closely cropped brown hair, ruddy cheeks, and a rounded chin that threatened to disappear into a turkey neck. He always seemed to be smiling, even when tragedy struck.

Sykes—smaller, leaner, and more intense—had a bald spot on top of his head. Like Calvin Coolidge, he rarely spoke, letting Cannon do most of the talking. That's how he got to be assistant sheriff. Cannon hated to be contradicted, and many ex-deputies learned that lesson the hard way. By contrast, Sykes allowed Cannon to hog the spotlight without a single objection.

Cannon stepped up to the lectern, put on his wire-frame eyeglasses, and cleared his throat. The sheriff bowed his head and closed his eyes.

"Our beloved Father in Heaven," he began, and a good two-thirds of the men in the room—including me—closed our eyes and lowered our heads. The other third kept their heads upright and stayed quiet. "Thank you for your blessings of family, nourishment, and employment in these difficult times. You have indeed been kind to us, and we are truly grateful. We ask that you extend another blessing unto us, oh Heavenly Father—the blessing of safety. Please continue to guide us, to help us to do what's right, to always seek justice and uphold the law. We ask this in the name of Jesus Christ, amen."

Prayer time always spotlighted divisions in the sheriff's office. Only the Mormons—Sheriff Cannon, Assistant Sheriff Sykes, me, and a number of other deputies—participated in the morning prayers. The non-Mormons, even the very religious ones, refrained. A Catholic deputy named Jim Boyd once told me he didn't pray because the morning prayers were "Mormon prayers," and he said a lot of the other religious men who weren't Mormons felt the same way.

Sheriff Cannon lifted his head. A soft chorus of amens echoed across the room.

"Gentlemen, I am sure by now most of you have heard the news," he said, lifting a copy of this morning's *Salt Lake Telegram* so we could all see the story and photo. From where I sat, I had to squint to see the headline. WIFE OF S.L. PHYSICIAN SLAIN. Below that: SOCIALITE RUN OVER BY OWN AUTO, FEW CLUES FOUND. The picture next to the story showed the victim in happier times, wearing a cloche hat and fur coat.

Cannon continued. "The body of Helen Kent Pfalzgraf was found by Deputies Arthur Oveson and Roscoe Lund on Saturday morning out at Pole Line Road. I don't need to tell you all that a resolution to this case is a top priority for this office. I also need not remind you of Hazel Hamilton's murder on New Year's Day of last year. We had four suspects before the trail went completely cold. Well, I assure you, gents: That will not happen again."

He dipped his head, tightened his mouth, and momentarily seemed too choked up to speak. Then he raised his head again and summoned the strength. "This past New Year's Day marked the first anniversary of the Hamilton murder. And guess who had to sit down with her parents and explain why the sheriff's office hadn't found the killer yet? Believe me when I say it was one of the worst moments of my life. I hope none of you ever have to do that. I hope I never again have to experience anything remotely like that."

Cannon stepped aside and turned to Sykes. "Al?"

Sykes nodded and moved up to the podium. The light overhead gleamed on his badge. He read from a dossier. "The victim's name is Helen Kent Pfalzgraf. Her birth name was Helen Joyce Higginbotham. Date of birth: August the twenty-fourth, 1897. That'd put her at age thirty-two at time of death. Place of birth: Twin Falls, Idaho. Her father, Walter, owned a dry goods store up there. She relocated to Salt Lake City to attend the University of Utah for one year, where she majored in speech and dramatics. She's listed in the 1921 *Utonian,* the University of Utah's yearbook, under the name Helen Kent, and it says her interests are stage acting, painting, crocheting, and baking. Approximately five and one-half years ago, she married Dr. Hans Pfalzgraf."

Whispers filled the room when Sykes said the doctor's name. Pfalzgraf enjoyed a reputation as one of the most successful and revered physicians in Utah, serving primarily an upscale clientele. Sykes glowered at the men as if to say, *Cut it out.*

"Early word from the coroner's office indicates Mrs. Pfalzgraf was struck on the head by a heavy object of some sort, which either killed her or knocked her out cold. Then she was run over by her own auto, a nineteen-and-twenty-eight Cadillac, possibly as many as seven times. Her car was later found abandoned in a parking lot on Washington Boulevard in Ogden. Hair and skin samples were removed from the front and rear bumpers of the auto, and they matched Mrs. Pfalzgraf's hair and skin. We aren't sure if robbery was a motive. Some of Mrs. Pfalzgraf's jewels were stolen, including her wedding ring, but the assailant—or assailants—left a lot of jewelry on her and left her purse in her car, which contained six hundred and twenty-five dollars in cash." Sykes closed his dossier. "That's all for now. We'll share any additional information with you as soon as we are privy to it ourselves."

Sykes stepped aside to make room for Cannon, who pressed his plump stomach against the lectern. "Teams of men will comb the area around Pole Line Road and up in Ogden where her Cadillac was found. Because the crime occurred outside city limits, it falls into county sheriff's jurisdiction. Still, I anticipate our friends over at the Public Safety Building"—that was Cannon's way of saying "the police," as the Public Safety Building housed the Salt Lake City Police Department—"will horn in on this case if they haven't already started to do so. Stay vigilant, keep an eye out for clues, and report back to Sykes or myself at all times. Constant updates are a must. Understand?"

Scattered yeses greeted his question. "Gents, go out and do good."

While deputies streamed out of the briefing room, I heard my name called.

At the front of the room, Sheriff Cannon smiled at me, hands on his hips. "Can I have a word with you?"

Roscoe frowned, and I arched my eyebrows at him, then walked over to Cannon with Roscoe following.

"Just you, Oveson. Lund, maybe you can wait outside."

Roscoe eyed me, and I tipped my head, as if to say, *What choice do you have?*

He scowled for a second at Cannon, but the sheriff was too focused on the mostly empty room to notice. The grin stayed on his face as his eyes met mine and he said, "Let's walk and talk. The walls have ears."

We found our way to the least desirable place in the entire building: the boiler room, hidden in the southeast corner of the basement. It being a cold day, the boiler was working overtime, and through the iron grate I could see rows of flames blasting away inside. The subterranean stone room was filled with noise—metal clanking, hissing steam, crackling flames—and inside of a minute, I was wiping the sweat off my brow with my sleeve.

Cannon turned to me. That smile didn't go anywhere as he held up a pack of Lucky Strikes and tipped it toward me. "Cigarette?"

"No thanks. I don't smoke."

He shook the package so a tip jutted out, and he put it between his lips. When he lit the cigarette, his face glowed for a few seconds before he closed the lighter and blew smoke at the boiler. "The missus doesn't care for me partaking, so I do it strictly in private."

"Yes, sir."

He blew smoke toward the ceiling. "I like you, Oveson. You're ambitious, but your ambitions don't conflict with mine."

"Thank you, sir."

"I knew your father. He and I were friends—sort of."

"He spoke highly of you," I said. It was a lie. Dad never once mentioned Cannon. I had misgivings about lying, but I knew with a man like Cannon, a compliment always builds trust.

Cannon arched his eyebrows, genuinely surprised. "Oh yeah? What'd he say?"

"He told me you're a fine lawman."

"Well, I'll be," he said. "Darn good fellow, your father. My condolences on his passing. It was awful—him getting gunned down. What's it been? Fifteen, sixteen years?"

Being reminded of my father's death filled me with an unexpected sadness, yet I hid it well. "Yeah, about that. Was there something you wished to talk to me about, sir?"

As he spoke, the glowing tip of his cigarette jumped up and down. "I remember when this city used to stop at Fourth South and everything beyond that was farms and houses. You probably weren't even born yet."

"I'm sure I wasn't."

He plucked his cigarette out of his lips and blew smoke. "Now they're building out beyond Twenty-first and the streetcars run clear out to Murray. It's crazy how much this town has changed since I was a youngster."

"Yes, sir."

"Salt Lake City isn't what it used to be. It's no longer the City of Saints. It hasn't been for a long time. Place is full of crime." He paused and looked me up and down. "I guess you know about Lorenzo Blackham?"

"Yes, sir."

"What do you know about him?"

"I see his billboards by the side of the road. I know he's running for sheriff."

Cannon nodded. "He's campaigning dirty—real below-the-belt stuff. Bastard is making speeches about Hazel Hamilton, saying I never even tried to find her killer. It gets me, Oveson. It *really* gets me. Then there was that brouhaha two years ago, which he insists on calling a *scandal*. Scandal, my foot! Wun't no scandal. All in the heck we done was tax gamblers. Sure, there was some arbitrariness about the whole setup, but that was our way of pushing the bad element out of the city."

I considered saying, *It wasn't a tax. It was extortion, and you personally pocketed all the money and fired six deputies who were in on it with you.*

I didn't. I wanted to stay employed. "Yes, sir."

"The Pfalzgraf murder has brought everything to a head. Things like that aren't supposed to happen in Salt Lake City. This is a big-city homicide. New York, L.A., Chicago—sure, but not in this place."

He smoked for a moment. "I'm already getting calls from newspapers, asking a lot of dang fool questions . . ."

His sentence tapered off so he could take a final drag of his cigarette. He dropped it on the floor and mashed it with his heel. "If this case isn't solved right away, Blackham will use it against me. I need someone I trust working on it—someone who'll keep me posted. I'm thinking of you."

I arched my eyebrows in surprise, and said, "What do you want me to do?"

"I want you working on the case, but I also want you to be my eyes and ears with the other deputies. I got a feeling a lot of them have it in for me."

"Are you asking me to spy for you?"

"I don't like the word 'spy.' It makes you sound like Mata Hari or something. I want to keep it low-key. There's an election coming up, and I don't want to be caught with my pants down. I need you to update me on the performance of my deputies out in the field. You have to lead by example on this investigation. Show the other fellows how it's done. They need to see someone with a positive work ethic."

I managed a grin. "Yes, sir."

I turned to leave, but Cannon said, "Oh, and Art?"

"Yes, sir?"

"Do whatever it takes to find Mrs. Pfalzgraf's killer. Dig up what you can. Report your findings regularly to me. Understand?"

I nodded. "What about my partner?"

"Oh, I know all about Lund. Real hothead. Used to be a paid strikebreaker. Loved cracking skulls. He's muscle, and you look like you could use some muscle. Just keep a leash on him."

Easier said than done, I thought. I said, "I'll try, sir."

"Good man. You're my eyes and ears, Oveson. Don't let me down." He patted me on the shoulder. "I do right by those who're loyal to me. You'll see."

"Yes, sir. I'll bear that in mind."

four

Everything emanated from the temple.

On the northern side of the oval Salt Lake Valley, the earliest Mormon arrivals set aside ten acres for what they called Temple Square. In those days, the valley was full of dry grass, meandering creeks, and trees—firs, quaking aspen, horse chestnuts, box elders, and others. Brigham Young selected the exact spot for the temple on July 28, 1847, four days after he looked out at this valley and told his traveling companions, *"This is the right place."* The prophet oversaw the groundbreaking ceremony six years later, but he had no idea at the time that the temple wouldn't be dedicated for another forty years.

The Salt Lake Temple, as it came to be known, was under construction for much of the second half of the nineteenth century. My grandfather Samuel Oveson found work on one of the many crews, laying the foundation and carving quartz monzonite. The work strained Grandpa Sam's muscles and ate up big chunks of his time, and the job wasn't steady. In fact, long periods passed without any progress, and there were times when Grandpa and other locals wondered if the temple would ever be completed. Meantime, Sam's younger brother, Lyman, was one of the workers in Little Cottonwood Canyon, south of the temple site, chipping away the canyon walls and hauling monzonite twenty miles to the temple grounds.

The coming of the Transcontinental Railroad sped up the transportation of the massive gray blocks from Little Cottonwood. The prophet, in fact, ordered the construction of a temporary railway line that fed straight into Temple Square, which gave Grandpa Sam and Uncle Lyman more work laying track. Sadly, Brigham Young never lived to see the completion of the temple he envisioned. The prophet died on August 29, 1877. The temple, with three towering spires on the east side topped by the gleaming Angel Moroni blowing his trumpet, was dedicated on the sixth day of April, 1893, by then-Prophet Wilford Woodruff, president of the Church of Jesus Christ of Latter-day Saints.

When I say everything emanated from the temple, I mean the city's founders created an orderly grid and chose the temple as its epicenter. They built streets wide—so wide, in fact, that early visitors to the City of Saints couldn't help but marvel at them. Every prestigious journeyer, from explorer Richard Burton to author Mark Twain to moving picture comic Charles Chaplin, voiced astonishment over the size of the city's streets. On the other hand, the men and women who lived their entire lives here seldom, if ever, stopped and thought about the streets. Salt Lakers were used to them, the way they were used to the tall buildings that had been sprouting downtown since the 1870s.

Salt Lake City was my city, just as it had been my grandfather's city in the last century. I knew each corner and every side street. I walked its dusty roads and absorbed its history, soaking up every seemingly trivial piece of information. Its people—even the odd and crazy ones—had a familiarity about them that I found comforting. By 1930, Salt Lake City had grown to 145,000 inhabitants within the city proper. That didn't count all of the nearby hamlets dotting the valley: West Jordan over at the base of the Oquirrhs; Murray in the dead center of the valley; and Sandy—mostly farms and scattered wood-frame houses, with the occasional dry goods store and filling station—built against the Wasatch Mountains to the south.

Those of us in the sheriff's department did most of our work in these outlying areas, outside the city limits but still inside the county. I guessed much of the Helen Kent Pfalzgraf investigation would keep us within the city proper, which is where I was that day when I drove east on South Temple, in the direction of Salt Lake City's ritziest neighborhood. South Temple was the street of the nouveau riche in Salt Lake City: mining tycoons, newspaper owners, men who had struck it rich in one western enterprise or another and built palaces that served as conspicuous reminders of their newfound wealth.

I drove too fast through the falling snow, but Roscoe didn't object. I was preoccupied the entire way, and he seemed lost in his thoughts as well—stone-faced, staring out the window at the mansions. I could not be bothered with him right now. I still felt squeamish over my conversation with Sheriff Cannon earlier that morning. *Why did he choose me as his go-to man? What was he really hoping to get out of me?* I hardly knew Cannon, and he had a bad rep. The first time we met was the previous year, for my job interview. Since then, he'd only ever said about a half-dozen words to me, most of them variations of "Howdy."

The Pfalzgraf mansion was near the corner of South Temple and 1300 East, at the foothills of the Wasatch Mountains, close to Federal Heights, Salt Lake City's most affluent neighborhood. Pfalzgraf commissioned a castle for himself and hired a high-priced New York architect who designed a French Chateauesque building made out of polished limestone, with rounded towers on both sides of the front and stone columns on the portico. Rumor had it the house cost $350,000 to build, which in 1916 was a lot. Still is, fourteen years later.

We reached the mansion gates, and there were several cars and a truck parked out front. Newspaper reporters with press passes tucked in their hatbands paced on the sidewalks and street. A scuffed black camera, emblazoned with a label that read MOVIE-TONE NEWS, and below that WESTERN ELECTRIC SOUND, was attached to the top of a wooden tripod, and a cameraman filmed exterior shots of the mansion. When the reporters noticed we were from the sheriff's office, they started shouting questions at us.

"J. L. Crabb, *Los Angeles Times.* I have a few questions . . ."

"Can you give us any new information about the Pfalzgraf murder?"

"Any updates?"

"What's the latest word on Dr. Pfalzgraf?"

"We've heard allegations that Mrs. Pfalzgraf kept a separate bank account containing a large sum of money. Any truth to this?"

Roscoe shoved a reporter who got too close. "Touch me again and I've got a blackjack with your name written on it!"

I excused my way to the gates. Snowflakes fell on my face and melted when they touched skin. I recognized the man standing behind the bars—Floyd Samuelson—dressed in a black security guard's uniform and matching cap. Hired muscle. He smiled when he saw me. He was a redhead with blushing cheeks, a squared-off chin, and hospitable green eyes. He and I attended the police academy together, and I recall him fervently trying to convert all of the non-Mormons in our graduating class to the Church of Jesus Christ of Latter-day Saints. I heard the Salt Lake City Police Department skipped over him because they thought he wasn't smart enough. Ogden and Provo also said no. He was a nice enough man, but his lack of smarts—book smarts, street smarts—made me think maybe he deserved those police department rejection notices. From everything I'd heard, he had done pretty well as a rental guard at the Pfalzgraf house for the past two years.

"Hello, Art!"

I slipped gloved fingers between the iron bars, and we shook hands. "Floyd. How's every little thing?"

"Busy as bees. This murder is the biggest thing that's happened in Utah." He raised his eyebrows, as if remembering something important. He fished out a billfold, opened it, and held up a picture of a chubby boy in a Buster Brown suit. "His name is Elbert Snow Samuelson. We call him Bert. This was taken a year ago. He's taller now."

I smiled at the picture. "Cute."

"Ain't he, though? I'm so proud of him." He tucked the wallet away. "Yeah. We've had press people camped out here all day. There was one fella from a pulp magazine, *Real Mystery Stories,* who actually went and climbed the wall. Police came and hauled him downtown. I don't mind, though. The doc's misfortune is puttin' meat and potatoes on my table. I'm working double shifts, and it looks like I'm gonna be in a newsreel."

"That's grand, Floyd." I winked at him. "We'd like to ask the doctor a few questions, if we can."

Floyd leaned in close to me and whispered so the reporters couldn't hear. "Doc slipped off to work. He's at County, on Twenty-first. He also has an office at Brooks Arcade on State. Second floor. But he's a busy man. Not easy to catch."

"What about his daughter?" asked Roscoe.

Floyd went white, as if somebody'd shot his dog. "How do you know about his daughter?"

"Because you just told me, you stupid sonofabitch. Besides, I see the papers. Her mug turns up in the society page all the time. Her old man is always trying to one-up her last birthday party."

"Anna's in awful shape," said Floyd in a nervous voice. "She and Helen were like sisters. She's holed up in her room, not eating anything."

"Can we have a few words with her?" I asked.

Floyd shook his head, and clouds of steam shot out his nostrils. "I don't think that's such a good idea."

I looked at him and said, "You can either let us in or I can ask Judge Bringhurst to swear out a warrant. You decide."

He stared a long second, then fumbled for a ring of keys and stuck one into the gate's padlock. He slid the iron bars wide enough for me to squeeze through, followed by Roscoe. The press hounds moved in and shouted out questions as Floyd closed and padlocked the gate.

The three of us trudged through the snow. "Pfalzgraf's lawyer is Parley Tanner," said Floyd. "He's doing all the talking, and believe me, it isn't much."

With my hands buried in my pockets, I strolled around the doctor's library, sizing up the place. Bookcases covered the walls from floor to ceiling and required sliding ladders to reach the top. Medical volumes lined the west wall, classic literature to the east, history north, and books about art, music, and theater on the south. Framed photographs covered a gap between the southern bookcases: Pfalzgraf and Utah senator Reed Smoot; Pfalzgraf and '28 Democratic presidential contender Al Smith; Pfalzgraf and Charlie Chaplin; Pfalzgraf and Charles Lindbergh; the doctor and Helen standing in the White House with President Herbert Hoover and First Lady Lou Hoover.

Anna Pfalzgraf, the doctor's daughter by his first marriage, entered the room, sat on a love seat, and gestured to a floral-print couch on the other side of a marble and glass table. "Please, sit," she said quietly. We sat across from her, and the radiance of her face, accentuated by her brunette bobbed hair, momentarily took me aback. She could easily make it as a fashion model or moving picture star. Her tight-fitting black dress was part lace, part silk, and maybe some chiffon, and it covered her up to the base of her swan-like neck. She had the whitest, most perfect set of teeth I'd ever seen in a woman's mouth. I could tell she had been crying because her eyes were red and she had on no mascara, and in all of those framed photos on the wall, she had on plenty of mascara.

"We're trying to reconstruct Helen Kent Pfalzgraf's final hours," I said. "We'd like to know more about your contact with her . . ." I cleared my throat, squirmed a little, and considered my words carefully. "Toward the end of her life."

"The last time I talked to her was Thursday," said Anna. "Thursday night. She said she wouldn't be home for dinner on Friday."

"Did she say where she was going?" I asked.

Anna shook her head, then buried her face in her hands, and her body convulsed in sobs. "She was my best pal. Who else am I going to play Chinese checkers with?"

I eyed Roscoe, looking for a reaction. He shrugged. We gave her a minute.

"I keep thinking I'm going to see her again," she said, lifting her moist face out of her hands. "I keep thinking this is all a bad dream. I miss her so . . ."

"How did they get along?" asked Roscoe. "Your father and Helen?"

"Fine," she said, but she didn't sound convinced. "As far as I could see."

Roscoe said, "It's important you level with us."

"They loved each other. I think."

Roscoe pressed. "You *think*?"

"They always seemed happy. Most of the time."

"Which was it?" asked Roscoe. "Always? Or most of the time?"

"*Almost* always," she said.

"Something tells me you're holding back on us," said Roscoe. "If there's anything you're keeping from us, we're going to find out what it is. You might as well tell us."

She balled her fist, put it in front of her mouth, and cleared her throat. "The three of us—me and Daddy and Kitty . . . I've always called Helen Kitty—"

"Why?" asked Roscoe.

"It's a nickname. I started calling her Kitty right after she and Daddy met."

"How did they meet?" I asked.

"He met her at a Christmas party at Parley's—Parley Tanner. Daddy's lawyer. I've known the Tanners ever since I was a little girl. The Tanners had a Christmas party. This would've been the Christmas of '24—so a little over five years ago. The Tanners live right around the corner. They're like family to us. They *are* family to us."

"So the doctor met Helen at the party and the two of them got married a short time later?" asked Roscoe.

"Six months later."

"What did you think of her?" I asked.

"Kitty and I were always close. We were more like sisters than stepmother and stepdaughter. We were each other's confidants. We traveled all over Europe together."

Roscoe said, "Where in Europe? What part?"

"Everywhere—England, France, Denmark, Germany, Spain, Italy, Greece. We journeyed by rail from country to country. Kitty and I loved the Old World."

"How many times did the two of you go to Europe together?" I asked.

"We went every summer, but we'll never go together again," said Anna. She shed more tears. We gave her another minute as she dabbed her eyes with her handkerchief.

Roscoe said, "What did she do when the two of you were over there?"

"She loved to shop . . ."

"And?"

Anna wiped her eyes with a handkerchief and blinked quizzically at Roscoe.

She said, "Kitty visited art museums . . ."

"And?"

"Roscoe," I said. He eyed me, and I shook my head, code for *Ease off her.*

"What exactly do you wish me to say, Deputy Lund?" she asked, her voice tightening.

"Start with the truth. The two of you sailed off to Europe each summer. When you got there, she liked to shop and visit art museums. Now, my question to you is, What else did she like to do over there?"

"I've been telling you the things she liked to do. I wish you wouldn't keep pressing me. I don't know what it is you want to hear."

"The truth," said Roscoe.

I followed a different line. "Did your father go on these trips?"

"Mostly, it was just Helen and me who went," said Anna. She blinked at the ceiling, as if remembering. "Father joined us at the end of one, but this was our time—Helen's and my time—together. I've been on lots of trips with Father, of course, to Germany, to see his relatives, but those are different."

"You say the two of you were like sisters?" Roscoe asked.

"Yes . . ."

"So I imagine she talked to you a lot about her personal life?"

"Yes."

"Was there another man?"

"Pardon?" she asked.

I didn't like the line of questioning, so I leaned in close to him. I could smell the mix of cigarette smoke and aftershave absorbed into his uniform. "Roscoe . . ."

He leaned toward me with an angry gaze. "Let me question her *my way.*"

"Yes," she said—a response that surprised both of us. "There was."

We waited, but she didn't add anything. Roscoe said, "Who?"

"She met him in Paris. He was a Persian prince."

Roscoe's face stretched with a mix of surprise and skepticism. "You don't say. A bona fide Persian prince?"

She nodded and wiped her nose. "Prince Farzad. He had a longer name. Farzad . . . uh . . ." She strained to remember. "I can't remember. I'm sure it's all in the letters."

Roscoe said, "He wasn't some charlatan trying to pass himself off—"

"No, he was a real prince."

"You mentioned letters?" I asked.

"Please don't tell Daddy. She didn't want him to know."

Roscoe said, "Know what?"

"About the love letters that Farzad sent her."

"Did you see these letters?" asked Roscoe.

"No." She wasn't much of a liar, and she knew it. She recanted fast. "Well, yes, I did, but Helen swore me up and down to secrecy."

"Do you know where we can find them?" I asked.

"No." Her lower lip quivered; her eyes moistened. Roscoe flashed me a *Here come the waterworks again* look. She managed not to sob, but it wasn't easy. "I'm not sure where she kept them. She showed them to me once, last summer. They smelled of perfume."

Roscoe said, "How many?"

"I'm not sure. Nine, maybe ten. Possibly more. They were in those red, white, and blue airmail envelopes, tied together by a ribbon.

They were addressed to a post office box. I guess that's how Kitty got them past Daddy."

I said, "Did Helen let you read the letters?"

"No. She read snippets to me."

Roscoe said, "Did you meet this Persian bird?"

"Once. In Paris. The three of us went out to dinner, to a little restaurant on the Seine. He was charming. He spoke perfect English, with the Oxford diction."

"How'd they meet?" asked Roscoe.

"I don't know. I wasn't there when it happened. Kitty never told me." She stopped talking and looked at me with pained eyes, then at Roscoe. "I'm tired."

He and I spoke in overlapping sentences. Me: "We've taken up enough of your time." Roscoe: "Just a few more questions . . ."

I stood up and nudged Roscoe. "Let's go."

"But I'm not finished—"

"Let's go!"

Roscoe grunted as he stood and trailed me to the front door. Outside, Floyd led us to the gate, and we dodged reporters all the way to the county auto.

We motored west on South Temple, toward downtown. The Walker Building came into view, the tallest building between Chicago and San Francisco at sixteen stories high, with a huge neon sign on top flashing the building's name. A few blocks away from the jail, I broke the silence.

"She lost her stepmother."

"Christ, Art, those were softballs you were tossing her." Roscoe rolled the window down a crack and lit a cigarette. "Next time I can't get to sleep, I know where to go."

Neither of us said another word as I steered into the county jail lot. What could either of us have said at that moment? I didn't like him, and I sensed, probably correctly, the feeling was mutual. It wasn't just because our methods were different, nor was it his re-fusal to compromise. No, a more fundamental rift existed. Roscoe's rage troubled me. We had been partners for a few months, and here I was, wondering how on earth I was going to make it through this investigation one more day working with such a hard-bitten man.

five

"Are you sure you want to see this?" asked Tom Livsey.

"Yep. I'm sure. Let's have a look."

He pulled the chrome lever until it clicked, opened the white door, and wheeled out a stretcher with a corpse under a sheet. Roscoe stood behind me, and I could sense him looking over my shoulder. Tom tugged the sheet off the head, and the odor almost overwhelmed me. He noticed the color in my face draining away and gestured to a sink behind me.

"If you have to upchuck . . ."

I shook my head.

He smiled. "I figured it wouldn't hurt to point it out."

Roscoe tapped my shoulder, and I faced him. He dangled a white handkerchief in front of me, which I accepted with a nod of gratitude and then held over my nose and mouth. I surveyed the damage. She hardly looked human anymore. They had cleaned all of the mud and blood and debris off of her and brushed back what greasy hair remained. Her one remaining eye was closed, and her body was so badly discolored that you'd never guess she had been pale-skinned in her lifetime. I forced myself to look at her body, but I couldn't for very long.

At my side now, Roscoe smirked at me. "She's seen better days. You don't look so good, either. What say we go outside, get some fresh air?"

"No. I've got to see her."

With my eyes fixed on the row of light globes on the ceiling, I steeled myself to resume examining her. I tilted my head down and tried to take in the rest. One of her breasts had been torn clean off, and bones were showing in spots. She was missing some fingers, and her left foot was almost entirely severed.

I felt my partly digested breakfast surging up my throat like molten lava, and that's when I turned to the sink and vomited in one violent heave as I grabbed porcelain and closed my eyes. It took a few seconds for me to catch my breath, and I felt Roscoe's big hand patting me on the shoulder. A bitter taste coated my tongue.

"Sorry, fellas," I said, my eyes closed, everything dark. "I guess I wasn't ready."

"Don't apologize," said Tom. "It's a normal reaction. It took me time to get used to this job. I suppose I'm still not all the way there yet."

I blinked to adjust my eyes and smiled at Roscoe, who leaned against the wall with folded arms, watching my every move. Everything was so white in that room: the octagon-shaped floor tiles, the freshly painted walls, the door with painted words on pebbled glass that read COUNTY MORGUE—DR. L. NASH, COUNTY CORONER on the other side, even the frame on the transom above the door. What wasn't white was stainless steel—cold to the touch.

Tom read from his clipboard. "Helen Pfalzgraf suffered a severe blow to the head before being hit by her automobile, so she was either unconscious or dead when the car ran over her. We found the piece of ore used to bash her skull, in the trunk of her Cadillac, of

all places." He paused to turn the page and skimmed the next
document. "Her stomach was empty, but she had liquor in her system. Her blood alcohol level was approaching point thirteen, so she
must've had a fair bit to drink that night."

I said, "Were you here when Dr. Pfalzgraf identified her body?"

"As a matter of fact, I was," he said. "Funny thing: He didn't appear to be very shaken up. He walked in with Dr. Nash, I pulled
down the sheet, and he looked at her for about ten seconds, nodded,
and left. Sheriff Cannon questioned him out in the hall. And that
was it."

"Do you remember what the sheriff asked?" Roscoe wanted to
know.

Tom shook his head. "I didn't get most of it, although I did hear
Cannon ask Pfalzgraf when was the last time he saw her alive."

Tom pulled the sheet up over the body and pushed the drawer
closed until something metallic clicked.

"And?" Roscoe prompted.

"I heard the doctor say he saw his wife last on Friday afternoon.
He wanted to spend the evening with her, but she had other plans."

"Did the doctor say anything else?" I asked.

It took a second, but Tom remembered. "When he identified the
body, he said there were some items missing: her wedding ring and
an antique oval locket with a picture of her mother in it. There were
no signs of these articles at the murder scene. The sheriff ruled out
robbery, only because Pfalzgraf had four thousand six hundred
dollars' worth of jewelry on her or scattered near her at the murder
site, and she was carrying hundreds of dollars in cash in her purse,
which the police found in the backseat of her car up in Ogden."

"Thanks, Tom," I said.

Tom's face lit up from remembering something. "Oh yeah. One
other thing. She was pregnant."

I tried to conceal my shock, but I have a feeling Livsey picked up on it. If the news left Roscoe dumbfounded, he hid it better than me. I said, "How far along?"

"About three months. Give or take a week." He walked over to a desk, pulled out a swivel chair on wheels, and sat down. "Every bone in her body was broken. I've estimated she was run over by the car at least seven, maybe eight, times."

I took a deep breath and let out a shaky exhale, still trying to come to grips with Helen being pregnant at the time of her death.

Tom looked up from his report. "You gonna be OK, Art?"

"Yeah. Thanks, Tom."

Roscoe put on his Stetson and pulled it low. "I'm starving," he said. "S'get the fuck outta here."

The Vienna Café at 144 South Maine was a narrow eatery with booths and a checkerboard linoleum floor. The long counter had chrome swivel barstools bolted to the floor, each with a corresponding condiment rack nearby. The sign out front proclaiming the Vienna to be UTAH'S FINEST EATING ESTABLISHMENT was sheer hyperbole, although they did serve the best seafood downtown. You couldn't go wrong with the fish and chips, but I hardly touched mine due to a loss of appetite after seeing Helen Pfalzgraf's remains. Meantime, Roscoe devoured his chicken fried steak like a man who'd just emerged from the mountains after days of not eating, unfazed by what he'd witnessed a half hour earlier.

The lunch crowd filled the place. A hunched man on a barstool caught my attention. The homely son of a gun—chinless, buckteeth, John Gilbert mustache—was dipping his toast in egg yolk and kept peeking at us. His worsted suit was too big for him, and the material on the elbows was frayed. He noticed me, too, and he sipped coffee and eased backward off his barstool. He rubbed his hand on his jacket as he approached us, then extended it and flashed one of the homeliest smiles in modern history.

"Seymour Considine," he said. I shook his hand, which was either moist or greasy (I couldn't tell which). When Roscoe didn't shake Considine's hand, he lowered it out of sight. He said to Roscoe, "Remember me? Fort Collins? The Chester Hicks case. I covered it for *Real Mystery Stories* magazine. You wouldn't talk to me."

Roscoe's mouth was full, and he wiped the corners with his linen napkin before speaking. "Sure. I remember you. Now get lost, chump, before I up and give you the heave-ho myself. There's a foul odor, and it's ruining my lunch."

Considine ignored him, eyeing me instead. "Maybe you read my coverage of the Ruth Snyder–Judd Gray trial. I was nominated for the Golden Magnifying Glass for those stories. I didn't win, but I was one of five finalists."

"We don't like to associate with lawbreakers," said Roscoe.

"What do you mean?" asked Considine.

"I know you got your ass thrown in jail for jumping the wall at the Pfalzgraf place," said Roscoe. "Now leave us the hell alone."

Considine said to me, "I dig up all kinds of information the law can't find. You know, *real dirt*. I could be of use to you, and I know you could be of use to me. I was thinking of an exchange of information, a little quid pro quo. What do you say, Deputy"—he squinted to read my nameplate—"Oveson."

"Maybe you don't hear so well, Considine," said Roscoe. "I said get lost."

His face sagging in defeat, Considine returned to the counter, leaving Roscoe and me to eat in silence.

"I gotta take a leak," said Roscoe at the end of his meal. He got up and walked back through a door at the rear of the restaurant.

This is my opportunity, I thought. I walked over to where Considine was sitting and leaned against the counter near him. He glanced at me and raised his eyebrows in acknowledgment.

"Your friend could use a few lessons in manners," he said.

"I'll be quick, because he won't be in the restroom long," I said. "I'd like to take you up on your offer. It's probably better that you don't to call me at work. I'm at home most evenings. My telephone number is Wasatch four-eight-four."

He uncapped a pen and wrote the number on the back of his hand, looked past me, and made a long face. His signal for *Your partner is coming.* I dropped a couple of coins by the cash register and told Roscoe I was treating. He snatched a cinnamon toothpick and let it dance on his lips for a minute but didn't bother saying thank you.

At the cash register, Annie, the owner's redheaded, apple-cheeked wife, punched in our bill. "You hardly touched your fish and chips, Art," she said. "Everything alright?"

"Fine, thanks, Annie. I guess I just wasn't hungry."

"It's not like you," she said as I dropped coins in her palm. "You usually clean off your plate. Want a box, to take it home in, for your daughter?"

"No thanks. I don't think my appetite will be returning anytime soon."

Considine eyed me over his plate of food. Roscoe stood two feet away. Even though he wasn't studying my every move, I played it safe by pretending to ignore Considine. As we exited the café, a little brass bell on the door rang.

"Daddy, Daddy, does this piece fit?"

Sarah Jane, a freckly sprite with brown hair in pigtails, held up the puzzle piece. Cerulean sky. We sat side by side at the dining room table. She pressed the blue piece against another piece with colorful tulip bulbs but couldn't fit them together.

The cathedral radio in the next room played violin music while outside a snowstorm pummeled the valley.

"It doesn't go there, S. J.," I said. I held up the box and showed her the windmill, the blue sky, and the tulip bulbs. "This is Holland. The blue sky goes above the hill and the windmill."

"Have you ever been there, Daddy?"

I smiled as I set the lid on the table. "Nope, but I'd love to go."

She blinked at the puzzle for a moment and snapped her blue-sky piece with another blue-sky piece. She smiled triumphantly as she sorted through other pieces with her index finger. "Where'd you go on your mission, Daddy?"

"Los Angeles."

"What was it like?"

"Hot," I said. "Big, too. There were lots of palm trees. And if you reached up . . ." I lifted my arm high. "You could pick an orange. I'd grab one off the branch and rip the peel off and eat the sections one at a time. Nothing hit the spot on a hot day better than that."

"What else was there?"

I snapped two tulip pieces together. "They had these big Pacific Electric streetcars. They called 'em Red Cars because of their color. You could hop on one and in twenty minutes you'd step out at the ocean."

Clara entered the room through the swinging kitchen door holding a glass of lemonade on ice. She passed it to me and smiled at Sarah Jane, who triumphantly snapped two more pieces together.

"Thanks," I said, sampling the lemonade.

"You're welcome. How much longer until you two are finished?"

"Mommy?" said Sarah Jane.

"Yes, dear?"

"Can we go to Holland?"

"We'll see. Let's focus on putting this puzzle together, so we can get you to bed soon." Clara walked over to the table and winced when she got a good look at all the pieces. She picked up the lid and inspected it. "My goodness, Art. Two hundred and fifty? Couldn't you have picked one with fewer pieces?"

"It was the smallest one they had at Skaggs," I said.

"You two had better finish this tomorrow."

"We can't," said Sarah Jane. "We've got another puzzle to put together tomorrow."

Clara's mouth fell open. "Another one?"

"The Grand Canyon," she said. "Right, Daddy?"

Clara glared at me. I spoke haltingly. "I meant to tell you. There was a sale on puzzles."

Sarah Jane burst into giggles, and I could tell it was going to be a late night for her, which meant it was going to be a late night for me as well.

For most of my life, I've been plagued by insomnia. I spend hours staring at the shadows on the ceiling and listening to the ticking of the alarm clock. Insomnia comes in different forms. Some sufferers can't get to sleep for a long time, while others—and I fall into this category—have an easy time drifting off to sleep but wake up in the middle of the night and can't fall asleep again. For as long as I can remember, I've been a light sleeper, and on Saturdays—my only day to sleep in—I was incapable of sleeping beyond about seven thirty in the morning.

In general, lawmen are more susceptible to insomnia than other people. Insomnia, like the nightmares that often precede it, comes with the job. Each lawman thinks different thoughts while tossing and turning in the darkness, but at some point, many of us are haunted by that one unsolved homicide case. For me, the murder of Hazel Hamilton, six months before Sheriff Cannon deputized me, was that case.

At the time, I was working as a dispatcher at the Provo Police Department, a job I landed thanks to the behind-closed-door machinations of my older brother Grant. Newspaper headlines and radio reports told and retold her tragic story. She was twelve when it happened. Born in Duluth, Minnesota, Hazel moved with her family a few times and finally settled in Salt Lake City. She had a five-year-old sister and three-year-old brother and lived with her family in a two-story brick house on Fourth South and Fifth East. She went missing on New Year's Eve day 1928. Her parents telephoned the police midmorning to report that she had been gone a few hours and it wasn't like her to leave without telling them. Her younger sister, June, told the police that a car had pulled up and the driver had lured Hazel inside. June didn't see the driver's face, but she said Hazel smiled and nodded while talking to the motorist and willingly climbed in, which led police to theorize that the murderer was someone Hazel knew.

The next day, county deputies found Hazel's badly beaten and mutilated body in a rural canal that ran parallel to Redwood Road, a wide, dusty street full of potholes. You couldn't find a more desolate stretch of the valley—snowy fields that turned to weeds in May, no houses for a few miles.

When news of the killing broke, a wave of panic spread across Salt Lake City. Frightened parents escorted their children to school and picked them up in the afternoon. In many instances, children were not allowed to leave their yards on the weekends and holidays. You could feel fear in the air well into the fall.

In the dead of summer, late July '29, shortly after starting my deputy job, I drove out to where the deputies found the body. I squatted at the edge of the canal to get a better look at the stone marker her family had placed there. HAZEL HAMILTON, 1916–1929. OUR BELOVED DAUGHTER & SISTER. WE WILL BE TOGETHER AGAIN.

Nothing grew in the fields near the spot where the body was found. It was as if a curse had been placed on the earth there. Staring at the canal's murky water, I dwelled on how terrifying her final moments on earth must have been. I remembered the coroner's report: *raped and assaulted*. I couldn't think about it for very long.

How could anyone focus on such a ghastly crime without going a little bit crazy?

Four months into the investigation, Sheriff Cannon touched off a fierce public outcry when he accused the girl's father, Raymond Hamilton, of direct involvement in the "foul deed." "I am not sure what his exact role was in this tragedy," Cannon told a room full of reporters and radiomen, "but I have reason to believe, based on evidence in our office, that he played some part in the tragic death of his daughter. Only time will tell if I'm right, but I believe I am."

Turned out Cannon had no evidence to back up his accusation, which he later admitted. By the spring of '29, most of the leads in the Hamilton case had gone cold. Cannon's future as sheriff was more precarious than ever. He still faced accusations of corruption arising from a scheme he concocted a year before Hazel disappeared to tax local gamblers. Allegations of ineptitude and corruption were taking a toll on his reputation. It only made matters worse that his opponent, Lorenzo Blackham, the respected sheriff of Weber County (north of Salt Lake City) looking to return to his hometown, had already won the endorsements of key local politicians and businessmen.

Now here I was, "Cannon's spy"—a lackey for a man whose days as sheriff were numbered. I wanted as little to do with him as possible, yet I feared for my future if I didn't cooperate. The election was still months away, this November, so I sought a cautious middle line: stall him, feed him as little information as possible, keep him wondering—but not too much. The way I saw it, sometimes not doing anything is actually a way of doing *something*.

These were the kinds of things I thought about while I roamed the halls of my house in the wee hours of the morning, hoping Mr. Sandman would pay another visit soon.

Six

Naked and dripping water, I tried to remember my locker combination.

A dozen deputies were in the locker room across the hall from the gymnasium in the county jail building. Sheriff Cannon insisted his deputies take part in an hour of rigorous calisthenics each morning before going out on patrol. "It clears your mind of all cobwebs," he once told us, "and makes you better lawmen." The men obeyed, despite grumbling among the heavier fellows.

So here we were, carrying out his directive before the A.M. rounds. Men leaned in close to mirrors as they ran straight razors over their lather-covered necks. Metal slammed against metal with the opening and closing of locker doors. Showers hissed, filling the air with steam, and the soles of bare feet slapped tile. For some reason, I was blanking out on the last number of my locker combination. Roscoe sat on a bench bolted to the tile floor, already dressed, tying his shoes and eyeing me.

"Sixteen," he said.

"Come again?"

"Sixteen is the last number."

"Oh." I arched my eyebrows. I turned right to 16. *Bingo.* "Thanks."

"Don't mention it."

Three men—Romney, McKitrick, and Glendon—stepped out of the showers with white towels wrapped around their waists and began turning the dials on their lockers. Glendon was fat, while the other two men were lean and pale-skinned.

"I'm just saying the man is inept," said Romney.

Glendon laughed. "That's one word for it."

"I'd say that's about the *only* word for it," said Romney. "Cannon wouldn't know how to solve a murder case with the confessed killer in custody. The other day, I stuck five dollars in an envelope and mailed it to the Lorenzo Blackham for Sheriff Campaign. If Cannon's reelected, I'm quitting my job. I don't care if times are hard. Unemployment can't be worse than working for that SOB."

I scooped my temple garments out of my locker and put them on, avoiding eye contact with the others. Their talk made me feel uncomfortable in the extreme, and I did everything in my power to stay out of it.

"Cannon is pussyfooting, sending us on one wild-goose chase after another," said McKitrick. "It's like he isn't even trying."

"All he gives a shit about is getting voted back in office," said Roscoe. He eyed me with a grin. "What do you think, Art?"

I glanced at him as I buttoned my shirt, hiding my anger about being asked the question. "I guess I don't have much of an opinion, one way or the other."

"C'mon, Art," said McKitrick. "You must feel *something*. This is our future we're talking about here. I don't see how you can sit on the fence."

I put one leg in my pants, then the other, and tugged up the zipper. "Put yourself in Cannon's shoes," I said. "He's faced a lot of challenges these past few years. Think about it: the Hazel Hamilton murder, thefts, homicides on the rise, and now this. The newspapers are turning it into a soap opera."

"Sounds to me like you're on his side, Oveson," said Romney, running a comb through his thin hair and gazing at the mirror in his locker. "Are you?"

I closed my locker and faced the men getting dressed. "Last I checked there were only two sides: the law and the lawbreakers."

"I'll shoot straight with you, Art," said McKitrick. "I noticed Cannon calling you aside the other day. Just you. I have to admit, it got me wondering about you, where your loyalties lie. The men don't care for a snitch, you know."

I glared at McKitrick. "If I run into any snitches, I'll tell 'em you said that. Now if you'll excuse me . . ."

"We're just looking out for you," said Romney. "Sooner or later Cannon's going to be out on the pavement. We don't want to see the same thing happen to you. You seem like a decent sort. And your father—well, he was the best in the business. It's too bad he didn't live to become chief of police."

"I appreciate you looking after me," I said, "but I can take care of myself."

Glendon moved his chunky body in my way, dangling a piece of paper in his fingers. I stared at him a few seconds, and he wiggled the paper. "We're circulating this letter for the deputies to sign. It's calling for Cannon's resignation. Our goal is to get all the deputies to sign on. We've only got five signatures so far, but I understand Boyd has agreed to sign. We figure if we can get a few more John Hancocks, maybe some of the other fellows won't be so yellow about adding their names."

"We plan on sending it to the *Examiner,* and they're gonna print it word for word and have a reporter do up a story on it," said McKitrick. "We're endorsing Blackham for sheriff. What do you say, Art? Care to sign?"

All eyes were on me. I sighed and gazed down at the checker-board tiles on the floor. "No thank you. I don't want to get involved."

"You're already involved," said Roscoe. "You're in it like the rest of us."

At that moment, I loathed Roscoe worse than anybody else in my life. His shiny bald head, sunken eyes, toothy grin, gravelly voice—everything about him I disliked. I noticed the contempt in his eyes as he watched me. I said, "Maybe if you men spent a little more time searching for Helen Pfalzgraf's killer and a little less time grousing, we might actually bust the criminal for once."

I walked out. I could feel all eyes on me.

Sometimes a man reaches a point where he simply doesn't care anymore.

The Wednesday morning after we found Helen Pfalzgraf's body down by the Pole Line Road, I sat alone in a long common room full of desks. Most of the men were out on patrol. I had no idea of Roscoe's whereabouts, and truth be told, I didn't want to know.

I telephoned Dr. Pfalzgraf. Leaning back in my swivel chair, I lifted the receiver on the candlestick telephone and raised the transmitter to my mouth. The party line popped with static, but I heard the operator's voice. "Number, please?"

"Operator, ring State nine-ninety-eight."

"Now ringing. Please hold the line."

"Thank you."

Party line chatter: *"I'm going to make it up to the dry goods store on Wednesday . . ." "Yes, our water line froze down here late last night and now it's leaking everywhere . . ." "We're hoping it'll be a warmer March than it was last year . . ." "Sorry, LaMarr told me you was comin' next Tuesday . . ."*

"You may go ahead," said the operator.

A woman's voice said, "Dr. Pfalzgraf's office, may I help you?"

"Hello," I said. "I'm Deputy Art Oveson, Salt Lake County Sheriff's Office. To whom am I speaking, please?"

"Eunice Mickelson, Dr. Pfalzgraf's secretary."

"I wish to speak to Dr. Pfalzgraf."

"If this is about his donation to Sheriff Cannon's reelection—"

"No, I just had a question for him."

"Oh." A good ten seconds of silence followed. I almost spoke, but I thought I should wait for her to say something. "Well, Deputy, you may wish to contact his attorney—"

"Parley Tanner?"

"Yes. He's at Grand seven-eighty-five."

I nodded and stared out the windows at the snow falling on downtown Salt Lake City. "Thank you. I'll try Mr. Tanner. If the doctor suddenly finds himself in a talkative mood, maybe you can let him know that I can be reached at County nine-ten."

"I'll pass him the message, Deputy. Mind you, I can't guarantee anything."

"No, of course not," I said. "Until tomorrow."

I lowered the receiver on the metal cradle, pushed the telephone aside, and massaged my temples, hoping to offset the effects of a headache.

"Oveson! My office!"

I turned to see Cannon, sleeves rolled up, snapping his suspenders. He turned and ducked into the twin doors of his office, leaving the left one open for me. I momentarily feared the worst. What if he heard me telephoning Pfalzgraf's office? I walked past rows of desks, past a bulletin board covered with WANTED posters, past a watercooler and a large, unused carpeted space to his office entrance.

He had an enormous office with spinning ceiling fans, plush green carpeting, and huge arched windows looking out to the City and County Building across the street. Brass lamps with green glass shades furnished soft light. Cold wind blew snowflakes through an open window and brought the office's temperature to meat locker levels. Cannon squirmed in his thronelike chair behind a long oak desk, and Sykes sat off to the side, right leg over left knee. Cannon smiled. Sykes frowned.

"Have a seat, Art," Cannon said, "but please close the door behind you first."

I did as asked, pulling the door gently shut until the knob clicked, then sat on one of two high-backed leather chairs that faced his desk.

"It's Wednesday morning," said Cannon. "The coroner's office will begin a public inquest in less than a week. The coroner says his goal is to bring together all of the information from the police and sheriff's department investigations into one hearing, to make all the evidence available to the public. Frankly, I think it all stinks."

"Yes, sir."

Sykes said, "I understand Nash has already subpoenaed Helen Pfalzgraf's younger sister and a fellow who claims he got a look at the suspect who ditched her Cadillac up in Ogden. If you ask me, I think Nash and Livsey are just trying to make Sheriff Cannon here look bad, like he's not on top of the investigation."

I nodded, trying my best to stay out of the fray. "It sounds like they've built quite a case."

Cannon scrunched his face in displeasure. "Truth is, I haven't been happy with the progress of this investigation. I've put all of my men on this case and all we have to show for it are a bunch of lurid headlines."

He opened a file folder that contained a few newspaper clippings. He held one up and read from it. "From the *Los Angeles Times*: MURDERED SOCIALITE CAUGHT IN LOVE TRIANGLE." He dropped it and picked up another. "From the *New York Times* . . . Let's see, what have we got here? SLAIN UTAH WOMAN ROMANCED BY PERSIAN PRINCE BEFORE DEATH." He put it down and arched his eyebrows at the next one. "This is my personal favorite. From the *Salt Lake Examiner*:

SHERIFF'S DEPUTIES MAKE LITTLE HEADWAY IN PFALZGRAF INVESTI-
GATION."

He closed the folder and nudged it aside. His smile never left.
"Do you know what gets me the most about all of this? These newspaper reporters know more about this investigation than me. I'll
give you a for instance. They knew about Helen Pfalzgraf's secret
bank accounts totaling . . ."

He opened the folder, picked up another clipping, and read
from it. "Seven thousand eight hundred dollars. That includes her
accounts in banks in Los Angeles and San Francisco, and that's just
for starters. I knew nothing about these accounts until I read the
newspapers. As if that wasn't bad enough, I get a telephone call this
morning from"—he glanced at a yellow pad on his desk—"a Mr.
Con . . . Conside . . ."

"Seymour Considine?" I asked.

He looked up at me and blinked a few times. "Goes by the ini-
tials S. J. Do you know him?"

"Sure," I said. "He writes for one of those true crime magazines.
I just barely met him at the Vienna. He came up and introduced
himself to Roscoe and me."

"Well, Considine delivered a major sucker punch this morning,"
said Cannon. "He said Dr. and Missus Pfalzgraf paid a visit to Pfalzgraf's attorney, Parley Tanner, the day before the murder. Considine found a stenographer from Tanner's law office who went on
the record saying she overheard the word 'divorce' used repeatedly.
Of course, the woman has been dismissed from her job, but the
damage has been done. What's worse is I knew nothing about it
until that Considine fella flapped his mouth. Most of what I know
about this case, I've learned from the newspapers."

"I'm sorry, sir," I said. "I want to assure you I've been earning
my keep. The other day, I telephoned Helen's father in Twin Falls,
Idaho. He said he hasn't seen her for years and he's not even plan-

ning on going to her funeral. He shouted at me to leave him alone and hung up on me. One of Helen's sisters, Constance Higginbotham, still lives in Salt Lake, and Deputy Evans has questioned her, and I've requested a copy of the transcript as soon as Faye has it typed up. I've been out to the murder site twice looking for additional clues, but I've come up empty-handed. We've been sorting through two hundred telephone calls, letters, and eyewitness reports. I've called around to the local mining companies to trace the piece of galena ore that was used to hit Helen Pfalzgraf in the head. I've placed a call to—"

He cut me off with a wave, and his smile grew even wider, which surprised me. "Art, I don't need a rundown of your weekly activities. I know you're no slacker. If all my deputies were like you, I wouldn't be losing sleep at night."

I gulped nervously, and, despite icy wind blasting through the open window, beads of sweat formed on my brow. "Well, sir," I said, "is there something I can do to help?"

Cannon jerked an upbeat nod at Sykes. "See what I mean about this boy? He's just the type of capital fellow I'd like to be on my team in the final minutes of a nail-biter. Isn't he something?"

"Yes, sir," said Sykes, deadpanning all the way. "He *is* something."

Cannon looked at me and said, "I need you to speak frankly and tell me what the general sentiment is among the deputies toward me at this time. I would very much like to hear your observations."

"My observations, sir?"

"Yes. Please tell me your impressions."

How to tell him his deputies detested him? He struck me as the kind of person who'd slay the messenger if the news were bad, and in this case, positive words eluded me. Yet here he was, staring at me with that permanent smile on his face, waiting for an answer. The clock ticked on the table behind him.

I picked the wrong time to have a severe case of cottonmouth. I could see from his slight wince that he detected my uneasiness. Finally, I managed to speak. "Well, sir, I think it is safe to say that in all the time I've been here, the esprit de corps of the men has never been higher."

He blinked as though trying to make sense of what I just said. Lucky for me, he didn't try too hard. The smile only faded for a few seconds, before it returned in full force. "That's what I like to hear," he said, banging his desk with the palm of his hand. "It's a proven fact that high morale makes for good crime fighting."

Sykes nodded and said, "It is the basis of any effective law enforcement organization."

"You're darn right!" said Cannon. He chuckled, which petered out into a grunt while his eyes studied me. "I understand you paid a visit to Dr. Pfalzgraf's place the other day. Talked to his daughter."

"Yes, sir. I felt it was important to find out what she knew—"

Cannon cut me off. "There's something I forgot to tell you the first time we discussed this case."

"What's that, sir?"

"Leave Dr. Pfalzgraf and his daughter out of it."

"Begging your pardon, sir?"

"I questioned him already, Oveson. I'm convinced he had nothing to do with his wife's murder. He's a solid, upstanding citizen in every respect. His daughter has an alibi, so I took the liberty of ruling her out, too."

"Well, don't you think I should at least—"

"The Pfalzgrafs are distraught. The man just lost his wife. I could tell when I questioned him he's innocent. Something else . . ." His words trailed off.

"What's that?"

"What I'm about to tell you is just between you and me and Sykes here. The doctor gave me a generous donation toward my reelection campaign. It'll enable me to put up some new billboards along Highway 91. I happen to know Lorenzo Blackham's billboards are getting a lot of attention, and—well—I'd like a few of my own, just to show the public I'm serious about winning my bid for reelection."

Even with my instinct to avoid conflict, I could not hide my disgust with what Cannon was proposing. "So you don't want me to investigate Dr. Pfalzgraf because he gave you a campaign donation?"

"That's a crude way of putting it," Sykes said angrily. "A better way of saying it is that Sheriff Cannon interrogated Pfalzgraf already and he's convinced the doctor's innocent. It's hard times we're living in, Oveson, and we've got no business wasting taxpayers' money chasing after someone who's clearly innocent."

"With all due respect, I think he should be treated like every other suspect in this case—"

"I don't care what you think, Deputy," said Cannon, scowling at me now. "I'm not accustomed to having my orders challenged. Understand?"

"Yes, sir. I understand."

What was I going to say? Men were losing their jobs all over the place. What about Clara and my children? What of my monthly mortgage payment? There were bills to pay, too—hydroelectric, coal, the iceman, the milkman, water. We would never get rich from my salary, but it kept a roof over our heads. Clara received a steady income from her teaching job, but I couldn't let her be the family breadwinner. What would my brothers say? The Oveson name would be shamed.

My heart raced. I squirmed, squeaking against the leather chair, and the cold wind sliced my ear like a straight razor.

"So I can count on you to play ball?" asked Cannon, smiling once more.

I said, "Yes, sir. I can be counted on."

"Didn't I tell you?" Cannon asked Sykes. "A real go-getter."

Sykes nodded, and for the first time his lips formed something vaguely resembling a smile. He said, "The genuine article."

"You're someone to watch out for, Oveson," said Sheriff Cannon. "You're the bird who's going places in this business."

I stood up and walked over to the door. Cannon said, "Remember, Oveson. I reward loyalty. And so far, you've got a blue-ribbon attitude, son."

"Yes, sir," I said, glancing over my shoulder, mustering a smile. I overheard Cannon say, "Now there goes one heck of a kid."

Seven

The dream always plays out the same way.

Blinding whiteness envelops me as I walk forward. The contours of a hospital hallway slowly take shape. Nurses wheel patients on gurneys, and a woman's voice pages a physician on the loudspeakers. I reach room 402 and notice Dad's name on a medical chart attached to a clipboard. Dad, in a medical gown, lies on his back with an intravenous tube in his arm, eyes closed. His brown hair is combed back, which makes his hairline seem even more receding than usual, and his chin is pulled into his neck. The doctor had removed the bullets and bandaged the wounds where he got shot. Outside, the largest storm in Utah history blankets the valley with snow. In here, radiators bang and rattle, filling the room with warm, thick air.

I am twelve years old, about to turn thirteen. It is 1914 again. There is so much I want to tell him. We are reading *The Adventures of Huckleberry Finn* in English class, and I yearn to talk to him about it, ask him if he'd read it, share my impressions.

Dad's eyes are closed, and his chest rises slightly with each breath. His right hand dangles over the bed's edge, so I lift it by the wrist, lay it across his chest next to his other, and pull the sheet higher, bringing it nearly to his neck. I slide a chair closer and sit at his bedside, waiting for him to open his eyes and say something. *Anything.*

Dad opens his eyes. I am no longer eleven. I am twenty-nine and it is 1930.

I want to tell him everything that has happened in the last sixteen years. I'll show him pictures of my wedding reception—me in a rented tuxedo, Clara in a white wedding dress—and remind him that she and I fell in love in the seventh grade. I'll describe his grandchildren and tell him how strongly they resemble him. I'll hold up my polished deputy's badge so he can see it, and I'll ask him what one piece of advice he'd pass on to a beginning lawman.

The three words we had such a difficult time telling each other when he was alive—*I love you*—will come out of our mouths so naturally.

Dad rarely said he loved me, but he showed me every day with his actions: taking me fishing; teaching me how to cook frankfurters over an open fire; leading me on the best hiking trails at Zion and Bryce and Canyonlands and in the high Uintas. He showed his love for me by waking up each morning and going to work.

So much I had to tell him.

But our time is up.

His eyes widen, he places his hand over his heart, his face twists in pain and the life leaves him.

I search for serenity in his eyes but find none. All I see is terror. I have no reason to believe he went somewhere else. He simply ceases to exist, and when his bodily functions stop, his consciousness ends.

At least in my dream, that is how it played out.

I will not see him again, and I did not have a chance to say a proper good-bye.

The dream ends there. With each awakening, I jerk upright to catch my breath, drenched in sweat, heart racing.

When I awoke this night, I leaped out of bed and stumbled to the bureau drawer where I had left my star-shaped badge. The moon illuminated the engraved words: SALT LAKE COUNTY DEPUTY SHERIFF. I ran my fingertips along the lines and grooves and tiny canyons.

"I wish you could see this, Dad," I whispered.

Each time I dreamed the dream, I would cling to the hope of glimpsing calmness in his eyes. Maybe once, *once,* he'd die peacefully and I would feel as though he had moved on to the other side.

My dreams are not so cooperative. They torment me. The father in my dreams has only agony in his eyes.

The coroner's inquest convened at 9:00 A.M. sharp on the morning of Monday, March 3, 1930. It was held inside the city council chambers, a big room with twinkling chandeliers and plenty of space for a jury of six and a hundred spectators. I arrived a half hour early, hoping for a good seat, but the place was almost full. No surprise. This case had evolved—or should I say *devolved*—into a nationwide soap opera, and we Salt Lakers had the best seat in the house. This was the biggest homicide case to happen in Utah since the murder of Hazel Hamilton. In fact, the coroner, Dr. Laird Nash, announced that he would set up loudspeakers in the packed hallway for the overflow crowd.

When the inquest opened, I spotted Dr. Hans Pfalzgraf in the front right corner of the room, sitting next to his attorney, Parley Tanner. Pfalzgraf was straight out of Hollywood central casting for the kindly old doctor role, with his round face, wire-rimmed glasses, thinning white hair, and white mustache.

On the other side of Pfalzgraf sat my old friend Floyd Samuelson in his dark security guard outfit and matching cap. He turned in his chair until he made eye contact with me, smiled, and gave a wave.

I looked back over my shoulder and made eye contact with Buddy Hawkins, two rows behind me, seated beside Wit Dunaway. Buddy nodded, I nodded back, and I faced forward. Roscoe and I squirmed on the hard, pewlike bench. He opened the color Sunday funny papers and began reading "Mutt and Jeff," laughing under his breath.

"All rise," said a bailiff.

Everybody stood, and in walked Dr. Nash in a navy blue three-piece suit, white shirt, and yellow tie. He took a seat at the center of a long table in the front of the room, placed a stack of file folders to his right, and tipped a stainless steel pitcher to fill a glass with water. "Please be seated."

He waited a moment for the sound of creaking benches and scooting chairs to settle. "This is the coroner's inquest into the death of Mrs. Helen Kent Pfalzgraf, resident of 1285 East South Temple here in Salt Lake City. I am Dr. Laird Nash. I would like to remind you that this hearing is purely for informational purposes. I shall summon a series of witnesses, review professional reports, and present evidence that I hope will clarify all relevant issues. This is not a civil or criminal trial, and, as you can plainly see, it is open to the public."

People in the room laughed. Roscoe ignored him, having moved on to the color panels of "Toonerville Folks."

"The first witness I would like to call to the stand is Constance Higginbotham," said Nash.

With a wavy platinum bob, blue eyes, a red lipstick grin, and a green dress that hugged her tiny body, Constance Higginbotham seemed to share her sister's penchant for film-star fashions, but she possessed a sort of imperfect beauty—namely, a pug nose and slightly crooked teeth—that would've kept her out of the movies. She raised her right hand and placed her left on the bailiff's Bible and swore to tell the truth, the whole truth, and nothing but the truth, so help her God. She sat down.

"Please state your name," said Nash.

"Constance Lola Higginbotham." She had a surprisingly deep voice for such a small woman.

"Where do you reside?"

"The Kensington."

"Address?"

"Come again?"

"Can you give me an exact street address of the Kensington?"

"Oh sure. Second North and Main. Apartment three-oh-two, third floor."

"And you are the sister of . . ."

"Helen Kent Pfalzgraf. She used to share my last name. Higginbotham. She added the Kent on her own. I don't know why. Her middle name was Joyce."

Nash read his notes, and I could see his lips moving. Then he looked up at Constance Higginbotham and said, "It says here that you testified you were in Farmington on the night Mrs. Pfalzgraf was murdered."

"Yes, that's right. I was on a date. We went to Lagoon."

"The amusement park?"

"Yeah. I'm partial to the roller coaster. And there was a dance orchestra playing that night."

"Oh yeah? Which one?"

She rolled her eyes like Clara Bow. "Ray Miller was the bandleader."

"When did you learn of your sister's death, Miss Higginbotham?"

"Uh, that would've been the following afternoon. About three o'clock. A couple of deputies dropped by my apartment and told me the news."

"Did they explain the cause of death?"

"No. They must've seen I was busted up over it. They didn't say much. They were sweet fellas."

"When and how did you find out about the cause of your sister's death?"

"The following day, in the afternoon. Hans—um, Dr. Pfalzgraf identified her body at the coroner's. His attorney telephoned my apartment to tell me what happened to Helen. He said she was run over by a car a bunch of times, and he said the sheriff thought her own car was used to kill her."

Nash jotted notes and nodded as she spoke, even though a stenotype operator was hard at work at the table next to the jury box. Nash dipped his pen in the inkwell and made eye contact with the witness. "My condolences to you for your terrible loss, Miss Higginbotham."

She arched her eyebrows, as if his remark took her by surprise. "Thank you, mister. I puzzled over it for a long time—you know, who'd want to kill her? She was going through problems at the end of her life . . ."

"What sort of problems?"

"Marital problems. Hans treated her fine. He was more patient than any man I've ever seen. But Helen was—ah, you know—*restless.* Always going out, rushing off somewhere—parties, dates, jumping on trains to California. All the time telling me she was going to be in movies."

"You two were close?"

"We lived together a while, back when she was a secretary in a downtown office, before she met Hans. I was the only member of my family still speaking to her at the time of . . ." Constance couldn't bring herself to say the words "her death." She sighed shakily and gazed down into her lap.

I felt sorry for her. The pain of her loss was visible in her face. Every few minutes, I'd catch a glimpse of Dr. Pfalzgraf's profile. No emotion was evident there.

"I'm sure there are sisters out there closer than we were," she said. "We talked on the telephone most days, and once or twice a month we'd go to lunch. She always had more money than I did, so she always treated. She loved to eat at Lamb's on Main. We talked. I knew she was seeing a few different men . . ."

"This Persian prince who's all over the newspapers," said Nash. "Is that who you're talking about?"

"Yeah. Him. There were others, too. Helen saw the prince a couple of times when she was in Europe. She claims he swore his undying love for her, but I'm pretty sure he was just leading her on to . . ." She paused as if screening her words and then decided that what she was about to say wasn't proper for a public inquest. She cleared her throat and drank water from a nearby glass. "She made it out to be a storybook romance, claiming he wanted to marry her, but I'm sure she exaggerated it. He had plenty of opportunities to come here and sweep her off her feet, and he didn't."

"You said there were others?"

"Uh-huh. One was a movie actor she met in Los Angeles, big shot in the silent pictures, star of a couple of talkies, Roland Lane." Lane's name triggered a flurry of whispers, laughs, and even outright talking. Nash banged his gavel, and the audience eventually fell silent. Constance resumed. "They spent time together. She hinted it was something more than friendship. She wanted to be in pictures and thought he was the ticket. I don't think there was much going on between them. I'm sure it was another case of wishful thinking on her part."

"Anyone else?"

She blinked a few times and nodded. "Yeah. The mining man."

"Mining man?"

She tilted her head back and gazed at the ceiling, then looked straight at Nash. "Clyde—er, uh, C. W. Alexander. He has an office in the Newhouse."

"The Newhouse? Isn't that a hotel?"

"They rent office space. You can look him up in the city directory if you want."

"No. I believe you. So your sister was involved with this Mr. Alexander?"

She nodded. "Yes. She met him at a Labor Day picnic last year and saw him a bunch of times after that. They went on a long drive on Saint Valentine's Day, but it got cut short when that snowstorm moved in. He was crazy about her. She didn't return his affections. I think the prince sort of let her down and Alexander didn't stack up. She was sweet on him at first, but she turned cold real fast. She did that with men. He telephoned her all the time, always pressuring her to leave Hans. I remember one time Helen told me, 'I would not have Clyde. The lop-eared fool.' Those were her exact words."

"Do you know where they went on their Saint Valentine's Day outing?"

"I'm not sure. Helen said he had to put the top up on his car because it was snowing so hard. She said he drove her to a quiet place out in the west valley."

"Did she give you an address?"

"No."

"When you say this Alexander fellow was a mining man, what do you mean?"

She shrugged her shoulders. "Mister, do I look like an expert? All I know is the fella was involved with mines somehow. He was all the time driving around the state, looking for mines and trying to get big shots to invest in them. Sorry I can't be more helpful. That's all I know. Helen called him a speculator. You'll have to find him and ask him what he does to put meat and potatoes on the table. I'm sure he'll tell you everything you want to know."

"Did you ever meet C. W. Alexander?"

"Yeah, once."

"What was your impression of him?"

"We went on a drive up the canyon to see the changing leaves. There were three of us—me, Clyde, Helen. This was in, oh, early November, maybe late October. I can't remember. He didn't talk much, and when he did, he didn't have much to say. I've had week-old bread less stale than him."

The audience laughed, and the coroner banged his gavel a few times. "Order in the chambers. Thank you for speaking so frankly, Miss Higginbotham. You may be excused. If we have any further questions for you, we will summon you again."

The coroner excused the jury before noon for a lunch break. In front of the City and County Building, vendors did a brisk business selling hot dogs, tamales, and ice-cold bottles of soda pop to long lines of customers. Roscoe and I stood in the slush drinking Nehi Colas through straws and eating lukewarm frankfurters. Some of the crowd gathered around a lanky radio announcer in a gray suit standing at a microphone with a KSL logo above it.

"I cannot begin to convey the drama, the tragedy, the intrigue that pervade this chamber," he said. "In all my years covering events for the press and the radio, the murder of Helen Kent Pfalzgraf is unique in its sheer brutality and ability to captivate the citizens of this fair city . . ."

Roscoe fed a stick of Black Jack chewing gum into his mouth and offered me a piece with a tilt of the pack. I shook my head and listened to the announcer for a moment, but Roscoe pushed his Stetson back on his head and said, "I've heard enough of this horseshit, Art. Let's go inside and find some seats."

Roscoe said it loudly enough that the mike probably picked up his words, and the announcer went pale, but Roscoe didn't care. Ruffling feathers was his specialty, and I noticed him cracking a grin as our footsteps echoed across the marble lobby.

When the clock on the wall said one, the chamber filled up and

we heard Parley Tanner's testimony. Tanner was in his early fifties
with salt-and-pepper hair, a lean and handsome face, and small gray
eyes. You could tell this was a man with the most expensive taste in
clothing imaginable, right down to his gold cuff links. He came
across as calm and sure of himself, and he looked around the room
making eye contact with just about everybody whenever he spoke.

Nash said, "You're the head partner of the firm Tanner, Smith,
and Wells."

"Yes."

"And you've said you are testifying on behalf Dr. Hans Pfalzgraf?"

"Yes. As his legal counsel, I am allowed by the state of Utah law
to testify in his stead in these proceedings."

"Of course. How long have you known him?"

"We—my wife and I—met Dr. Pfalzgraf and his first wife,
Nellie, back in 1908, not long after Pfalzgraf opened his office in
the Brooks Arcade. We liked each other right away. He offered to
be our family physician and we said yes. We needed no coaxing. He
had—*has*—a reputation as the finest physician in the state."

"So your relationship with him is closer than arm's length?"

"He's my client and dearest friend," said Parley Tanner. "Miriam shares my fondness for him. We'll never forget when the doctor
made a house call in the middle of the night two years ago to bring
medicine to our daughter, Elizabeth, when she was ill. He's a true
saint, the most generous man I've ever known."

Nash cut off the praise. "Were you with him when he identified
Helen Kent Pfalzgraf's body?"

"Yes, as a matter of fact, I was. Her death left him devastated.
I've been worried about him ever since."

I turned on the bench to see Pfalzgraf's profile across the room.
He sat still, and his expression did not change. If this testimony was
causing him grief, he wasn't showing it.

"Worried? How so?"

"I wouldn't want Hans's melancholy to get the best of him," he said. "He's one of this city's finest citizens."

"What was Dr. Pfalzgraf's reaction to the allegations that Mrs. Helen Pfalzgraf was seeing this . . ." Nash stared down at his notes for a long second and shook his head. "Oh, for Pete's sake, I can't say his name. The Persian prince."

There was light laughter. Tanner propped his right leg over his left knee. "The newspapers have made a real to-do out of that whole deal. I'd like to underscore what Mrs. Pfalzgraf's sister said in her testimony. The gossip about the Persian fellow was just that—*gossip*. Mrs. Pfalzgraf was a lovely woman with an active imagination."

"Are you saying she made it up?"

"No. I'm sure she really met him in Paris. But a romance?" He shook his head as he picked a piece of lint off his thigh. "Helen once said she was being considered for a role in a Cecil B. DeMille movie. That's how she was. She enjoyed boasting, but her achievements were hardly remarkable. Then again, she was only thirty-two when she died. Who knows what she might've accomplished had she lived longer?"

"What about the newspaper claims that she and the doctor visited you the day before her death to discuss divorce proceedings?" asked Nash.

"There's no truth to the claims. I'm sure this talk of divorce was a gimmick cooked up by the press to sell papers."

"Do you know C. W. Alexander?"

"I've never met him."

"Had you heard of him before today?"

"No. "

"You weren't aware of this Saint Valentine's Day outing of theirs?"

"No."

"Dr. Pfalzgraf never voiced any concerns about this man?"

"To me? No."

Nash read from his dossier and jotted notes. Without looking up, he said, "I understand you were with Dr. Pfalzgraf the night Mrs. Pfalzgraf was murdered."

"Yes. We were at the Majestic on Ninth watching wrestling. It was one of those touring road shows—ten matches for two and a quarter, including Lippert versus Barnett. I know the doctor isn't an avid wrestling fan, but I thought he seemed to be gripped by melancholy, and I find that wrestling, for all of its ballyhoo, possesses a certain thrilling quality that I hoped would cheer him up."

Nash smiled as he stared at Tanner. "Who won?"

"Lippert. He pinned Barnett in less than ten minutes. The match was broadcast on the radio, but you had to be there to fully savor it. Worth every nickel."

"Thank you for your testimony, Mr. Tanner," said Nash, capping his fountain pen. "You may be excused."

"Thank you, Mr. Nash."

Eight

Sheriff Cannon staged a photo shoot in front of the Newhouse Hotel, and the weather was on his side. That Tuesday was our first cloudless day in a month, and the skies offered plenty of natural lighting when the *Examiner* photographer arrived. He wasn't much more than a kid, late teens I guessed, pimply and dressed in a baggy suit. His press badge said his name was Ephraim Nielsen. He set up a tripod in front of the Newhouse, opened his folding camera, and expanded its leather bellows outward like an accordion.

Near me, three other deputies—Roscoe Lund, Billy Taggart, and Ralph Young—stood patiently, waiting for something to happen. A streetcar roared past us, dinging its bell and dropping off passengers half a block to the south. Moments later, *Examiner* reporter Frank Ferguson, a mustachioed man with a thin neck covered in shaving cuts, showed up with his notepad and pencil, ready for action. The six of us—two newspapermen and four deputies— formed a semicircle around Cannon and waited for orders.

"Here's what I'd like," Cannon told Nielsen. "I'd like a shot of me entering the lobby. I'll go in first, followed by Oveson and the other deputies. If need be, I'll do it a few times for so you can get the perfect picture."

"Yes, sir," said Ephraim, removing the lens cap from the camera.

Cannon pointed his thumb over his shoulder at the revolving door. "After that, you take photos of us in the lobby, heading to the elevator."

"Sure thing."

Cannon nodded and patted the shutterbug on the shoulder, then turned to Ferguson. "I've got a gut feeling this C. W. Alexander fellow is our man. I'm giving you the scoop. You think this will make front page?"

Ferguson bobbed his head up and down. "I have no doubt, Sheriff."

"Dandy. Let's get this show on the road. Look lively, fellows."

Cannon charged through the revolving door, and I reluctantly followed. I noticed the stony-faced expressions of the other deputies. None of us liked where this was going. Cannon was playing judge, jury, and executioner. He had a reputation as a lawman who would decide on the guilt or innocence of suspects based on nothing more than his hunches and gut reactions. If he thought someone was guilty, he'd pursue that individual relentlessly. If convinced of a man's innocence, he'd order his deputies to stay away from that person. That was one reason so many of his deputies hated him. If I had more courage, I would tell Cannon exactly what I thought. *There is such a thing as innocent until proven guilty. We have no business zeroing in on one person like this. Any decent lawman would . . .*

"Oveson, snap out of it!" said Cannon, leading the way. "This ain't no time for daydreaming!"

As we spun through the revolving door, Roscoe shared a wedge with me, leaned forward, and whispered, "If the cocksucker is right, this is his ticket to reelection."

"*If* he's right," I said.

The revolving door spit us out into a lobby with potted palms and glassy marble floors so shiny you could see your reflection. Cannon posed for more photographs inside the lobby.

CLICK: Cannon stopping at the front desk to inquire about the location of C. W. Alexander's office.

CLICK: Cannon gesturing to his deputies to follow him to the elevator.

CLICK: Cannon pushing the UP button while his deputies wait for orders.

The elevator's copper-plated doors slid open, and an operator in a maroon monkey suit and matching pillbox hat stepped out of the way, eyes wide with surprise, as Cannon pushed inside. I went in next, followed by Roscoe, but Cannon raised his palm to halt the other deputies. "Stay put, men. Let the press boys come with us. Remain in the lobby."

"Yes, sir."

"Yes, Sheriff."

"Gents," Cannon said to Ferguson and Nielsen, "there's room for two more."

The men stepped inside, and the operator threw a lever that closed the heavy doors. The elevator hummed as it lurched upward, climbing slowly to the eighth floor. The operator finally threw the lever again, and the five of us spilled out into a hallway.

"How's the lighting in here?" asked Cannon.

The photographer looked around the dimly lit hall and held his camera up to chest level. "Poor. I can see what I can do . . ."

"That's a boy. You're about to witness history in the making. The office is right over here."

CLICK: The silhouettes of Cannon and two deputies walking down the hall of the Newhouse's eighth floor.

CLICK: Sheriff Cannon knocking on the door of room 805. The

frosted glass on the door reads INTERMOUNTAIN MINING SPECULA-
TORS, LTD.—C. W. ALEXANDER, PROPRIETOR.

CLICK: Sheriff Cannon and his deputies entering Alexander's
office, a portion of the photo obscured by the glare of the sun piercing through the window against the lens of the camera.

A pale woman with an Irene Castle bob, a doughy face, and a
string of pearls jumped out of her swivel chair and crouched behind her desk when we charged into the room.

"Sheriff Fred Cannon." He held his badge high so she could get
a better look. "We're here for C. W. Alexander. Is he in?"

"What do you want with—"

"I take it that's his office," said Cannon, pointing at a door with
C. W. ALEXANDER painted on pebbled glass.

"Yes, but he's not—"

Cannon wouldn't hear her out. "This way, fellows."

"Do you men have a search warrant?" asked the secretary.

"We don't need one when we're arresting somebody," said Cannon.

"Arrest? Mr. Alexander? I don't understand. Why—"

"Ma'am," said Cannon, smile now gone. "This doesn't concern
you."

"He isn't in there!"

Cannon walked over to her desk, placed both hands on it for
effect, and leaned in close to her. "Where is he?"

"I don't know. He didn't show up today. Maybe it's all that stuff
in the newspapers."

Cannon slammed his hand on a little file card box on the desk,
startling the poor woman. "Reach in there and pull out his address.
Will you?"

She nodded, flipped open the box, and fumbled for a 3 × 5 file
card. Her shaking hand brought it out. Cannon snatched it from

her before she had a chance to pass it to him. He got a good look at it and dropped it on her desk.

"Much obliged."

C. W. Alexander lived in a bungalow on 500 East, one of those three-thousand-dollar brick jobs across the street from Liberty Park. It had a detached one-car garage with no auto inside and a sleeping porch containing a hammock. We parked next to the curb, two houses down. Roscoe got out of the car first and double-checked to make sure his revolver was loaded. Cannon's car pulled up next, followed by another county sedan and the press boys in a tan Pontiac. Water dripping from nearby eaves troughs fooled me into thinking spring was around the corner. We had a while of winter yet.

Cannon ordered shutterbug Nielsen to set up his camera near the Alexander place. Nielsen did as told and snapped pictures of us as Roscoe charged up the wet sidewalk, leaping every other step to the porch, and turned to Cannon for a signal. He and two other deputies opened a fence door at the side of the house and followed a path to the dwelling's rear, to make sure Alexander didn't try to make a run for it out the back door. I stood on the sidewalk watching Roscoe, waiting for him to do something and feeling uneasy about this operation.

"You ready to go in, Deputy?"

Cannon's voice jarred me out of my thoughts. "Yes, sir."

"Go ahead and ring the doorbell," said Cannon.

I moved up the porch stairs and passed an irate-looking Roscoe on my way to the door. I pressed the doorbell. Inside it buzzed.

Roscoe and I waited. Nielsen snapped photographs of us waiting for somebody to answer the door. I pressed the doorbell once more. Again it buzzed inside. My pulse picked up speed, and my hands developed a case of the shakes. At tense moments like this,

I felt myself gripped by a deep yearning to go home, to be with my family, the one place in the world I knew to be safe and warm and full of love.

I faced Cannon. "Nobody's answering."

"Step back and let Lund do his thing, then."

I opened the wood-and-wire screen door, and Roscoe stared at an arched white front door with three rectangular windows on it. He turned the doorknob, it clicked, and he pushed the door open a few inches. Inside, closed drapes darkened the room. Roscoe raised his revolver and nudged the door another couple of inches, enough to sidle in.

"Proceed with caution," Cannon called out from the front walkway.

I drew my gun and followed Roscoe into the darkness. The only light came from the glowing dial of a radio on the table next to the love seat. The fabric-covered speaker chimed with a man's voice while a quartet sang the Lifebuoy theme in the background. *"Remember to buy Lifebuoy Health Soap, and while you're at it, pick up a tube of Lifebuoy shaving cream for him, both available at your local druggist for ten cents . . ."*

I switched off the radio and scanned the room, every inch crammed full of furniture, with rows of dilapidated encyclopedias on bookshelves built into the wall. The furniture was probably about ten years old, frayed and faded but usable, with a Sears, Roebuck floral design. I'm guessing it came from a catalog—sturdy, but not built to last.

I stepped inside the kitchen, a box-shaped room with closed Venetian blinds, pots and glasses in the sink, and a table covered with breakfast food—sliced fruits, a box of Wheaties, and a bottle of milk. I lifted the bottle to my nose, and it smelled fresh and was still cold, as if it had only been out of the icebox an hour. Clearly, the breakfast had been made earlier this morning.

I advanced to a closed door near the icebox. Turning the knob, I flung the door open, pivoted, and aimed my gun around the corner. Wooden stairs descended into a pitch-black cellar. I held the railing and moved carefully down the stairs, and what little light there was grew dimmer with each step. When I reached bottom, I caught a glimmer of light from a chain dangling from the ceiling. I tugged it. A low-wattage globe dangling from an electrical cord above my head bathed the room with soft white light. Either C. W. Alexander or someone else in the house was a collector of magazines, because there were stacks and stacks of them. I scanned the rest of the basement. There were boxes everywhere. One had the Chero-Cola logo on top, along with the words AMERICA'S FAVORITE SODA—STILL 5 CENTS A BOTTLE. I opened the lid and lifted a bottle. It wasn't Chero-Cola. I stared at a sealed pint of Gordon's Dry Gin.

"Any sign of anything?"

Cannon's voice startled me, and I slipped the bottle back inside the box where I found it. "Bootleg liquor, sir. I'm guessing there's lots of it in these boxes here."

"I'll notify the dry agents."

"Find anything upstairs?" I asked.

"Looks to me like he's skipped town," said Cannon, stepping into the light. "Dammit! He's our man. I'm convinced. He was the last person to be seen with Helen Pfalzgraf. We have the telephone logs from Mountain Bell to show that he was telephoning her house over and over. Years ago, he bilked Doc Pfalzgraf out money to invest in some fraudulent mine down in Carbon County. This guy reeks to high heaven."

"What makes you think he's skipped town?"

"I can tell. Drawers have been pulled out of the bedroom bureau. Clothes are strewn all over the place. Somebody packed in a mad rush. Judging from the pictures on the mantelpiece and a room full of toys, it looks like he has a wife and a couple of children."

"What do you plan on doing, sir?"

Cannon stepped closer to me, smiling at a moment when nobody else would smile. "It's not what am *I* going to do, Oveson. It's what are *you* going to do. *You* are going to put out a statewide alert on C. W. Alexander, his family members, and his auto. While you're at it, send it out to the surrounding states. We're going to stop this cowardly murderer dead in his tracks. This is *not,* I repeat *not,* going to turn out to be another Hazel Hamilton case. Understand?"

"Yes, sir."

"If I have it my way, this murdering bastard is going to have a date with the firing squad at Sugar House."

"Yes, sir."

Cannon nodded. "You said you found liquor?"

I took off my Stetson and waved it at the box with the gin bottles. "Right there."

He stepped toward the box, opened the lid, and lifted a bottle. He made sure the seal wasn't broken before stuffing it inside his coat pocket. He noticed me watching him and winked. "Evidence."

"Sir, don't you think we should be following up with other leads in this—"

"I've already told you what I think," he said. "C. W. Alexander is our man. My gut tells me so. Nail him and good things will come your way."

Nine

On Tuesday night, Sarah Jane and I were locked in a life-and-death round of checkers in the living room. She was red, I black. Reds covered the board, several of them kings, but blacks had been reduced to one. I was a goner and I knew it.

"I'm beating you," she said with a giggle.

"True, you are," I said. "I've still got one checker on the board, though."

"You're bad at checkers," she said, "but you're good at other things."

I pointed to my last checker. "You just watch. I'm going to stage the greatest comeback in the history of checkers."

"I doubt it," she said.

"How did you get to be such a sassy girl?"

She smiled at me for a moment, resting her chin in her hand, then stared down at the board, waiting for me to do something. "Dad."

"What is it, little button?" I asked, plotting my next move.

"You know that lady who got hit by her own car?"

I looked up at her tiny heart-shaped face, her eyes darting from checker to checker.

"What about her?" I asked.

"Did she do something bad?"

I placed the tip of my index finger on my black checker and was about to move it, but I reconsidered. "How did you happen to hear about that lady?"

"Mary told me. She heard her parents talking about her. Mary's dad said the lady was bad. Is that why she got hit by her car?"

"Remember what the bishop told us last week?" I asked. "It's not good to judge other people. That's Heavenly Father's job. I'm guessing Mary's dad didn't know the woman who got run over."

"Mary's dad called the dead lady a tramp," said Sarah Jane. "What's a tramp?"

"When you get older, I'll tell you what it means. It's not nice to call someone a tramp."

"How come they call Charlie Chaplin a tramp if it's a bad thing?"

"Well, in his case, it isn't bad. But for everyone else, it is."

"Did that lady deserve to get hit by a car?"

"Nobody deserves that."

The telephone rang, distracting Sarah Jane from her line of questioning. I went over to the crescent moon table by the entry hall, lifted the receiver to my ear, and raised the transmitter to my mouth. "Hello."

"Oveson?"

"Speaking?"

"Is this Wasatch four-eighty-four?"

"Speaking?" I repeated.

"Seymour Considine," he said. "Remember we met at the Vienna and you gave me your number? We agreed we'd exchange information. Remember?"

"Oh yes," I said, turning slightly to see Clara behind me, her eyebrows furrowed into that *Who is it?* expression. She held Hi in her arms, and he was doing his restless dance, flailing his arms and whining, probably hungry for a dinner only she could provide. I mouthed, *I'll tell you later*, then said into the transmitter, "That is still something I'd like to do."

"Is this a bad time?"

"No. What did you have in mind?"

"I was hoping we could meet somewhere," he said. "I've come upon some tantalizing tidbits since we talked."

"Where do you want to meet?" I asked.

"You suggest a place, I'll be there. I'm easy."

"You like ice cream?"

"Ice cream?" There was a pause. "Don't you want something a little harder?"

"Ice cream is as hard as I get," I said. "What do you say?"

"Do they have rum ice cream?"

"That I don't know."

He sighed audibly. "Yeah. Sure. Ice cream will do. Where do you want to meet?"

"There's a great place called Keeley's," I said. "On Main, between South Temple and First. They also sell ice cream sodas and candy."

"Well, then, that seals the deal," he said. "Be there in fifteen minutes."

"OK."

I lowered the receiver onto the cradle and set the telephone on the table. Clara still stared at me.

"It's a lead," I said. "I've got to follow through on it."

"Well, don't take too long," she said, raising Hi so his head was level with hers, as if she thought I couldn't see him before. "He wants to see his daddy, too, you know."

I walked over to her, kissed her on the cheek, and rubbed Hi's soft head. "This shouldn't take long."

Keeley's was a bright place with rows of candy-filled jars and fine chocolates displayed in glass cases, a soda fountain with barstools, and tables where families feasted on frozen delicacies even in the depths of winter. I ordered a banana split made with rocky road ice cream and extra dollops of whipped cream. Considine came in wearing a yellow shirt and maroon cardigan with flakes of snow on his shoulders. He ordered a cup of coffee and joined me. He dropped his dossier on the table and was noticeably taken aback by the size of my banana split.

"That thing's huge," he said, sipping coffee. "Can you eat all that?"

"If you can eat a whole one of these on your birthday," I said, "you get another one free."

"You're putting me on, right? A whole one of those would probably kill you."

I shrugged my shoulders, spooning a big piece of ice-cream-covered banana into my mouth. "At least you'll die a pleasant death."

He tugged at his mustache. "You're nuts."

I spoke with my mouth full, a no-no when I was growing up. "Remind me to pick up my pint when I'm done."

"A pint?"

"Tutti-frutti," I said. "It's my daughter's favorite, and I like a midnight scoop."

"Let me get this straight: When you're done with that thing, you're going to have more ice cream?"

It took me a moment to chew and swallow what was in my mouth, and he gestured for me to dab the corners of my mouth with the napkin. "Ice cream is my favorite food. But I'll only have a small dish around midnight. It helps me go to sleep."

I pointed my long dessert spoon at the ice cream counter. "Go try a coconut cream cone. It's good. I'll give you a dime . . ."

He shook his head in disgust. "I don't want any ice cream. I don't care for it."

"Too bad," I said. "So what did you want to see me about, Considine?"

"Our swap. I give you information. You give me information. Remember?"

"Yeah. I recollect us agreeing on that in the Vienna."

"You go first."

"Alright," I said, resuming my quest to devour that banana split. "I suppose you must know all about C. W. Alexander?"

"The mining man who's in the newspapers?" he asked. "The last man to be seen with Helen Pfalzgraf? What about him?"

"We drove out to arrest him this morning. He wasn't at work or home. Sheriff thinks he skipped out after his name came up at the coroner's inquest."

He slapped a copy of the *Salt Lake Examiner* on the table and pushed it closer to me so I could see the headline at the top of the page. MINING MAN LINKED TO SLAIN WOMAN.

Considine said, "C'mon, Oveson. Is that all you've got? Surely you can do better."

"The sheriff seems certain Alexander's the killer."

"What do *you* think?"

"I don't know," I said. "It's all been happening so fast. I know one thing: I don't feel good about the way we've been handling it. There have been so many lawmen working this case, and I haven't been able to get a bird's-eye view of it all."

"You aren't telling me anything I don't already know," said Considine, lowering his coffee cup so abruptly it clanked loudly against the saucer. "Please tell me you've got something else. Otherwise, this won't strike me as much of a fair trade."

"That's it," I said. "For now."

"You're not holding back on me, are you?"

"Nope. I'm giving it to you straight."

He reached for a container of cream and poured some in his coffee. It spread across the black coffee like a cloud, turning it brown. I hadn't ever touched a cup of coffee in my life and I had no plans to, but I'll admit: I loved the smell of it. I inhaled deeply through my nose and savored the aroma.

He looked at me and said, "Want a cup?"

"I don't drink the stuff."

"Is that a Mormon thing? Not drinking coffee?"

I shrugged my shoulders. "Sort of. I don't like it, either."

"Have you ever tried it?"

"No."

"Well, then, how do you know you don't like it if you haven't tried it?"

I shoved a maraschino cherry in my mouth and chewed it for a moment. "I just know I won't like it."

He sighed and shook his head. "Get a load of Philo Vance here. *I just know I won't like it.*"

"Remember our deal?" I asked. "Well, I just gave you something. Alexander skipped town. Now, what have you got for me?"

"Your information is useless. Why should I tell you *anything*?"

"It's not useless," I said. "Maybe Alexander is our man. Maybe the sheriff is right."

"Yeah? Well, I'll tell you one thing, Deputy: You're not going to dig up anything sitting in that goddamn coroner's inquest. You've got to get outdoors, look under rocks, down alleys, in railroad yards and bars, at the bottom of cellars. You've got to go where desperate people go to do desperate things. I'm sure Sheriff Cannon doesn't ask you to do that, does he?"

I shook my head. His shoulders slumped, and his steely gaze relaxed. I could tell he was easing up. "Alright, Oveson. I'll share. But I'm not going to give you everything I've got. I've worked damn hard to track down this information."

He opened his dossier and thumbed through the documents, stopping to read one to himself. He pulled out the piece of paper—onionskin, it rattled at a touch—and gently set it near me. "Don't spill ice cream on that, Deputy."

I wiped the corners of my mouth and drank from a glass of ice water. The top of the paper read "Los Angeles Police Department—INVESTIGATIVE REPORT."

My eyes moved down to handwriting on the police form. "CASE NUMBER: 0057834. REPORT OF: Auto accident. Vehicular death. DATE AND TIME REPORTED TO PD: 01-26-1917, 11:45 (with P.M. circled). VICTIM'S LAST NAME: Pfalzgraf. VICTIM'S FIRST NAME: Nellie (Eleanor). AGE: 29. DOB: 06-22-1887. MIDDLE INITIAL: P. ADDRESS: 1272 E. South Temple. CITY: Salt Lake City. STATE: Utah."

I skipped lines to get to the meat of the report. "INCIDENT OF OCCURRENCE: Pico Boulevard Hill, near South Ocean Avenue, Los Angeles. VICTIM'S VEH: 1915 Dodge Brothers Touring." Below that was a road map with the words PICO BLVD. HILL written in the middle of the road, along with two rectangles side by side—CAR A and CAR B—and several little arrows tracing the trajectories of the two vehicles. Someone with poor penmanship had scribbled below the map: "Veh. #1 runs Veh. #2 off the road a block past 3rd Street, before Pico intersects with South Ocean. Veh. #2 breaks through guardrail, ejects victim, throws her 10 yards, then rolls down hill & lands on victim. Victim taken by ambulance to St. Catherine Hospital in Santa Monica, where she is pron. dead."

Considine tapped the paper. "That's a copy of the police report from thirteen years ago, showing Nellie Pfalzgraf was the victim of a hit-and-run driver who ran the Pfalzgrafs' car off the road. It was night, and they were returning to their hotel after drinking high-balls at a local roadhouse."

"Intriguing," I said, eyes fixed on the police report.

"Of course it is." Considine passed me four yellowing press clip-pings. "They're all from the *L.A. Times,* all about the auto accident. Apparently, the L.A. police chief put up a reward for the mystery hit-and-run driver. Please be careful with those. I had to purchase offprints from the *Times,* so those are my only copies."

"I will." I leafed through them, and all the headlines sounded similar. HIT AND RUN MOTORIST CLAIMS WOMAN'S LIFE. POLICE QUES-TION S.L. PHYSICIAN. POLICE RESUME SEARCH FOR DEATH CAR DRIVER. PHYSICIAN RETURNS TO S.L. TO BURY WIFE, POLICE CONTINUE SEARCH FOR MYSTERY DRIVER.

Considine said, "According to the *Times,* Dr. Pfalzgraf was so distraught over his wife's death that his attorney, Parley Tanner, had to come down to Los Angeles to escort him back to Salt Lake City. The Salt Lake press ignored the story completely, except for Nellie's obituary in the *Examiner,* which mentions she was killed in an auto accident. They laid her to rest at the city cemetery."

I shook my head, trying to make sense of this new information. "What a strange coincidence that both of Pfalgraf's wives died in auto-related incidents."

"I have a couple more press clippings for you." He opened the dossier and scattered a few more tattered papers in front of me. "That one's from the *Salt Lake Examiner,* October 18, 1916. Just months before Nellie was killed, the doctor and his brothers inher-ited a fortune from a deceased German uncle. The article says Pfalzgraf's share was slightly over a million."

I raised my eyebrows as I scanned the headline. LOCAL PHYSI-CIAN HEIR TO BIG GERMAN ESTATE. Above it, somebody—likely Considine—had scribbled the date.

Considine waved his finger at another clipping. "The story was big enough to find its way into the *New York Times*. Apparently, this Pfalzgraf's uncle had a hell of a lot of money. He was some sort of big-shot industrialist."

I said, "Can I take these with me so I can read over them?"

Considine smiled, revealing horse teeth. "I'm not a lending library, Oveson."

"Got anything else?" I asked, passing the police report and clippings back to Considine.

"Isn't that enough for you?"

"I'd like to see more if you've got it. It would help with the investigation."

He shook his head, his show of contempt for a novice deputy who couldn't keep up with him. It annoyed me, but I didn't show it. Considine was a valuable source of information. Alienating him would serve no purpose. "I'll show you two more items and that's it. Then you're going to have to do your own dirty work."

"Please."

He handed me an obituary and an article, both from the *Ogden Post*. The article, from November 3, 1928, ran under the headline CONTROVERSIAL DOCTOR FOUND DEAD. The next was an obituary, same date, for Everett Alvin Wooley, an Ogden physician with a second-floor office on Washington Boulevard.

"Gunshot with a large-caliber weapon to the back of his head," said Considine. "It was gruesome. The crime scene photos are available for viewing at the Ogden Police Department."

"What does this have to do with Pfalzgraf?" I asked.

"Wooley was an abortionist, willing to operate on any woman for a hundred bucks. For years, he ran a clinic on Second South. Some of his patients ended up dying horrible deaths. They'd come down with infections, fevers, cold sweats, abdominal pains. You name it. The Salt Lake police believe at least seven local women died as a result of Wooley's bad surgeries. And guess who waged a one-man crusade to get the state board to yank Wooley's license?"

"Pfalzgraf?"

Considine nodded. "The very same. He submitted a complaint on July the first, 1926, on behalf of Harmony Tattershall of Salt Lake City. It was this complaint that led to the suspension of Wooley's license by the Utah State Medical Board. A few weeks later, in late August, Wooley had an ugly confrontation with Pfalzgraf at a Mex joint. The police were called in. They dragged Wooley away hollering and left Pfalzgraf bruised and shaken. Wooley spent the night in city lockup and left town the next morning. At some point, he resurfaced in Ogden and reopened his clinic, only to end up with a bullet in his brain a year later."

"Do you think Pfalzgraf had anything to do with Wooley's death?"

"You tell me, junior," he said. "You're the deputy. I'm just a lowly pulp writer who spins yarns for five cents a word. I'll tell you one thing. I've interviewed several people who paint a poor picture of Pfalzgraf. They say the kindly doctor was a hell of a miser. Wouldn't even listen to your heartbeat if you couldn't pay first."

I ate as much of my banana split as I could—almost half—before nudging it aside to watch Considine sip his coffee. In my mind, I tried to connect all of this new information to what I already knew about the Pfalzgraf murder. I kept coming up blank, and I knew I would need more time to make sense of it all. Meantime, the evening crowd at Keeley's was thinning out. Several patrons stood in line to settle their bills at the cash register. The clock on the wall said it was quarter to nine, which meant Keeley's was closing in fifteen minutes.

"We don't have much time," I said. "You said there was something else."

He reached inside his coat and pulled out a gray film canister and set it on the table between us. "It's a reel of film. The clapboard at the start of the film bears the date December the ninth of last year."

"What's on it?"

"Helen Kent Pfalzgraf's screen test. She was obviously trying out for a part in a talkie. Actually, she's surprisingly good. They had a famous guy reading the man's lines." Considine snapped his fingers as he tried to remember. "What was his name?"

"Roland Lane?" I asked.

His eyes widened, and he pointed at me. "That's it! Roland Lane. Famous actor. He lives in a white stucco castle at the top of the Hollywood Hills, where you can see L.A. on one side and the San Fernando Valley on the other. I drove up there and tried to talk to him, but the security guard wouldn't let me inside. His number isn't in the city directory, either. These movie stars are damn near impossible to get to, unless you have connections with studio big shots, and I'm afraid I don't."

"You mean you were in Los Angeles?"

He nodded. "Just got back on this morning's *Zephyr*. It's a lot nicer there than it is here. Sixty-eight degrees and sunny. Can you beat that?"

"May I borrow the film?"

He slid the canister across the table to me. "Go ahead. I've watched it already. Be careful with it, though. I want it back. Understand?"

"I understand."

He stood and buttoned up his cardigan, then dropped two bits on the table near my banana split. He said, "Next time, I want something better out of you, Oveson. Or I'll cancel our future chin-wags."

"OK," I said.

"Don't forget your pint," he said with a wink.

I ran the palm of my hand along the dented and scratched film canister. Then I carried it with me to the counter and ordered a pint of tutti-frutti to take home to Sarah Jane.

She was still up when I walked in the front door.

Ten

Every so often, it pays to have connections. I was on good terms with a man in my ward (when we Mormons say ward, we mean a local congregation) named Owen Vanderhoff, a portly fellow with no hair on the top of his head, a nose squared off at the end, and ruddy Santa Claus cheeks. He had a big belly and was partial to singing loudly. He loved to discuss all of the choirs he was in—four, to be exact—and I listened to him with a patience that would make Job envious. Now it was my time to collect. I knew Owen was a projectionist at the Isis Theater on 300 South, and he could show me what was in that film canister.

Roscoe and I stood out on the sidewalk in front of the Isis so he could finish smoking his hand-rolled cigarette. He asked me where I got the film. Much as I hated lying, I told him I lifted it out of evidence, that it had been confiscated with Helen Pfalzgraf's other personal effects. Telling Roscoe about my meeting with Considine would only set him off. I tilted my head back to get a good look at the arch that towered above the front entrance of the movie theater.

It wasn't old—the year 1908 was carved into the foundation stone—yet it had that ancient quality to it, and when you walked inside, the cold air enveloped you, making you feel like you had reached the depths of some great Egyptian tomb. As we crossed the green lobby carpet in the direction of the ticket booth, Roscoe took out a bottle of gin, unscrewed the top, and took a hard swig, gasping as he pulled it away from his lips.

"I'd offer you some," he said, tucking the bottle away, "but I've got a feeling you'd turn me down."

"You never know. I might actually say yes."

He took the bottle back out of his pocket and tilted it toward me. "Snort?"

"No thanks."

"Your loss, choirboy."

By now, his sullenness had taken on a joking quality. All bark, no bite. It was his shtick, as they say on the vaudeville circuit.

Owen stood behind the snack bar, preparing a batch of popcorn. When he saw me, he smiled with recognition and hobbled around from behind the glass counter and shook my hand.

"Howdy, Owen," I said.

"Howdy, Artie," he said. "How's my favorite lawman?"

"Never better. It's swell to see you, Owen, and it's awfully kind of you to let us use your movie theater like this."

"I'm honored to have you fellas using it. You got lots of time before the matinee crowd shows up." He faced Roscoe. "I don't think we've been introduced."

He held out his hand, but Roscoe glared at it, so Owen dropped it and offered a smile instead. "I'm Owen Vanderhoff."

"Roscoe Lund. I'm Oveson's partner."

Owen waved his thumb in my direction. "He's a keen fellow, isn't he?"

Roscoe nodded. "He's a Grade-A peach, alright. It's good of you to let us use your projector."

"Think nothing of it," said Owen. He gestured to a door on the other side of the lobby. "Right this way, fellows."

We followed him, and he talked while we walked. "I don't know what you fellows know about running a thirty-five millimeter projector. I figured it'd be best if I were to operate it."

"That makes sense," I said. "I operated one at a summer job I once had in Provo, but it's been years. How about you, Roscoe?"

"No, but I once played piano in a joint that showed silent pictures on a hanging bedsheet," he said.

I threw him a crooked smile. "Sometimes I actually learn something new about you."

Roscoe smirked. "Let's keep it to sometimes."

"Why don't you fellows go inside and find yourselves a seat," Owen said when we reached a curtained door. "I'll go up to the booth and get this set up."

"That's swell," I said. "Thanks again, Owen."

Roscoe and I entered the palatial theater. Ornamental flowery paintings covered its ceiling, and air-conditioning blew in our faces, despite frigid weather outside. We had five hundred seats to choose from, and we ended up smack-dab in the middle, close to the aisle. We both crossed our legs over our knees and waited for Owen to start the projector.

I leaned in close to Roscoe. "I didn't know you played the piano."

"What you don't know about me could fill Fenway Park—and we might have to set aside part of Wrigley Field, too."

I grinned as lights dimmed and a projector light flickered. Movie countdown numbers in the middle of circles started at 5 and worked down to 0. A production clapboard flashed on the screen, and the black-and-white bar clacked down. It happened fast, but I caught a glimpse of the date—12/09/29—and the words HELEN PFALZGRAF SCREEN TEST—FIRST NATIONAL PICTURES—VITAPHONE (SYNCHRONIZED SOUND). PRODUCER: EDGAR KING. DIRECTOR: CHARLES LEWIS.

The image of Helen Pfalzgraf flashed on the screen. She wore a light-colored jersey dress with a skirt that stopped at her knees. She had on a cloche hat, plenty of eye shadow and heavy lipstick. Her chin jutted out, and she had pretty teeth that gleamed in the light.

A male off-screen voice—so melodious it sounded like a bird's trill—said, "The camera is rolling, Miss Pfalzgraf. You may begin anytime you wish."

"Thank you, Roland." She rolled her eyes, as if trying to think of something to say. "I shall be reading from *The Greatest Gift of All*, scenario written by G. S. Erwin."

She dipped her head, and when she raised it again, her expression changed as she got into form. She clasped her fingers, as if praying, and held them over her chest. "You can't go, Ralph. I won't let you. Why should you join the army and go fight a war thousands of miles away? Stay here with me."

She paused as Roland Lane read the man's dialogue off-screen. "This is my war too, Gladys. You heard what President Wilson said. We are making the world safe for democracy."

"Words! Just words," she said. "But what do they really mean, especially when you're in that terrible charnel house, surrounded by the dead, and all you wish to do is see another day? Those words mean precious little on the battlefield!"

Roscoe leaned near me and cupped his hand on the side of his mouth. "Talk about stilted dialogue. A monkey could write a better photoplay than this."

I smiled and said, "She isn't bad, though. She's got some natural talent."

The dramatic exchange lasted a few minutes longer, but the part that interested me most about the screen test was when Helen Pfalzgraf finally relaxed and the director began to quiz her.

"You say you're from Salt Lake City?" asked a low voice from off-screen.

She smiled and nodded her head and showed off her perfect teeth. "Yes."

"What is it like, Salt Lake City? I've never been."

She laughed, and her eyes looked around. "It's a hick town. I'm ready to leave. It has always been my dream to be in the pictures. I've wanted that ever since I was a little girl, when I used to watch the Biograph pictures at the nickelodeon."

A long silence followed as the camera zoomed in on Helen looking around and smiling. Noises could be heard coming from other parts of the set—a buzzer going off, distant voices calling out to each other. By the end of the film, her radiant face took up most of the screen, her eyes gleaming, dark lips smiling, pearly teeth reflecting the light from above.

Then the film ended.

The theater lights went on, and we got up and walked into the lobby. Owen waited for us, reel in hand. He presented it to me, and we shook hands again.

"I didn't mean to snoop, but I recognized the fellow reading the lines," said Owen. "Roland Lane. I showed one of his pictures here two weeks ago. He played a big-shot Broadway producer who falls for a pretty showgirl. Wasn't half bad. You should bring Clara back tonight for the picture show, Art. I'll let you two lovebirds in free of charge."

"That's mighty nice of you, Owen." I laughed. "Look, if there's any way I can repay you—any way at all . . ."

He mentioned some old yard clippings that had to be taken out to the dump. *Me and my big fat mouth,* I thought.

• • •

I spent my lunch hour in the deserted common room placing a long-distance telephone call to Edgar King, a producer at First National Pictures in Burbank, California. It took a half hour for the operator to finally reach the studio because of all the interference on the cross-country lines. It took another forty-five minutes for the studio operator to find someone who knew where to locate King. His secretary asked if she could help me and I said no, unfortunately I had to talk to the head honcho. More waiting through a popping connection. More veering into party lines. *"What time are you coming over tonight?" "Half past six. Will the supper still be warm?" "I'm not even sure it'll be done by then."* I sighed. I hated hearing other people's conversations, but such was the world of long-distance telephone calling. I had to keep the receiver pressed against my ear so I wouldn't miss King if he came on, which made eavesdropping a necessary evil. *"How hot is it out there?" "I think we broke fifty."* I rolled my eyes, opened my desk drawer, took out a freshly sharpened pencil, and began doodling on a pad of paper. Outhouses were my specialty.

The secretary's high voice came on. "Deputy, are you still there?"

"Yes, ma'am."

"Sorry for the long wait. Here is Mr. King. I'm going to patch you through. You'll hear a few clicks. Please do not hang up."

"Yes, ma'am. Thank you, ma'am."

Three clicks sounded, followed by a dial tone. I slammed the receiver on the cradle and pushed the telephone aside. I felt like saying *Sonofabitch!* and throwing the telephone against the nearest wall. Restraint won out.

It took another hour and fifteen minutes to get through to King. This telephone call ate up a goodly portion of my afternoon.

"This is Ed King," said a gravelly voice at last.

"Hello, Mr. King. My name is Deputy Art Oveson, Salt Lake

County Sheriff's Office. I'm calling about a woman who auditioned to be in one of your pictures. Her name was Helen Kent Pfalzgraf."

"Ah, yes, Helen, I remember her," he said, sounding more somber now. "I heard about what happened to her. Awful. Simply awful. Such a tragic end for one so promising."

"Yes, it is. I just finished watching Miss Pfalzgraf's screen test for First National—"

"Her screen test?" he said, surprised. "How did you get hold of that? That's studio property."

"I know someone who knows someone."

"Who?"

"I'd rather not say his name."

"All screen tests are studio property, not meant to leave the grounds."

"I see. She gave a good performance, Helen Pfalzgraf."

"Remarkable," said King. "I would very much like that screen test returned. You can send it to the studio, care of me. As for Miss Pfalzgraf, she acted like a pro. Roland Lane pushed for her audition—and pushed hard. I'm glad he did. I think Mr. Lewis, the director, wanted to offer her the part of Gladys, but I demanded he cast her as Gladys's older sister, Sylvia. We needed a big name to play Gladys, like Anita Page. Plus, Helen was perfect for Sylvia. The character has this protective streak and . . ." He paused. "Never mind all that. You don't want to know all the details. We drew up a standard studio contract for Miss Pfalzgraf, a five-picture deal, and I telephoned her at her house in Salt Lake City to tell her we were wiring her a train ticket to come to Burbank and sign the contract in person. We had a splendid conversation. She was thrilled—and I could hear someone else, a young lady, squealing for joy in the background. Less than a week later, Helen was dead."

King's revelation of Helen's Hollywood coup caught me off guard, but I remained calm. "When did you talk to her?"

"On a Monday. Let me check my datebook . . ." He paused for a moment and then came back on the line. "February seventeenth. Yes, it was a Monday."

"When were you planning to have her come out to First National for the contract signing?"

"A week later. The twenty-fourth. We were going to notify the trade press. *Photoplay, Variety*—you know, the usual suspects. A contract signing always makes for great publicity. She was going to change her name and everything."

"To what?"

"Helen Hopkins."

"Hmm. Did Helen talk to you about her preparations for coming out to Los Angeles?"

"No. She told Roland that she had some personal matters to attend to before coming out. That was all."

"Did she happen to indicate the nature of those personal matters?"

"My conversation with her was brief, and she said very little, other than expressing her excitement over the contract. She was closer to Roland. She knew him from social functions. Frankly, he's the only reason she got past the studio gate."

"Do you have a number where I can reach Roland Lane?"

"No. He's unreachable, Deputy Oveson. You won't find his name in any telephone directories, and no operator will be able to patch you through to him. He's too big. He lives in a secluded house with a big wall. He's got a big-shot agent who protects him like a guard dog. Besides, I happen to know he set sail to England a week ago."

"England?"

"Yes. He owns an estate in the countryside. Splits his time between here and there."

"Is there a telephone number there where he can be reached?"

"Not that I know of."

"What about an address?"

"I'm afraid I don't have that information. Now, if you'll excuse me, Deputy, I am a man on a tight schedule." He pronounced schedule "shed-you-el." I'd never heard it said that way before. "Is there anything else you'd like to ask?"

"No, you've pretty much covered everything I wanted to know. I'm grateful for your time, Mr. King."

"I would appreciate it if you could seal that screen test in a box and put it in tomorrow's post, care of First National, Deputy Oveson," he said. "This studio does not like its screen tests to be floating around out there for viewing by the general public."

I was about to say, *I'll do that*, but I am a man of my word. If I say I'll do something, I'll do it, and I knew that Considine wouldn't be happy if I mailed his reel off to First National. So I gave King the best noncommittal answer I could think of. "I'll consider it," I said. "Thank you, Mr. King."

The line went dead.

I lowered the receiver into the cradle, folded my arms, and stared for a long moment at the candlestick telephone. It seemed to be silently goading me to track down Roland Lane. I lifted the earpiece again and, for the next two hours, attempted to connect to an operator in London. Much of that time I spent waiting for a cross-country line to take me to New York, then a transatlantic line the rest of the way to the British Isles. The English operator, a faraway-sounding woman barely audible above the line static, informed me there was no Roland Lane in the local directory. She said unless I had a specific address for him, locating his telephone number would be impossible. I thanked her and said good-bye. My next telephone call went out to Los Angeles. Less of a wait this time, but I was still holding a long while. "There's no Lane, *L-A-N-E,* first name Roland, listed here," the operator finally told me. "Sorry, mister." I said thanks, hung up, and opened the city directory to the residential section to look for Harmony Tattershall, the name given to me by Seymour Considine at Keeley's. Dr. Pfalzgraf had filed a complaint on her behalf against Everett Wooley. There was only one Tattershall in the entire phone book, "Tattershall, Geo. T."—listed at 1466 East 1300 South, telephone number Wasatch 594. I lifted the earpiece. "Operator, give me Wasatch five-nine-four, please."

"One moment." Minute-long pause. "Sorry, that number has been disconnected."

"Is there another number?"

"No. I'm sorry. There isn't."

"How about Harmony Tattershall. Do you have a number for her?"

"One moment." Clicks. More time passed. "Sorry, I have nobody by that name."

"Thanks very much," I said, returning the earpiece to the cradle. I leaned back in my chair, ran my palms over my face, and sighed.

Eleven

"Why the fuck are we here, anyhow?" asked Roscoe.

I lowered my issue of *Field & Stream* and stared across the room at him. He had his rump planted on the davenport, mine was on the love seat, and we kept the drapes closed, so nobody outside would know we were in the house. *"Heigh-ho everybody,"* said Rudy Vallee on a little tabletop radio while Roscoe thumbed through a book, something by Booth Tarkington, a surprise to me because I never pegged him as a reader. I think it was one of those *Reader's Digest* condensed deals, but it was better than nothing. I shrugged my shoulders, raised my magazine, and went back to the primer for trout fishing in front of me. Rudy and his Connecticut Yankees performed a sentimental orchestra tune.

"Sheriff's orders," I said. "In case C. W. comes home to pick up his toothbrush or something."

"We're wasting our time," he said. "How the hell are we supposed to catch Helen Pfalzgraf's killer if we're holed up in this place?"

"Don't slay the messenger. I don't want to be here any more than you do."

"Somehow I find that hard to believe," said Roscoe, glaring at me. "You know, Art, there's still time for you to sign that letter calling on Cannon to resign. The men would see it as a good thing if you was to add your name."

"I said I wasn't interested."

"I wish you'd reconsider." I didn't answer. He squinted to see the cover of the magazine in my hands. "At least tell me what the fuck you're reading."

"It's called 'How to Fish for Trout.'"

"Sounds fascinating." His sarcasm did not lacerate me the way he hoped it would.

"I've read worse. I haven't learned anything new yet."

"Well, then why the fuck you reading it?"

Flipping to the next page, I said, "I'd prefer it if you didn't use the F-word. I don't like it."

"Oh, you don't, huh?"

"No, I don't. Vulgar language is for men who can't find the right words to say."

"Sometimes the right word is 'fuck.' Did you ever think of that?"

"That's never the right word," I said, narrowing my eyes at him. "If you want to use that kind of language, please take it outside. It pollutes the ears and the mind. I don't care to hear it."

"Good God almighty, are you for real, Oveson?"

I closed the magazine, keeping my index finger on the page where I left off. "What do you mean?"

"You don't drink. Don't cuss. Don't blow half your paycheck on whores. As far as I can tell, the closest thing you have to a vice is eating too much ice cream."

I feigned reading some more and said, "I've got a side to me you don't know about."

Roscoe slammed his book shut and tossed it on the table. "Now we're getting somewhere. C'mon, Oveson. Talk. You can't jackass around like that and then clam up. What's this other side you're talking about?"

It's time, I thought, *to add an element of levity to this grim conversation.* I looked over my left shoulder, over my right shoulder, and whispered, "Jacks."

He gave me a look of disbelief. "Jacks?" I nodded. "Jacks, the game?" I nodded again. "That's your *hidden* side?"

"I'm up to my foursies."

"I can't believe it. I've got Tom *fucking* Sawyer for a partner."

"I'll teach you if you want."

"Teach me what?"

"To play jacks."

"I don't want to play jacks, Oveson! For fuck's sake!"

Roscoe uncapped a bottle of liquor and took a few swallows. While he drank, I said, "What about you?"

"What *about* me?"

"Have you got a side you don't want anybody to know about?"

"Everybody does. Even you do, though you won't admit it."

"What's your hidden side all about?"

He laughed and ran his palm over the dark peach-fuzz bristle on top of his head. He said, "If I was to broadcast it, it wouldn't be hidden, now would it?"

"It might make you feel better to talk about it."

"Art," he said, sitting up straight and resting his elbows on his knees, "when you get to be my age—"

"Which is?"

"Nice try. When you get to be my age, you end up with a head full of bad memories. It doesn't make you feel any better talking about them." His face brightened, and he said, "Hey, I've got an idea. Why don't you come to Evanston with me this weekend?"

"What's in Evanston?"

"A whorehouse."

I laughed uncomfortably. "Now what on earth am I going to do in a whorehouse?"

"Brother, if you need me to explain that, you're in worse trouble than I thought."

I held up my ring finger and showed him my silver wedding band. "No, I mean I'm married. You knew that."

"Don't matter. Most of the men who go there have got wives. I go up there just to see this Chink whore goes by the name of Glenda—calls herself that because nobody can pronounce her Chink name. It sounds like a bunch of pots and pans falling down the stairs. For ten dollars, this dame will ride you till you're bow-legged."

"That's a foul way to talk about a woman," I said. "Did the thought ever cross your mind that she's somebody's daughter?"

"Not till now. Tell you what, Art. You find her parents' address and I'll drop 'em a picture postcard letting 'em know what a great lay their daughter is."

He's a lost cause, I thought, and I went back to reading my magazine and listening to Vallee crooning softly on the radio.

A few minutes later, Roscoe said, "When do we shove off? I don't like being in another man's home. It doesn't feel right."

"The other deputies are supposed to spell us at two. We've got about three more hours. Well, three and a half. We might as well make ourselves at home. Maybe he has some decent food in the icebox."

"So do you think this shitbird murdered Helen?" asked Roscoe.

"It doesn't look too good for him," I said. "Especially him taking a powder like this." For a second, I considered telling Roscoe about the conversation I had with Considine—about Pfalzgraf inheriting a fortune and his first wife dying in an auto accident a few months later; about Pfalzgraf's one-man crusade to drive Dr.

Everett Wooley out of Salt Lake City; about Wooley getting murdered in Ogden. I reconsidered, though, knowing Roscoe wouldn't be happy with me for sharing information with Considine. So I held back and instead simply said, "But I do think we ought to be investigating other leads."

"Now you're talking," said Roscoe. "Got any ideas?"

"Let's just say I've been keeping my eyes and ears open. Sometimes you have to think against the grain."

"Grain?" He looked perplexed. "The fuck you talking about, grain?"

"I agree with you that we should be out there," I said. "Not in here."

Roscoe grinned. "I like what I'm hearing."

In the afternoon, Roscoe and I were relieved by a couple of deputies so I could testify on the next-to-last day of the inquest. In the witness box, I spoke about finding Helen Pfalzgraf's body. Reliving that moment was harder than I'd thought it would be, but I didn't show it. Once it was over, all my words became a blur. The same day I testified, Anna Pfalzgraf took the stand, but she didn't say anything in front of that packed room that she hadn't told Roscoe and me when we questioned her. After she stepped down, Deputy Coroner Tom Livsey spoke about the condition of the body. Before he could show slides of the badly mangled corpse, the coroner asked the women to leave the courtroom, including the stenographer. The black-and-white slides unleashed a torrent of memories for me. Looking at those images ended up being far more difficult for me than testifying.

A few more testimonies followed Tom's. The managers of three local banks were called in to discuss Helen Pfalzgraf's big deposits, which greatly exceeded the regular allowance given to her by Dr. Pfalzgraf. At least three of the deposits were traced back to the bank account belonging to Intermountain Mining Speculators, the company owned by C. W. Alexander.

Testimonies on Friday, the final day of the inquest, were equally damning for Alexander. A resident of the Van Buren Apartments in Ogden recalled seeing a man ditching Helen Pfalzgraf's car in a parking lot in the middle of the night. His description of the man closely matched Alexander. A waitress at a dance joint called the Club 40, located on the highway between the airport and the Great Salt Lake, remembered seeing Helen and C. W. cutting the rug lots of times. Their last outing at the 40 came four days before Pfalzgraf's death, and the witness said she saw the two of them having a terrible spat before they left. She couldn't hear what they were fighting about.

The coroner's inquest officially ended in the late afternoon on Friday, March 7, with an inconclusive verdict. Basking in camera flashes, Cannon announced to the press he still suspected C. W. Alexander was Helen's murderer.

Our alert for all lawmen to be on the lookout for C. W. Alexander had gone out via Western Union across Utah and the surrounding states on Tuesday, and over the next several days, the fish kept nibbling. Men resembling Alexander were spotted in towns across the state—as far south as Panguitch down around Bryce Canyon, as far east as Vernal a little ways from the craggy hills of the Utah-Colorado border, and as far north as Cornish, a postage-stamp-sized town on the Oregon Shortline Railroad near the Utah-Idaho border. So far none of the look-alikes had turned out to be the real Alexander.

On Friday, as the inquest concluded, Roscoe and I found ourselves on telephone duty, but a radio tuned to station KSL played highlights of the inquest in the background. It turned out to be much busier than guarding C. W. Alexander's house. Callers reported spotting Alexander near the vermillion cliffs on the outskirts of St. George in southwestern Utah; hiking a footpath in Echo Canyon, by Zion Park; riding on a Pullman car outside of Fort Collins, Colorado; leaving a boardinghouse in Spokane, Washington; painting a roadside billboard in Phoenix, Arizona. One man on a crackly line even fessed up to being none other than C. W. Alexander himself, in the flesh and spending his days on Santa Catalina Island working as a fisherman. I asked him to prove it by telling me his birth date. The line went dead.

Ogden was Salt Lake City's besotted younger brother, a town that wore its wild past like a badge of honor. Like Salt Lake, it grew up pressed against the rugged Wasatch Mountains, a formidable eastern wall if ever there was one. Its earliest inhabitants were trappers; in fact, it was named after a legendary fur trader and explorer, Peter Skene Ogden, who explored the region in 1828 while on the payroll of the Hudson's Bay Company. I'm not sure Ogden would've been too pleased to witness the evolution of his namesake city as it transformed from a sleepy village into a bustling railroad hub that lured all kinds of gamblers, speculators, opium merchants, con men, outlaws, and just general dregs of humanity.

By 1930, it had shed some of its Wild West past, but traces of its dark history lingered. The streets west of downtown were still home to grimy flophouses full of desperate souls, lunatics, addicts, slummers, and others who gravitated to the periphery. Prostitutes with wavy hair, empty eyes, too much lipstick, and runs in their stockings still roamed the sidewalks. Plenty of Ogdenites, whatever their station in life, thought Salt Lake City was a snooty Mormon burgh, too uptight for its own good. If only they knew that many Salt Lakers regarded their town as the armpit of Utah.

I made the forty-five-minute drive north to Ogden on a cold and wet Saturday that marked the two-week anniversary of Roscoe and me finding Helen Pfalzgraf's body. Clark Peterson, a patrolman

with the Ogden Police Department who also happened to be a
friend of the family, offered to let me in the police station after
hours to have a look at records on the Everett Wooley file. I arrived
equipped with a spiral notebook, a pencil, and a brown bag of
candy I picked up on the way at Kolitz Kandy Kitchen in downtown Ogden.

Clark was a bearish blond man who always wore his black uniform, even to church. He led me down a hallway on the second floor
of police headquarters to the last room on the right. He unlocked
the door and punched a button that switched on a ceiling light. I
walked over to a barred window and admired the view of Weber
Valley. I pulled out a chair, and he set a stack of files on the table in
front of me. I opened the bag of candy and held it in front of him.

"Want some?"

He peeked over the edge of the bag, his face long with interest.
"Whatcha got there?"

"Butternut taffy from Kolitz." He reached in the bag and snatched
a piece, tore the wrapper off, and stuffed the taffy in his mouth. I
said, "Best butternut taffy in the West."

"You can say that again," he said, chewing madly. "Mind if I
take a few more?"

"Go right ahead."

He grabbed a small handful out of the bag and gestured to the
files. "These are all on the Wooley case. I'll be across the hall. If
you need anything, holler."

"Thanks much, Clark. I hope you take me up on that chicken
dinner."

"Any chance of Clara making it instead of that old greasy
spoon?"

"Let me have a word with her," I said, smiling. "It'd be the perfect excuse to have you and Jean over."

"Sounds swell, Art. I'll check on you in a half hour."

"Much obliged, Clark."

He closed the door behind him, and I opened the file on top of the stack. A blue piece of paper with the words CASE FILE STATUS SHEET at the top and Wooley's name in someone's longhand below. Next: "DOB: May 4, 1872. PLACE OF BIRTH: Logan, Utah." Then: "DOD: Friday, November 2, 1928. PLACE OF DEATH: Wooley's office, Washington Boulevard, Ogden. AGE OF DECEASED: 56." My eyes dipped farther down the page to "CASE STATUS: CLOSED/UNSOLVED."

The black-and-white photographs taken at the crime scene showed him sitting in his wooden swivel chair, facedown over his desk with a bullet wound in the back of his head. Angle from top (*flip*), behind (*flip*), left (*flip*), right (*flip*). Coroner's verdict on canary yellow paper: "DEAD OF GUNSHOT WOUND TO REAR OF SKULL FROM .45." (*flip*) "SUMMARY OF THE CRIME: Dr. Everett A. Wooley, a physician residing in North Ogden, was found shot to death Friday, November 2, at his second-floor office in the 2400 block of Washington Boulevard. Ogden Police patrol officers responded to a call at approximately 11:15 reporting the sound of a gunshot coming from the said office. Police arrived at Wooley's office to find the victim unresponsive."

On page three, I came across something interesting. "Officers detained a white male, late 20s, who identified himself as Sam Louis. Suspect was seen fleeing building where Wooley's office is housed. Louis explained that he was leaving the premises to catch a bus. Ogden police held Louis for four hours while they performed a background check. When the officers were satisfied the suspect played no role in the homicide, they released him from custody."

I opened my spiral notebook and jotted the name "Sam Louis." I tapped my pencil against my lips, eyed that name, and thought about it. I stuck my hand in the brown paper bag and pulled out a piece of taffy, ripped off the wax paper, and stuck the candy in my mouth. "Sam Louis, Sam Louis, Sam Louis . . ."

The name seemed familiar, but it didn't set off any bells right away.

I thumbed through the file and came across a snapshot of Wooley while he was alive. Taken outside somewhere, it showed him standing next to a pine tree. He had on a fancy suit—three piece, pinstripes, with a gold watch chain and patent leather shoes. He was a lean man, with thick glasses, a pointed nose, thinning white hair, a weak chin, and a self-conscious smile. He appeared too mousy to be the "dangerous abortionist" the press made him out to be. But one cannot base much on looks.

I opened a folder marked WOOLEY, EVERETT—PRESS CLIPPINGS, 1925–1928. A cluster of articles in August of 1926 detailed the efforts of Dr. Hans Pfalzgraf to drive Dr. Wooley out of Salt Lake City. PHYSICIAN FILES COMPLAINT ON BEHALF OF S.L. WOMAN (*Salt Lake Examiner,* Thursday, August 12, '26). MEDICAL BOARD HEARS PFALZGRAF'S COMPLAINT (*Ogden Post,* Saturday, August 14, '26). WOOLEY PERFORMED HARMFUL SURGERY, BOARD AVERS (*Salt Lake Telegram,* Tuesday, August 24, '26). BOARD SUSPENDS WOOLEY'S LICENSE (*Salt Lake Telegram,* Thursday, August 26, '26). WOOLEY ASSAULTS PFALZGRAF IN DOWNTOWN RESTAURANT, and below that, RESPECTED S.L. PHYSICIAN TO PRESS CHARGES (*Ogden Post,* Saturday, August 28, '26).

The next series of clippings was from October of '28, all from the *Ogden Post,* about a citizens group called the Ogden Protective League filing a complaint with police about a surgeon practicing in the city without a license. If you guessed the name of the surgeon to be Dr. Everett Wooley, you get a cigar. One of the clippings referred to two women, Pearl Hickmore (of Pleasant View) and Maxine Granger (of Brigham City), coming down with "mystery illnesses" after visiting the doctor. No word on the ultimate fate of either woman.

Peterson gave a knock and poked his head in. "How's it going?"

I had taken up enough of his Saturday. I closed the clippings file and set it on top of the others. "I think I've seen everything I needed to see. Thank you for your time, Clark."

He walked in the room and I handed him the files. He said, "It's a shame, Wooley getting it like that. But most folks in this town don't miss him. Not after what he did to all those poor girls."

"Have there been any new leads in this case?"

"I don't know, it wasn't mine," he said. "I'm just a lowly patrolman walking the beat. The case has been closed for a while, though. We must've interviewed twenty, thirty people. Nothing but a lot of dead ends."

"What about this Sam Louis?" I glanced at the name on my notebook. "Last name spelled *L-O-U-I-S*. According to the file, eyewitnesses saw him fleeing the building where Wooley's office was located."

"Hang on a minute," he said, and he left the room with the files in his arms. A few minutes later, he returned and slammed a 1929 city directory on the table, opening the page to the *L*'s. He ran his finger down a column, then shook his head and backed up a step, glancing at me apologetically. "Nope. No Sam or Samuel Louis in the city directory. You sure it was *L-O-U-I-S*?"

I nodded. "That's what the report said."

He checked just in case. "Sorry," he said. "No Samuel or Sam Lewis, *L-E-W-I-S*."

"That's OK," I said. "I'm grateful that you looked."

His eyebrows bounced up and down, and he cracked a smile. "Don't forget about that chicken dinner, Art."

"Oh, I won't."

Twelve

Sunday dinner at the Oveson family compound once again drew perfect attendance. The women complimented each other's hairdos and talked about the challenges of canning homegrown vegetables. All of the Oveson brothers except me gathered around the fire crackling in the hearth to discuss their latest law enforcement exploits. A radio in the sitting room played the Mormon Tabernacle Choir. The place was full of children, running, laughing, and dashing in and out of the back door, enjoying Nature's first breath of spring and the longer days outside.

If you haven't been to Utah, let me tell you March is a wild-card month. March can either be bitter cold or springlike, with the season's first buds poking out of branch ends. The children left the door open each time they dashed out in the backyard to play, but Mom didn't object. She was too focused on preparing dinner—a hefty pot roast that dripped juice into the pan—and I assisted by setting the long tables with the proper place mats, plates, and silverware.

By half past six, the two long tables were packed, the north one with adults, the south with children. Plates made the rounds—roast beef, mashed potatoes, peas with pearl onions, asparagus, gravy, a basket of hot rolls, a plate of softened sweet butter. People were too busy eating to make small talk, although I was simply moving food around my plate and hoping nobody would notice. My appetite had flown south, and I wasn't keen on sitting at the same table with my competitive brothers, especially with the Helen Pfalzgraf investigation unresolved.

A spat erupted at the children's table. Sarah Jane got into a shoving match with her cousin Stephen.

I grabbed my panting daughter while Grant wrapped his arms around Stephen. I said, "What on earth are you two fighting about, anyhow?"

"Stephen called you a tenderfoot, Dad!"

The word took me aback. "Tenderfoot?" I echoed. "Do you even know what that means?"

"No," shrieked Sarah Jane, "but nobody can call my dad names!"

"He *is* a tenderfoot," said Stephen, a bristly buzz-cut kid whose white shirt and red tie were now disheveled. "That's what my pop says, and Pop's always right!"

Grant, a huskier version of me, was shaking his head and blushing. "Now, you know I didn't say that, Stephen. I never called Uncle Arthur a tenderfoot."

"Sure you did, Pop," he said. "A few days ago, at the dinner table. You said Uncle Arthur is a tenderfoot. I heard you."

"You misunderstood me," said Grant, leading Stephen back to his chair. "Now you sit down there and enjoy the wonderful dinner Grandmama made for us."

"Yes, sir."

I returned to my chair, and Clara reached over and squeezed my hand. She leaned in close and whispered, "Don't mind him. He had no call to say that."

Grant sat next to his wife, Bess, a double-chinned brunette in a green dress. He scooted his chair closer to the table and tucked his napkin into his collar like a bib.

Mom ran her fingers through her white hair and stared through her bifocals, first at Grant, then at me, then Grant again. "I don't want you two quarreling over anything. You hear?"

Grant, all smiles, said, "Oh, we weren't quarreling, Mom. I said something a few days ago and Stephen misunderstood me. That's all."

I said, "So you didn't say I was a tenderfoot?"

"I was talking to Bess about the Pfalzgraf investigation," he said. "I might've said the Salt Lake Sheriff's Office was full of tenderfoots. Something along those lines. But I didn't mean any harm by it, Art. Honestly."

"Why would you say something like that?" I asked.

He took a deep breath as he drowned his piece of roast beef in gravy. "It's been over two weeks, Art. The crime scene was full of clues. The Keystone Kops could've—"

"Grant!" said Frank, my oldest brother. "That's quite enough."

Grant nodded, cut into his roast beef, and forked a bite into his mouth. He watched me as he chewed and arched his eyebrows, tauntingly.

"The Keystone Kops could have what?" I asked. "Finish your sentence."

He spoke with his mouth full. "Every criminal in America knows that Salt Lake City is the place to go if you want to get away with murder."

"Grant," said John and Frank at the same time.

John said, "Gosh, leave him alone, Grant. Eat your supper."

Frank said, "Don't fight back, Art. There's a time and a place. Cool down and eat your supper, kid."

I said to Grant, "If you're so doggone smart, why don't you come up and show us hayseeds a thing or two. I'm sure one hour of Sherlocking and you'd crack this case wide open."

"I bet I'd do a better job than any of you," he said, his mouth forming a crooked grin. "Tell you what. I'll take a day off, come up and show you fellows how it's done."

Clara moved so close to me her lips touched my ears when she whispered. "Think of all the work your mom has done. Be the bigger man."

She sat straight, still looking at me—all eyes were on me at this point—and I took a deep breath. I faced Grant, who watched me intently, rocking back and forth subtly, perhaps waiting for me to strike back. I tossed my linen napkin on the table as I stood and headed for the back door.

Most of the snow outside had melted—big patches of mud and grass showed—and the days were lasting longer and getting warmer. I went to my favorite spot inside the barn and boosted myself up onto the leather chair of the tractor. The din of livestock kept me company out there as I blew warm air into my hands. Water dripped everywhere, Mother Nature's whisper that April was coming. I was alone a good ten minutes, but footsteps told me my solitude was about to come to an end.

Mom stood in the doorway with a black knit stocking cap on her head, a gentle smile on her face, and her dark green coat buttoned up to the very top. She walked past bales of hay and metal farm implements and made herself comfortable on top of a big wooden crate.

"I had a feeling I'd find you out here. You aren't like your brothers in one respect. They're always surrounding themselves with other people, but you—you like to be alone. Always have."

I nodded. "It helps me clear the cobwebs out of my head, Mom."

"Won't you come back in, Art? I know Grant was out of line, but he didn't mean any harm. He sometimes gets carried away and says things he shouldn't, and this was one of those times. If you could find it in your heart to forgive him . . ."

"He was right. I am a tenderfoot." I ran my fingers along the red surface of the tractor's body, now dented and scratched by years of use. "I'm not like this old tractor here. It's been making the rounds on these fields for years and years. I've always followed the easy route. I'm a year away from thirty and I haven't done much of anything with my life."

"Don't say that," said Mom. "You've achieved great things. Maybe you are the type who doesn't go looking for big challenges. Nothing wrong with that."

I nodded. "I've spent a lifetime running away from the things that scare me. I don't know why." I looked down at my feet, not able to make eye contact with her. "Maybe it's my poor health. Maybe it was Dad's death. I don't know. I feel like I'm always so frightened by the world."

"Don't sell yourself short, Arthur," Mom said, squeezing my wrist. "That's always been your biggest problem—not giving yourself enough credit. All of you Oveson boys are smart, but you, Arthur, have got something more. You've got a heart full of kindness."

She nodded her head firmly and gave my wrist another squeeze. "Life is full of adversity. You don't need to seek it out. It's how you respond to it when it finds you that counts."

I looked into her warm eyes. "What they say about Sheriff Cannon is true. He's no good. All he wants to do is pin the Pfalzgraf homicide on this one fellow, and he might not even be our man."

"Times like this, you have to listen to your heart. It'll serve you well." She paused. "Do you want to come inside?"

"Maybe not quite yet. I think I'll sit out here for a few minutes."

"Well, I'll stay, too. Keep you company."

She inched back on the top of that crate to get more comfortable. We stayed in the barn together a while longer, eyeing the snow-covered peaks to the east, reflecting the last streaks of daylight.

Roscoe didn't show up to Monday morning calisthenics. In the short time I'd been a deputy, he had never missed a day of work. Three other deputies also failed to appear at the gymnasium: Harold Romney, Bill McKitrick, and Ed Glendon. I didn't think much of it as I endured the daily exercise routines with the other deputies. After, I took my usual piping-hot morning shower, toweled myself off, opened my locker, and gazed at my dripping reflection in the little mirror. Once I dried off, I got dressed in less than two minutes, stopping to run a comb through my hair before I put on my socks and shoes. Jim Boyd, a brown-haired deputy with pale skin, big ears, and an overbite, emerged from the showers, opening up a locker near me.

"Tough break, Art," he said as I was tying my shoelaces.

I looked up at him. "What do you mean?"

"About your partner and all," he said, slipping on his temple garments.

"What about my partner?"

He stood motionless for a few seconds and winced at me. "You mean you ain't heard?"

"Heard what?"

"Cannon canned him, along with Glendon, Romney, and that other fella. What's his name?" He snapped his finger twice and his eyes widened. "McKitrick. Cannon called 'em all into his office on Saturday, said they were the ringleaders, and fired each and every one, right on the spot."

"Ringleaders? Ringleaders of what?"

Boyd walked over to a nearby sink with toothpowder, a toothbrush, and a metal cup. He filled the cup with water and glanced at his protruding pearlies, which in his case weren't so white. "Cannon found out about that little letter they wrote to the *Examiner* calling for his resignation and endorsing Blackham."

I stood still, mouth open, too dumbfounded to speak.

Boyd began brushing his teeth, side to side, up and down, and I gave his words a minute to settle in. He tipped his metal cup, gargled with water and spit. "I thought Lund would've called you over the weekend. He's your partner, ain't he?"

"Yeah. But . . ." I stopped. I thought about telling Boyd that I didn't know Roscoe very well. Then I reconsidered. I had a lot of mixed feelings running through my head about Roscoe at that moment, and Boyd didn't need to know about them.

"But what?"

"Nothing."

I rushed out, heading straight for Sheriff Cannon's office. Walking down the hall, I thought of exactly what I was going to tell him—that nobody liked him. He was inept. His reputation was in the gutter. Probably his own mother even thought him corrupt. I couldn't remember being this furious at any other point in my life. I charged up the sets of stairs and cut across the common room full of desks, until his office door came into view. *This is it,* I told myself. *I'm finally going to say all of the things I've wanted to say to him.*

Something happened a few feet away from his office door, though. My feet didn't just go cold—they went full-fledged iceberg on me.

Cannon was in there, sitting triumphantly at his desk, looking every bit the king, stuffing a sweet roll into his mouth and washing it down with a cup of hot chocolate. He saw me and arched his eyebrows, stood up, and wiped his mouth with a napkin. He waved his hand toward the chair, chewing food as he beckoned me inside.

Sykes was sitting in his favorite chair, to the side of Cannon's desk, breaking open roasted peanuts from a brown paper bag.

"Have a seat, Deputy," said Cannon. "Just the man I wanted to see."

"Sir," I said, "I've got something I want to talk to you about—"

"Good, I've got something I want to talk to you about, too," he said. "I'll go first. Deputy Oveson—"

I blurted out, "Sheriff Cannon—"

"Uh, uh, uh. Let me go first. You've probably heard the news that I fired four disloyal deputies who were fomenting all kinds of trouble in these corridors."

"That's what I wanted to talk to you about, sir—"

"Good. I'll finish what I'm going to say, and then I'll give you a turn. At first I was disappointed that you didn't tell me about this little escapade of theirs. After all, I did ask you to be my eyes and ears. Your failure to convey that information to me had me wondering about you, Deputy—about where your loyalties lie. I thought about calling you in here with the four of them and telling you to hit the road, too. But Sykes here told me something."

I glanced at Sykes, who was busy eating peanuts and tossing the shells into a spittoon.

"What's that, sir?" I asked.

"Sykes said that the other fellows probably didn't let you in on their little plot because they had you pegged a Cannon loyalist. I gave it some thought, and what Sykes says makes a lot of sense. But now that you're here in my office, I want to hear it from you, Oveson."

"Hear what, sir?"

"Were you in on it?"

The March wind whipped in through the open window and ruffled my hair. Car horns blared, streetcar bells clanged, and Old

Glory at the City and County Building across the street flapped high on a pole alongside the state beehive flag. I sat paralyzed in that chair, unable to say what I was really thinking, and terrified of going home and breaking it to Clara that I no longer had a job.

"How about it?" he asked. "It really shouldn't take you this long to come up with an answer."

"No. I wasn't in on it."

I spoke the truth. I wasn't in on it. Uttering the words was still agonizing. I felt like I was betraying Roscoe.

He slammed his palm on the desk, and the bang startled me, making me leap out of my chair an inch or so.

"What did I tell you, Sykes?" he asked. "Didn't I say he was loyal to the end?"

"Actually, I believe that was me who said that," said Sykes, who looked up from his peanut shelling to wink at me. Cannon smiled at me as he leaned back in his chair, hands clutching the armrests. "Now what was it you wanted to say?"

My entire body trembled, from head to toe, as I looked at him, and I couldn't help but wonder if he noticed my bewildered expression. "W-w-what?"

"You were going to tell me something, Oveson. Go right ahead. I'm all ears."

"Tell you . . ." I licked my lips and nodded my head really fast. "Oh yeah. I was going to tell you something. I was going to tell you . . ."

Peanut shells rattled as they hit the spittoon. My mouth eventually formed the words. "I was going to tell you that I had nothing to do with writing that letter. Had I known about it, I would've shared that information with you and tried to help nip it in the bud."

Cannon's smile returned. "That's what I thought. You know darn well how much I prize loyalty. And your loyalty to me will never again be brought into question, Deputy."

I stood up from my chair, turned around, and headed for those arched doors, thanking my lucky stars the men's room was nearby.

"Oh, and Oveson?"

Slowly, I pivoted toward him.

"Go out and find C. W. Alexander for me. I'm starting to really dislike the lack of resolution on this case. I read in the *Examiner* this morning that Doc Pfalzgraf is offering a ten-thousand-dollar reward for the man who apprehends his wife's killer—dead or alive. Bring Alexander back and you'll get a good chunk of dough for your family. Also . . ."

He opened his drawer, lifted out a little gray box, and opened it, revealing a shiny gold star. "You'll get a promotion. It'll up you a grade. I'm sure your missus will be thrilled when you come home wearing this beaut on your chest."

"Yes, sir," I said. "I have no doubt she will."

I left. There was nothing else to say.

Thirteen

Sitting at one of the desks in the common room after my unsettling conversation with Cannon, I made it my mission to find C. W. Alexander.

I possessed a newfound determination to apprehend the man for questioning. Perhaps Cannon's offer of a promotion prodded me. Or maybe I simply needed something to keep me focused after the loss of Roscoe. Exiting Cannon's office, I'd felt a combination of restlessness and nausea, but I couldn't figure out why. Then it occurred to me as I raised the earpiece from the telephone. I missed Roscoe. I never thought I would. It's funny how a friendship can develop between two men without either of them realizing it. Maybe Roscoe was aware of it. I sure hadn't been, not until now, anyway.

I put in the first call to Alexander's secretary at Intermountain Mining Speculators in the Newhouse, where Sheriff Cannon had stationed a deputy. Her flinty voice left nothing to guesswork. "I haven't seen him. I haven't heard from him. Please stop telephoning me about this—you're tying up our lines."

I went through some court records, confirmed that Alexander was indeed married, and found out his wife's maiden name—Hicks. A midmorning search through back issues of the *Examiner* also proved fruitful. I found their May 18, 1921, marriage announcement on page B-8. Her parents, Elmer and Rose Hicks, were listed as living on a rural road in Bountiful. Next, I went to the '29 Salt Lake City directory and found "HICKS, E & R," located at 400 East in Bountiful. I stared at their name in print and wondered why none of the other deputies had done this since we started our search.

I put on my Stetson as I cut through the parking lot behind the county jail and climbed into the driver's seat of a county Model A. The sky had turned dark with clouds, and gusts of wind shook the car as I steered onto Fourth South. The day was fixing to snow, but it hadn't started yet. Most of the winter snow in the Salt Lake Valley had already melted after days of warmth, so we were about due to be walloped.

I raced up the highway to Bountiful in record time. Close to Salt Lake City—in the next county to the north, at the foothills of the Wasatch Range—it's a town of scattered farms, a café, a market, a filling station, and new suburban streets with freshly constructed bungalows. I took the 400 East exit, drove along a stretch of road where the houses were spaced far apart, and parked in front of one I recognized from an old Sears, Roebuck catalog—two stories, wood frame, gambrel roof, veranda and rocking chairs out front. A detached garage out back had been built to resemble the main house. These joints were the craze fifteen, twenty years ago. A buyer would order a house out of a catalog, pick it up when it arrived on a freight train, and assemble it, often with the help of dragooned neighbors.

I went up to the front door and gave a knock. It creaked open a few inches. I lifted my .38 out of my holster, switched off the safety, and cocked the hammer back. It was dark inside. My eyes needed a

moment to adjust. The place had a lived-in feel, but the closed curtains blocked out the daytime light, and there wasn't much of that
due to overcast skies. Somewhere Ruth Etting sang "Deep Night"
on either a phonograph or a radio—I couldn't tell which. Wood
floors moaned under my feet. A steep front-hall staircase rose to an
even darker second floor.

Etting's voice filled my ears . . .

"Deep night, stars in the sky above . . ."

I crept forward, down a hall lined with framed photographs
barely visible in the darkness.

"Moonlight, lighting our place of love . . ."

At the end of the hall, I whipped through a door, gun aimed. I
stood in a kitchen. Pots and pans dangled from hooks above the
counter, and in the center was a table covered with a checkered
tablecloth and five of everything: place mats, plates, sets of silverware.

I lowered my .38 and walked across the linoleum, past a stove
and porcelain sink, and the back door came into view, its window
concealed behind blinds. I unlocked the door latch and opened it,
stepped out onto the back porch, and went down four stairs to a
path behind the house. It started to snow as I headed in the direction of the two-car detached garage. The twin doors were closed
and latched shut, but each had a square window. I fished a piece of
paper out of my pocket and read my own scribble: *Forest green 1927
Hupmobile 4-door sedan, LP UT 8347.*

I cupped my hands around my eyes and peered into the garage.
It was dark inside, but light enough for me to see a cream-colored,
four-door Willys-Knight sedan. No sign of a green Hupmobile.

The sudden crack of gunfire rolled from one side of the valley to
the other, and a geyser of dirt erupted three inches away from my
foot. I bolted. My Stetson fell on the ground as I lunged and rolled
behind the garage, where I crouched with my .38 leveled. I peeked

around the corner at the house. A flash went off in the second-floor window, followed by a jolting crack. A bullet pinged off the garage. I couldn't see the shooter, although I noticed a ghostly shadow between the curtains.

Another shot went off, clipping the branch of a nearby box elder tree. A fourth bullet shattered a garage door window. The shooter was aiming wildly. This wasn't a pro.

I inched closer to the corner and shouted as loudly as my lungs would let me, "My name is Deputy Arthur Oveson, Salt Lake County Sheriff's Office! I didn't come here to hurt you or anybody else! I'm only here to help!"

Snowflakes tapped my face. I squatted between the garage and fence, debating in my mind what to do next. A hundred yards separated the garage from the back door, and I opted to run for it. I counted down: *Five, four, three, two, one* . . . A mad sprint, my legs moving as fast as they could carry me, and a pair of shots ripped out of the upstairs window. Earth burst a few feet away from me, and my Stetson, lying on the ground, jumped suddenly with a new hole blown clean through it. I leaped onto the back porch and tore through the back door.

I slipped inside the house, .38 in my right hand, and bumped things as I moved through the darkness—a kitchen chair, a table, a coat tree in the front hall. I stepped on every other stair on my way to the second floor. The door at the top of the stairs was closed. That was the room I wanted, the one overlooking the backyard. The transom window above it was open. I crouched low on the right side of the door and called out, "Listen up in there. My name is Deputy Oveson, and I aim to leave this house without firing a single shot! I don't have a beef with you! I wanna talk. *That's all.*"

First I thought the only sound in the house was the radio downstairs, now playing a quiz show. Then my ears picked up something else: a soft whimpering coming from behind the door in front of me. I reached for the crystal knob. "I'm going to open the door slowly. I'm not going to make any sudden moves. The last thing in the world I wish to do is hurt you."

I turned the knob clockwise, and the door jumped out of the frame half an inch. I gave the door a gentle poke and crouched on the left side of the doorway. The door creaked open a few more inches. "All I really want is for us to walk out of here together."

I spied around the corner into a room containing a full-sized bed with a brass headboard and footboard and a patch quilt, a bureau with a mirror and metal washbasin, a rocking chair, a framed photograph of the Salt Lake Temple, and a little boy, armed with a pistol almost as long as he was, sitting cross-legged and sobbing. With his free hand he covered his eyes. He couldn't have been more than twelve, and his cheeks were sprayed with freckles. He was dressed in thick black denim pants and a plaid shirt with shades of maroon, black, and yellow. I spotted a box of bullets a few feet away from him. I holstered my .38, so as not to scare him.

"What's your name, son?"

"Scotty," he said, sniffling, voice trembling. "Scotty Alexander."

I nodded and stared at that long-barreled pistol in his hand. "That's a good name. I like that name—Scotty. That's a big gun you've got there. Might I be able to persuade you to lay it on the floor in front of you? It's a dangerous item, and I don't want it to discharge and hurt you or me. I've got a daughter who's not quite your age—her name's Sarah Jane—and I want her to see her dad tonight."

Convulsing with sobs, he leaned forward and placed the gun about a foot away from his toes.

"Now, son," I said, "I'm gonna reach out and switch on the safety on that gun. It's your firearm—I don't intend to take it. I just don't want it going off. OK?"

He raised his knees to his chest and pressed his forehead against them. He nodded his head slightly to my request. I leaned close to the gun and pushed the safety switch, then let out a quiet sigh of relief.

"I'm going to give you a handkerchief," I said. "It's clean. You can use it for your nose and eyes."

I passed him a cotton hankie, and he took it and held it against his nose. By now he'd eased to a gentle weeping.

"Are you gonna arrest me?" he asked.

"I'll make you a deal, Scotty. If you don't fire that gun anymore, I won't arrest you. It's too dangerous for a boy your age. How old are you, anyhow?"

"Twelve."

"That's what I guessed. Last week, I read in the paper about a couple of fellows in North Carolina—not much older than you—who got a hold of a revolver. They started by shooting tin cans off of a fence. Then one of the boys put a tin can on top of his head and told his pal to fire. Well, the kid who put the can on his head is now in the cemetery, and the poor boy who fired the shot has to live with what he did for the rest of his life." I pointed to the gun on the floor. "The moral of the story is, not much good comes of those things."

He looked up at me. He had a pug nose and crooked teeth, but he was a cute kid—full of innocence. "Sorry about your hat."

I chuckled. "You have a good aim."

He snickered, for the first time since I got there. "I've got money in my piggy bank."

"Nah. I was due for a new one anyhow." I glanced over my shoulder, taking in the quietness of the house. "How come you felt the need to use that gun?"

"I was scared."

"Of what?" He didn't answer, so I didn't press it. Instead, I said, "Aren't there any grown-ups around here?"

"My grandma and grandpa own a restaurant by the highway. Mama works there, and my sister helps out, too."

"What's it called?"

"The Pioneer."

"Oh yeah. I drove past it on my way here. What's the best thing on the menu?"

"Steak and french fries."

"I'll have to give it a try. What about your father?"

He rubbed his tiny red eyes, and I was relieved he wasn't crying anymore. "He's hiding. Why are you looking for him? My dad didn't hurt anybody."

"I want to help him, but I need to be able to find him first."

"They think he killed a lady, but he didn't. My dad wouldn't do that."

"I believe you. In order to help him, though, I've got to know where he is."

"C'mere. I got something to show you."

He led me downstairs into the kitchen and pressed a button that turned on a light fixture above. He gestured me to follow him, and when we reached a wood box telephone, he pointed to handwriting on the wall above it. "Here."

I leaned in close to read the shaky scrawl: *79 SUMMIT, P.C., TEL SUM 387.* I guessed the *P.C.* stood for Park City, a mining town in the mountains.

"Didn't that other man help him?" asked Scotty.

I looked down at the boy, and said, "What other man?"

"The man who came here looking for him. He wasn't as nice as you. He aimed a gun at me. That's why I shot at you when you got here. I thought you were him."

"Did you give him this address?"

Scotty nodded—then his eyes widened and he suddenly looked

horrified, and his lower lip began to quiver. "He scared me. Did I do something wrong?"

I crouched so I was eye to eye with him. "No. Stay calm. I need your help, son. This other man—what'd he look like?"

"He had a hat and coat."

"Was he a police officer or a sheriff or a deputy, like me?"

The boy shook his head. "I don't think so. He didn't say. He said he was my dad's friend, and he even shook my hand. He told me he needed to find my dad. He said it was real important that he talk to him right away. I said I didn't know where he was. Then the man got angry and called me a liar. He aimed a gun at me and told me I'd better tell him where my dad was or my whole family was gonna go to jail. The gun scared me real bad. So I showed that to him."

He pointed to the address above the telephone.

"What did he say his name was?" I asked.

Scotty tapped his chin. His eyes opened wide with recognition. "Sam."

"Sam? Sam what?"

More finger tapping. "Sam. Sam. Lou. Loom."

I remembered the name in the Wooley file at the Ogden Police Department. The name I jotted on my pad of paper: Sam Louis. A witness saw him fleeing Wooley's office around the time a gunshot was heard. A short time later, Wooley was found dead. I said, "Was it Sam Louis?"

He snapped his finger. "Sam Louis! That's his name!"

"When did he come here? Was it recently?"

"A while ago . . ."

"How long ago?"

His face lit up again. "Thursday."

"This past Thursday? March sixth?"

"I don't know what the date was, but yeah, it was last Thursday.

Is my dad going to be OK? Mama says he isn't answering the tele-phone. She thinks Bell disconnected it."

I took a deep breath and looked into his pleading eyes. "I'm go-ing to go see him right now. I promise you this. I'll do everything in my power to help him."

He smiled. "Thanks. I'm sorry I shot at you."

"No harm done," I said. I rubbed the top of his head, and he smiled. "Except my hat went to the dogs. Maybe you oughta be one of those Wild West Show sharpshooters."

He laughed.

Five minutes later, after giving him my Stetson with the new hole in it and saying good-bye, I was on the road, driving the Model A as fast as it would go up the canyon to Park City.

A green cabin with white shutters, a little porch, and a picket fence, 79 Summit stood at the end of a steep gravel road at the forest's edge. Down the road a stretch, Park City was on the verge of be-coming a ghost town. Most townsfolk had left long ago, and a lot of the dwellings were boarded up and decaying from years of neglect. There were a few signs of life. Some houses were still occupied. The center of town still had a five-and-dime, a diner, a Chinese laundry, a couple of merchants, a candy store, and a local branch of Zion's Bank. Park City had seen far better days, though. At first glance, 79 Summit appeared to be one of its many abandoned places. Pine trees towered above it on all sides and a small garage kept the cabin company. I slid the garage door open a few inches and, sure enough, that '27 Hupmobile was parked inside.

The front door was locked. I reached into my coat pocket for my pick set and played around with the lock until I felt a click. I turned the knob and pushed the door open. The foul stench hit me head-on like an airplane, sending me reeling to the hedges to upchuck. I was on my knees on the pine-needle-covered ground, clearing out my system.

I'd given my only handkerchief to Scotty Alexander, so I fetched an oil rag from the Model A's backseat and held it over my nose and mouth as I entered the cabin. The puny interior—two rooms, a kitchenette, and a bathroom with a claw-foot tub—at least meant that I wouldn't be searching long.

C. W. Alexander was sitting in a floral-pattern armchair in the living room, dressed in a brown three-piece suit with a shirt and tie. His right hand still held a .45 caliber revolver, his index finger resting on the trigger. There was a hole in his chest that I guessed to be large enough for me to stick my index finger into, but I wasn't about to put that theory to the test. I breathed steadily through the oil rag, and believe me when I say the smell of petroleum beat the stench of a days-old corpse any time. His eyes were still open, his mouth agape, head bent back.

I saw a note on a table next to the chair, and next to the note were a locket and a wedding ring that I guessed were Helen Pfalzgraf's. The note was typewritten. Peculiar, since there was no typewriter in the cabin, as far as I could see. I didn't touch the note, but I craned my head so I could get a good look at it.

> I killed Helen K. Pfalzgraff. I am a lowly coward with a black heart. I can no longer live with myself. I am ending my life. (Signed,) CLYDE W. ALEXANDER.

He misspelled his lover's last name. He didn't bother putting his signature above his name at the bottom of the note. Hard to say what smelled worse: his decomposing remains or this sham setup to make his death look like a suicide.

I walked into the kitchen, dropped the oil rag on a table, and found a wall phone near the back door. I lifted the earpiece and turned the iron crank at the bottom of the box. The line crackled as I stepped close to the mouthpiece.

"Operator."

"Operator, give me the sheriff's office in Salt Lake City, please. This is an emergency."

"One moment and I'll connect you."

While I waited, I picked up the oil rag and held it over my face, because the rotten odor coming from the next room was too much to take.

Fourteen

A snowstorm did not prevent a crowd of hundreds from forming a semicircle around the steps of City Hall. The press hounds came out in full force. Cannon in his overcoat showed up with his wife, Ida, and Sykes hovered over a group of newly hired deputies as they set up the podium near the building's entrance. Nearer to the center of the vast audience stood Buddy Hawkins in a fedora and overcoat, side by side with Chief Otis Ballard. White-haired and lean-faced, Ballard startled me with his presence. He had once been my father's partner, many years earlier, and I had vague memories of him coming to the house when I was a little kid. His appearance at today's function did not shock me, but it heightened my nervousness. My eyes continued scanning the crowd, stopping at Seymour Considine, bundled up with his hat titled sideways and a toothy grin on his face. I wondered what he was grinning about.

I turned to Clara, who looked strikingly beautiful in a long coat over a dress made of green velvet and black lace; she held hands with Sarah Jane, whose smile never let up. I leaned near and whispered, "Oh no," when I noticed a gaggle of Ovesons—my brothers, their wives, and their sizable collection of offspring—seeking out prime locations in the audience. Cannon's assistant, Faye, had planned this event at the last minute and informed me about it the previous day with a telephone call. Cannon raised his eyebrows at his pocket watch, turned my way, and gestured for me to follow him to the podium.

"I love you," said Clara before I pulled away.

"I love you, too."

We kissed each other, and then I hurried over to where Cannon and Sykes stood. I spotted Dr. Pfalzgraf, bundled up and wearing a bowler, squeezing past others on his way up the steps, followed by Floyd Samuelson in his uniform and cap. Watching him carefully, I wondered why such a private man would be making such a public appearance. I saw my mother in the crowd and inhaled deeply, licked my dry lips with my even drier tongue, and did my best to appear calm. Camera shutters clicked as Cannon took his place at the podium.

He began speaking, but I was too nervous to hear his words. I kept looking out at my mother's smile through a veil of falling snow, wishing this press conference would end so I could pile into the family auto with Clara and Sarah Jane, pick up Hi from her sister Joyce's house, and go home to a hot meal and time with my family. In my moment of anxiety, bits and pieces of Cannon's speech stuck with me: "... *great day for law and order in the state of Utah ... Deputy Oveson behaved heroically in the line of duty ... Alexander died as he lived: a craven killer, without an ounce of decency ... now I'll turn the time over to Deputy Oveson ...*"

People clapped. Why? What had I done to deserve it? I gulped and my hands trembled as Cannon put his arm around my shoulder and guided me over to the podium. In that instant, all I could think about was young Scotty Alexander—terrified and alone, firing a gun at me because he thought I was the same man who'd visited the week before. The applause subsided, and I looked out at that sea of faces, smiling at me, waiting for me to say something meaningful.

"I'm proud to present you with this badge," said Cannon, opening a small box and revealing a gold-plated deputy's star. "With this promotion, Deputy Oveson, you're now a senior deputy in the Salt Lake County Sheriff's Department. I'll let you say a few words."

Light applause crackled.

"I . . . um . . ." I bit my lower lip and looked down at my loose-fitting shoes. I shut my eyes tightly and pictured my father's face. Smiling. He leans close to me in the boat and shows me how to hook the bait. When I opened my eyes, the crowd was still there. Still waiting. "I just want to say that I didn't do this alone. I was only one man in a department full of fellows who are, in my estimation, a heck of a lot braver than I am. We all did this together, under the guidance of Sheriff Cannon and Assistant Sheriff Sykes." The crowd clapped. "My father, who was a police officer when he was alive, used to tell me that the only way for justice to prevail is if brave men and women stand up and make it happen. I only hope that my actions, in some small way, helped bring about justice. Thank you."

I moved away from the podium, and the audience erupted in applause and whistles. Out of the corner of my eye, I noticed Cannon and Pfalzgraf talking about something or other; they were far enough away and the cheering so loud that I couldn't hear them. Cannon turned in my direction and pointed at me, and Pfalzgraf nodded and headed this way. A silence fell over the scene in front of City Hall as Pfalzgraf arrived at the podium, holding a slip of paper in his hands.

He cleared his throat and spoke in his thick German accent. "I have asked the bank to make a check for ten thousand dollars out to Deputy Arthur Oveson. I give this money to him with my personal thanks for apprehending my wife's killer."

To the cheers of those present, Pfalzgraf turned to me, crinkly-eyed and smiling, and shook my hand while I eyed the check in his other hand. "Thank you, Deputy Oveson."

"You're welcome, sir."

He handed me the check, and cameras clicked away, capturing a moment that I didn't want to be remembered.

Nobody warned me I'd have to pose for so many snapshots. One after another: Huddled between Cannon and Sykes. Lined up with my brothers. Embracing my mother. Crowded together with all of the other deputies—at least those who managed to hold on to their jobs. Arms around Clara and Sarah, all smiles. Standing in the center of the enormous Oveson clan. Shaking hands with white-haired Salt Lake Police Chief Otis Ballard. I was exhausted when it was all over.

The crowd dispersed. People climbed into their cars and drove away. Every last Oveson either hugged me or shook my hand before they left. My mother told me she was proud of me, and I handed her the check that Pfalzgraf gave me.

"What is this?" she asked. "I can't take this, Art . . ."

"You can," I said, "and you will. I love you, Mom."

"No mother's ever been more proud of her son," she said, holding back the tears as best she could and not succeeding entirely.

By the time my mother and I parted ways, the crowd had thinned to only a few. Imagine my surprise when I saw Roscoe Lund, dressed in a fancy worsted three-piece suit, standing on the sidewalk, collecting snow on the brim of his fedora. He offered a big smile and approached me with his hands buried deep in his pockets. I held out my hand, but he didn't bother shaking, and somehow, I'd known he wouldn't.

"Hello," I said.

"Art." He looked me up and down. "You look none the worse for wear."

"You're looking pretty dapper yourself. What are you up to these days?"

"Oh, you know. Pounding the pavement, looking for work. I think I might have something lined up."

"No kidding? What?"

He shrugged and released a chuckle. "Mum's the word. I don't like to jinx anything. I guess you're the hero of the hour."

"I guess so."

"The public doesn't know what I know. You're wet behind the ears, sonny."

His words stung me for a second, and I responded with a slow nod, as if feeling the truth of what he said. "Yeah, maybe so."

He paused thoughtfully. I worried another insult was coming. He surprised me. "But I'm happy for you, Art. Because one day, you're gonna make a hell of a lawman."

He squinted up at the swirling clouds. "Goddamn March snow." He lowered his head and winked. "See you around."

I watched him cross the street to a dark-colored sedan, get in, and drive away. Away to where, I can only guess.

The next day, a surprise awaited me at work.

In the front reception area, Faye Meadows, a bobbed brunette with a thing for bright floral dresses, worked the switchboard. She arched her eyebrows when she saw me coming and said, "Hold on," into her transmitter tube. She plucked the earphones off her head, rose, and hurried over to me, glancing into the waiting room. The last person I expected to see sitting on one of the waiting room's benches was Scotty Alexander, but there he was, his flat cap pulled low, eyes swollen from tears, lower lip quivering, clutching a folded newspaper against his chest.

"He was standing out front when I opened this morning," she said softly. "Crying. I tried to console him, but no luck. He said he wanted to talk to you. I would've asked him to leave, but he's just a kid. I don't even know how he got here. I didn't see any grown-ups with him."

"Did he say what he wants?"

"Just that he wants to talk to you. Said he won't leave until he does. I'm so sorry, Art. I didn't know what—"

"Don't apologize," I said, smiling reassuringly at Faye. "You did the right thing. I'll have a word with him. See what he wants."

"Good luck."

"Yeah. Thanks."

I entered the bright waiting room, filled with natural light from arched windows. There were three pewlike benches in the room, and Scotty sat on one facing the windows. Some days the room was full of people, but not today. Scotty sat alone. When he saw me approaching, his face tightened with rage. He got on his feet, met me halfway, and handed me the folded newspaper. The front page of the *Salt Lake Examiner* greeted me with a banner headline, PFALZ-GRAF SLAYER KILLS SELF. Oval photos of Helen Pfalzgraf, smiling in her cloche hat and fur, and C. W. Alexander, lean-faced, hair slicked back, bow tie on—overlapped with a photo of the cabin where I found Alexander's body. Adjacent to the main story was a small sidebar with a grainy image of me accepting my badge from Sheriff Fred Cannon. The headline on that story read SLEUTH IN PFALZ-GRAF CASE PROMOTED TO SENIOR DEPUTY.

"Remember what you said?" Scotty had a hard time speaking through his sobs. "You said you wanted to help him! But you didn't! You lied to me."

"Listen, maybe there's somewhere we can sit down and talk—"

"I don't want to sit down! I don't even want to look at you!"

"I can explain what—"

"You can't explain anything! You're a bad man! Just like Mr. Louis!"

Hearing his breaking voice, seeing tears streaming down his cheeks, was more than I could take. I felt terrible. I folded the newspaper like it had been when he gave it to me and reached out to squeeze his shoulder. He yanked his shoulder free and ran over to one of the windows, leaned into the glass, and cried. He kept his back turned to me. I watched his body convulse.

I eased closer until I stood next to him, and I let him get some of that crying out of his system before I said anything. I could tell he was a kid who needed to sob some of his pain away. I always understood that crying had tremendous healing powers, like sucking the poison out of a rattlesnake bite. Even so, seeing a kid cry because of something I did left me forlorn.

"You have to believe me when I say that all of this has happened so quickly, my head is spinning," I said. "I wanted to help your father—"

He looked at me with red eyes. "He's dead! You didn't protect him, like you promised! Now the papers are saying he killed that lady! He couldn't have! My dad never hurt anybody!"

He shoved me in the chest. I didn't expect it. He could really shove, young Scotty. I almost toppled on my hind end. Lucky for me I had fast reflexes. Only my Stetson fell on the floor.

To give him more time to cry, I reached down and picked up my hat. "You're right," I said a minute later. "I didn't protect him, but maybe there's a way we can make things right."

"How? He's dead! You can't do anything to fix it!"

"I can't bring him back. That's true. But I can do something else."

"What?"

His crying let up, and he was blinking at me now. A good sign.

"Let's talk some more and see if I can come up with something," I said. "You like ice cream?"

He sniffed and let out a shaky exhale. "Who doesn't?"

His eyes dropped to my hat, which I held by the brim. He smiled and said, "I see you got a new one."

I smiled back. "C'mon. Let's go for a walk. It's a nice day out."

Our outdoor stroll took us to Keeley's Ice Cream Parlor on Main Street. On the way, Scotty explained that he found the address of the sheriff's office in the city directory at his grandparents' house. He used a hammer to bust open his piggy bank to retrieve a dime for the early-morning transit bus. While he spoke, he kept staring up at the downtown buildings in amazement. He missed his home, he said, and wanted to return.

At Keeley's, we sat at a round corner table, and he must've broken a speed record with his banana split. I sat back and let him munch away. He came to the end and scraped the glass dish with his spoon to get the last of it.

"Aren't you going to have one?" he asked, wiping chocolate off his face with a paper napkin.

"Awfully tempting, but I'm not hungry."

"Best breakfast I've ever had!"

I posed a long-shot question. "Is there anything you can tell me about your dad? Anything that might help me clear his name?"

He stared thoughtfully at the hanging lights above. "He was left-handed."

"What?"

"I overheard my mom telling my grandma and grandpa yesterday that my dad was left-handed. I don't know what that has to do with anything, but the way she said it, was like it was real important."

I instantly thought of that revolver in Alexander's right hand, but I spared Scotty the gruesome detail. "That's helpful. Is there anything else?"

He nodded. "The last time he called me on the telephone, he told me he wanted me to get good grades in school and listen to Mom and help take care of my sister. And just before he hung up, he said, 'I keep my cans in the hurricane.' "

I looked down at my hat on the table and considered the words. *I keep my cans in the hurricane.* What on earth? My eyes shot back up to Scotty, who waited expectantly, perhaps for me to say something that would help him understand his final conversation with his father. I sighed. "He didn't say anything else?"

Scotty's facial features loosened, and there was no missing his disappointment. "I guess you don't know what it means?"

"I'm sorry. I don't. I'll try to find out for you, though."

I led Scotty to the telephone booth and dropped a dime in the phone box so he could call his mother and tell her he'd be home soon. We walked together over to the bus depot, and there a Beehive transit bus idled before its trip to Bountiful in five minutes. I bought his ticket, made sure he got on board safely, and paid the driver an extra dollar to deliver Scotty safely right in front of his house.

From the sidewalk I waved to him, and he waved to me, as the bus drove away from the depot, heading north for Bountiful.

"Oveson! May I speak to you for a moment?"

Sheriff Cannon stood in front of his office beaming, opened the timepiece attached to his vest by a gold chain, and turned around. "This shouldn't take long."

I followed him into his office—that colossal office, larger than a Ringling Brothers circus tent—and sat in my usual chair, opposite Cannon. His wide smile made me wonder if his facial muscles ever got tired. *All that smiling must be exhausting,* I thought. Sykes perched at his favorite spot, his sourpuss expression unchanging with my entrance. I squirmed in the chair until I was as comfortable as I was going to get, kicking my right leg over my left knee, jiggling my foot, admiring the blue sky through the arched windows. The dailies covered Cannon's desk, all celebrating the outcome of the Pfalzgraf case with triumphant headlines. He held up a local newspaper so I could see the words: SHERIFF'S OFFICE SOLVES PFALZGRAF MURDER.

"I'm getting this one framed," he said. He turned it toward his face and gave a prideful nod. "Ain't she a beaut?"

"That's a swell headline, sir."

"That it is, Oveson. That it is." He folded the paper and tossed it on his desk. "This is precisely the outcome I was hoping for with this case. The people of Salt Lake City once again feel safe. And when they feel good, I feel good. All of us owe you an enormous debt of gratitude."

"I was just doing my job."

Cannon looked at Sykes. "Always so modest. You can tell it's not an act."

"He's the genuine article," said Sykes.

Cannon looked at me. "The office at the end of the hall is yours. The man from the sign company is coming today to paint your name on the door. Arthur J. Oveson. Senior deputy. What a nice ring that has to it."

"It was good of you to promote me, sir. I don't deserve it—"

"So! How are you going to spend that reward money?" Cannon leaned forward and whispered loudly, "You gonna give me my cut?"

He burst into laughter and looked at Sykes, who stretched his mouth into a smile.

Cannon's laughter died down, and he said under his breath, "My cut. That's rich." He cleared his throat and got official. "How do you plan to spend it?"

"I don't know. I guess we'll see."

Cannon nodded with bobbing eyebrows. "I get it. You have to consult with the missus first. Not only is he a good egg, Sykes. He's pragmatic."

"I think the expression I've used before is 'levelheaded,'" said Sykes.

"That's why I keep Sykes around. To expand my vocabulary." Cannon's lips curled up into a smile again, and he said, "I've called you in here to tell you that I've changed the description of your new job. You're now the public liaison."

"Public liaison?"

"Yes. You're the human face of the Salt Lake County Sheriff's Office. In that capacity, you'll go out and speak to civic groups, churches, schools, and you'll keep men, women, and children posted about the wonderful things we're doing in this office to safeguard lives and property. Understand?"

I nodded. "Sir, I'd like to—"

"No need to thank me, Oveson. You're a natural for it. We've needed a position like that in this office for a long time. I wish I could take credit for creating it, but it's Sykes's idea. I always give credit where credit is due. Don't I, Al?"

"That you do," said Sykes.

"Sir," I said, trying to conceal my trembling voice, "with your permission, I'd like to continue investigating the Pfalzgraf homicide."

Silence—thick as molasses. Cannon's smile went away, and his eyebrows twitched. No amount of squirming on my part alleviated the uneasiness I felt at that moment.

"Come again?" asked Cannon.

"This Alexander suicide stinks," I said. "He's left-handed, but the gun was in his right hand. He didn't own a .45, but that's the type of gun he used. There's no typewriter at his cabin—"

"He could've typed that note at his work," said Cannon. "Remember, he had Helen's wedding ring and locket on him."

I shook my head. "Those could've been planted. He misspelled Helen Pfalzgraf's last name, even though they were supposed to be intimate. Here's the really strange part: A man stopped by his in-laws' house a few days before me looking for him—a man named Sam Louis. Louis is also connected to the Everett Wooley homicide in Ogden a year and a half ago. I suspect this Louis fellow had a hand in Alexander's—"

"Hold on." Cannon stood up, circled his desk, walked past me, and closed his office door. He returned to his chair and sat down. "The sensitive nature of this conversation calls for privacy."

I said, "Thanks. With your blessing, I'd like to—"

"Permission denied," said Cannon.

"What?" I asked. "With all due respect—why, sir?"

Sykes said, "Haven't you read the papers? The case is closed. It's been solved."

"Helen Pfalzgraf's murderer is still out there," I said. "I know it."

Cannon's friendly gaze went nasty glare on me real fast. "Look, Oveson, the people of Salt Lake City wanted swift justice in this case. I don't mind telling you I think this investigation lasted longer than it should've, but it's a done deal now. Alexander confessed to the murder. He killed himself. The case is closed. I can tell you right now the voters in this county won't be happy if they find out we're reopening a murder investigation I said was solved."

I said, "That's just it. It hasn't been solved. Not yet."

Sykes said, "What exactly are you proposing, Oveson?"

I looked at Sykes. "I want to find out who this Sam Louis is. I want to talk to Dr. Pfalzgraf. Campaign donation or not, I want to ask him questions about the death of his first wife. I want to get to the bottom of how Dr. Wooley's murder connects with all of this—"

"I know what this is all about," said Cannon. "You've been working hard on this case, and now that it's solved, you don't want it to be over. I suspect you'd like to relive a little of your glory from the past few days. Heck, that's to be expected. But this case is over, and I'm ordering you to drop it and move on to your new position as public liaison."

I said, "But—"

"Oveson," said Cannon, frowning now. "Don't do this. OK. I'm being civil. Don't make me angry. I like you. You're a good fellow, and your presence in this office improves the general state of affairs greatly. But if I have to, I'll let you go. Just like that." He snapped his fingers. "Understand?"

"Yes."

"Good." He signed. "Now, before you go, I got a call from a Mrs. Lorlene Kelley at . . ." He read from a pink message slip. "Hawthorne Elementary on Seventh. She'd like you to come and talk to the students at an assembly on Friday morning. She wants you to give a general safety spiel—you know, crossing at crosswalks, avoiding strangers, going straight home after school. All that jazz. I hope you don't mind. I said yes for you."

I stood up and put my hands in my pockets. "This Friday?"

"Ten A.M." He blinked at me a few times, but his smile remained on hiatus. "That's all, Oveson. You may go now."

With that reward of ten G's, I could tell Sheriff Cannon where to go, I thought. Alas, I was better at imagining myself as a tough guy than actually being one. Timidity visited me, poured himself a glass of milk, propped his feet on the ottoman, and made himself right at home. I left Cannon's office, tail between my legs, thanking him for promoting me to public liaison, yet feeling a painful sting somewhere inside.

I awoke at half past one and could not get back to sleep. Clara slept beside me in a long-sleeve flannel nightgown, breathing gently. I lay on my back for ten minutes, staring at the ceiling and listening to a distant locomotive whistle. I got out of bed and crossed the hallway into Sarah Jane's room to check on her. Same as her mom—out like a light. I poked my head in Hi's room and found him sleeping in his crib. I pulled the blankets higher on him and ran my hand over his downy hair. A mobile of farm animals hung from the ceiling above his bed. I tapped a cow and the rest jumped up and down and danced in circles, eventually slowing down. I left before they came to a halt.

In the kitchen, I lit the gas stove and heated a pan of milk. I poured the warm milk into a mug, sat down with a pencil and spiral notepad, and began jotting notes. *Sam Louis,* I wrote, then I drew a horizontal arrow, followed by the name *Dr. Everett Wooley.* A second arrow, this one diagonal, went from "*Sam Louis*" to *C. W. Alexander.* Above this very rudimentary schematic, I wrote *Harmony Tattershall* with a question mark beside her last name and circled it. Considine told me about Harmony. Pfalzgraf had filed a complaint on her behalf against Dr. Wooley. There was no telephone number for her with the city operator or in the phone book, but maybe there was another way of finding her. One thing was certain, though: It wasn't going to happen at this hour of the morning.

I opted to go back to bed. I capped the milk bottle and carried it back to the icebox. Clara had taped a newspaper article with my picture to the icebox door. The headline read, DEPUTY SLEUTH IN PFALZGRAF CASE PROMOTED. The grainy picture showed me shaking hands with Sheriff Fred Cannon in a press ceremony at the county jail. I opened the icebox and put the milk on the top shelf, closed the door, and saw the article again. DEPUTY SLEUTH. I shook my head and sighed. This sleuth was going take another shot at sawing logs.

Fifteen

There was no way humanly possible that someone searching for the Salt Lake County General Hospital could miss it. White, three stories, with elaborate cornices along the top, long rows of rectangular windows, and marble-columned front steps, it was by far the largest building on 2100 South State, a newly developed area at the city's southern boundary with lots of eyesore billboards, thick utility poles, and cheap restaurants that weren't much more than glorified shacks under shade trees. In the late afternoon, I sat in my car, parked in the lot south of the building, thumbing through an issue of *Real Mystery Stories*. I glanced at my wristwatch—4:45—then watched the entrance, people coming and going. Earlier that afternoon, I had driven all the way down here to see Dr. Pfalzgraf and ask him about the murder of his wife. I knew the doctor worked a shift until five o'clock in the evening, and I sat there working up the nerve to confront him as he was leaving the building.

Thumbing through *Real Mystery Stories,* I came to Seymour Considine's latest installment on the Pfalzgraf murder. The story contained no surprises. It was about what one would expect from such a lurid magazine. He wrote florid dispatches, full of fifty-cent words and artist's renditions of key moments in the Pfalzgraf case. One illustration showed Helen Kent Pfalzgraf (poorly rendered) in the center of a big heart, surrounded by the Persian prince, C. W. Alexander, and Dr. Pfalzgraf.

My eyes wandered down to the prose: "Dear Reader, one can only imagine the terror that Helen felt as her attacker raised that chunk of ore high and it came down, splitting the top of her skull. The diabolical caitiff who committed this ghastly crime realized Helen might not be dead, so he dragged her through the snow and mud and dropped her to the bitter cold earth. Then, sensing this was the time to strike, he got behind the wheel of her posh Cadillac, revved the engine and shifted to 'drive.' The car roared forward and Helen—poor Helen—feasted her eyes on an oncoming pair of yellow lights, barreling toward her at high speed. Then came the smack of the bumper against her skull, a crunch reminiscent of a cracking eggshell, the blow of blows! No piece of ore could do this sort of damage to the human head, no matter how forceful the attacker's arm!"

"Caitiff?" I said out loud, making a face. "I'll have to look that one up."

I rolled the magazine into a tube and tossed it on the seat next to me. My timing was perfect. I watched Dr. Pfalzgraf pass through the hospital doors, shadowed by Floyd Samuelson in his black security guard getup. On the opposite side of the parking lot, they reached the doc's car, a dark blue Essex sedan, and Samuelson opened the back door for him. I stuck closely to the Essex's red taillights, heading northbound on State. We stayed on the wide street all the way to the Brooks Arcade at the 300 South and State intersection. I turned left at 300, flipped a U-turn, and parked next to the curb, which gave me a view of the alley behind the building where Floyd parked Pfalzgaf's car.

The Brooks Arcade was a queer place, a sprawling center of commerce that offered a little bit of everything: a millinery, a cigar shop, a dressmaking school where women could buy cheap clothing, a sandwich joint, a studio specializing in pricey china, a men's clothier, the Politz Candy Company (which I happened to know sponsored a basketball team in a local league that played Thursdays at the police gymnasium), and a plethora of offices—doctors, lawyers, dentists. Outside, dusk brought shadows, but there was still enough light for me to see Doc Pfalzgraf going in the Brooks Arcade through the service entrance, tailed closely by Floyd.

I got out of my car, jogged across the street, and headed down the alley until I reached the heavy steel door. I grabbed the handle and shook it. Locked. I hurried around the building to the State Street entrance, passed under a green and white awning, and shoved a door with chicken-wire glass. In the lobby, I went straight to the glass-case directory, and my eyes dropped to DR. H. PFALZGRAF, ROOM 268.

The second floor had green carpeting with tan patterns and elegant brass-and-glass light fixtures on the ceiling. All the doors were oak with pebbled glass and serif black-and-gold lettering. It was a long hall, and I eventually turned right and kept walking until I reached a door that read, DR. H. PFALZGRAF, MD. Below that: OBSTETRICS AND GYNECOLOGY. I jiggled the knob. Locked again. I heard footsteps approaching. The door opened, and Floyd poked his head out.

"Art!"

"Howdy, Floyd. How's every little thing?"

He was shocked to see me. "What are you doing here?"

"I've come to talk to Dr. Pfalzgraf."

"About what?"

"I have some questions—"

"Look, Art, if this is about the reward—"

"This has nothing to do with the reward. I won't take up much of his time. I'm putting the finishing touches on the Mrs. Pfalzgraf matter, and I have a few routine questions before I close the case for good."

"This isn't a good time, Art." His voice shook with panic, and his face turned marshmallowy. "Couldn't you come back again later? Please . . ."

"What's wrong, Floyd? I don't see why Pfalzgraf can't take a few minutes out of his day and answer a couple of questions."

"Art, I'd consider it a personal favor to me if you'd scram and call him another time, when he doesn't have so much work to catch up on."

I tilted right to see if I could catch any sign of Pfalzgraf behind Floyd, but he also moved right (or to his left, I should say), blocking my line of vision. A slant to my left produced the same result. Dr. Pfalzgraf wasn't in the anteroom. He must have been back in his office, or perhaps one of the patient rooms. I ran my fingers through my hair and looked down at Floyd's spiffy patent leather shoes, which almost seemed nailed to the floor. At that moment, I needed Roscoe to rattle the gate for me, to strong-arm Floyd into letting us waltz inside the office to have a word with the doctor. While Roscoe was at it, he could shove Pfalzgraf against a nearby wall and twist his arm for answers. My attack dog was gone, though, and Sheriff Cannon had made it clear he didn't want me touching this case, so I aimed for the lower-profile approach. No tough talk. No warning about judges swearing out warrants. The moment called for tact.

I said, "Maybe you can tell the doc I stopped by and I'll come back later."

"I'll do that. Thanks, Art."

He stepped back and slammed the door. His footsteps faded on the other side.

The Floyd Samuelson I knew—showing off pictures of his son,

making small talk about the weather and his job—was nowhere to be seen. This was another Floyd altogether, a version I'd never seen before: agitated, frightened, eager to get rid of me. Something was up.

I consulted with the city directory I kept in the trunk of my car, turning straight to the *T*'s. Tanner, Parley. Arlington Drive. My eyebrows shot up. *Ritzy address,* I thought.

Tanner lived in Federal Heights, the most affluent neighborhood in Salt Lake City—probably in the entire state—and a short drive from the Pfalzgraf mansion. Rumor had it the real estate developers shipped in the tallest trees they could find and planted them on both sides of the road. The Tanner house surpassed my wildest expectations. Parking across the street, I pegged it at five thousand square feet, with two of everything: two doors, two chimneys, two stories, two columns on the porch, and two gardens, not yet humming with life because of the cold weather, divided by a concrete walkway. It was probably suppertime, but I cared more about this investigation than about interrupting the Tanner family's dinner. I stepped up on the porch, balled my hand into a fist, and pounded on the outer screen door. I pushed the doorbell. Chimes clanged.

A gray-suited servant showed me to the living room. A framed oil painting of a woman as tall as me hung above the hearth. If there is such a thing as being too pretty, the woman in the painting would be a candidate: golden hair styled into a wavy bob, blue eyes, a thin swan's neck, a jutting chin with a dimple, and a white summer dress with pearls and lace and a low V-neck. In the fireplace, flames danced and crackled and spit sparks. Hundreds of books— their spines colored black and green, maroon and brown, many with gold lettering—covered the entire wall from floor to ceiling. There was a French theme to the room, from a knotted pile carpet to the four Louis XVI chairs. Candlelike lighting fixtures lined the walls, and there was lots of dark cherry woodwork.

In walked Parley Tanner wearing duds that for anyone else would've been extravagant but for him were informal: a green wool sweater, white oxford underneath, brown corduroys, and brown leather slippers lined with soft fur. Behind him was a woman who bore a haunting resemblance to the one in the oil painting, only older and with hair that was curlier and grayer. She wore a brown tunic and dress with tan dots splashed all over both and a matching bow tie at the neckline. The dress was tiered, and I bet the outfit must have set her back a small fortune. She probably had to go overseas—Paris, I'm guessing—to get it. She had a Mona Lisa smile, and she passed her husband and extended her hand to me. I squeezed it gently, but she didn't squeeze back.

"Miriam Tanner," she said. "And you are?"

"Art Oveson." I wasn't used to saying my new rank, senior deputy. Art Oveson would have to suffice for now. "We've met, Mr. Tanner."

"Yes, hello again, Art," said Parley Tanner. "I meant to call and congratulate you on a masterful job of solving the Pfalzgraf case." I thanked him, and he said, "Very well done. Executed brilliantly in every respect. Please, let us sit."

Following handshakes, we fanned out and each chose a Louis XVI chair.

I sniffed the air. The aroma of cooking food warmed my body.

"You're welcome to join us for dinner," said Miriam. "It's just Parley and me. We're having a roast I prepared."

"That's mighty kind of you, but I don't intend to intrude," I said.

"You wouldn't be intruding," she said. "Please join us."

"Much obliged, ma'am, but my wife and children are expecting me home in a little while."

The Mona Lisa smile widened subtly. "Of course. You wouldn't want to disappoint them. Perhaps another time? Ever since Elizabeth left us, it's just been Parley and me. We always end up with leftovers in the icebox."

"They make for great lunches the next day," said Parley with a grin and a wink.

I looked up at the painting above the fireplace. "Did she go off to college?"

Miriam's eyes turned to the ornate rug. "She passed on."

Her words caught me off guard, and it took me a moment to snap out of my initial shock. "I am sorry. How did she . . ."

I could not say *die*.

Miriam opened her mouth to speak, but Parley interrupted. "Poliomyelitis. We rushed her to the hospital, but we didn't get her there in time. The virus entered her bloodstream and . . ."

He watched me, as if studying my expression. I said, "I'm terribly sorry. I can't imagine . . ."

"Don't be," said Miriam. "She lived a good life. She left us before her time, but we'll see her again."

I nodded. "Was she your only . . ."

My words tapered off, but I'd said enough to get a nod out of Parley.

"My condolences."

"Thank you, Art," said Parley. "That means a great deal to us. Now, what can we do for you today? Is this regarding the Pfalzgraf investigation? I was under the impression the case was closed."

"Yes," I said. "That's true. I just have a few minor clarification questions to ask before I close the file. Do you mind?"

"Ask anything you wish," said Parley, with genuine warmth in his voice.

I opened a spiral notebook and licked the tip of my pencil in order to take notes. "In 1917, Dr. Pfalzgraf's first wife, Nellie, died in a hit-and-run accident in Los Angeles. Can you tell me more about it?"

Parley eyed the chandelier above and shrugged his shoulders.

"Not much to tell. They were vacationing in California, the doctor and Mrs. Pfalzgraf, and motoring home from a function in late January. It was night. It was dark. Another driver ran their touring car off the road. Nellie was thrown out of the car and then the car rolled over on top of her. The doctor survived with minor injuries, but Nellie was killed instantly."

Miriam Tanner spoke up. "The accident affected Hans terribly. Right after it happened, Parley and I went to Los Angeles to pick him up and bring him back here. I've never seen a man hit so hard by the loss of a loved one. On the trip home, he kept breaking down and wailing in agony. For years and years, he'd do that—just break down and cry out of the blue. Parley and I started a sort of family tradition after the accident. We'd invite Hans and Anna to dinner every Sunday night. Anna and Elizabeth got to be quite close in that time, but I'll never forget that Hans would suddenly start crying, for no reason that I could see. He was never the same after Nellie's death. He blamed himself for it."

"I'm sorry to hear that," I said, glancing at the name *Sam Louis* scrawled on the notepad. "Do either of you know of someone named Sam Louis?"

The Tanners shook their heads at the same time and said no quietly.

"What about Dr. Everett Wooley?"

"He was a terrible man," said Miriam. "A murderer of innocent women and unborn babies. We knew *of* him. Everybody in this city who followed the newspapers or radio knew about him. The Butcher of Salt Lake, people called him. If it weren't for Hans, that vulture would still be operating his clinic downtown."

Parley Tanner had cooled, staring at me with uncertainty in his eyes. "What, if you don't mind me asking, does Wooley have to do with this case?"

I said, "I'm trying to rule out any connection between the two homicides."

"I'm sure they're not connected," Parley said. "I don't see how they could be."

"Maybe you're right, but that doesn't change the fact that there are a lot of strange loose ends surrounding the Pfalzgraf case," I said. "I'm just trying to make heads or tails of it all."

"For instance?" he asked.

"For instance, Helen Pfalzgraf was pregnant at the time of her death—but who was the father?"

"Gossip fodder for the newspapers," he said with a dismissive wave. "Does it really matter?"

"Sure it does," I said. "All loose ends matter. It matters that Helen went out to Los Angeles in December and auditioned to be in a First National movie and the studio offered her a contract to be a supporting player. I've seen the audition reel, and she's not half bad. Other details matter, too. It matters that she was close to three men other than her husband—C. W. Alexander, Roland Lane, and the Persian prince. It matters that she had bank accounts full of money that nobody can account for. It matters that a witness overheard you talking to Hans and Helen Pfalzgraf on the afternoon before her murder about divorce proceedings—"

"That's a lie, and I fired the stenographer who said it." His angry twitch shifted back to the easygoing demeanor that preceded it. "These don't sound like the sort of questions one would expect from a lawman who's trying to close a case."

I lowered my spiral pad, tucked my pencil behind my ear, and leaned forward so my elbows were resting on my knees. "Here's what I've got so far. I think Helen Pfalzgraf wanted to leave town, probably to pursue a career in Hollywood pictures. I believe she found a few rich benefactors—a movie actor, a prince, and a mining speculator—who kept filling her bank accounts. Then, right as she was about to leave town, somebody lured her out to Pole Line Road and ran over her several times, using her own Cadillac. Why, I don't know. I do know that before I close this case, I want to find some answers to these questions."

"What would the answers change?" asked Miriam. "I'll speak candidly with you, Arthur—if I may. I never cared for Helen Pfalzgraf. In fact, I disliked everything she stood for. She was selfish, money-hungry, man-starved. The only thing she cared about in the world was her own gratification. She used men and women and then tossed them aside when she got what she wanted. She had no values that I could see. No convictions. No sense of right and wrong. Forgive me for saying this, but she opened her legs for any man with a hefty bank account—"

"Miriam," said Parley, looking sideways at her. "Please . . ."

"Arthur ought to know what sort of woman Helen Pfalzgraf was," she said curtly. She looked at me. "Every day of my life, I regret that we introduced her to dear, sweet Hans. He doted on her every whim, treating her like a spoiled schoolgirl. He didn't even treat his own daughter that way. I guess you could say I came to hate Helen. That doesn't mean I think she deserved to die in such an ugly way, but I don't lie awake nights wondering who killed her, and I haven't shed a tear over her sad fate."

I nodded and pushed my notebook and pencil into my coat pocket. "I see."

Parley stood and gestured in the direction of the hall. "I hope that, in spite of the rather unpleasant tenor of the last few minutes of our conversation, you'll reconsider joining us for supper, Art."

I rose, too, at the same time as Miriam Tanner. I turned once more to admire the painting of Elizabeth above the mantel.

"She was a lovely young lady," I said. I glanced at Miriam. "I had polio when I was a little boy. Come to think of it, I had just about everything, but polio was the worst. People who haven't been through it have no idea of how bad it is. That makes me extra sorry for your loss."

She held out her hand, and I clasped it in mine. This time, she squeezed back. "Thank you," she said.

I could tell my words meant something to her.

Sixteen

It's 182 miles from Salt Lake City to Twin Falls, Idaho. If you can somehow maintain a sixty-mile-per-hour speed limit—a decent clip for a four-cylinder sedan—you can make the drive in about three hours (that is, if you don't stop a lot and dillydally). I packed a couple of sandwiches, some carrot sticks, and a bottle of milk for the journey, and I was on the road by 6:00 A.M. I'd called in sick the previous day, and Cannon, being in a generous mood, volunteered Sykes to cover my duties as public liaison until I returned. I did not tell him it bought me time to work on the Pfalzgraf homicide. I drove my brown Plymouth to Idaho, noticing the first signs of spring—stubs of grass, mud where snow had been days earlier, and droplets of rain dabbing the windshield.

Twin Falls is southeast of Boise. The north side of town abruptly stops at the natural border of the Snake River Canyon, a deep, winding gorge that's spectacular to look at. It's a short drive to Shoshone Falls, a 210-foot-high roaring wall of water that sends clouds of mist in all directions. Picture postcards of the falls, sold at most stores in town, call it "the Niagara of the West."

Thanks to a breakfast stop along the way (turns out I developed a hankering for flapjacks en route), I rolled into town past ten. The sun shone brightly on Twin Falls, and the air smelled of April arriving. The decision to come here was spur-of-the-moment. My investigation felt stagnant. What it needed was a jump-start. Meeting her parents, finding out what—if anything—they knew, struck me as a fresh starting point. Yet I second-guessed my decision as I steered off the highway and turned left at a stop sign into town. I stopped for directions at a restaurant and ordered a bottle of orange Nehi and fried cinnamon dough for the road. Five minutes later, I reached my destination. The Higginbotham family home was a white wood-frame house with an enclosed porch sandwiched between homes that looked exactly like it on Second Avenue North, off a main drag called Addison. I parked, got out of the my car, and put on a Stetson I'd purchased the day before at a Salt Lake hat shop.

I hated paying surprise visits to people I didn't know almost as much as I hated getting them, which probably accounted for the queasiness I felt as I crossed the street and walked up the porch steps. I balled my hand into a fist and pounded on the screen a few times. That set off a dog barking inside the house. I waited for a moment and watched a convertible roadster speed past, in an awful hurry to get somewhere. The door opened, and out stepped a beefy man with a lot of curly white hair, a set of bloodshot eyes, and a face covered with white stubble. His faded plaid shirt and trousers appeared well worn. I guessed him to be in his late sixties. He was a man who had done a lot of hard living.

"Who are you?" he asked, frowning.

"I'm Salt Lake County Senior Deputy Arthur Oveson," I said. *What a mouthful.* "I'm here to ask you a few questions."

He shook his head and held up his palm. "Ah no. No. No. Someone from your office called me the day Helen was killed. Was it you? Well, whoever'n the hell it was, umma tell you the same thing I told

him. I'm glad that cunt is dead. Good riddance! The world is a better place without her. Now, get the fuck off my property!"

I looked down at my patent leather shoes, dumbfounded by his
words. I shook my head and took a deep breath. "What?"

"You heard me. Want me to spell it out? *C ... U ... N ... T.
Cunt.*" He spat the word and took great pleasure in it. "That's what
she was. She broke her ma's heart. She left her fiancé at the altar.
She never called, never wrote, not so much as a fuckin' postcard—
which is fine by me, because I couldn't stand the sight of her nohow.
Now, why don't you get lost?"

Behind him stood a woman—a phantom in dim light. She, too,
had white hair but was diminutive, with a narrow face, eyes like
the bottom of hardboiled eggs, sagging jowls, and a floral dress that
dipped to the middle of her shins. Her lips moved, as if she were
attempting to speak, but nothing came out of her mouth. Her eyes
gave off sorrow, almost more than I could take.

I stepped forward, positioning myself face-to-face with him. "I
have a daughter. Her name is Sarah Jane. And there isn't anything
she could ever do or say that would make me talk about her the way
you spoke about your daughter just now. You, sir, have a shriveled-
up soul."

For a second, I thought he was going to deck me. He instead
slammed the door in my face. I heard him holler something inside
his house, but the closed door muffled his words. On my way back
to my car, I thought, *So much for the long drive to Twin Falls.* The
car engine turned over right away when I started it, and I was about
to drive away when the phantom woman waddled across the street
toward me. She motioned that she wanted to talk to me, and I
rolled down the window. She held up a framed photograph showing four rows of young men and women—the women in sailor tops
and matching skirts, the young men in knickers and ties. COLUMBUS
HIGH SCHOOL, TWIN FALLS, IDAHO, 1915. She pointed to a pretty teen-

ager in the picture with her hair pulled back tightly and a large bow keeping it in place.

"That's my baby," she said. "My Helen. The day I found out she died, part of me died with her. You know what the hardest part was? Not being able to talk to Walter about it. He hated her. He still does. I never knew why. Maybe it was because Helen and I were so close. He used to take out his anger on her. He used to beat her. He used to . . ." She stopped, and once again her mouth moved but no words came out.

"What? He used to what?"

"I can't say it." Tears streamed down her face and she shook with sobs. "It wasn't her idea."

"What wasn't?"

"The blackmail. She didn't want any part of it . . ."

"Blackmail?"

"C. W. cooked it up. It was his idea for her to find a doctor who'd get rid of her baby, too. He told her if she was gonna be in movies, she shouldn't have a baby. But she wanted to see it through. She planned to leave C. W. and the doctor, to raise the baby alone, without either of 'em helping her. That's why she wanted to go to Los Angeles. She hoped the small part she landed in that picture would be her break in the movies. Her plan was to leave Salt Lake City and raise her baby in Los Angeles. She hated Clyde's blackmail. That's God's honest truth."

"I believe you. I need you to tell me more about this blackmailing—"

Across the street, the screen door of the Higginbotham house banged shut, and Walter moved out onto the porch and squinted in our direction. She glanced over her shoulder, then back at me with terror in her eyes.

He called out, "Git back here! Don't you be talkin' to that fuckin' sonofabitch!"

She held the framed photograph in her hands. "I'll always hate Walter for what he did to her. He was the one who killed her, even if he wasn't there the night she died. The only good thing he ever did in his whole rotten life was to give me my angel."

"Mrs. Higginbotham, I need to know about the blackmailing."

"Get over here, woman!" he shouted. " 'Fore I come over there and slap you upside your fuckin' head!"

I said, "If I'm going to help find who did this to Helen . . ."

She walked backward several steps, almost stumbling, and nearly dropped that framed photograph. I wanted to lunge out of the car and whisk her away from here, to someplace safe, but I knew if I tried she'd run. "It doesn't have to be this way," I told her through the car window. "You don't have to stay with him."

"This is how it's always going to be," she said through a veil of tears. "His lot in life is to hurt women. Mine is to be hurt. So was hers . . ."

She swiveled around and strode back to her house, cradling that picture of her daughter, and when she reached the sidewalk, her husband slapped her hard in the face. "Git on inside!" he shouted into her ear.

He cocked his fist back as if about to slug her, and she instinctively guarded herself by turning her shoulder to him, but he froze, perhaps conscious of me watching. His arm fell by his side and his lips moved, but he was far enough away that I could not hear a word he said.

She obeyed him and stepped inside. He followed her, glowering at me from afar. The door slammed hard.

Seventeen

Inside the gymnasium of the recently built Theodore Roosevelt Grammar School, hundreds of schoolchildren listened in rapt attention. A row of windows above the bleachers let sunshine flood the room. An American flag hung above one of the basketball hoops.

A teacher, whose glasses were so thick I couldn't see her eyes, introduced me, and the kids clapped and quieted. I delivered my grammar school spiel. *Work hard. Do your homework. Obey your teachers. Read whenever possible.*

I lifted a glass of water off the wooden stool, drank three gulps, and cleared my throat. Maybe it was my gleaming gold badge, maybe it was the squad car parked out front, or maybe it was my power to arrest people—whatever it was, I impressed these kids. There wasn't a pair of half-closed eyes in the place.

The teacher walked up to the front of the room, fingers knitted together as if praying, and gestured to me with the tilt of her head. "Please join me in giving Senior Deputy Oveson a big Theodore Roosevelt Grammar School thank-you!"

The children applauded, and one boy put his fingers in his mouth and let out a shrill whistle. I had my hands on my hips, grinning at the kids, and mouthing the words "thank you." When the applause subsided, the teacher took two steps forward, and her eyes surveyed the audience from one side of the gym to the other. "Maybe Mr. Oveson wouldn't mind if we asked him a few questions about his job. Does anyone have any questions for him?"

Dozens of hands shot up.

I said, "Before you ask your question, please say your name. That helps me get to know you all."

I pointed to a freckle-faced boy with spiky red hair. He leaped to his feet in the center of the gymnasium and said, "I'm Dickie Morgan. Is that your very own patrol car parked outside? Do you get to keep it?"

"Very good question, Dickie," I said. "Is that my patrol car? The answer is no. It belongs to the taxpayers of Salt Lake County. That's why I always make sure to take extra special care of it. Next question?"

More hands shot up, and I called on a girl in the fourth row. She stood, and when her face came into view, my heart nearly stopped.

"Hazel Hamilton. Why didn't you try harder?"

She had a porcelain doll's face—white with wide eyes and curly locks over her ears.

"Why didn't I . . ."

All of the children stared at me and the adults whispered to one another.

"Why . . . ? Good question. Why . . ."

"Dad . . . Dad . . . Hey, Dad! Snap out of it!"

I blinked a couple of times and turned to Sarah Jane, who held up a picture of a girl in a boat on the blue sea. Behind the boat was a small island with a palm tree. She had used her shoebox full of Dixon crayons to color it.

"What do you think?"

"That's a lovely picture," I said. "I especially like how happy the girl is. She looks like she really loves being in her sailboat."

"She does."

We sat side by side at the kitchen table. The radio played a jaunty tune by Charlie Straight's Orchestra that on any other day might make me want to don a straw hat and fur coat and do the Charleston.

Not today. Today I was in a gloomy way, although I tried my best to hide it around Sarah Jane. This was our time together. Yet she could tell I was not all the way there.

"Let me see what you drew, Daddy."

I showed her my crummy stick figure. She shook her head and furrowed her eyebrows, not making an effort to conceal her disappointment.

"Is that the best you could do?"

I pulled the drawing closer to me. "Maybe not."

"You tell me I should always do my best," she said, "but that's not your best."

I sighed. "There's an old saying. Do as I say, not as I do."

She giggled, and her blue eyes reflected the light above. She went back to coloring, this time a new picture.

"Daddy?"

"Yeah?"

"Is it true that God punishes people who do bad things? That's what Mary's dad says."

"Oh, he does, does he?" I thought about it for a moment. "I like to hope so. But I also happen to know that some people do bad things and never get punished for it. They get away with it."

She stopped coloring with her purple crayon and looked over at my gold star, sitting on the table near my elbow. "Can I see that?"

"Sure."

I handed it to her, and she moved it around in her hands, touching each point, turning it around and running her finger along the pin in back. She passed it back to me. "Is that why you got that star, Daddy? Do you stop people from doing bad things?"

I shrugged my shoulders and ran the palm of my hand over my clammy forehead. "It's hard to prevent bad things from happening. The best we can hope for is to capture the men and women who do bad things, make sure they get punished, and hope others learn from it."

"Daddy?"

"Yeah?"

"Promise me nothing bad will ever happen to you."

The telephone rang. She watched me, her eyes begging me to speak the words.

"Excuse me for a second, jelly bean," I said.

"OK. Hurry, Daddy."

"I'll do my best." I winked at her, and she winked back.

I walked over to the wall nook, lifted the telephone's earpiece, and held the transmitter up near my mouth. "Hello."

The line crackled and party line voices came and went.

"Hello," I said again.

"Art! It's me, Seymour."

"Considine?"

"Yeah, Seymour Considine. I think it's about time we had one of our powwows. I'm sitting on a gold mine with this Pfalzgraf case."

I turned sideways to see Sarah Jane sitting at the table, smiling, looking at me expectantly, probably wishing I would join her again. I maneuvered into the kitchen, as far as the telephone cord would stretch.

"Haven't you heard?" I asked. "The case is closed."

"Yeah? Well, I've been digging deep for a follow-up story, and there's a hell of a lot more to this case than meets the eye. For starters, Clyde Alexander was the wrong man. Sure, he was a no-good grifter and blackmailer, but he wasn't a killer. Pfalzgraf's murderer was a button man, I'm sure of it. Hired by someone who's loaded *and* connected."

"So what's next?" I asked.

He laughed—a little too uproariously given the question I posed. "I hope you don't think I'm going to tell you my plans over the telephone, Oveson. We've got party lines all the way to Omaha listening in. No, we have to talk in person."

"I don't have much to give you in exchange for your information," I said. "I put aside my investigation. Sheriff's orders."

"So you believed that hogwash about Alexander?"

"Sheriff Cannon closed the case after I found Alexander's body with a suicide note," I said. "You can't blame me for giving up. Alexander had an awful reputation. I'm still not convinced he was innocent."

"What about Sam Louis?"

I needed a moment because that name unexpectedly paralyzed me.

"Oveson! You still there?"

"Yeah. I'm here. How do you know about Sam Louis?"

"I found out about him the same way you did," said Considine. "I bothered to get my ass off the chair and actually do some legwork, which is more than I can say for most of your pals in the county sheriff's office. The police haven't done much better, either. I thought mentioning Sam's name would shake you up."

"Well, it worked. You've definitely got my attention now."

"Something else," he said. "Dr. Pfalzgraf knows people in high places. He's protected. You and I need to talk, Oveson. I'm staying in town."

"Where?"

"You know the Valley-Vu Motor Court?"

"Thirteenth South and State?"

"That's the place. Number eight. Come around nine o'clock tonight. Wait till you see what I've uncovered."

"I'll be there," I said. I heard a click, my cue to drop the receiver on the cradle.

Sarah Jane called out from the other room, "C'mon, Daddy. Let's finish our coloring."

Her voice warmed my heart. "Coming."

I pulled into the parking lot of the Valley-Vu Motor Court at five minutes to nine. The Valley-Vu consisted of two rows of ten identical cabins made to look rustic, complete with green shutters, flower boxes under each window, and attached carports. A neon VACANCY sign burned red and yellow into my retinas. The stars were out, but it was too early in the year for the crickets to chirp their nocturnal symphony.

I passed between the buildings and arrived at cabin 8. A 25-watt globe lit the porch and a couple of rocking chairs. I gave a knock. Nothing. I knocked again. From the cabin to the left came sounds of moans and groans—a man and a woman making whoopee. Music played in another cabin, something jumpy, heavy on the horns with a little percussion thrown in to keep rhythm.

I broke out the lock pick and a minute later pushed the door open.

There wasn't much to the cabin: one room with a bed, bureau, settee, and rolltop desk; a kitchenette with a small icebox and hot plate; and a toilet-and-shower restroom with cold tile floors. The room was empty, but I knew when I walked in and saw all the bloodstains on the bed, carpet, and walls that something terrible had happened to Considine. My gut told me he wouldn't be churning out any more five-cent-a-word stories. I took out my .38 and cocked back the hammer. I made sure not to touch anything. The drawers

had been yanked out of the bureau. Clothes were strewn everywhere. The top mattress was halfway off the bed, and the blood-
saturated linens had been pulled off and thrown into piles in the
corner of the room. Even the complimentary copies of the Gideons'
Bible and the Book of Mormon were on the floor. The icebox door
was ajar, open enough for me to see that Considine had stocked it
with Ward's Strong Wyoming Ale. He probably picked it up from
one of the downtown bootleg joints.

The telephone rang. The clock said nine, the time I was supposed to arrive. I walked over to the bedside table and, using my
handkerchief, picked up the earpiece receiver. I waited for the person on the other end to speak.

A high-pitched woman's voice said, "This is the front desk. I
have a telephone call for room eight."

"Put 'em through," I said.

A man's voice said, "You made your nine o'clock appointment,
Art."

I instantly recognized the voice. "Roscoe? Is that you?"

"None other. I hate to break it to you, my friend, but it looks like
your little motor lodge conclave with Considine ain't gonna happen."

"I guessed as much."

"You better meet me at Saltair—a mile west, to be exact, at the
South Point turnoff. You can't miss it. You'll see all the police car
headlamps. Make it snappy, will ya?"

I didn't wait to say good-bye. I wiped my prints off the exterior
doorknob, then got in my car and sped up State to North Temple,
took a hard left from North Temple onto U.S. Route 40, and kept
on 40 all the way out to the Great Salt Lake.

Fifteen minutes passed, and Saltair came into view. If Coney
Island and the Taj Mahal could give birth to a runt offspring, it
would be Saltair, a Persian-influenced fun park, with rides, slides,

games, and eateries, located on the southern shore of the Great Salt
Lake. The sprawling pavilion juts out into the water, and its big
brown minarets give the place a certain Near Eastern exoticism. As
you stroll the grounds, though, it quickly becomes evident that this
place—its nickel arcades, its red-white-and-blue bunting, its carou-
sel and rickety roller coaster—is about as American as it gets.

The Mormons built Saltair in 1893, twenty miles from Salt Lake
City, hoping it would be Utah's Coney Island. They wanted to persuade the federal government that we Utahns were just like everybody else. In those years, there was stiff resistance in Washington
to allowing Utah to be admitted into the Union because of the
territory's long history of allowing plural marriage. The Mormon
Church stopped sanctioning polygamous marriages in 1890, but it
would take more than that to convince the United States government to admit Utah as a state. The church also embraced all things
American, including amusement parks, which happened to be the
big craze at the time. Not only did the church fund the construction of this massive pavilion filled with rides, games, and sweet things
to eat, Church authorities also footed the bill to build a Saltair railroad depot with lines coming in daily from Ogden, Salt Lake, and
Provo.

The original pavilion burned down back in the big fire of '25,
but the Church quickly rebuilt it, better than it was before. Today,
thirty-seven years after Saltair's grand opening, the place still drew
big crowds and was open late for wholesome family fun under the
stars. As I neared it—about a quarter to ten—park lights flashed in
different colors, merry-go-round music cheered the darkness, and a
few intrepid bathers braved the still-cold waters of the Great Salt
Lake. I lead-footed it across the causeway in my Plymouth, keeping pace with a locomotive roaring west toward the park. Yellow
lights burned inside the passenger car windows, and the people

inside—men, women, and children—moved freely, talking, laughing, full of merriment.

I passed Saltair, accelerating into the darkness and admiring the park's resplendent glow in my rearview mirror. I turned off at the South Point exit and followed the short, very dark road north to the shore of the Great Salt Lake. The headlamps on my car illuminated the scene before me: five Salt Lake City Police Department patrol cars, two sheriff's vehicles, and the county morgue wagon. Spotlights attached to autos beamed on the lake. An army of uniformed cops stood on the shore, watching two of their own wearing green chest waders pulling something out of the water.

I parked and got out of my car. Walking to the scene, I came face-to-face with Roscoe Lund, dressed in patrolman's blue with a Salt Lake City Police Department cap pushed back high on his head. He stood next to a black-and-white, looking every bit the policeman.

I wanted to hug him, yet I settled for a handshake.

"Well, well, well," he said. "If it isn't—"

"Yeah, I know. The choirboy. The Boy Scout. The goody-two-shoes. Am I forgetting anything?"

He nodded. "The Mormon Marauder. Mr. Vanilla. Saint Art. Deputy Squeaky Clean. You know, I could go on . . ."

"No. That's OK. I get the picture."

Roscoe grinned, showcasing that gap between his front teeth. "How the hell are you, Art?"

"I'd be a lot happier if we were partners again. How about you? You look like you've done well for yourself."

He made a long face and rolled his eyes. "I landed a job on Night Watch, Pioneer Patrol. The hours are late, but I don't mind. Beats the shit out of being unemployed."

I nodded. "You're sorely missed in the sheriff's office."

"Yeah, well, I hope for your sake the voters give that cocksucker Cannon the boot and elect Blackham."

Now's the perfect time to change the subject, I thought. I said, "How did you know to call me at the Valley-Vu?"

"Your name and home phone number turned up on Valley-Vu stationery I found inside the glove box of a late-model Oldsmobile belonging to Seymour Considine. The car is parked up the road about a hundred yards. I was the one who found the car, and when I saw your name on the stationery, I pocketed it, so the homicide dicks wouldn't find it. Not that you'd get in any trouble. You're just a lawman like the rest of us, doing a day's work. Still, Detective Hawkins can be a pain in the ass, even if you wear a badge. Along with your name and number, Considine wrote *9:00 p.m.* I figured the two of you must've had an appointment. When I found the stationery, I drove to a nearby call box to call and see if you were there. Sure enough . . ."

"Thanks for doing all that," I said. "I owe you."

"You could say that." He winked.

I turned in time to see the police dropping a waterlogged corpse on the shore.

Tom Livsey came sloshing out of the water toward us, wearing the same type of green chest waders as the police. We shook hands as water cascaded down his rubber-covered legs.

"Art. We've gotta stop meeting like this."

"No kidding, Tom. How's every little thing?"

"I'm fine. Can't say the same for him . . ."

I walked over to the body and, by the light of the automobile headlamps, saw it was Considine. His face was sliced up in several places, much of his nose and part of his mouth had been cut off, and his shirt was covered with bloody tears where a knife had punctured his torso.

"He's a human pincushion," said Livsey. "We won't know how

many times he was stabbed until Nash gives him a good going-over."

"What happened?" I asked.

Livsey scratched his nose and gazed out at the shimmering water. "He was stabbed somewhere else, thrown into the trunk of his own car, and driven out here. Some bathers from Saltair were walking along the beach and saw the body floating facedown."

"Obviously the killer wanted the body found," said Roscoe.

Livsey looked at him. "Why do you say that?"

"There are a thousand places in the West Desert where you can dump a body and nobody will ever find it," said Roscoe. "The perp picked a stretch of water near Saltair, the busiest resort in the state."

Livsey shook his head and stared down at the lacerated corpse. "There's nothing obvious about it. We might be dealing with a rank amateur who doesn't know any better." He began to unbutton his chest waders and started off toward the morgue wagon. "If you gentlemen will excuse me . . ."

"See you later, Tom," I said.

Roscoe scowled as he watched Tom walk away. Tom was probably still in earshot when he said, "I can't stand that cocksucker."

Roscoe looked at me. At that point, I could not hide the shock of seeing Considine so thoroughly sliced up, and I think Roscoe sensed that. He said, "What did Considine want with you?"

"He was researching a story on the Pfalzgraf murder for that true detective magazine he writes for," I said. "He was going to share some of his information with me. He telephoned me at home earlier and asked me to meet him at the Valley-Vu."

"How did you know him?"

Time to fess up, I decided. "Remember when we saw him at the Vienna?"

"You cut a deal while I was out back taking a piss?"

"Something like that."

Roscoe nodded and made a slight face, what I'd call a partial glower. He said, "Well, if you did it, I know you meant well, Art."

"He said he dug up a lot of dirt on the Pfalzgraf homicide," I said. "He insisted there's more to it than the public knows. He was going to show me what he had at our meeting tonight. I showed up at the time we agreed on. He didn't answer the door, so I jimmied the lock and went in. Somebody ransacked his room. Gave it a good going-over. Did you find anything in his car other than that pad of stationery?"

"Yeah, a couple of pints of blood in his trunk. No other papers, though."

I was quiet for a moment, staring at the lines etched into Roscoe's face, the smoothness of his clean-shaven chin, the tiny razor cuts on his neck. He was looking at the body, but he sensed my eyes on him and turned to me. "What is it?" he asked.

"C. W. Alexander didn't kill Helen Pfalzgraf," I said.

"Who did?"

"I don't know, but I'm going to do my darnedest—" I saw him smile at my language. "I'm going to do my *damnedest* to find out."

"Good luck with that," he said.

"I need your help."

"My help?"

"Yeah."

"Sorry, Art. I got fired. Remember? I'm off the case."

"You can still help me. I can't do it without you," I said.

"Sure you can." He rubbed his hands over his face, took a deep breath, and exhaled shakily. His eyes were weary and full of sadness. He said, "Don't sell yourself short. You're a damn good lawman. You're young. You've still got a few things to learn. You're getting the hang of it, though, and you can do anything if you put your mind to it. Hell, all I am is an aging night cop, halfway over the hill and on my way to the bottom. I've got a lot of shit going on in my life that you know nothing about. I'm tired. I get paid chicken feed, and I'm in debt up to my chest. My joints ache. Every day, I'm amazed I have the juice to get the fuck out of bed. Excuse the French. I'm tired, Art. The last thing I want to do is stick my neck on the chopping block. Don't ask me to get involved."

I nodded, and the two of us watched the morgue boys loading the body onto a stretcher and covering it with a white sheet. Buddy Hawkins and Wit Dunaway, in hats, ties, and buttoned-up coats, stood near the morgue wagon and watched the vehicle speed off into the darkness. Buddy walked over to me, looking me up and down.

"What brings you out here, Art? And please don't tell me you just happen to be out for a late-night drive to savor the cool lake air, because I won't buy it."

I gestured to Roscoe. "He and I knew the deceased. Seymour Considine. He was a writer for the gossip rags."

"I know," said Buddy. "I talked to Considine a couple of times. Arrested him once, right after Helen Pfalzgraf was murdered. He was a real pain in the neck. Let me ask you. Do you think his death had anything to do with the Pfalzgraf homicide?"

"I don't have the faintest idea."

Buddy made a pained face and shook his head. "C'mon, Art. I have a sneaking suspicion you have a good idea whether this is connected to the Pfalzgraf case. How about you level with me?"

"I can't," I said. "Cannon doesn't want me sharing any information with the police. If it bothers you, talk to him."

Buddy looked in both directions—east and west—and then at me. "I don't see Cannon anywhere near here. It's just you and me and Roscoe, and I've got this nagging feeling that you know something that might actually help me in getting to the bottom of Considine's death. Now, out with it."

"I don't know anything."

Buddy smiled, hands in his pockets. "Uh-huh. I see. Well, if you change your mind, you'll see me in church on Sunday."

He turned and walked along the shore, heading to the cluster of police cars with their bright headlamps and spotlights bathing the water in light. We watched him until we could no longer see him.

Out of the corner of his mouth, Roscoe said to me, "Ever think of quitting that goddamn church of yours?"

"See you around," I said, smiling. "Good luck, Roscoe."

"You, too, Art. You, too."

Eighteen

I stood at a lectern facing rows of folding chairs. Half a dozen reporters were scattered around the room, mostly men but also one woman (a dead ringer for Marion Davies), along with four radio technicians and a pair of silver microphones, one from station KSL, the other KDYL. In my blue suit and red necktie, I held a stack of messages typed onto index cards by Faye Meadows. I developed a case of cottonmouth halfway through the presentation and drank from a nearby glass of water. Reporters jotted notes in their spiral pads as I spoke.

"Henry D. 'Puddinhead' Morgan—" I stopped and glanced up at the reporters. "With a name like Puddinhead, he must be a dangerous outlaw." The audience laughed, but Sykes, standing in the corner, shook his head disapprovingly. I resumed. "Mr. Morgan was captured yesterday by sheriff's deputies while running a fifty-gallon still in a barn in Murray. Deputies Lester Hansen and G. T. Fisher destroyed the still and smashed four hundred and fifty gallons of mash and twenty gallons of rye liquor. The deputies retained two gallons of the illegal brew for evidence."

I sipped more water. Switching cards, I said, "Once again, deputies from the sheriff's office have clamped down on John Papacostas's South Town Roadhouse at 501 West Thirty-third South, due to the serving of illegal liquor inside of the said enterprise. Mr. Papacostas insisted that this was a soft drink establishment, serving only legal beverages with their dinner specials. Deputies worked closely with J. L. Francom, a federal dry agent from Salt Lake City, in carrying out the raid. We felt vindicated when Mr. Papacostas, while being booked and fingerprinted, boasted of being cited more than one hundred and forty times for liquor law violations and other offenses without being convicted a single time. We sincerely hope that the latest charges against Mr. Papacostas stick. He has long been an undesirable element within this community, and unless he's punished for his flouting of the law, he will more than likely resume roadhouse operations soon."

I glanced at the clock. Closing in on nine. "I see our time is almost up, but I will take questions from the reporters now."

A hand went up, and I called on the blonde in the green dress, Amelia Van Cott, a reporter for the *Ogden Post*. "Mr. Oveson, there's a body in the morgue identified as Seymour Considine, a writer. He was working on a story about the Pfalzgraf homicide. The coroner says he was stabbed fifty-three times and then dumped into the Great Salt Lake. Is there a connection between the Considine and Pfalzgraf homicides?"

Sykes glared at me and shook his head forcefully. My sights switched to Miss Van Cott. "We have not found any sort of link between the two murders."

A hand shot up. I pointed to Leonard Bennion of the *Telegram*. He stood up. "Since you masterminded the capture of Clyde Alexander, is the sheriff's office going to assign you to solve the Considine homicide?"

Sykes strode to the podium and did his best to put an artificial smile on his face. He said, "Mr. Considine has spent the last ten years writing sensational stories for gutter magazines, and plenty of underworld types had it in for him. We are cooperating with the Salt Lake police and sheriff's departments in other states and expect that Considine's killer will be apprehended soon. But let me assure you this case does not—I repeat, *does not*—have anything to do with the Pfalzgraf investigation, which is now officially closed."

Sykes stepped back and gave a slight wave. "This concludes today's Roundup. I'd like to thank Senior Deputy and Public Liaison Arthur Oveson, for doing such an exemplary job with the announcements."

The radio technicians began disconnecting their mikes, and the reporters filed out of the room. I started for the exit.

"Oveson."

I took a deep breath and faced Sykes, who sprinkled snuff on the back of his hand and took a snort. He blinked his eyes, opened his mouth, and flared his nostrils, then blew air through pursed lips and jerked his head.

"So far I've been finding your performance on this job a little lackluster."

"How so, sir?"

"You act like you're going through the motions. And you were downright flippant when you mentioned that Puddinhead fellow."

"Sorry you feel that way," I said. "I take my job seriously."

"I'm glad to hear you say that," he said. "Because I've booked a speaking engagement for you for tomorrow afternoon. The Daughters of the Utah Pioneers are having their monthly meeting at 2:00 P.M. at the chamber of commerce, and they've asked if you'd be so kind as to give your law-and-order, crime-doesn't-pay talk. I said sure you would. I don't want to disappoint these ladies, and I know you feel the same way. Their votes mean a great deal to Sheriff Cannon. How say you?"

"Yes, sir," I said with a grin and nod. "I'll be there."

"And Oveson?"

"Yes, sir?"

"You're not still snooping around the Pfalzgraf case, are you?"

"No, sir."

"That's funny. Dr. Pfalzgraf telephoned Sheriff Cannon and told him that you paid a visit to his office. After that, you met with Parley and Miriam Tanner at their home in Federal Heights. Ring any bells?"

I started to speak, but he cut me off.

"I got where I am by playing it smart." He tapped his temple with his index finger. "I thought you did, too. But if you don't smarten up, you're going to miss out on some golden opportunities. I'd hate to see that happen. Get me?"

"Yes, sir."

"Good. Bear in mind we are always—*always*—one step ahead of you."

"Yes, sir."

He placed his hand on my shoulder. "Stay levelheaded, boy. Lincoln said it best. 'Don't go swapping horses in midstream.' "

"Thank you for that advice, sir."

I stood next to a mosaic of WANTED posters pinned to the bulletin board and watched Sykes leave the room.

"Hello, Art."

"Oh! You almost gave me a heart attack."

"Sorry."

Roscoe Lund was sitting on a guest chair in my windowless box of an office, right leg propped over left knee. He wore a straw boater and a buttoned waistcoat, but he'd come tieless. His kept his brown leather jacket draped over his arm. I closed the door behind me, took a seat on the swivel chair on the other side of the desk, and placed my sack lunch and bottle of milk in front of me.

"When did you get here?" I asked.

"Don't worry, choirboy. Cannon didn't see me."

He looked around. Not much to see. I had my chair and two more for visitors, a green filing cabinet, and an electric globe dangling from a ceiling cord. Two framed pictures hung behind my desk, a family portrait (taken a few weeks before Christmas '29) and a color photo of the Salt Lake Temple. Roscoe shook his head when he saw that one.

"Why the fuck have you got that thing on your wall when you can step outside your office and see it from the window?"

"It's for inspiration."

"Oh yeah? Well, I have a couple of French postcards that are a damn sight more inspiring than that thing. 'Course, you'd have to take 'em off the wall when the missus drops by, if you get my drift."

"Drift gotten. No thank you."

His focus, thankfully, shifted to my sack lunch and milk bottle. "What've you got there?"

"Lunch," I said, narrating as I removed the contents. "Baloney sandwich, carrot sticks, apple slices, and . . . the pièce de résistance." I lifted a big object wrapped in wax paper. "My wife's apple cinnamon cake. You want to try some?"

"Let's go halfsies on it."

I unwrapped it, gave him half, and took the other, and we munched quietly for a few minutes. I unscrewed the lid on my bottle of milk and gulped down a third of it in one shot.

Roscoe said, "Moist, but it could use a little kicker."

He uncapped a flask he kept hidden in his jacket and took three swallows. He tilted it toward me.

"I don't drink that stuff," I said. I lifted the bottle of milk, covered with condensation drops. "This is my poison."

"Well, you know what they say, Art," said Roscoe, swigging more. He gasped and capped the bottle. "Candy's dandy, but liquor's quicker."

I leaned back in my chair and popped an apple slice in my mouth and chewed it. "What brings you here?"

"That little matter we discussed the other night over Considine's body."

"The Pfalzgraf case?" I asked. "Haven't you heard? It's closed."

"Bullshit," said Roscoe, pocketing his flask. "Tell me something, Art. What are you willing to do to solve this case?"

"Whatever it takes."

He shook his head and gave me a skeptical squint. "Too vague. Spell it out for me."

"What do you want me to say?"

"I want you tell me how far you're willing to go," said Roscoe. "Are you going to turn this into some kind of happy-valley Mormon cakewalk, with a performance by the Tabernacle Choir and lots of pretty balloons and all the fuckin' ice cream you can eat? Or are we gonna roll up our sleeves, wade into the shit, crack skulls, and get some results?"

"The latter."

"That's what I wanted to hear," he said. "Then I'm in."

I raised a skeptical eyebrow as I capped the milk bottle. "What made you change your mind?"

"It's a long story. I'll tell you some other time. Right now, we've got plenty to keep us busy. Starting with a visit to Miss Harmony Tattershall."

"Where'd you get that name?"

"Considine wrote it on the Valley-Vu stationery with yours. She works in a joint called Caroline House—it's a home for pregnant, unwed teenagers, the girls that nobody else wants."

"She was in the Ogden police file on Dr. Wooley. Pfalzgraf filed a complaint against Wooley before the state medical board on her behalf."

"Let's not sit around here socializing anymore," said Roscoe, lurching out of his seat and tugging the boater lower on his head. "Let's go have a word with her and find out what she knows."

I put my coat on and said as I went for the doorknob, "This won't involve breaking any laws, will it?"

"Only a half dozen or so."

He saw my face lose color and laughed loudly. "Relax, choirboy. We're finally going to figure out who really ran over Helen Pfalzgraf out at the Pole Line Road. That's what you wished for, isn't it?"

The block of A Street that rises steeply above South Temple offered plenty of parking spots along the curb. I slowed my Plymouth to a halt next to a telephone pole, across from a rooming house that played home to a mix of college students, bohemians, indigents, and Mexicans. Small lawns in front of nearby houses had recently turned from dormant winter yellow to spring emerald. Roscoe and I got out of the car and hiked up the steep hill to a Victorian mansion on First Avenue that had been converted to a communal house for unwed pregnant teenagers. The place presented an eclectic mixture of styles: part Queen Anne, something vaguely resembling a castle tower on the southwest corner, a few hints of Italian villa, and a porch reminiscent of a midnineteenth-century Mormon pioneer farmhouse. Somebody in the house was practicing piano scales, and the sound of laughter floated out the upstairs windows. We went up wooden porch steps, and Roscoe gave the front door a good pound.

We didn't have to wait long for an answer.

The door flung open so abruptly the knocker banged once, and there appeared a woman on the other side of the screen with long black hair tied into a bun in back. She had on a pair of wire-frame glasses and a long dark dress. The dimple in her chin was pronounced. "May I help you?"

Roscoe flashed ID. "Patrolman Roscoe Lund, Salt Lake City Police Department. This here is—"

I leaned my chest in near the door so she could see my sheriff's badge. "I'm Senior Deputy Arthur Oveson, Salt Lake County Sheriff's Office."

"We're looking for someone named Harmony Tattershall," said Roscoe. "Do you know where we might find her?"

"I'm her," said the woman. "Only I go by Harmony Baker now."

"Miss Baker, we would appreciate it if you'd let us ask you a few routine questions," I said. "This shouldn't take long."

She nudged the door open a few feet. "Please . . ."

She led us through the first floor of the house, where young women (I couldn't keep exact count of how many) were engaged in various activities—practicing piano scales, cooking food, crocheting, sitting around a blackboard and learning lessons—and into a huge kitchen with a tiled floor, where a pair of pregnant teens were scrubbing dishes in soapy water. She pushed another screen door open, and we followed her out. On the screened-in back porch, there were a half-dozen white wicker chairs with green cushions. We each sat down.

"Would you gentlemen care for something to drink?" she asked. "Milk? Tea? Lemonade?"

"No thank you, ma'am," I said. "We're fine." I cleared my throat. "Four years ago, Dr. Hans Pfalzgraf filed a complaint on your behalf to the state medical board. As a result of that complaint, Dr. Everett Wooley was barred from practicing medicine in the state of Utah."

She nodded. "Yes. That's correct."

I said, "We need you to tell us what that was all about."

"I'll make a long story short," she said. "I got pregnant. I was sixteen at the time. The father of the baby was also my father. I didn't want to have the baby. I tried different things to get rid of it. Jumped off the roof of our house. Drank insecticide. Dry heaved for an entire week, but it didn't do anything to the baby. I rode my horse as hard as I could, but the baby kept growing in me. So I visited Wooley, and he operated on me. Afterward, I got sick. I came down with a fever and an infection. I remember sweating so badly . . . and the pain—it was like someone threw a spear into me. I would've died if it weren't for Margaret."

"Margaret?" I asked.

"Margaret Collins. She runs this place. She runs another one just like it in Denver. Goes back and forth between the two. The woman's a saint. She took care of me. She nursed me back to health and convinced me to adopt my mother's maiden name. She made me read a book by Charlotte Perkins Gilman called *The Yellow Wallpaper*. At first I didn't get the book, but I read it a second time, and it opened my eyes like nothing else. Margaret helped me to understand that women have to fight for their rights—"

Roscoe cut her off. "So you completely recovered, thanks to this Margaret lady?"

She shrugged, and her thick glasses could not conceal the pain in her eyes. "I can't ever have a baby again. My uterus was damaged, thanks to Dr. Wooley. But I am happy to be alive. I volunteer here, to help the girls."

I said, "Why did Pfalzgraf agree to submit a complaint in your name to the state medical board?"

She kept rubbing her hands against her forearms, as if trying to warm herself. I'd written it off as a nervous tic, but she wasn't letting up. If anything, she was doing it with even more frenzied intensity now. She took a deep breath and said, "I think he had a number of reasons for helping me. He's got a decent side to him. Part of him wants to help people. No question about it."

"Why else?" I asked.

"Guilt."

I looked at Roscoe. Roscoe looked at me. We both looked at Harmony Baker. I said, "Can you elaborate? Why did he feel guilty?"

"Because I came up fifty bucks short. That's why he turned me away."

Roscoe's eyebrows twitched. "Who turned you away? What are you talking about?"

"Dr. Pfalzgraf," she said. "He charges two hundred and fifty for his surgeries. That's why all of his clients are rich women. And girls."

I was nearly too stunned to speak—I felt my body shaking—but I managed to spit out the words. "You mean . . . Pfalzgraf . . . Dr. Hans Pfalzgraf . . . was . . . is . . ."

"He's an abortionist," said Harmony. She smiled and let out a pained laugh. "You mean . . . you didn't know? You guys are cops, right? How can you not know?"

"We know now," said Roscoe. "So among other things, Wooley was competition for Pfalzgraf?"

"I guess you could say that," said Harmony. "He was the only other abortionist in town. He charged a hundred bucks. I thought I was getting a good deal. Pay a hundred, go home with a hundred."

"How did you find out about Wooley?" I asked.

"I asked around. If you talk to enough people, you find out who's who."

"How did you meet Pfalzgraf?" I asked.

"Margaret called him when I got sick. He paid several house calls. I got to know him. He wasn't such a bad guy. I'd describe him as considerate. He made a couple of follow-up visits." She chuckled again. "If only he'd been so kind when I came up fifty bucks short. I later found out that Pfalzgraf has one of the best reputations in this country as an abortionist. I can't say the same for Wooley. He used his clinic to mutilate innocent women and girls."

"Did Pfalzgraf approach you about going after Wooley?"

"No. It was Margaret's idea. Margaret said Wooley's operation killed a lot of young women. She said somebody needed to stand up to him. Pfalzgraf was Margaret's physician, so she talked to him. She convinced me to go after Wooley. I did. I'm glad I did. The board stripped him of his license. I remember the day it happened. He was upset. He hollered at Pfalzgraf. He hollered at me real good. I laughed at him. What was he going to do to me worse than what he'd already done? I heard he later hit Pfalzgraf in a restaurant. Then he vamoosed. Turned up in Ogden later, and I'm sure you fellows know what happened to him. Although you didn't know Pfalzgraf was an abortion doctor, so I shouldn't assume anything."

"We know what happened to Wooley," I said.

She pushed her glasses higher on her nose and said, "We didn't lose much when he died. So is that why you're here? He was murdered a year and a half ago."

"Partly," I said, "and partly we're looking into Helen Pfalzgraf's murder."

She said, "But I thought—"

"It's complicated," said Roscoe. "You'll be doing us all a big favor if you don't ask us to explain. I've got one more question, then we'll leave you be."

"Shoot."

"Do you know somebody named Sam Louis?"

She scrunched her face, shook her head. "Loomis?"

Roscoe said, "No. Louis. *L-O-U-I-S.* Ring any bells?"

"Oh, Louis. No. I don't know anybody named Sam Louis. Never heard of him."

We rose from our chairs, and she stood and shook hands with us.

"If you fellows ever have supplies you'd like to donate to Caroline House, we'll gladly accept them," she said. "We could use everything. Books. Aspirin. Toilet paper. Baby food. Diapers. You name it."

"It's a great place," I said. "I didn't even know it was here."

"It's been here ten years," she said. "Margaret named it after her daughter. I guess you could say helping out here is my religion now. About the only thing I believe in now is helping these girls get a good start on life. We all need to look after each other. Girls are strong, but they're also delicate at the same time."

On my way out, I turned to Harmony, took out my billfold, and donated a few dollars to the cause, even though I couldn't easily afford it. As we left the house, I noticed Roscoe rolling his eyes and muttering something about me being a "sentimentalist."

"Guilty as charged," I told him.

Nineteen

It takes a couple of minutes to get from A Street to the Brooks Arcade. I parallel parked between two cars next to the State Street curb. The day was overcast, and the lunch crowds had thinned out as the dashboard clock hands ticked toward one. We got out of the car and walked in through the office entrance, took the elevator to the second floor, and found our way down the carpeted hall to room 268.

Eunice Mickelson, whose voice I'd heard so many times on the telephone, sat at the desk fielding switchboard calls. She had wavy hair the color of honey and a V-necked dress, short-sleeved, in an earthy brown. She wore a silver necklace with a purple amethyst, and her fingernails were painted a shade that matched the gem. She saw us entering the office and removed her cumbersome headphones with the attached transmitter.

"Hello, gentlemen," she said. "May I help you?"

We flashed badges and made with the introductions.

"I know you," she said to me. "Why haven't you called me lately?"

I blushed. "I thought you'd be happy to stop getting those calls."

"To tell you the truth, I was starting to think you didn't like me."
She smiled and winked.

"Can it, you two," said Roscoe, looking around. "Where's Pfalz-graf? We've got some questions to ask him."

"He's not here. He's—"

Roscoe put his hands on the desk and leaned in so close, he made her rear back. "Listen, doll face, we don't wanna talk to that shitbird Berkeley-educated attorney of his. We want the doc himself. Where is he?"

"I was about to tell you, you rude sonofabitch," she said, eyebrows furrowed. "Why don't you shut up long enough to let me answer?"

Roscoe looked at me and said, "This is my kinda dame." He looked at her. "Well?"

"He's gone for the day. You may wish to try him at his home."

Roscoe pulled his trousers higher on his waist and said, "C'mon, Art, let's go have a look around."

She stood up so abruptly she sent her wheeled swivel chair rolling in the other direction. "Wait! You need a warrant to search this place!"

Roscoe stopped, turned to Eunice, and pulled a piece of yellow paper out of his coat pocket. "I've got that taken care of, doll face. Judge Bringhurst signed it this morning. It's right here if you'd care to read the fine print."

She eyed the warrant, then Roscoe, then the warrant. She licked her lips, took a deep breath, and eased back toward the switchboard. "Go ahead."

Roscoe started off down the hall, and I followed him. As we neared Pfalzgraf's office, I said, "How'd you cop a warrant out of Bringhurst that quickly? I thought he was stingy with those things."

Roscoe faced me, unfolded the yellow paper, and held it up, and the first thing I noticed was the Firestone logo in the corner. "It's for two pair of vulcanized tires. Four bucks and fifty cents apiece, down at Sam the Tire Man. You think I actually got a warrant from Bringhurst? I avoid that cocksucker like the plague."

"So you lied to her?"

He glared at me as he tucked the receipt back in his pocket. "It was for the greater good. C'mon, choirboy. Shake a leg. Let's get results."

DR. HANS PFALZGRAF—PRIVATE OFFICE, it said on the pebbled glass. Roscoe opened the door and walked inside. I followed him.

Pfalzgraf's office was larger than the waiting room and filled from floor to ceiling with bookcases packed with medical volumes and enclosed by glass doors. The eastern wall was covered with photographs of Pfalzgraf with big shots. On the west wall, behind Pfalzgraf's huge long desk, an oil painting of Helen Pfalzgraf dominated. The painting of Helen shared the wall with a framed mirror to its left, and left of the mirror was a closet door. Roscoe rummaged through a few drawers and filing cabinets while I checked the view from the south window.

"Come in here, Art," said Roscoe from the closet. "There's something you ought to see."

I stepped inside a narrow walk-in closet, startled to discover a motion picture camera mounted on a tripod and aimed at a two-way mirror. Sitting atop a table next to the camera was a big, box-shaped object with a metallic green surface that resembled a phonograph machine, only larger and without the horn-shaped speaker. A logo on the side of the machine read WESTERN ELECTRIC NO. 555 RECEIVER. There was a red light on it and a row of switches and dials.

"What is this?" I asked.

"This, my friend, is the latest in motion picture technology," said Roscoe. "A motion picture camera with synchronized sound. Used for shooting talkies. This baby right here has a perfect panoramic view of Pfalzgraf's office. It's wired to a control panel behind

Pfalzgraf's desk. There are hidden microphones in his office so the recorder can pick up the sound. All he has to do is throw a couple of switches and he films everything that's going on."

Roscoe ran his hand along the camera's black surface, stopping when he reached the lens. "Must've set him back a pretty penny."

"Why?" I asked.

"Insurance. He may be good at what he does—hell, he might even be the best—but he's still vulnerable. If a district attorney or judge gets any fancy ideas, Pfalzgraf can put in a telephone call to one of his rich friends, someone with pull who has a lot to lose if Pfalzgraf hands over the right film to the local newspapers."

I nodded, and the significance of what I was seeing hit me. "So if he has filmed everything . . ."

"He's got leverage," said Roscoe.

"Do you think Alexander got ahold of those films?" I asked. "And that's what he was using to blackmail people?"

"I wouldn't be surprised. Come on. Let's check the operating room."

We left the cramped space, passed through the office, and crossed the hallway. I opened the door to a room opposite Pfalzgraf's office and switched on the lights. The whiteness of the room stung the eyes: white tile, a white bed with stirrups, white counters, bright white lights on adjustable, wheeled chrome stands. Adjacent to the bed was a long table on wheels covered with steel instruments— pointed, twisted, unnatural, used for cutting, poking, scraping, and sucking. Roscoe walked up to what I guessed was another two-way mirror and checked his reflection, mumbling the word "handsome," then pushed open a closet door beside it, went inside, and found a setup similar to the one in Pfalzgraf's office. Same type of camera. Same type of recording equipment.

"I bet these things set him back a hundred G's," said Roscoe.

"He probably had to go out to Hollywood to get them. I'm sure he sends the undeveloped films out there to be processed, too."

"Hollywood," I said. "Roland Lane."

"The actor?" asked Roscoe.

I nodded.

"What about him?"

"It's a hunch . . ."

I returned to Pfalzgraf's office, to a file drawer marked J-K-L, and walked my fingers through the files until I reached a dossier marked LANE, DOROTHY.

Roscoe came in with his hands in his pockets. "Well?"

I read enough of the file to get the picture: Roland Lane had brought Dorothy Lane to Utah five years ago for one of Dr. Pfalzgraf's famous "surgeries." I closed the dossier and tucked it back into its proper place.

I said, "So that's how the doctor and Helen Pfalzgraf met Roland Lane."

"Do you suppose that's how Helen landed her audition at First National?"

"I don't know," I said, closing the filing cabinet.

"Why don't we go straight to the source?" asked Roscoe.

I faced him. "You mean . . ."

"Let's go see what the doctor has to say."

Floyd Samuelson, in his black security guard getup, lowered his copy of *Outdoor America* and eyed us as we pulled up to the curb in front of the Pfalzgraf mansion. I waited for a red trolley to pass and watched it round the corner onto Thirteenth East, then I checked my Bulova: 2:30. Crossing the street, I thought about how much things had changed since I came here in February. The snow had all melted, thanks to the arrival of warm spring weather. The first buds

poked out of the ends of tree branches. No newshounds. No newsreel cameras. No shutterbugs. Normality had returned to South
Temple and, once again, the loudest sound was the birdsong coming from the towering trees. Floyd grimaced when he noticed Roscoe, closed his magazine, and tipped his cap at me.

"Hiya, Art."

"Floyd, how's every little thing?"

We shook hands through the gate.

"Everything's jake. Hey, I've got something to show you!" His
grin widened as he scooped his billfold out of his pocket and flipped
it open to a snapshot of his son, bundled up outdoors and holding a
fishing pole. The boy was grim-faced, and his freckled cheeks puffed
out to make him look even more sullen. "This is Bert with his first
rod and reel."

I nodded. "You must be proud. He's a handsome kid."

"He's a chip off the old block," said Floyd, admiring the photo
for a moment before tucking it back in his trouser pocket and patting the lump for good measure. "Hey, are they hiring down at the
sheriff's office?"

"I don't know. Maybe," I said. "Why? You thinking of applying?"

Floyd went shifty-eyed and lowered his voice. "I'm getting tired
of this job. Long hours with nothing to do but sit here and read
magazines and pick my nose. It's for the birds. Not what I signed up
for when we went through the academy."

I bowed my head and laughed. "Well, come on down and fill out
an application form sometime."

"I might just do that, Art," he said, cheered up again. "I might
very well."

"I need to talk to Dr. Pfalzgraf, Floyd. Is he here?"

"I'm sorry, he can't talk to you," said Floyd. "He's busy."

Roscoe cut in front of me, grabbed an iron bar, and gave the gate
a good rattle. "Horseshit. Open this gate and let us in."

Floyd backed up a few steps, shaking his head. "You don't scare me, Lund."

"You want me to make a scene out here?" said Roscoe, pacing back and forth in front of the gate. "I'll do it, if I have to. I'll make one hell of a racket. I'll wake up the dead. I'll let the whole world know what the doctor *really* does for a living."

Behind Floyd, the twin doors of the Pfalzgraf mansion opened, and the white-haired doctor in a black suit and string tie came hobbling out of his house. He crossed the lawn slowly and reached us at the gate, steadying himself with a silver-handled cane. He wore bifocals and a suit that, like everything else he owned, probably came from Germany and cost a small fortune. He was taller than I thought—about six one, neck bent forward. He had a soft face with wrinkles around his mouth and eyes and white hair around his ears.

"Gentlemen," he said, in a voice softer than rabbit's fur. "I expected you to show up sooner. Floyd, let them in."

"But Doc . . ."

"You heard me. Please let these gentlemen pass through the gate."

Floyd reached for his ring of keys, unlocked the padlock, and slid the gate open for us. Pfalzgraf started across the lawn, and we followed past the side of the house and into the backyard, a place full of flower gardens that weren't yet blossoming due to the earliness of the season, with a burbling stone fountain that attracted birds. We ended up at a stone picnic table, under a canopy of trees that shielded us from the mild March sun.

"I love to sit out here," he said, still holding tightly to his cane. "It's peaceful. It's a pleasure to see you again, Mr. Oveson."

"You as well," I said.

"I don't believe we've ever met," he said, offering his hand to Roscoe, who glared and refused to shake it. Pfalzgraf lowered his arm with a shrug and sideways tip of his head, as if to say, *Your loss.*

"This is Officer Lund," I said. "Of the Salt Lake City Police Department. We're conducting an investigation together."

"I know why you're here," Pfalzgraf said. "It's about Helen."

"That's right," I said.

"I owe you a tremendous debt of gratitude, Mr. Oveson," he said. "I hope that reward money I gave you has been of some help."

"You were too generous, Doctor," I said.

Roscoe said, "Let's leave out the mutual dick sucking for another time, shall we? You best level with us, Doc, or I'll haul your pruny hide down—"

Doc cut him off. "What's your name again?"

"Officer Roscoe Lund."

"Don't you ever speak to me that way again, Officer Lund," he said, raising his cane ominously. "You may think you're tougher than me, but I promise you are not."

Roscoe looked Pfalzgraf over, knowing he was outranked. Glad as I was to be partnered with him again, it was refreshing to see him humbled by this elderly man.

Pfalzgraf said, "Do you think I would've let either of you onto the grounds if I'd been the one who murdered Helen? I had nothing to do with her death. I am more eager than anybody to find out who murdered her. That is why I gave you the reward money, Oveson, because I thought you solved this case. And that is why I let you in here, on the grounds."

"Thank you," I said, glancing sideways at Roscoe. "I'll get right to the point, Doctor. Where were you the night your wife was murdered?"

"I believe Parley Tanner answered that question at the coroner's inquest. He and I attended a wrestling match at the Majestic, and there were many witnesses who saw us there and can confirm this fact."

"It's strange," said Roscoe.

"What is?" asked Pfalzgraf.

Roscoe tapped the marble with his fingers. "Your first wife was crushed to death thirteen years ago when your own touring car rolled on top of her. Your second wife was pulverized under the wheels of her own Cadillac. Doesn't that strike you as a little too coincidental?"

"I suppose it is . . ." He searched for the right word. "Unusual."

"To say the least," Roscoe said quietly.

I said, "Did Helen want to divorce you?"

"Yes."

He blurted out the answer before I finished asking the question.

I said, "But Parley Tanner said at the coroner's inquest that—"

"Dear Parley was trying to avoid embarrassing me in front of all those people. He was wrong. She wanted a divorce, and she asked me for it the day before she was killed. We quarreled for almost two hours, and we continued fighting even after we visited Parley's office. I begged Helen to stay married to me and promised her that we could work out whatever problems we had. I reminded her that I lost my Nellie in a car accident all those years ago and I didn't want to lose her, too. I also told Helen how much Anna loved her— adored her like a sister, in fact—and that her leaving would devastate Anna as much as it would me. I tried so hard to convince Helen to stay, but she said she could not remain married to me. She ran out, and I never saw her again. After Helen left, I experienced what you might call a change of heart and decided to give her the divorce she requested. The next morning . . ."

His voice trailed off, and he shifted his gaze to the ground.

"Why did you change your mind?" asked Roscoe.

"Helen did not want to stay married to me. That much was

obvious. I did not wish to force her to live a life she did not want to live. I knew she was pregnant, but the baby wasn't mine. We had not been intimate for over a year."

"Who was the father?" I asked.

"I think C. W. Alexander, but I don't know that for a fact. The two of them had been sleeping with each other for months, as you probably know."

"What about this Persian prince everybody was talking about after the murder?" asked Roscoe. "How does he fit into it?"

Dr. Pfalzgraf bowed his head and wrinkled his forehead thoughtfully. "The fellow took her out on the town a few times in Paris and London. I thought it nice that she was having a delightful time with a man closer to her age. The newspapers exaggerated the extent of the relationship."

"Do you think he had anything to do with her murder?" asked Roscoe.

He blinked through his bifocals at Roscoe and shook his head. "Theirs was a surface relationship, no depth to it at all. Purely superficial. Helen boasted about him to anyone who would listen. She liked that a real prince liked her. She was always very conspicuous when it came to status symbols, no doubt because she was raised in such modest circumstances. That is one of the reasons she auditioned at that movie studio. She wanted the fame and fortune, but she also wanted to be able to say she accomplished great things on her own, without anyone's help."

"She did have help, though," said Roscoe. "Roland Lane, the actor, helped her land an audition at First National. Lane also brought his wife to you for an abortion last year."

"That was not his wife," said Pfalzgraf in a testy way. "She was his sister. She wanted to be in motion pictures, too, like her older brother, but she had had a relationship with a young Mexican fellow who got her pregnant. Roland knew this could destroy any hope she had of being in the movies. So he brought her here for surgery, out of the spotlight, and sure enough, after I performed it, she was cast in her first movie."

Roscoe seemed unimpressed. "I'm guessing C. W. strong-armed Lane into landing Helen that audition last year with First National. Probably using the film you shot of Lane's sister."

I thought Dr. Pfalzgraf was a pale man who could not have possibly gotten any paler. I was wrong. He got paler when Roscoe said that. "How did you know . . ."

I said, "We've been to your clinic at the Brooks Arcade, and we know your office and operating room have been rigged with two-way mirrors and synchronized sound cameras, the kind the studios use to shoot talkies."

Roscoe said, "Helen knew where you were hiding the films, and she knew how to get her hands on them. She helped C. W. get ahold of them, or at the very least she told him where they could be found. The films fell into his hands and became the basis of his blackmail racket."

The doctor did not utter a word but instead sat speechless, looking from Roscoe to me. I said, "Your clients are mostly prosperous and educated people who know that in exchange for two hundred and fifty dollars, you'll perform the safest operation available in the country. Those movies protected you. They kept you out of hot water with the authorities, shielding you against lawsuits, preventing the medical board from stripping you of your license the way they did with Wooley."

Roscoe cut in like a dancer, nudging me aside to trip the light fantastic with a beautiful woman. "C. W. Alexander used those films to threaten the people in them, and his scheme paid off, for a while at least. The money flowed into bank accounts opened under Helen Pfalzgraf's name, so nobody would ask any questions. The bankers probably figured the rich doctor's wife was just making another deposit. No big deal. Nothing unusual. But at some point, C. W. blackmailed the wrong man. Maybe he was an industrialist. Maybe he was a mobster. Maybe he was a Hollywood actor or a Persian prince. Who the hell knows? Whoever this big shot was, C. W. wasn't expecting the man to dispatch a torpedo to run over Helen with her own car and then turn around and knock him off at his cabin in Park City."

The doctor inspected the silver head of his cane for a moment, frowning and inhaling deeply through his nose. "I have no comment on your little theory, but I do have a business proposition for the two of you. Return those films to me—all of them—and I'll give each of you fifty thousand dollars as a reward. Nobody need know of it. We will transact our business quietly and put the matter behind us."

"How many films are we talking about exactly?" I asked.

"Over the past ten years, I've shot close to two thousand films," he said. "I keep them in a secure room in my basement—or what I thought was a secure room. They're short, and they're in small canisters. I keep them on shelves in alphabetical order. The films shot before May of 1929 are accompanied by sound disk recordings, which are kept in paper sleeves. Whoever took the films did not take all of them. Eighty-two of my films have vanished. At first I didn't even know they were missing, but then I noticed gaps between some of the canisters. I counted eighty-two such gaps. I am afraid Mr. Alexander knew precisely what he was doing. He chose films of some of my most affluent patients, including the wives of many prominent local figures."

I said, "Describe a typical one of these movies."

"Most of the footage consists of the initial meeting between the patient and me, followed by preparations for the surgery—me administering anesthesia, the patient falling asleep. The films were shot in such a way as to document the process and show it was consensual at every step along the way. Nobody was coerced into having the surgery."

"Did the patients know you were filming them?" I asked.

"God, no," he said. "This was for my protection. I must take steps to guarantee my safety. I am sure you gentlemen understand. *So.* What do you fellows say to my business proposition?"

"That's not good enough, Doc," said Roscoe.

"Okay. If you insist, I'll pay you more," said Pfalzgraf. "What do you think is a fair—"

"This isn't about the money or your movies," I said. "Three people ended up in the morgue before they should have. We're going to find out who put them there and why."

Roscoe rested his elbows on the marble table, clasped his fingers together, and stared skeptically at the doctor. "Tell me, Doc. What was to stop you from getting behind the wheel of her Cadillac and running her over? Hell, we're all human. If my wife had a mattress tied to her back the way yours apparently did, I'd probably turn her into mashed potatoes with my car."

Pfalzgraf shook his head and said, "I loved her with every little atom of my heart, Officer Lund, and I would never do something so horrible to her. When I found out how she died, I felt the same terrible sense of loss that I did when I lost my dear, beloved Nellie. Now that Helen is gone, I plan to retire, and all I want is my daughter, my films, and my friendships so I can leave this business and spend my remaining years living in peace and quiet."

I said, "Why did you file that complaint against Dr. Wooley?"

"He was inept, and his surgeries were killing his patients," said the doctor. He looked at Roscoe. "You're a policeman, Officer Lund. I suggest you ask someone in the missing persons bureau to let you look at the files of all the young ladies who've gone missing in the state of Utah over the past ten years. I am certain at least half of them were victims of Wooley's dreadful work."

"Do you know a man named Sam Louis?" I asked.

His eyes wandered a moment as he considered the question, but they returned my way as he shook his head. "No. I do not know anybody by that name. I have an uncanny memory for names."

Roscoe scowled, with arms folded. "Never met him? Never heard of him?"

"No. I have not. I am sorry, Officer Lund."

My behind was getting uncomfortable on this marble bench, and I squirmed to find a better position. "I can't say I approve of this line of work you're in, Doctor."

"Mr. Oveson," he said, turning up his palms, "I've gotten where I am today by being the very best at what I do. The top obstetricians across the country send their patients to me for my surgeries. I get telegrams from women pleading with me not to leave on trips abroad so that they won't have to wait for an operation. I have performed surgeries on patients from as far away as Japan and Austria. The daughter of one of the vice presidents of the United States paid me to travel to Washington, D.C., to provide my services. These women trust me, because they know I am the ablest practitioner in America. Maybe the world." He leaned forward to get closer to me, so he could speak low. "Ask yourself this, Mr. Oveson. What if someone you loved insisted on having one of these surgeries and refused to tell you she was going to do it? Who would you want to be her physician? Me? Or a Dr. Everett Wooley?"

A twig snapped. Roscoe and I turned to see Anna Pfalzgraf standing nearby, smiling at us. Rays of sunlight broke through the tree branches above her and illuminated her face and shoulders. There was something ethereal about her in that turquoise dress and matching cloche hat.

"Hello, gentlemen. I remember you," she said. She looked at Pfalzgraf. "Father, the fellow from the travel agency telephoned. He wishes to finalize the dates of our trip to Germany with you."

"I'll be along shortly, my dear," said Pfalzgraf.

She gave us a tiny wave, turned, and walked back in the direction of the mansion. Roscoe and I turned around at the same time and faced the doctor.

"When are you leaving?" I asked.

"Next week," he said.

"I see. Do you have relatives in Germany?"

He nodded. "A brother. He's a dentist. We received a rather large inheritance some years ago, and he used his share to purchase a castle. Anna and I are going to stay there for a month. I thought it would do Anna good to get away from here. Helen's murder hit her hard—harder than anybody else. Harder than me, even."

I held out my hand, and he shook it. This time, Roscoe extended his as well. The doctor smiled, and they clasped hands together and shook rigorously.

"I hope you find Helen's killer," he said, rising to his feet. He leaned on his cane and started on a slow walk toward his mansion. Partway up the path, he half-turned to us. "Remember—if you deliver those films to me, I shall be true to my word and present each of you with a check for fifty thousand dollars. On top of the ten-thousand-dollar reward you've already received, Mr. Oveson, you may very well be able to afford a house in this part of the city."

He hobbled away toward his daughter, waiting in the sun.

Twenty

SEE ME AT ONCE.

I stared at that note on my desk. Dread filled me on my brief journey from my office to Cannon's office, akin to a man on his final walk from a jail cell to the gallows. I knew why he wanted to see me, although how he found out was beyond me. I had been performing most of my investigation after hours and never discussed it with my co-workers. Still, that writing on the paper told me he was angry and knew exactly what I was doing. His door was ajar, so I knocked gently and stepped inside under the withering stares of the duo I expected to find inside—Cannon and Sykes—in their usual spots. I loosened my necktie as I entered and let my shoulders slump, a sign of humility.

"Come in, Oveson," said Sykes. "Please, close the door behind you."

I did as asked. Gone was Cannon's trademark smile, replaced by one of the surliest frowns I'd ever witnessed. I pinched my pants at the thighs and raised them slightly as I planted my rear in the chair.

Cannon was silent. If it weren't for the slight movements of his chest rising up and down from breathing, I would probably have begun to wonder whether he had passed away in his favorite place. His fingers were clasped together, and both of his index fingers touched his lips. The look on his face spelled ferocity, and his neck had turned red the way it did when he was exceptionally enraged.

"I found a note out on my desk," I said. "Did you wish to see me, sir?"

"I did." He pushed a piece of paper across his desk, with his favorite tortoiseshell fountain pen lying across it. "Sign this if you want to keep your job."

I craned my neck to see a the typewriting on the paper, packed with as much legalese and boilerplate as one can squeeze onto a single piece of paper and still have room for a signature line at the bottom.

"What's that?" I asked.

"It's an oath, stating you'll obey the orders of your superiors and carry them out to the best of your abilities, or you'll lose your job. I've decided to make all of my men sign one, starting with you."

"What if I don't—"

"I'll fire you. Look, I know you paid a visit to Dr. Pfalzgraf yesterday. There's no point in denying it."

"If you'll give me two minutes to explain, sir, I'm convinced that—"

He smacked his palm against the desk, and the sound echoed across his office like a firecracker. "Did I ask you what you think?"

"No."

Rage glowed in his eyes. "I know you've been investigating that case. Your actions are an embarrassment to this office and to me personally. I've warned you, Oveson . . . Didn't I warn him, Sykes?"

"You gave him ample warning," said Sykes, glowering at me.

"Darn right," said Cannon. "This case has been a political hot potato from the get-go. If it's reopened, I can guarantee you Blackham is going to use it against me for his campaign. Would you say so, Sykes?"

"Utterly."

Cannon showed his gratitude to Sykes with an exaggerated nod. "You found Helen Pfalzgraf's killer, Oveson. Notice I'm giving you full credit, because I believe in giving credit where credit is due. The public feels safe once again. With this case solved and put to bed, my second term will be handed to me in November. Now you're getting funny ideas about flushing all that down the toilet. Why? What the heck are you thinking? Let me ask you something, Oveson. In the scheme of things, do you think it matters the world is short a chiseler and a nympho? Do you really lose sleep at night wondering about all this? I sure as frick don't."

He was quiet for a moment, studying my face, perhaps waiting for me to say something. Sitting there in stunned silence, I wondered how this man, who shared my faith, could be so callous and indifferent. I thought it wise to stay quiet.

He took a deep breath. "Now, I think you'll find I'm a forgiving man, Oveson. I'm willing to give you one last chance."

He pushed the paper and fountain pen forward. "Sign at the bottom. I'll sign as a witness, and Sykes here will notarize it. By the way, I've booked you for a noon-hour speaking engagement at the salt sellers convention at the Hotel Utah. I'd like you to talk about why Utah is the perfect place to do business from a law-and-order standpoint. Emphasize the low crime rate, the cleanliness of our city, the charm of our natural scenery, that sorta stuff. You'll get a free chicken lunch out of the deal."

I looked at the paper, at Sykes, at Cannon. "No."

Cannon didn't hesitate. "You're fired, Oveson."

Those words, harsh as they were, filled me with relief bordering on euphoria, as if a pair of hands strangling me had just let go.

I exited Cannon's office, and this time there were no parting shots about what a "stand-up guy" I was.

Roscoe devoured a hamburger later that day at Grant's Luncheonette, a busy eatery on the first floor of W. T. Grant Co. Grant's, as the locals called it, was a popular department store on Main where you could buy just about everything, from console radios to family silverware sets to cheap men's suits. Roscoe hummed contentedly while he ate, stopping to glance at me and wonder why I had no appetite. He took another enormous bite—probably a fourth of the burger at once—sending ketchup, pieces of lettuce and onion, and sesame seeds raining down on the plate, next to a pile of french-fried potatoes. Before he even swallowed all the food in his mouth, and there was a lot of it, he washed it down with piping hot coffee, drinking it as fast as I might down a glass of lemonade on a hot day.

I ordered a banana split, but what on earth was I thinking? My appetite had flown south, along with my job, and there was no way I was going to consume that mountain of banana, three flavors of ice cream, topped with a whipped cream Matterhorn, crushed nuts, and a maraschino cherry. Not even a Grant's banana split—the best banana split in the Intermountain West, possibly the best banana split on this side of the Mississippi—held much appeal for me at that particular moment.

Roscoe lifted a pad of paper off the seat next to him, slapped it on the table, near his plate, and scanned his notes. "I've placed telephone calls to the widows of Considine and Alexander. Neither knew a thing about Pfalzgraf's home movies. Who knows if Alexander even had them? It's possible Helen Pfalzgraf held on to them for safekeeping."

Roscoe bit into his hamburger again, raised his head, and saw that I was preoccupied with other matters.

"Did you call him a bastard to his face?" asked Roscoe, his mouth full of food. "Or better yet, a good-for-nothing yellow sonofabitch?"

I smirked. "I don't talk that way to anybody."

"What a waste," he said, lifting his coffee mug high so the waitress would give him a refill. She came over and topped it off. Roscoe winked and said, "You're getting an extralarge tip, sweetie."

The young waitress, blond and no more than twenty, blushed and giggled on her way back to the kitchen.

Roscoe sipped coffee and said, "So what's next?"

"I have to figure out a way to tell my wife," I said, poking the vanilla-ice-cream-saturated banana from side to side with my fork. "I'm worried about how she's going to take it."

"You think she'll flip her lid?"

"That's the thing," I said. "I know she'll be sweet about it. She'll remind me she's getting a teacher's salary and everything will be fine. Then she'll probably hug me."

"That doesn't sound so bad," said Roscoe.

"Yeah, but I'll be ashamed of myself," I said. "And my brothers . . . Oh, good heavens, my brothers."

Roscoe pushed his picked-over plate aside and reached for his can of smoking tobacco. It took him less than thirty seconds to roll a cigarette. He slipped the end between his lips and lit the tip; it crackled orange. He blew smoke at the ceiling. "Tell you what, Art, I'll have a word with Ballard. I bet you'll be working out of Public Safety this time Monday morning."

Seeing my hands tremble, Roscoe grimaced as he flipped ash into a glass ashtray. "You alright?"

"Scared," I said. "Petrified, if you really want to know. What if this is it? What if I turn out to be one of those fellas I read about in the newspaper who can't ever find work again? There was a story just the other day in the *Telegram* about a man in Washington state who—"

I stopped. The words seemed too grim to speak.

"Who what?"

I slid my dish away and sighed. "He couldn't find work, and he shot his whole family. Then he turned his shotgun on himself and—"

"Knock it off, Art," said Roscoe. "Things aren't as bad as all that. Look at it this way: Seymour Considine is in a pine box on a train heading to Asbury Park, New Jersey, where his widow is waiting to identify his remains. Sure, he was a prick, but getting carved up like that and then that being the last thing you ever experience in your life . . . Shit almighty. Now there's someone I feel sorry for. But you, Art, you've got a daughter, a son, and a wife who all love you. Plus, you've got all that reward dough from Pfalzgraf. Ten G's. That should hold you over for a little while."

"I gave it to my mother," I said, blinking wearily at him.

He reared his head back. "Huh?"

"I figured she needed it more than I did."

"Hmm." His eyebrows shot up. "Well, you know what they say about one good deed. Maybe she'll divvy it up with you. Point is, Art, there's no way you're gonna end up like that cocksucker in Washington. Christ, I bet you'll live to be an old geezer, ass parked on a rocking chair on a front porch somewhere, bird nests in your beard, watching your great-grandkids running around the yard and playing in the sprinklers. You'll see."

I smiled at him. "That's awfully nice of you to say."

He stubbed out his cigarette in the ashtray, and the weight of my stare got to him. He looked at me and said, "What?"

"How come you changed your mind?"

"What do you mean?"

"The other night, at the Great Salt Lake, you said you didn't want to get mixed up in this," I said. "I was just wondering. Why the change of heart?"

He shrugged his shoulders and began twirling a bottle of Heinz ketchup. "You wouldn't understand."

"Try me."

He shook his head and kept his focus on that ketchup bottle. "Before I became a cop, I used to be a strikebreaker, on the payroll of a company called Donovan and Sons. I was hired muscle."

He leaned back against the booth seat and finally made eye contact with me. "Eleven years ago—1919, it was—me and a bunch of my pals were hired by the lumber bosses up in Centralia, Washington. Centralia was a crazy place in them days. The radicals in the IWW had their guys up there, stirring the pot, calling on lumber workers to join the One Big Union. When I jumped off the train in Centralia, I was like a kid in a candy store. All them labor agitators just waiting to be drubbed. And I was the one gonna do most of the drubbing."

He sipped coffee and looked at the cash register. "It was the first anniversary of Armistice Day, and we got to drinking—me and my buddies, along with some rowdies from the American Legion. Fuck, we were getting blotto and we wanted blood. All hell broke loose in Centralia. Guys fighting, breaking glass, lighting shit on fire, shooting guns. There was supposed to be a big parade in town, but it got cut short. Place was a real mess. Brawls went on for hours. It got to be nighttime, and a bunch of us gathered outside the IWW hall and beat the shit out of anyone we thought was a Red. One of the radical lumberjacks was a fella named Wesley Everest. A real kook. He still wore his army uniform issued to him when he was a doughboy in the war. We chased his ass down, and the crazy bastard tried to ford the Skookumchuck. He got panicky out in the middle of the river when he saw us coming, so he took out a gun and shot and killed a Legion fella. I don't think he meant to do it.

He was scared. Scared as hell. Shit, any of us'd be if we were in his shoes. The sheriff showed up in time and hauled Everest to jail, but the strikebreakers and Legion boys were so crazy drunk we took the law into our own hands. We broke into the jail and pulled Everest out of his cell. We drove him way out to a bridge that crossed the Chehalis. He was bawling like a baby, and I think he shit his britches. The bunch of us ended up beating him within an inch of his life, until he screamed like a woman and begged us to put him out of his misery. Then we put a rope around his neck and hanged him from the bridge. Right there on the spot."

Roscoe stared down at the table, scratched his chin, and bit his lower lip. "At the time, I thought it was funny—but something happened I didn't expect."

"What?"

"A few days later, I woke up in the middle of the night to the sound of Wesley Everest screaming. And that started happening every night. Every fuckin' night, without fail. The crazy thing is, the screaming isn't in my mind, either. It's as if the sonofabitch is right there in the room next to me, screaming the way he did when we beat him. Eleven years of this. Wesley Everest screams and I sit up in bed, sweating, shaking, and I can't go back to sleep. Hell, I don't want to go back to sleep after hearing that sound."

His words got to me. At that point in my life, I still had no idea men and women were capable of doing such things to each other. These depths of depravity were terra incognita for me. He gulped down the rest of his coffee and slammed his cup on the table. I thought he wanted me to say something, but how could I respond? What could I possibly say? Then I realized that he probably didn't want me to say a word. Someone who'd listen—that's what he wanted.

He said, "I keep thinking that if I do something to make things right, maybe that prick will quit screaming in my ear every night."

He chuckled and stuck a toothpick in his mouth, counting out coins to pay for his hamburger. "I guess you could say I changed my mind for selfish reasons," he said. "All the fuck I want is a good night's sleep."

I gave him a minute to spread out his money on the table, and then I said, "Clara wants you to come to dinner at our house sometime. You and . . ." I hesitated. "Whoever it is you live with."

He laughed as that toothpick danced on his lip. "Tell her I said thanks. Maybe I'll take you up on it some other time."

"Fair enough."

He plunked a few extra coins on the table. "I'll cover yours, Art. This one time. C'mon, let's drift. This Pfalzgraf case isn't going to solve itself."

I don't know why, but Roscoe's violent tale soothed me like nothing else that morning.

Twenty-one

The tray of ham reached my plate, and I nailed a slice with the carving fork. Dinnertime at the Oveson homestead in American Fork, following prayers, kicked off with food making the rounds as voices overlapped with voices. Silverware clanked, and food commentary flared up. I glanced over my shoulder at the children's table, and Sarah Jane took a break from giggling with her cousins to give me a wave. She wasn't at the age where I embarrassed her yet. I waved my fork back at her and gave her a little smile. Hi bobbed up and down in his high chair, sticking peas and tiny pieces of ham in his mouth with his fist.

Sitting at the table, poking at my food with my fork, I was preoccupied with my experiences of the past few days: telling Clara I lost my job (as expected, she hugged me and told me everything would be alright); making fruitless phone calls from my home and chasing down a bunch of dead-end clues with Roscoe; visiting the employment agency in search of something even vaguely resembling law enforcement work, only to be told there were no jobs to be found. I left that grim place Friday afternoon feeling worse than ever. On

Saturday, Roscoe telephoned me at home to tell me he was going to follow up on a lead in the Pfalzgraf case. He didn't want to say anything over the telephone because of party lines, but he'd call me soon and tell me whether it panned out.

Grant broke my train of thought when he leaned over his plate, eyes on me. "There's an opening in my office."

I was chewing potatoes au gratin and washed them down with gulps of milk. Clara shot me a nervous look, fearing I'd start a quarrel with Grant. I wiped off my milk mustache and said, "Oh yeah? Do tell. What is it?"

"Dispatcher," he said. "Now hear me out, little brother. Everybody who starts out at the PPD"—PPD meant Provo Police Department—"begins at dispatch. You'll love it because there are plenty of big changes in store. I read in the latest issue of *Police Gazette* that the Chicago police are already talking about installing two-way radios in their patrol cars. Can you imagine that? It won't be long before they make it out here and we can finally get rid of those annoying call boxes. When that happens, being a dispatcher is going to be the most thrilling job on the force."

I pierced a pearl onion with a prong of my fork. "Dispatch, huh?"

He pursed his lips and nodded. "You have to start somewhere. Dispatch is where I started. If it was good enough for me, I'm sure it's good enough for you."

"I already worked dispatch for two years," I said. "Remember? All those promises of a beat never went anywhere."

"No one's forcing you to take it, kid," he said. "But if I was in your shoes, the last thing I'd want is my wife bringing home the bacon."

Grant's wife, Bess, chimed in. "You two can sell your house in Salt Lake and move to Provo. It's so much nicer down here. There's less crime, less auto traffic, and there aren't as many vagrants. And fewer Mexicans!" She closed her eyes and chuckled merrily, then turned serious. "I don't see why anybody would want to live in Salt Lake when Provo is so much cleaner."

Clara dipped her head, but her eyes still watched my every move.

Mom tried to change the subject. "Frank has his work cut out for him. Don't you, Frank?"

Frank smacked his tongue along his molars. "It's this darn Hoover visit. It's still three months away, but there are a thousand tiny details we have to work out with the Secret Service Division, the municipal people, and the president's press secretary."

One of Frank's sons sitting at the children's table said, "Do we get to meet President Hoover, Pop?"

Frank rocked his head back and forth vigorously. "Anybody in this family who wants to meet President Hoover will get the chance. And if you all want, you can have your picture taken with him. A bunch of us Bureau fellows will be posing with him in the rotunda of the state capitol."

Bess ignored Frank and all the chatter about Herbert Hoover. "You'll love it here. It's a much nicer place to raise a family. You could buy a bungalow up the street. That way, we'd all live closer together. Clara, we could trade recipes."

Clara mustered a smile and a slow nod but went back to watching me—nervous that Grant was prodding me toward a fight.

"How say you, Art?" asked Grant. "Might we expect you at the station tomorrow?"

At that moment, Dad's platitudes raced through my mind and prevented me from saying something I knew I'd regret. *Choose your battles carefully. This isn't the time or place. Don't let your foes pick your fights for you.*

Dad also had what he called "the twenty-four-hour rule." The idea is, when you feel yourself getting steamed, wait twenty-four hours before expressing your outrage. If in twenty-four hours the anger is still simmering, then say what is on your mind, but not before.

I opened my mouth to speak, but Clara beat me to it.

"We have no desire to move to Provo. Salt Lake is perfectly safe. The auto traffic isn't too congested. Sure, we have vagrants, but every town does. We're in a depression, even though President Hoover is pretending we aren't. Most of the Mexicans I know are decent people, just like the rest of us. All things considered, I think we'll stay in Salt Lake City. Don't you agree, Art?"

"Yeah. I agree."

We smiled lovingly at each other. The room fell silent after that. Her words seemed to have killed the conversation, at least until Mom said, "Who wants some pie?"

When we walked in the door, with me carrying my sleeping son in my arms, the telephone was ringing. I handed the boy to Clara, and Sarah Jane shot past me, to turn on the radio. I picked up the candlestick telephone and raised the receiver to my ear and transmitter to my mouth. "Hello."

"Art. Buddy here."

"Buddy!" I said, smiling. "I didn't see you in church this morning. How's every little thing?"

"Roscoe Lund has been shot. He may not make it through the night."

I dropped the telephone on the floor in shock. Clara entered the room. "I just put him to bed, so we can all listen . . . Art. Are you OK?"

"It's Roscoe," I said. "He's in the hospital. He might . . . He might . . ."

"Go," said Clara. "I'll look after the kids. You go as fast as you can."

Moments later, I was racing up the steep Avenue roads as quickly as my car would take me, sending up clouds of dust in neighborhoods of bungalows and streets with high trees. As I rounded a corner, the LDS Hospital came into view.

The five-story building sat high on a hill, at the corner of Eighth Avenue and C Street, overlooking the valley. When construction was completed twenty-five years ago, it was called the Dr. W. H. Groves LDS Hospital, after the wealthy English dentist who bequeathed the money to build it. That was too much of a mouthful, and the locals knocked the dentist's name off and just called it the LDS Hospital. Behind the building was a dirt patch where drivers parked their autos in long rows. I skidded to a halt, shut off my car, and ran so fast to the hospital doors my Stetson fell off my head and I had to stop and pick it up. I pushed through the swinging glass and steel doors into the lobby, which—thankfully—wasn't very full.

"May I help you?" said a kind-faced woman in her fifties.

I leaned against the counter, trying to catch my breath, and managed to say, "Roscoe Lund. What room is he in?"

She checked a typewritten list in front of her. "Emergency care. This floor. Room one-oh-eight. Go straight back down this hall and turn right."

I walked fast down the hall, swerving around gurneys and medical personnel dressed in white. I passed under a big sign with red block lettering that read EMERGENCY CARE. Room 108—eight rooms away—couldn't come fast enough.

A police officer, uniformed and armed, stood guard at the door. Inside, two other policemen in black stood on either side of the bed as a doctor in a white coat jotted notes on sheets of paper attacked to a clipboard. Beside him, a nurse in a cap and white dress looked over his shoulder at his notations. Near the window, Detective Buddy Hawkins leaned against the wall, arms folded, watching the doctor's every move. Over in a corner, Detective Wit Dunaway sat in a chair, his right leg propped up on his left knee. When Hawkins saw me walk in, he moved around the foot of the bed, coming toward me.

Roscoe's brawny body was lying on the hospital bed, eyes closed, head bandaged, upper body elevated. Gauze covered his chest and his left upper arm and shoulder. Most of his facial color was gone, and his lips appeared parched. The urge to weep was great, but I fought it.

"I'll need a few of you to clear out," said the doctor, a middle-aged man with thinning brown hair and a lean face. "We need space in here."

Buddy motioned for me to follow him out into the hall.

"What happened to him?" I asked.

"He was leaving the Grand Central market on Ninth and Main, about midnight last night. End of his shift. The parking lot was mostly empty, and an auto rolled up out of the darkness and opened fire. Luckily, a store clerk acted fast and called the hospital. The ambulance boys brought Lund in conscious. Doc had to sedate him to remove the bullets."

"How many times was he shot?"

"Dr. Morrison said three times, although he only had to remove two bullets. One of them apparently grazed his head. He's lucky it didn't enter his skull. He was hit in two other places—the left bicep and chest, up near his left shoulder, so it missed his lungs and heart."

"Why didn't someone call me last night?" I asked.

"The doctor was operating on Roscoe through the night," Buddy said. "Wit and I have been going nonstop since early this morning, chasing down leads. We don't have much to go on. Tire tracks, and not very good ones at that. I wasn't even going to call you, because I heard Cannon fired you. Sorry to hear about that. Tough break, Art. Then earlier today, Roscoe regained consciousness briefly and started calling out your name."

"My name?"

"Over and over. 'Where's Art? I need him.' I figured I'd better call you and see if you knew anything about this."

"I don't have the faintest idea."

Buddy's expression turned thoughtful, as if he were mulling over something meaningful. "If you were to cooperate with this investigation, Art, I could put in a good word with my superiors. I can't promise anything, but maybe if there were an entry-level opening in the department . . ."

"What do you want to know?"

"That night at the Great Salt Lake, when we found Considine's body. You and Roscoe were talking about something. What was it?"

I dodged the question with one of my own. "Is Roscoe going to make it?"

Buddy shrugged. "Doc says a lot depends on how he fares tonight. He lost quite a bit of blood between the time he was shot and when the ambulance boys wheeled him in here. He's had several transfusions, and now they're just waiting to see if it takes. All we can do now is wait and see." Buddy's eyes widened. "One other thing. When Roscoe first came in, he said he didn't get a good look at the driver's face, but he's pretty sure he shot him in the left hand."

"Oh yeah?" I said. "The left hand, huh?"

Buddy nodded. "Apparently, the driver slowed and shot Roscoe with a pistol in his right hand. While he was doing this, he kept his left hand braced against the outside of his car door to support himself. Before Roscoe got put under with anesthetic, he said he fired a round and thought the bullet passed through the shooter's hand and lodged in the car door."

I watched the doctor lift Roscoe's eyelid, click on a small flashlight, and check both eyes. He shut off and pocketed the flashlight and scribbled on Roscoe's chart. The motionless Roscoe reminded me of a dead man, just lying there in that hospital bed, hardly even breathing.

"You didn't answer my question," said Buddy.

"What question?"

"That night at the Great Salt Lake, when we found Considine's body, what were you two talking about?"

"It was personal," I said. "I don't want to share it just yet."

"You want to know what I think?" asked Buddy. I watched him and waited. "This shooting outside of Grand Central wasn't random. Somebody targeted Roscoe. My hunch is that it has to do with whatever it was that brought you out to the Great Salt Lake that night. I want some answers, Art. You and I have known each other a long time, but that won't stop me from arresting you if I have to. And then you can kiss any prospects of a police job good-bye."

He waited for a reply, staring intently at me. I just blinked in the direction of Roscoe, in that cold room, without any family or friends there to support him. I felt a deep sorrow in my heart. I wanted to be there for him right then, but with all of those police around, I knew I had no choice but to leave.

Buddy finally shook his head and sighed. "Have it your way, for now. You can either put all your cards on the table with me, Art, or I'll get to the bottom of all this on my own. One way or another, I'll find what I'm looking for."

He reached in his pocket, took out a key chain holding four dangling keys, and handed it to me. "When Roscoe came to, and started calling your name, the last thing he said before he went back under is he asked if you would stop by his apartment and feed his cat, Barney. He named you specifically. The black door key will do the trick. His place is on the corner of Eighth East and Second South."

I nodded and stuffed the keys in my coat pocket. He said, "If you change your mind and want to help me out, Art, I'd look upon your actions very favorably."

We shook hands. "Thanks for calling me, Buddy. I'll take your offer into consideration."

As I was heading away, past nurses and patients in wheelchairs and the sick on gurneys, I heard him say, "Don't take too long to think it over."

In the early morning hours, I pulled up to the curb in front of a two-story brick apartment building at the northwest corner of 800 East and 200 South. Inside, at the foot of a staircase, I came across four mailboxes. One—apartment 201—had Roscoe's name taped to it. I ran up the flight of stairs to 201, opened the door, and switched lights on. The place was small and cluttered, with an electric light globe dangling from a cord in the ceiling. The front room had a small matching couch and armchair. Stacks of magazines were everywhere. Back issues of *The National Police Gazette* and *National Geographic, Modern Radio* and *Scribner's, Thrilling Detective* and *Real Western Tales.* An orange tabby came trotting out of the bedroom. He leaped onto the couch and got on the armrest, arching his back for me to pet him. I reached over and ran my hand across his soft fur, and he purred loudly and meowed at me.

"You must be Barney. Dinner's coming."

I switched on a light in the kitchen—which was really a tiny kitchenette with turquoise and white tiles, a modern gas stove, an icebox, and cabinet doors with glass windows. I searched the cupboards for Barney's food. There wasn't much in there: a few clean cups and plates, a sugar bowl, a box of cookies, a can of soup, and a can of tuna fish in oil. I came upon a blue box of Purr-Fect Cat Food with a grinning cartoon cat on the front. I poured some in Barney's dish, and he came running to it and began eating voraciously, like a starving cat. I found a bottle of milk in the icebox, uncapped and sniffed it (alright), and poured some in the next bowl over for Barney.

"Bon appétit."

I was about to shut off the lights and leave Roscoe's apartment when I spotted what appeared to be a scrapbook on a little table next to the couch. I sat down on the couch, reached for the book, and opened it. The first photo was an oval-shaped picture of a boy who looked like Roscoe standing beside a pretty woman in one of those big, puffy, turn-of-the-century Gibson Girl dresses. Pages rattled as I turned them. Roscoe as a teenager in front of a boarding-house. Roscoe standing beside a biplane with an aviator hat and goggles. Roscoe in his doughboy uniform. Roscoe in a Stetson and three-piece suit, standing with four other men dressed similarly, wearing a gold star on his chest. A yellowing certificate with a gold seal from Donovan & Sons of Denver, Colorado. *This certifies that Roscoe Henry Lund has attained the rank of detective for the firm of Randolph Donovan & Sons in the year* . . . In pen someone had written *1909* on the certificate.

The cat pounced in my lap, licking his chops. That was my cue to put the scrapbook away, despite my burning curiosity to learn more about Roscoe. I closed it and placed it on the table where I found it. I petted the cat awhile, and he kept pressing his head and arched back against me.

"You must be starving," I said to him, as if he understood my words. I let out a slight chuckle, a forlorn laugh if ever there was one. "Hey, want some tuna?"

Barney chased me into the kitchen, and I found a can opener and opened the lonely can of tuna, then scooped flakes into Barney's bowl with a fork. Barney went to work on the tuna, loving every morsel. I crouched and petted him while he ate.

"I must've been crazy, thinking I could tackle this mess," I said to Barney. "It's bigger than me. If all those deputies and police working on the case couldn't crack it, what made me think I could? Maybe I'll take that dispatcher job in Provo. Who knows? I might end up getting promoted to patrolman. Better than nothing. Wouldn't you agree, Barney?" I shook my head and sighed. "If you think this town is dull, wait till you see Provo. Grass growing is the most exciting thing going on there."

I picked the can of tuna up off the counter. "Maybe I can find some tinfoil to cover the rest . . ."

That is when it hit me. I ran my fingers over the jagged edge of the can and thought of those cans that stored film reels. "It's a can."

The words that Scotty Alexander spoke at Keeley's ice cream parlor echoed in my head. *I keep my cans in the hurricane.*

It was too late at night to act on my hunch. It would have to wait until morning.

Monday bright and early, I arrived at the Newhouse Hotel, room 805, a little too late.

Intermountain Mining Speculators was no more.

I jimmied the lock with my set of picks and made my way inside. The place was deserted. Movers had carted out all of the office furniture and filing cabinets. All that remained was crumpled pieces of paper littered on the floor and a disconnected candlestick telephone sitting on a solitary chair.

I had another idea. Nearby, the federal building on Main housed an office of the Department of the Interior, which kept records on Utah mines, including lists of deed holders. Interior maintained a sizable presence in Utah, monitoring fish and wildlife, overseeing water and mineral rights, and conducting public land transfers. They took up a big chunk of the first floor of the federal building.

I walked down the linoleum halls, stopping at double doors with UNITED STATES DEPARTMENT OF THE INTERIOR on the frosted glass. I entered to find a rawboned fellow with hair parted in the center and a prominent Adam's apple at the front desk.

"Welcome to the Department of the Interior," he said with a toothy grin. "May I help you?"

I closed the door and surveyed the plush office with wood paneling and framed photographs of scenic Utah places. The place felt like the inside of an icebox. They kept the air conditioner blasting frigid winds, despite chilly weather outside.

"Thank you," I said. "I'm looking for a mine. How do you keep them cataloged?"

"By reference number, by county, by type, and by status—active versus inactive," he said. He heard my sigh and noticed my look of discouragement.

"No site names?" I asked.

"I might be able to help you," he said, holding his hand to his chest in a slightly prissy manner. "Was there a particular mine you were looking for?"

"Yeah. It may—or may not—be called Hurricane."

"Right off the top of my head I know that we have two Hurricanes in Utah, one in Daggett County and one in Summit." He closed his eyes tightly, as if deep in thought. "The Daggett mine is copper and operational. It's owned by the Great West Mining Company, which is headquartered in San Francisco. The Summit County mine was classified as inactive, but someone purchased it a few years ago, I believe. A private individual. I'm not as good with names, I'm afraid."

"C. W. Alexander?"

"I don't know. I'd have to check. The mine was mixed mineral—zinc, gold, silver, lead, and, uh, possibly copper."

"How on earth do you remember all this stuff?"

He let out a high-pitched giggle, tilted forward, and whispered, "That's my job. Be right back."

I waited, pacing and whistling. A beautiful framed photograph of Arches National Monument caught my eye—a giant sandstone fin jutting out of the desert floor, taken with color film that turned the sky into a saturated blue and brought out the splashes of reds and oranges in the rocks.

The clerk returned with a red leather-bound book and placed it on the desk near his typewriter. He opened it and licked his fingers as he turned pages. "Records of land transfer," he said in response to my quizzical stare. "Here we go. It says here the Hurricane Number Eight was sold in 1925—Monday, August the tenth, to be exact—to a Mister Clyde W. Alexander. The address is given as the Newhouse Building here in town. He purchased the mine from Tintic Enterprises for the sum of fifteen thousand dollars."

"So it wasn't cheap."

He looked at me and shrug-tilted his head. "I'm guessing it probably still had a lot of deposits. There's also a mill on the site, which probably added to the cost."

"Does that give the exact location?" I asked.

He looked down and ran his finger along a list of pencil notations. "It gives longitude and latitude coordinates." He reached behind his desk and opened another hardcover book. "When in doubt, consult with the atlas. It should help."

He paid close attention to the atlas for a minute, then jotted on a pad of paper, tore off the sheet, and handed it to me. Directions: how to get to the Hurricane mine from the Salt Lake Valley.

"I don't know how to thank you," I said. "You've been so helpful."

"Please," he said, blushing and wiggling a few fingers. "This is my job. It's what I get paid for. Have a pleasant day, sir."

"You, too. Thanks again," I said, taking the piece of paper with me.

Twenty-two

I came upon the mill late in the morning. The rusted-out building—brown streaks on gray, with broken windows—had been built into the side of a pine-tree-covered peak, and now that most of the snow had melted, the first weeds were poking out of the earth. *Give it till July,* I thought, *and tall grass will overrun this place.*

A newspaper headline stared up at me from the passenger seat. SALT LAKE POLICEMAN CAUGHT IN MIDNIGHT AMBUSH. Subhead: OFFICER IN CRITICAL CONDITION FOLLOWING MYSTERY SHOOTING. Earlier in the morning, I'd visited Roscoe in the hospital, but he was sleeping when I arrived, and I didn't want to wake him. The doctor assured me Roscoe was still in critical condition. I left for the ninety-minute drive to the mine, stopping at Roscoe's apartment to feed Barney on the way.

At the Hurricane, I parked my car, locked the doors, and started up a path, sizing up the neglected place. I had on my Stetson, held a flashlight in my right hand, and carried a pair of long, coiled ropes draped over my left elbow. I explored the mill grounds, taking a guess at the construction date based on its corrugated metal siding and brittle girders. I thought 1890s but couldn't be sure.

A pair of abandoned water tanks at the top of the hill overlooked the desolate structure. I peeked through an opening in the wall, and it looked to me as though the furnace and boiler, both tipped over in the mud, had become chipmunk dwellings. I continued up a stony embankment, my feet slipping occasionally on the way, until I reached a set of corroded ore-car tracks that dipped into a ravine. I followed them all the way to the black, rectangular mine entrance, framed by ancient timber.

I passed a chunk of wood as tall as me that had a tin sign nailed to it with letters so bold you could not possibly miss them. DANGER: UNSAFE MINE—STAY OUT, STAY ALIVE!

I arrived at the opening in the side of the mountain. More signs: DO NOT ENTER. BEWARE DEEP SHAFTS. DANGER: CAVING GROUND. Finally: ENTRANCE PROHIBITED. I got the picture—but not enough to stop me from going on this fool's errand.

Time to switch on the flashlight. The beam danced around in the mine, illuminating the craggy rounded walls. I was deep inside now, feeling uneasy about the daylight diminishing with each step I took.

I kept going, driven by an inner compulsion I did not understand, passing under heavy beams and soon rounding a corner. I switched off my flashlight for a moment and, just as I suspected, stood in total blackness. I could not see my hand in front of my face, and the only thing I could hear was my breathing.

I turned the flashlight back on and continued.

Deeper . . . deeper . . . deeper . . .

Following the rails . . . taking each step carefully . . .

It was not my imagination. The ceiling was getting lower. The walls were closing in. I stopped, still as a statue in the stale air, sensing movement above. Tipping the ray of the battery-powered light upward, I felt my worst phobia flare up as I surveyed a thousand furry black pods dangling from the ceiling. I lowered my flashlight, and my heart sputtered like an airplane engine.

"Oh no," I whispered to myself, my body shaking. "*Bats.* What am I going to do? OK—alright—OK. Take a deep breath, Oveson. They don't like you any more than you like them."

It took every bit of strength in me to press on into the bowels of the earth.

I maneuvered my feet as stealthily as I could. At one point, my shoe crunched glass. Somebody had busted a soda pop bottle on the tracks. I avoided aiming the flashlight at the ceiling, yet I could still sense bats quivering over my head.

The tunnel widened dramatically into a cavernous stope where all of the ore had been extracted to carve out an area with cathedral-high ceilings. In the center of the room, water dripped from the ceiling into a crystal pool. The air smelled and tasted bitter, and I began to worry about what was in it. I took off my Stetson, reached in my pocket, pulled out a cloth face mask, put it over my nose and mouth, and secured it in place by pulling its rubber strap over and behind my head. I put my Stetson back on.

I now faced a trio of drifts, each a possible hiding spot for C. W. Alexander's box of films. Or maybe, I thought, Alexander did not actually hide his films down in the mine. Maybe he hid them somewhere else. But why would he tell his son that he hid his cans in the hurricane if . . . I could tear myself up asking these sorts of questions, and what good would it do? I approached the three timber-reinforced openings, my heart racing.

Which direction should I go? "Stop wondering and start searching," I told myself. I picked the middle drift and walked for a ways, holding my flashlight at chest level, waving the beam right, then left. I closed my eyes and said, "Heavenly Father, help me make the right decision . . ."

My shoe soles scraped gravel. It only made my jitters worse that the floor on either side of the ore cart tracks dropped at a forty-five-degree angle into deep crevices. My flashlight beam danced. I turned it up at the ceiling. "Good," I said aloud. "No bats—"

I halted and held my breath. *No bats may mean poison gas,* I thought. I considered turning back, but I had come this far and was still in one piece, so I continued forward.

Twenty feet later, I saw it, hidden in a level nook: a cardboard box, a couple of feet high by a couple of feet wide, sealed shut by strands of twine wrapped around it. I pointed my flashlight at a label: CLYDE ALEXANDER, C.O. INTERMOUNTAIN MINING SPECULATORS, LTD., NEWHOUSE HOTEL, SALT LAKE CITY, UTAH.

"Thank God."

As I said that, a timber brace groaned like a ghost, and dust and tiny particles fell from the ceiling.

Silence. I tipped my flashlight up at the rotten timber and caught my breath. Then I lifted the box. It was heavy enough that I needed both arms to carry it, but I was still able to hold the flashlight in my right hand while I walked.

Balancing the box and flashlight was tough. My strides grew longer, and the dust-filled light beam bounced more dramatically as I picked up the pace.

Then it happened.

My flashlight went out. Everything went blacker than black.

I lowered the box to the ground and began fiddling with the flashlight, but I couldn't see anything. I was one hundred percent blind. My hands shook something fierce. I panicked, silently reprimanding myself for not bringing a backup flashlight. I shook the

flashlight, switched it on and off, screwed and unscrewed the bat-
tery cap, tried switching it on again. Still nothing.

Only one option remained. Clutching the flashlight, I lifted the
box with both hands and started walking in what I thought was the
direction of the stope. I could not be sure, though, because not so
much as a ray of light broke through that far beneath the earth's
surface.

I tried talking to myself—"Keep going, Art . . . You're going to
make it"—which I found strangely comforting. It felt as though
someone else, a friend, was down there with me, sharing in the
grief. "When you get out of here, you can take Clara and the kids
out for—"

My feet slipped out from under me. I slid down a gravelly forty-
five-degree slope. I kept sliding for what must have been fifty feet.
The box fell out of my hands. The ground and roof kept narrowing
until rock closed in on my waist like a pincer and stopped my fall.
The good news: I was no longer sliding. The bad news: I was stuck
at the waist. Below my waist, the crevice was so narrow I could
hardly move my legs. The box slid to a halt next to me, and even
though it was an inanimate object, I felt like it was taunting me,
telling me I was a fool to creep down into this Stygian hole in the
earth.

Funny thing is, even though my religion taught me that if I died
I would be reunited with my family in the hereafter, I found little
comfort in that thinking. Instead, the fear of never seeing my wife
or kids again dogged me.

Staying where I was, lodged in a crevice, was not an option. I
summoned what strength I had left and pried my body loose. The
warm sensation of blood on my shin came from a deep cut on my
knee.

"If you make it out, Art," I said, "you can take your family to
Keeley's for ice cream . . ."

I dislodged myself and hooked my arm around that box. Then I inchwormed up the slope, tugging the box with me. This continued for a half hour until I felt the slope leveling. I shoved the box to the level surface at the top of the incline. I slid several feet backward but dug into the rocky ground with my fingernails and clawed myself to a halt.

By the time I made it to the level path, I was exhausted and my lungs ached when I breathed. I picked up the box and resumed my trek to the stope. Soon I could feel myself inside of that enormous room thanks to the sound of dripping water. I was almost out.

When I finally emerged from the Hurricane, my body was bruised and cut up in dozens of places, and I had abrasions all over my front and back from sliding into that crevice. I no longer had my Stetson, either. It was somewhere back in that black hole, and I had no intention of returning for it.

The sun never felt so wonderful, the air never cleaner, and I considered dropping to my hands and knees and kissing terra firma. I dropped the box into the back of my car, and I used my pocketknife to cut the pieces of twine that held the lid shut. I opened it and feasted my eyes on those eighty-odd canisters of film, and below those, a stack of about half that many phonograph albums, all labeled with the name of the interviewee. I closed the flaps and figured I would soon find out whether my foolhardy escapade into that abandoned mine was worth it.

Twenty-three

The movie marquee at the Isis advertised a double feature of *Song of the West.* starring John Boles and Vivienne Segal, and *On with the Show,* starring Joe E. Brown and Betty Compson. Below those head-liners, a smaller sign promised ICED AIR, AUDIBLE SCREEN, NEWSREELS, SPORT REVUES & CARTOONS. Not quite 10:00 A.M. and storm clouds brewed over the valley, spitting droplets on my windshield as I got out of my car. I had on my new Stetson, my third in a month. At this rate, I was running the risk of going broke buying hats.

I carried the box of films in my arms, and my body ached from yesterday's ordeal in the Hurricane mine, especially the cuts on my back and chest. I got a good earful from Clara when she saw me in my dusty and battered state after I narrowly escaped that deep hole in the earth. She insisted on taking me to see Dr. May. He bandaged me, gave me free tins of Anacin, and sent me home. On the way, I stopped at Roscoe's apartment to feed Barney and used his tele-phone to call the hospital for an update. "Officer Lund is awake," the doctor told me. "It's a great sign." I sighed with relief.

At the Isis, my church pal Owen Vanderhoff had promised me

an hour of projector time. He told me to check for a key in the drop
box near the entrance. I fished out an envelope with a note and a
key inside. The note said, *Don't forget the leaves and branches you
promised to help me clear.* I laughed as I read it—I was running up
tabs all over the place—and stuffed it in my pocket. Then, balancing the box in one arm, I used the key to unlock one of the swinging doors.

In the dim lobby, I located a panel of black and white buttons
near the snack bar. A few finger punches activated lights, including
blinking globes around COMING SOON glass-case poster displays.
Only a few days left until the opening of William Haines and Leila
Hyams in *The Girl Said No.* "Hmm," I said. "Maybe I'll have to get
a babysitter and bring Clara to that one." I cut across the lobby to
the projector booth. Owen had left me handwritten instructions
on how to operate the machine, but I already knew how it worked.

I opened the box and took out the canisters, all eighty-two,
stacking them on a table by the projector. Many had notes taped to
them, presumably written by C. W. Alexander. I read the scrawls. A
few were illegible. They appeared to be notations, perhaps to remind Alexander of each film's contents. DAUGHTER OF SENATOR &
MRS. M—. MISTRESS OF THOMAS L—. WIFE OF CONGRESSMAN R.A—.
NIECE OF VICE PRESIDENT . . .

The notes listed the name of the woman in the film and her connection to someone powerful. Among the luminaries were baseball
players and movie stars, members of Congress and industrialists,
bankers and attorneys, investment whizzes, physicians, oil barons,
radio performers, and governors. The sound disks sat at the bottom
of the box in a neat stack, all of them in yellowing paper, most
dated between '25 and '29.

I popped open a canister, threaded a film into the projector, and
turned a dial, and the reel began spinning. The projector clackety-
clacked as it engaged the film's sprocket holes. For the next hour, I

watched as many films as I could thread and rewind, thread and
rewind, thread and rewind.

The sound warbled, and the lighting in Pfalzgraf's office was
not sufficient. Despite the poor quality, I could plainly see the
uniqueness of each woman. Some were shy, others gregarious. In
age they ranged from young women—girls, really—who couldn't
have been any older than their midteens all the way up to spinster
types, late thirties or early forties. High-pitched talk came out of
some mouths like squeaks, while a few women had throaty, almost
mannish voices. Nearly all appeared prosperous, and many could be
described as fashionable. Cloche hats. Bobbed hair. Vogue dresses.

After a while, they blended in my mind.

I rubbed my eyes and buried my face in my hands. Then a
thought flashed in my mind—Clara somehow ending up in a situation like this—and a bout of nausea gripped me. Each of those
women could have been Clara. All of those faces, voices—they
wouldn't leave me alone. They mixed together in my head, a kaleidoscope, swirling in circles. Long after I stopped the films, the
voices kept coming at me out of the darkness.

The clock on the wall warned me I had been in there more than
an hour. Owen would be returning soon. Time to pack up. I had
only had a chance to watch about a quarter of the films. I would
have to return later, maybe late at night, after the last picture of the
day.

I lifted a stack of reels and lowered them into the box, tucking
them in neatly next to the phonograph albums. That's when I saw it
at the bottom of the box. An object poking out from under a stack
of phonograph albums. I reached my arm all the way down and
pinched the corner of what turned out to be a large cream-colored
mailing envelope. I walked over to the light to get a better look.
Somebody had written the name PARLEY TANNER on the outside. I
sat on a nearby chair and opened it.

I tipped it open side down and shook it. Out spilled the contents: a canister of film and a bundle of letter-sized envelopes, each
torn open, and wrapped in a blue ribbon. The letters smelled of a
men's cologne. The film can had the name ELIZABETH TANNER, all
caps, handwritten on it.

"Elizabeth Tanner," I said. I flashed back to the Tanners' house
last month . . . my conversation with Parley and Miriam Tanner . . .
Parley's words: *Poliomyelitis. We rushed her to the hospital, but we
didn't get her there in time. The virus entered her bloodstream and . . .*

It was 11:12 A.M. Would I have enough time to watch it?

I snapped the reel onto the projector, fed the film into the metal
loading chute, and turned the start dial.

The silent black-and-white film showed Elizabeth Tanner—
identical to the woman in the painting in the Tanners' living room—
sitting in Pfalzgraf's office, carrying on a conversation with the
doctor. There wasn't any sound. I eyed the date on the canister:
May 18, 1928. This reel should have had a phonograph recording to
go with it. I tipped my head up at the movie screen again. The flick-
ering image showed Elizabeth shaking hands with Pfalzgraf, putting on her cloche hat, and leaving the office. The film ended there.

What on earth were they talking about?

I thumbed through the phonograph albums in the box, each labeled with the name of a different patient and recording date, but I
could not find one for Elizabeth Tanner. "Dang," I whispered in
frustration. I really wanted to hear what they were saying in the
film.

Next, I picked up the stack of letters and untied the ribbon.
There were eight in total, all inside of torn-open envelopes. Each
envelope bore the name HELEN PFALZGRAF, front and center. I
plucked all eight letters out of the envelopes and quickly skimmed
each one. They were love letters, full of flowery words in cursive,
clearly written by someone who was smitten. It made me squeamish,

reading other people's private letters, but I convinced myself it was
necessary.

Most of them began with "Dear Baby Doll." I skimmed lines
and flipped pages. *How I yearn to hold you again . . . I miss you terribly, and when I see you with the doctor, my heart aches . . . Let's go
away from here, far away, where we can love each other without any
interference . . . I can't go on living without you . . .* They were all
signed, "Your Lover Daddy." They all sounded the same, and a few
were filled with graphic descriptions of sexual intercourse between
the man who wrote them and the recipient. They were dated between June 28, 1928, and February 16, 1930.

The last letter differed starkly from the rest. For one thing, it
was typed on a typewriter, on letterhead from the law firm of Tanner, Smith, and Wells. "Dear Mrs. Pfalzgraf," it opened. "You will
henceforth cease and desist with your claims that I shall be the father of your baby once you have given birth." The letter went on in
icy legalese. "You have no evidence that your pregnancy is the outcome of our intimate relations together. We have not been with
each other in that manner for months and I believe you know this
to be the case. If you are being perfectly honest with yourself, instead of vainly hoping that I will cast aside my wife of thirty years,
you will move on and forget about our illicit companionship. I told
you when we spoke on the telephone last week that I intend to remain faithful to my wife and that there is no hope for a reunion
between the two of us. If you carry out your threat to tell her about
our affair, it will only devastate her. She is innocent and she does
not deserve to be hurt in such a dastardly way. Moreover, I ask you
right now to stop telephoning me at home, especially late at night,
as I do not wish for you to arouse her suspicion."

My eyes wandered to the end of the letter and the signature at
the bottom nearly made my heart stop. "Sincerely, Mr. P. Tanner,
Attorney at Law."

Prime blackmail material for C. W. Alexander, one of Utah's heavy hitters in that highly questionable line of work. How much money was Parley Tanner paying him to keep these letters a secret?

A knock startled me. I stacked the letters and envelopes and stuffed them, along with the canister marked ELIZABETH TANNER, back in the big envelope.

The door opened.

"It's me, Art," said Owen, all smiles and good cheer. "Didja get my note?"

My heart raced and I had the jitters something awful, but I hid it well. "I, uh, I sure did. Thanks so much for letting me use your projector."

"Don't mention it. Sorry I have to chase you out of here, but the matinee is starting soon." He scooped a pocket watch out of his vest. "Time to ready the reels and open the box office. What about you? Did you find what you were looking for?"

"Yeah," I said. "If it's alright with you, I'd like to come back and watch more of these things later."

"You can use the place any old time I'm not, Art." He glanced at the box of films, grinned, and said, "Short subjects, I see. Anything good?"

"Mostly dull stuff," I said, patting the top of the box. "Home movies."

"No kidding? That's surprising."

"Why?"

"Most home movies are shot on sixteen millimeter stock. Folks buy those dinky toy projectors to show 'em on the wall. Montgomery Ward sells 'em for forty bucks. These babies here are thirty-five millimeters."

I took a deep breath. "Yeah, well, they're different."

"How so?"

His prying made me squeamish, so I lifted the box and stepped out of the projection room. "Thanks again, Owen."

"Hey, Art."

I'd gotten a few steps out of the room when I turned. Owen stood in the doorway, wiggling the bulky envelope. "You forgot something." He read the name on it. "Parley Tanner. Name sounds familiar."

I set the box on the floor and opened the flaps, pried the envelope gently out of his hands, and placed it inside with the films and phonograph albums. "See you at church, Owen. Thank you again."

"Sure thing, Art."

This discovery gave me a rush that somehow alleviated the pain of my cuts and bruises. My mind raced with a hundred different thoughts, all mixed together. My urge to dig up more information outweighed any need I felt to nurse my injuries. I hurried across the movie theater lobby, out the swinging doors into the rain. On the sidewalk in front of the Isis, I loaded the box into the backseat, slammed the door, hurried behind the wheel of the car, started the engine, and sped into a U-turn, so fast I almost slid off the road.

My car roared through rain-slicked downtown streets at record speeds, and when I reached the City and County Building, across the street from my former place of employment, I parked illegally with my front tire on the sidewalk ("Let 'em ticket me," I mumbled) and dashed inside in a mad hurry. Glass display directory check—tiny white letters on black background: PUBLIC HEALTH—ROOM 310. Third floor.

I sprinted up marble steps, breathless by the second floor. I pushed myself to the next floor, banging through a heavy wooden door and maneuvering around the few scattered people in the hallway. They looked at me like I was crazy for running so fast.

I stumbled inside an anteroom with a couple of chairs, a receptionist at a desk, and a watercooler. A bespectacled redheaded clerk in a light blue dress was so alarmed by my heavy breathing and the rain dripping off me that she went straight to the watercooler and filled a paper cone. She passed it to me, and I thanked her between breaths and took a sip of water. I plopped down in a waiting chair, trying hard to catch my breath.

"Thank you," I panted.

"What's wrong with you?"

"I guess I came up here a little too quickly."

"You sure did. What is it that you needed so badly you had to rush like that?"

I wiped moisture off my brow with a handkerchief and drank the rest of the water, then crumpled the cup and tossed it in a nearby wastepaper basket.

I looked at her—she had freckles, like Clara, but more than Clara, and her soft hazel eyes put me at ease. "Are records of polio deaths available to the public?"

"Yes. We've tracked the disease for almost thirty years. There haven't been many cases. It hasn't reached epidemic proportions. Not like the influenza twelve years ago. Do you have a specific name?"

"Elizabeth Tanner," I said. "*T-A-N-N-E-R*. If she died of polio, it would've been two years ago."

"Tanner?" she asked. I nodded. She stood up and brushed off her dress. "Let me check. I'll be right back."

She left and was gone for five minutes. She returned, nodding her head and pushing her glasses higher on her nose. "Here she is. Diagnosed by Dr. Edmund Reid on the fourteenth of June, in '27."

"Ah. I see."

"But she recovered."

"Come again?"

"Reid gave her a clean bill of health."

"So she didn't die from it?"

"Evidently not."

"OK. Much obliged." My panting had eased up, and I stood.

She laughed and folded her arms over her chest. "Is that why you almost killed yourself running up here? To find out if that Tanner woman died of polio?"

I straightened my Stetson. "It'd take me a long time to explain it all to you, but yeah, that's why I almost killed myself. I'm grateful for your help."

Twenty-four

The postman requested I sign for the small parcel. I scribbled my signature, and he passed me the package. It came wrapped in brown paper and, sealed in twine, and the mailing label listed a return address in Asbury Park, New Jersey. Who could have sent it? I closed the door, took the parcel into the kitchen, and found a steak knife. Two upward slashes cut off the twine. I tore off the paper, opened the box, and pulled out a pair of Dictaphone cylinders wrapped in tissue paper. A note came with it. I unfolded it.

Dear Deputy Oveson: I am sending you two sound cylinders that belonged to my late husband, Seymour Considine. They are compatible with the Dictaphone machine. The first is a recording of his interview with Clyde Alexander, conducted in Park City on March 4, 1930. The second is his interview with Twyla Smoot, formerly of Ogden, dated March 9, 1930. He was in the process of transcribing these at the time of his death. You are the only lawman he ever mentioned by name, and he said you had worked with him. I found your name in his address book. I hope you will be able to make good use of these. Signed, Yours Truly, Mrs. Fern Considine, Asbury Park, New Jersey.

I needed a Dictaphone. Fast. Time to use one of my connections. I lifted the telephone receiver and thumbed the cradle up and down.

A woman's voice said, "Operator?"

"Sheriff's office, Salt Lake County, please."

"Hold the line, please. I'll ring that number."

Two rings—like cat purrs—and a woman's voice came on the other line. "Salt Lake County Sheriff's Office."

"Faye?"

"Speaking?"

"It's me, Art Oveson."

"Art, how are you?"

"Great, and how's every little thing on your end?"

"I've had better, I've had worse. Still breathing and that counts for something. We miss you around here. It's not the same anymore without your face brightening the place."

"That's kind. I miss you, too, Faye. I've got a favor to ask you . . ."

"Yeah?" She paused for a moment, perhaps expecting me to ask in that quiet patch. She prodded, "Out with it."

"Cannon has a Dictaphone in his office . . ."

"For dictating memos. What of it?"

"I'd like to borrow it."

Dead silence. "Faye?"

"I'm here. He doesn't want you around here anymore, Art."

"I know," I said. "That's why it has to be done on the hush. I need to come in and clear all my belongings out of my old office anyway. How about I kill two birds with one stone—listen to the cylinders with Cannon's Dictaphone, then box up all my stuff."

She took a deep breath on the other end. "I don't know about this, Art . . ."

"I figure he usually takes a long lunch at Lamb's Grill with Sykes. Right? I'll mosey in while he's gone, play these things, and leave before he comes back."

"Oh, Art, I'll probably regret this . . ."

"I'll see to it that you don't. I'll be there in ten minutes."

"If you get caught, I didn't know anything about it."

"Okay. Deal."

Ten minutes later, I stood in the sheriff's office, chin-wagging with Faye at the front desk. She led me to Cannon's office and switched on the lights, and the ceiling fans started spinning. The office didn't look as colossal with Cannon and Sykes away. A breeze blew through open arched windows, and birdsong mixed with streetcar bells, traffic cop whistles, and car horns.

"You have till twelve fifty-five," she said.

"Tell you what: I'll be out at twelve fifty," I said.

She winced at the sight of the cuts on my arm and neck. "You look pretty banged up."

"I was a little careless in my exploring," I said. "It won't happen again."

She laughed and pulled the twin doors closed. I pulled up a chair and sat down beside a rectangular black machine that had a tube and funnel jutting out of it. I checked the combination chamber and speaker on top, and it was empty, so I removed the first of the cylinders from its cardboard container and slipped it inside the machine. I pressed a button on top of the machine, and the speaker cracked and hissed.

Considine's voice came on, and he introduced C. W. Alexander. The recorded discussion lasted about a half hour, with Alexander briefly touching on his childhood, early career as a miner, and recent years as a speculator. It was mostly quite dull. The interesting part came about twenty minutes into the interview. I turned the volume knob on the side as high as it would go.

"Tell me, Mr. Alexander, why you are hiding in this cabin."

"I've been framed. They're trying to make it look like I killed Helen."

"Who's they?"

"The people responsible for her murder."

"People? More than one person was involved?" There was no answer from Alexander. "Was more than one person involved?"

"Yes."

"Who?"

"I would rather not say."

"But you had nothing to do—"

"God, no. I loved her. I wanted to start a family with her."

"Rumor has it she was going to leave you, and you—"

"Stop right there! Hold on just a damn second. I had nothing to do with killing Helen. I tell you, I've been framed!"

"Who's framing you?"

"Helen's killer."

"Dr. Pfalzgraf?"

"I'd rather not say . . ."

Alexander described his final outing with Helen Pfalzgraf the night she was murdered. He said they drove to the top of the Avenues and watched the twinkling lights of the Salt Lake Valley spread out for thirty miles. Then they motored out to the countryside in search of a more secluded spot. Their romantic time together turned ugly. They quarreled, and she asked him to take her home. He told Considine that he dropped her off at the Pfalzgraf mansion and she was alive when he last saw her.

"If you don't believe me, Seymour, ask that security guard fellow at Pfalzgraf's house. He was there."

"Do you remember his name?"

"Damn. What was his name?" There was the sound of snapping fingers. "Floyd! Ask him. When I dropped her off, he was there. He opened the gate. He's my witness. I don't think the sheriff's people or the police have talked to him yet—"

I backed up the Dictaphone a few seconds and pressed PLAY.

"Floyd! Ask him. When I dropped her off, he was there. He opened the gate. He's my witness . . ."

The interview played for several more minutes. C. W. admitted using Pfalzgraf's movies and sound recordings to blackmail others. "I wish I hadn't done it," he said. "I know I've fouled things up, painted myself in a corner, but I'm so scared, and I don't know how to make things right again." He discussed hiding out in his cabin and the toll it was taking on him and his family. "I'm considering giving up to the police," he said. "Maybe they'll give me a square deal. I know Sheriff Cannon won't. He's out to nail me, regardless of what I've done."

The machine buzzed, ending the recording. I popped out the cylinder and slipped it in its case.

In went the next one. *Let's see what Twyla Smoot has to say.*

"Please identify yourself . . ."

"Twyla Smoot."

Her voice was soft, and on a few occasions, Considine had to ask her to speak louder and closer to the microphone.

"And your address?"

"I'm not saying."

"As you wish. Do you know why I've requested this interview?"

"I think so."

Silence for a moment, but their breathing was audible in the background.

"Why?"

"Something to do with my old job as a nurse in Dr. Wooley's Ogden clinic."

"That's right. What can you tell me about that experience?"

"I'd prefer not to talk about it."

"This is your chance to tell the world about your ordeal, to set the record straight. And I promised you fifty dollars if you cooperated . . ."

"I can use the money." She paused. "I came to work for Wooley in the fall . . ."

"This would've been '27?"

"Uh-huh."

"You'd just finished the nursing program."

"Yeah. I had two daughters to feed. My husband ran out on us, the worthless—"

"What kind of fellow was he?"

"My husband? A failure if ever there was—"

"No. Wooley."

"Oh. Him. He drank a lot. He made passes at me. He loved to cop feels under the table. He wanted me to give him head, but I wouldn't. I woulda quit, but I needed the money."

"What was the doctor's specialty, medically speaking?"

"I'm not even sure he was a real doctor. A quack is what he was. He'd scramble any lady with a hundred bucks. No questions asked. If a woman was desperate and didn't have the money, he might cut her a deal after she sucked his cock. Sorry about the foul talk."

"I've heard his surgeries have killed a few women."

"I can name seven off the top of my head."

"Go ahead. Please."

"You want me to say their names?"

"Yes, please, if it's no trouble."

"No trouble. It's just that . . ."

"What?"

"You're the first person who's ever shown an interest."
She paused for a half minute. "Uh, let's see. There was, uh,
Esther Bowers. And Georgia Wright. And Maria . . . Maria . . .
Oh, darn, I can't remember. She had a Mexican name. San-
chez, I think it was. Maria Sanchez. Yeah, I'm pretty sure that
was it. Anyway, there was her and Zella Farr and Myrtle
Vincent and Edith Dahlquist. What is that? Six?" Considine
said, "Yes," in the background. "There was another one."

"Drawing a blank?"

"It'll come to me."

"Give it a minute and maybe you'll—"

"Tanner! That was her name! Elizabeth Tanner."

"Can you tell me more about her?"

"Who?"

"Tanner."

"What do you want to know?"

"The name sounds familiar. Who was she?"

"I don't know. The daughter of some big-shot lawyer."

"Do you remember anything about her?"

"Not really. I don't know why in tarnation she came to see
Wooley. Her parents were rich, friends of Dr. Pfalzgraf. The
rich ladies went to see Pfalzgraf. The poor showed up on our
doorstep. Elizabeth was the only well-off person I ever met."

"Why do you think Elizabeth didn't go to Dr. Pfalzgraf?"

"I asked her that, after she told me who she was."

"What'd she say?"

"Her beau got her pregnant, and she was frightened of her parents and his parents finding out. She went to Pfalzgraf first."

"How do you know this? Did she tell you this?"

"She told me while Dr. Wooley was outta the room. She was nervous. I tried to comfort her. You shoulda seen her. She was shaking like a leaf."

"So Pfalzgraf refused her an abortion because . . ."

"He said he loved her parents too much to do it. So Elizabeth went to Wooley, and he charged her a hundred and stuck dirty metal in her."

"Did she die in his clinic?"

"No. She was fine when her cousin picked her up. She died a few days later."

"Her cousin was with her at Wooley's clinic?"

"Yep. Waited in the waiting room and everything."

"What was her name?"

"Him."

"Sorry. Him."

"Sam. I can't recollect his last name. I quit a month before Wooley was shot. I moved outta Ogden with my daughters. I like this town better. I don't look back. After Wooley was murdered, I heard a rumor that Elizabeth's cousin Sam was the one done the killing—"

The Dictaphone buzzed, startling me. I ejected the cylinder and placed it inside its case. I ran my hand over the Dictaphone, and it was hot to the touch. I grabbed hold of my cylinders and darted out of Cannon's office. I entered my office, former office now, flipping lights on and placing an empty storage box on the desk. I began emptying the contents from the drawers—all mine because employees had to furnish their own office supplies—and loaded up a box, and when it was almost full, I added the framed wall pictures of my family and the Salt Lake Temple to the top. A wave of sadness hit me as I finished packing, and for a moment I considered crawling on my hands and knees to Cannon and pleading for my old job back.

Thankfully, that moment passed.

The door squeaked open. Floyd Samuelson, of all people, poked his head in a little ways. His face beamed with all the joy of the cat who caught the mouse. "Hello, Art! I didn't think I'd see you in here! I heard you were . . . you know . . ."

"Fired? Yep. I was. I'm here to collect my belongings."

"What a shame," he said. "You're fired and I'm hired, all at the same time."

"No kidding?" I said, genuinely happy for him. "Congratulations!"

I rose to shake his hand, and as I crossed toward him, he stepped inside to meet me halfway. When we shook, his grip was unusually tight. "I owe it all to you, Art," he said. "I wouldn't have applied if you hadn't mentioned it. Guess I was tired of that Pfalzgraf detail. I needed a change of scenery."

"That's swell, Floyd," I said. "I'm happy for you. Really I am."

"Thanks, Art," he said. His eyes widened, and he reached for his billfold. "I've got a new picture of Bert, taken at our family reunion last week."

I noticed his left hand was wrapped in gauze and white medical tape, with a tiny maroon blood spot on it. I had a difficult time concealing my shock. He held the wallet in front of me with his bandaged hand, and I struggled to focus on his boy dressed in a springtime church outfit.

"This was taken in Payson. Look how fast he's growing." He saw me staring at his hand and gave his wallet a wiggle. "See, Art. Right here. Ain't he something? My Bert! We bought him that outfit especially for this reunion."

I forced myself to look at Floyd's crooked mouth. "He's something, alright," I finally said. "I can see why you're so proud of him."

Floyd dropped his gauze-wrapped hand behind his back as he tucked his billfold away with his other hand. It wasn't my imagination: He began shaking and licking his lips, and his larynx wiggled. "I reckon I best get going. Gee, it's swell to see you again, Art."

"You, too."

He nodded and kept his left hand out of sight. "I only wish we could work together. I know we'd make great partners."

"Yeah."

"See you around, I hope."

"See you around, Floyd."

He closed the door behind him. I fell into a swivel chair. I jabbed the red button on my desk intercom. Faye's voice crackled over the speaker: "Yes?"

I pushed the TRANSMIT button and said, "One last thing before I go."

Hiss-pop. "Yes?"

PUSH. "Is it alright if I take a look at Floyd Samuelson's job application?"

"You're not supposed to, now that you don't work here any longer—but maybe I can pull a few strings. Hold on."

A few minutes later, Faye entered and placed his job application form on the desk in front of me. My eyes went straight to his handwritten name at the top of the page. "FIRST NAME: Louis—MIDDLE NAME: Floyd—LAST NAME: Samuelson." I covered the middle name with my index finger. Louis Samuelson. Reverse it: *Sam Louis.* I looked up at Faye. She was staring at me.

"Everything OK?" she asked.

I nodded and gave her the application. "Yep."

"Did you find what you were looking for?"

"Yes. I think I did."

She started to leave, then stopped at the door and faced me. "Maybe this November the voters will . . . Well, you know. Maybe you can get your old job back."

"Thanks, Faye," I said. "I guess we'll see what happens."

Twenty-five

A chill evening wind whistled through the streets of Salt Lake City as I steered my car into the parking lot of the local Mormon ward building where I attended church on Sundays. Tonight was Tuesday, not Sunday, so the parking lot was mostly empty, except for the blue '28 Oldsmobile parked near the entrance to the building. With the end of March approaching, the days were getting longer, and only the most defiant clumps of snow remained. I parked my car next to the Olds and went inside the ward, an austere brick building with a steeple out front. The door to the building was propped open with a chair, and when I went inside, I pulled the chair in with me and the door clicked lock-shut. The hallways were dimly lit, and my footsteps on the carpet made almost no noise. I reached the gymnasium, with its open doors and bright lights, and my ears were greeted by the squeak of shoes against shiny wood and a dribbling basketball echoing from one side of the high-ceilinged room to the other. Stepping inside, I watched Buddy Hawkins in a sweatshirt, sweatpants, and athletic shoes running down the court and shooting a basketball into the hoop. The ball rolled around the rim and sank into the basket. I clapped, and Buddy lunged for a rebound and faced me.

"Thanks for coming," he said. "I figured this is a familiar place for both of us. We see each other here every Sunday. Fine location to shoot the breeze."

"I didn't know you were such a good basketball player."

"You can't play basketball in those," he said, eyeing my weather-beaten black shoes. He looked at my clothes—trousers, coat, dress shirt underneath—and shook his head. "I told you I wanted to play you."

I took a few steps into the gym, and he tossed me the basketball. I caught it and dribbled a couple of times. "I'm afraid I'm not any good."

"Take a shot."

"Nah. I've got fallen arches. I can't run the way you—"

"Go up to the line and shoot, Art. Just give it a try."

I walked up to the free-throw line, raised the ball over my head, and hurled it. It sailed above the backboard, hit the brick wall behind it, and came rolling back toward us. Buddy shrugged as he retrieved the ball. "Like anything, it takes practice."

He dribbled a few times, turned, and took a shot. The ball went in. He rebounded it and took another shot. It went in again. *Show-off*, I thought. He stopped and walked to me, cradling the basketball in his arms. Perspiration covered his face, and a damp circle had formed on his sweatshirt. He stopped a few feet away and tossed the ball gently to me, and I caught it.

He said, "We've known each other how long?"

"A while."

"That's right. We see each other every Sunday. Our kids go to the same school. One might even describe us as friends. Or at least on friendly terms."

I stared down at the brown leather ball and pressed my fingertips into it, wondering where this conversation was going.

He continued, "I've got this funny notion—and, please, correct
me if I'm mistaken—that you know a great deal about the Pfalzgraf
homicide. More than you're letting on. Now, if you were to cooperate with me, I'd cooperate with you. I know you're out of work. I
can help fix that. But to do that, I need you to help me. See, Art, I'm
beginning to think that all of these recent homicides around
here—Helen Pfalzgraf, C. W. Alexander, Seymour Considine, and
the attempt on Roscoe Lund—are connected."

"But C. W. Alexander killed himself in his cabin in—"

"C'mon, Art. You don't really believe that. The only reason Cannon closed the case was so he could get all the glory from his deputy solving it. You and I know Alexander didn't kill himself. Now
there's some cockamamie theory going around that Considine was
murdered because of an exposé he was writing on Al Capone's criminal enterprises in Chicago. What a load of malarkey. If that isn't bad
enough, some of my fellow police detectives are dismissing Roscoe
Lund getting shot as the work of a thrill-killer who just gunned
down a cop in Omaha. I don't buy any of these explanations. I'm
certain these are all linked, and you know what else I'm sure of?"

"No. What?"

He stepped closer to me. Beads of sweat ran down his face. "You
know I'm right, and you can help me prove it."

"That's what you think, huh?"

He nodded. "Are you going to look me in the eye and tell me I'm
wrong?"

I couldn't stand him being so close to me, so I thrust the basketball into his chest, which pushed him back a step, and he grasped it
with both hands and grinned again.

"Yep," I said. "You're wrong."

"Why are you doing this, Art? I don't get it."

"Doing what?"

"Going it alone. I know Roscoe was working with you before he was shot. That's why I gave you the key to his apartment. You're a smart bird, Art. I'm just trying to figure out what's going through your head. Is it that you think you can see the big picture from all the angles more clearly than anybody else and only you know what's best? Do you think I'd botch this case? Are you afraid that once it's out of your hands, you won't be in control of what happens? Help me understand why you're holding out on me."

The polished maple floor under my feet served as my focal point. I didn't feel like staring at Buddy's face any longer. "I'm not sure what you're talking about."

"Or maybe you think if you crack this one, you won't be in your father's shadow anymore."

Now he had my attention. I glared at him so intensely he moved away from me. His words touched a raw spot deep inside of me, and I couldn't hold back. "Stop it!"

"Stop what?"

"You never knew him!" I shouted.

"That's it, isn't it? Will Oveson is why you won't—"

I forcefully ripped the ball out of his hands, which jolted him, and I threw it hard against the floor so that it bounced over to the corner of the room. "You don't know the first thing about him! So can it!"

"You're right. I know nothing about the man." Buddy stepped closer to me and jabbed his index finger into my chest. "But I know you, and I know you think you've got to prove something to the rest of the world. You've fooled yourself into believing you can do it all alone. Catch the culprit single-handedly, the way they do in the detective magazines. Show the world you're every bit as tough as your father."

I shoved him in the chest with both hands and he stumbled backward. "I said cut it out, Buddy!"

"You know, Art, you'd be a lot better off if you'd quit believing all the stories about your father being a bigger-than-life hero." He moved closer to me. "He wasn't Hercules, and you don't have to fill his shoes in order to be a good lawman—"

That's when it happened. It occurred so fast, all in a split second. I felt as though I stepped out of my body, stood off to the side, and watched me throw my clenched fist into Buddy's jaw, which sent him toppling to the floor, covering his mouth with his hand. The pain in my knuckles from bone meeting bone was instant, and it pulled me back into my own body. I didn't mean to punch him. Inside a church, no less. *Our church.*

"I'm so sorry, Buddy. I don't know what came over me . . ."

I offered my hand, but he refused. He rose to his feet on his own.

"No need to apologize, Art," he said. A droplet of blood plunged from his lip and hit his shoe. "I probably had it coming, and you probably had it in you for a long time. But that doesn't mean I'm letting you off the hook. I'll give you until the end of the day tomorrow to drop by my office and tell me what you know. If I don't see you, then Wit and I will pay a visit to your house and arrest you in front of your wife and children."

"On what grounds?" I asked.

His grin returned, despite the cracked lip. "You know me. I never tip my hand."

"Thanks for the warning."

He scooped up the ball and tossed it to me. When I caught it, I was a ways away from the basket, about halfway down the court.

"One for the road," he said. "Only you've got to get a little closer to the basket. You'll never make it from here."

I threw the ball into the air with all my might. I didn't expect it to plunge into the basket, but that's what happened.

• • •

No sleep again for me. The clock by my bedside said half past four in the morning and I went back to watching the ceiling. Clara was sound asleep, with her back turned to me. I reached over and lightly stroked her golden locks and thought about how much I loved her, and how I couldn't bear to lose her. I wanted to wake her up and tell her how much she meant to me, and thank her for putting up with me. *I know I'm not easy to live with,* I'd tell her, *but I love you with all my heart. No man ever loved a woman more.*

I didn't tell her these things. Instead, I let her sleep.

I crept into the living room, to Clara's desk with her Underwood typewriter in the center. I turned on a desk lamp, took a piece of bond paper off of a stack and rolled it into the carriage. I hit a key and then stopped. Why was I typing the message? What I wanted to write needed to be handwritten.

I found a piece of stationery and a pen and began writing.

Wednesday, March 26, 1930

My Dearest Darling Clara,

It was a little over eight years ago that you married me and made me the happiest man in the world. You blessed me with the joys of a family. Just as importantly, you blessed me with your love. All of those years ago, when we danced under the stars at Lagoon and promised each other our undying love, I never knew that I could be as happy as I am now.

We've stuck together, through good times and bad. But now I find myself in the middle of a situation I must confront alone. I may not make it out alive. Should anything happen to me, please go to Owen Vanderhoff at the Isis Theater and tell him you're there to pick up a box. Make sure you give the box to someone who will tell the world about its contents. I suggest a big newspaper. Believe me, what's inside that box is a big story.

Also know that no matter what happens to me, I'll always love you and Sarah Jane and Hyrum. A man couldn't ask for a better family. You've made me happier than I ever thought possible. Thank you.

Love,

Art

A tear ran down my cheek as I set the pen down, and the drop hit one of the words on the paper and pulled the ink into a black streak. I folded the paper three ways and placed it inside a matching stationery envelope, then licked the flap and closed it. I hid the letter in a leather-bound album containing our wedding photos, right next to the 8 × 10 black-and-white glossy of us kissing. I closed the album and returned it to the bookcase.

For the next two hours, I typed a letter explaining everything I knew to Clara. When I finished, I set it on top of the film canisters and closed the box. In the next room, I lifted the earpiece off the telephone and clicked the cradle a few times. An operator said, "Number, please?"

"Can you ring the residence of Owen Vanderhoff, please?"

Half an hour later, wearing my Stetson, I pulled up in front of the Isis Theater, with that box in the backseat. My coat concealed my .38, pressed against my ribs in a shoulder holster. It felt like somebody had placed a weight on my chest. The rearview mirror revealed a pair of headlamps slowing behind me, my cue to get out of my car and remove the box of films and phonograph discs from the backseat. I was careful to keep the envelope marked P. TANNER on the front seat, like a passenger traveling by my side to an uncertain destination. Owen emerged from his auto looking groggy, and what hair he had left flew in different directions like a bursting firework. He yawned and watched me lifting the big box, lugging it to where he stood by the ticket booth.

"What was it that couldn't wait till I opened her?" asked Owen.

"You mentioned your movie collection you keep below the theater," I said. "Would you mind if I store this box there?"

Owen raised an eyebrow. "Something tells me you weren't being entirely on the level with me when you said those are your home movies."

I laughed. "What gave me away?"

"All the secrecy, and the thirty-five-millimeter stock. I can spot the difference from a mile away. You gonna tell me what's in that box?"

"I'd prefer not to."

"OK," he said, not registering an iota of disappointment. "Follow me."

I tailed him through the Isis lobby and down a set of rickety stairs to a dark and cool cellar. He pressed a button near the door, and a tightly strung cord of dim bulbs on the ceiling lit long rows of high wooden shelves. He led me past what must've been thousands of reels of motion picture film, turned right at the end of the line, and took me to a far corner. He pointed to a space on the bottom shelf. I lowered my box onto the shelf and shoved it back as far as it would go.

I stood straight and smiled at Owen. He said, "Remember that yard work you were gonna help me with, Art?"

"I'm good for it. Call me sometime."

He glanced at my Stetson and made a long face. "You back at the sheriff's office again?"

"Not anymore. I'm on my own now."

He pointed his thumb at the box. "Don't you worry, Art. She'll be safe here." His eyes widened and he looked me up and down. "You aren't in any danger, are you, Art?"

For a long second, I considered giving Owen a brief account of everything I'd been through. I'm glad my hesitation won out. I knew

Owen was precisely the kind of big-hearted man who'd worry himself sick about me, so much so he might even pay a visit to Buddy Hawkins, a mutual friend and churchgoer, in an effort to help me. I couldn't have that. If there was ever a time to lie for the greater good, it was now. I gave him a pat on the shoulder to put his mind at ease.

"No," I said. "I'll be fine."

Twenty-six

The high walls surrounding the Pfalzgraf mansion came into view. Gone were the press hounds camped out front, back in the days when Helen's murder was generating front-page headlines. Hard to believe that was only a matter of days ago. It seemed as though years had passed since then. The wrought-iron gate was open, and I swerved my Plymouth into the driveway, behind the doctor's limousine. Sunlight reflected on the car's chrome. It wouldn't be around long. In the skies over the western side of the valley, storm clouds swirled, moving in our direction. I shut off the car. My hand still throbbed from when I punched Buddy. More painful was the guilt that burned inside of me.

A new security guard, younger and huskier than Floyd but wearing an identical cap and tie and suit, was loading luggage into the back of Pfalzgraf's car. As I stepped out onto the running board, I straightened my Stetson and tipped the brim to him. In my left hand, I clutched the envelope labeled P. TANNER. The guard lowered a suitcase next to the rear wheel and came toward me, furrowing his brow at my car.

"You gotta move that thing. Now. The doctor and his daughter have to catch a train—"

I cut him off—not my usual style. "They're not going anywhere."

He got close and shoved me in the chest. I unzipped my coat, took out my .38, cocked back the hammer with my thumb, and held it level with his head.

"Take it easy," he said with raised palms. "This is my job, you understand."

The mansion doors opened, and Pfalzgraf stepped out of the shadows, bowler on, relying even more on his cane than the last time I saw him. Anna escorted him, arm in arm, and I'm not sure who had the angrier expression as they headed toward me. I gently uncocked the .38's hammer, holstered the weapon, and swiped my Stetson off the car seat. Torrents of fear raged inside me. It would be hard to find someone more nonconfrontational than I am. Funny how seeing Dr. Pfalzgraf and his daughter approaching me with such anger in their eyes made me steel myself for a fight.

"What is the meaning of this, Deputy Oveson?" asked Pfalzgraf. "My daughter and I are leaving on a trip to Germany, and we have to go now, to catch a train!"

I shook my head. "The only place you two are going is back inside. Get moving."

Pfalzgraf grimaced. "Maybe I should place a call to your boss, Sheriff Cannon."

"Cannon isn't my boss any longer. He fired me." I poked my thumb into my chest. "I'm my boss now, and your little campaign donation to Cannon isn't going to stop me anymore. I've got a big box of your movies—more than eighty of them—just waiting to be delivered to my brother Frank, who happens to be an agent with the Federal Bureau of Investigation. I'm sure the films will be of great interest to him, especially the part about women crossing state lines for illegal surgeries."

Anna Pfalzgraf's expression went from anger to shock. She turned to her father. "Films? What films?"

"I suggest we go inside," I said, waving my Stetson at the mansion. "Talk where we can have more privacy."

I followed Pfalzgraf and Anna inside the darkened mansion, down a long and poorly lit corridor. All of the curtains in the house had been drawn, apparently in anticipation of the Pfalzgrafs' trip. We entered a room too dark for me to make out anything. The doctor switched on three electrical lamps, which furnished enough light for us to see each other's faces. We stood inside a reception parlor with expensive-looking art hanging on the walls, tapestries on tables, a grand piano, and furniture that looked like it belonged to ill-fated aristocrats at the time of the French Revolution. We sat—I on a floral armchair, the Pfalzgrafs on a similarly upholstered couch, with a coffee table separating us—and I wasted no time in confronting them.

I had to act tough, even if I didn't feel tough, even if I knew it was just an act.

I plucked off my Stetson, hung it on the armrest, and placed the long envelope on the coffee table.

"Tell me, Mr. Oveson," said Pfalzgraf. "What is it you wish to ask me now that you didn't get a chance to ask me last time you were here, with Officer Lund?"

"I was hoping to ask Anna a few questions." My gaze shifted to his daughter, whose immaculately styled brunette hair almost gave off a light of its own.

"Me?" she said, placing her hand to her chest. "Why? You already questioned me, right after—"

"I don't think you were completely honest with me that first time around."

"What do you want to know?"

"Where were you the night Helen was murdered?"

"I told you, the last time I talked to her was Thurs—"

"I didn't ask you when the last time you talked to her was. I asked where you were the night she was killed."

"With two of my friends," she said.

"What are their names?" I asked.

She shook her head angrily. "Why do you need to know—"

I shot up to my feet, my hat fell on the carpet, and I raised my voice as loud as it would go. "Because I've got enough evidence with those films to send your father to the penitentiary for the rest of his life. Because you're hiding something from me, and I want to know what it is, and I want to know now!"

She wept bitterly. The doctor put his arm around her shoulders and rocked her gently. I didn't know I had it in me. I reached down, picked up my hat, and returned to the chair.

"Give me the names of your two friends," I said. "I want to call them now and verify that you were with them."

"I wasn't with two friends," she said hesitantly, wiping the tears from her eyes with a handkerchief her father gave her. "I was here. Alone."

"Anna, you don't have to tell him anything," said Dr. Pfalzgraf.

"I have nothing to hide, Father." She looked at me, sniffed, and bit her lower lip. "I lied to the police about where I was Friday night because I was afraid they'd think I murdered Helen. You must believe me when I said I had nothing to do with her death. I was at home, alone, on Friday night. Father had gone off with Parley to the wrestling matches. I heard Helen come in the front door. I can't remember what time it was. Nine? Nine thirty? I didn't check the clock.

"I could smell liquor on her. She was stumbling around badly. I worried because she was carrying a baby. She had her purse with her, and there was a rock inside it. I thought that was strange. She showed me the rock and said it was gold ore. She said C. W. Alexander offered to sign a deed over to her for a mine that was full of gold if she'd stay in Utah and marry him. He vowed to leave his wife for her, according to Helen. I tried to convince Helen to go to bed. I told her to sleep it off, that we'd talk in the morning. She pleaded with me to come with her to Los Angeles. I told her again to sleep it off, we'd talk about it in the morning. She said she wanted another drink. I asked her if that was such a good idea. She said, 'Not you, too. Don't you start telling me how to live my life.' I couldn't take it anymore. I went to bed. I cried myself to sleep."

I said, "Where was Floyd Samuelson this whole time?"

She shrugged and mumbled, "I dunno," wiping tears with her handkerchief.

"You're not telling me everything," I said.

"Why do you say that?"

I leaned over the big brown envelope, opened the flap, and dumped the contents on the table. The canister of film landed spinning, like a coin, then settled. The letters spilled on top of it. Her eyes widened when she saw them, and I instantly knew she recognized them.

"You once said the two of you were like sisters," I said. "That you confided in each other."

"Please don't do this, Mr. Oveson," she said. Now tears streamed down her cheeks, one after another. "Not with Father in the room."

"Sweetheart," said Dr. Pfalzgraf as he scooted closer to her and stroked her hand tenderly with his. "What is it you're talking about?"

"He doesn't need to know," she said between sobs. "Please don't tell him. I beg you. It will break his heart."

The doctor stiffened and lifted his arm off of his daughter's shoulders. He snatched one of the letters and read it through bifocals. His lips moved as he read, and before long his eyebrows quivered and hands trembled.

"Helen wanted Parley to leave Miriam," I said. "It's possible Helen was pregnant with Parley's baby."

All of this was more than Anna Pfalzgraf could take. She stood and rushed out of the room, halting briefly at the door to scream, "You're a horrid man! Do you hear me? Horrid! There was no reason to do this to Papa!"

Her footsteps echoed through the corridors, as did her forlorn wails. He slumped back in his chair, and his hand holding the letter fell to the couch, as if the weight of the paper had become more than he could bear. He appeared defeated, too shocked and blindsided to be enraged at me for revealing the ugly truth to him. I decided not to speak until he did, to give him time to take in the awful pain that came from reading those words of love and lust in the letters Parley Tanner penned to Helen Pfalzgraf.

"I suppose I should've known," he finally said. "Helen started out as a stenographer in Parley's firm. He introduced the two of us. I really thought she . . ." He was quiet again for a while. "I thought she loved me. I guess I was a fool."

"You loved her and trusted her, and she ended up betraying you, in spite of that."

"Have you ever been betrayed, Mr. Oveson?"

"No. I can't imagine how painful it must be. I hope it never happens to me."

The doctor smiled. I think that was the first time I'd seen him smile today. I said, "I'm not quite done here, Doc. I need your help. Please."

"How can I help?"

"I have questions."

"Ask." He fell back deep into the couch.

"Floyd Samuelson. Who is he to the Tanners?"

"Parley and Miriam raised Floyd like a son. He came from a broken home. Floyd's father was an alcoholic and a violent man who beat Floyd when he was a little boy. His mother died when he was seven. Floyd went to live with the Tanners. Miriam thought she was blessed because for the longest time, she couldn't have children."

"So you already knew Floyd when he came to work for you as a security guard?"

"Of course, I'd known him for years. Parley provided legal representation to the agency that hired Floyd, Bonneville Security. I pulled a few strings to get him placed with me. I've been his family doctor for quite some time. I'm an obstetrician, it is true, but I'm also a general practitioner. He was always a lovely boy. Never the sharpest razor, but kind with a good heart."

"Did he have a violent side to him?"

"If he did, I never saw it."

"Why did you hire a security guard? Most doctors don't have them."

"After my films went missing, I contacted Bonneville and arranged to hire Floyd as my guard. By this time, my secretary, Eunice, was getting telephone calls from victims of C. W. Alexander's various blackmail schemes. They asked how on earth he got hold of the films. I feared my cover, which I've worked so long and so hard to protect, would be broken, and I'd be exposed in the press. That didn't happen, luckily. Having Floyd around helped. There weren't any more break-ins. No more stolen films. I felt safer with him around."

I changed the subject. "You said the Tanners couldn't have children. What about Elizabeth? Was she adopted?"

"No. Elizabeth came only after years of trying."

"I watched the movie of her visiting your office."

His eyes widened. "Do you have it?"

I pushed the love letters off the film canister. "Right here."

The doctor studied it for a minute. He reached out and ran his fingers along the scuffed and dented metal. "May I keep this?"

"It's all yours. It doesn't have the sound disk with it, though. I need to know what you two discussed that day."

"Mr. Oveson, there is something called doctor-patient confidentiality."

"There's also something called a box of eighty of your movies in my possession."

Pfalzgraf thought it over, then rose to his feet and walked to an enormous framed painting of a sailing ship at sea. He opened it like a door, thanks to three hinges that kept it fastened to the wall on one side. Behind it was a large gray wall safe. He turned the dial and pulled down a chrome handle. The heavy door squealed open, and a little electric lightbulb inside lit up, revealing jewelry boxes, stacks of papers, and assorted valuables. He took out a phonograph in a brown paper sleeve and walked over to a Victrola sitting on a three-legged table and put on the album. He turned a crank on the side and lowered the needle. The album opened with hissing and popping, and the first voice sounded clear, as if in the room with us.

"I am Dr. Hans Pfalzgraf. This recording is made at my office, second floor, Brooks Arcade, nine July nineteen twenty-eight."

A few clicks sounded, followed by a low humming in the background. From this point, the voices echoed like people talking into buckets.

"Please state your name, where you're from, and why you're here," said Pfalzgraf.

"I certainly will," she said nervously. *"My name is Elizabeth Tanner. I am from Salt Lake, born and raised here, and I have come here today to, uh, line up one of your surgeries. I've heard you are the very best man to see."*

"Why do you seek my assistance?"

"I am pregnant and I wish . . ." Elizabeth paused.

Pfalzgraf finished her sentence. *"You wish to halt the pregnancy through medical scientific means."*

"*Yes,*" she said. "*That is what I want.*"

A long pause followed. The next voice was Pfalzgraf's. "*I am sorry, Elizabeth. I cannot help you.*"

"*Wh-why? Why not?*"

"*Your parents are like family to me,*" he said. "*They are my family. To perform one of these surgeries on you would be a betrayal that I could not—*"

When she interrupted him, I could hear panic in her voice. "*I brought my money. It's right here. Two hundred and fifty—*"

"*No amount of money will make me change my mind, Elizabeth. My answer is no, I'm afraid. There are certain ethical lines I will not cross.*"

"*You don't understand. I think I'm already three months along—*"

"*I will not perform this operation on loved ones, and I regard you and your parents and Floyd as akin to my own family. This is a policy I will not violate.*"

"*I know, but I have the money right here—*"

"*The answer is no. I will not operate on you, I'm afraid. There is nothing else to discuss. I am happy to call you a cab—*"

"*I need this done right away. If the baby keeps growing, I won't be able to—*"

"*I'm certain your mother will help you take care of the baby.*"

"*No, you don't understand,*" she said, crying now. "*My father and mother will never approve—*"

"*Please do not ask me to go against my principles,*" said Pfalzgraf. "*I could never do this to your parents. I love all of you dearly. I am willing to be your obstetrician, and in that capacity I'll do what I can to ensure that your pregnancy is a healthy one.*"

For a long moment, the only sound on the phonograph was a faint, pathetic sobbing. "*I beg you . . .*"

Elizabeth spoke through a veil of tears I could not see, but I could plainly hear the agony in her voice. "*I can't let the baby grow more or I'll never be able to give it up.*"

"*I'm sorry, Elizabeth. I urge you to try talking to your mother and father. Tell them about it. Be honest with them. Give them a chance. I'm sure they will be—*"

"No! Never! They'll never understand . . ." Sobbing. "*I would rather die, Doctor.*"

"*I am sorry, Elizabeth. I can't. I just can't.*"

She seemed to regain her composure. "*Th-thank you, Doctor. I understand your reasoning. I . . . I just wish . . . Oh, never mind. I'd better go.*"

Pfalzgraf raised the Victrola needle, set it on its rest, and shut off the machine.

"That visit will always haunt me."

"You mean you wish you'd performed the surgery on her?"

"No, but I wish I had helped Elizabeth. I let her leave my office distraught. I now understand that her death is partly my fault. I let her go. I didn't help her."

He returned to the couch and sat motionless for a long while, not saying a word, deep in his thoughts. I was still trying to make sense of what I'd just heard. I had absorbed a lot of new information over the past several days. It reminded me of those puzzles that Sarah Jane and I put together on the big table at home. I was beginning to see a clearer picture, and my thoughts kept drifting back to that wound on Floyd's hand when we greeted each other at the sheriff's office. That he was like a son to the Tanners—and, presumably, like a brother to Elizabeth—gave me a clearer understanding of his involvement. Plenty of puzzle pieces remained missing, though, and there was a great deal I still could not see.

I broke the long silence. "How did Elizabeth go from your office to Dr. Wooley's?"

Pfalzgraf shrugged. "That, I do not know."

"I know."

I turned in my seat to see Anna Pfalzgraf in the doorway, no longer crying. She moved across the room, returning to the place beside her father, and took his hand in hers and squeezed it. He squeezed back.

She inhaled a deep, shaky breath and averted her eyes to the ceiling. I could tell she was preparing to say something significant, simply by the change in her posture. If there was ever a time for me to remain silent in spite of that investigator inside of me urging me to ask more questions, it was now.

"Before Helen was . . ." Anna couldn't bring herself to say "murdered." "She confessed something to me. It was Helen who told Elizabeth about Wooley. Elizabeth was desperate. She wasn't in her right state of mind. I knew she'd fallen for a young Mexican fellow named Juan. She met him at a dance, and they started seeing each other in secrecy. But Elizabeth was afraid her parents wouldn't accept him. She told him she couldn't see him anymore. It broke her heart."

"Because he was Mexican?" I asked.

She nodded. "And because he wasn't of the faith. You see, Mr. Oveson, the Tanners—unlike us—are Mormons."

"If you and Elizabeth were so close, why didn't she tell you about her plans to see Wooley?"

"She was ashamed. She didn't really want the surgery, but she was so fearful of her parents' reaction. I think she went to Helen because she hoped Helen could persuade Father to change his mind. Instead, Helen suggested she go to Wooley."

"Surely Helen knew Wooley wasn't safe."

Anna was biting her lower lip, resisting the tears. So far, she was winning. "Not every woman who went to Wooley died afterward. Hundreds survived before Elizabeth went, and she didn't know about all the deaths. I imagine Helen could see how desperate Elizabeth was—how frightened and alone she was."

I nodded, glanced at her father's forlorn expression, then returned my focus to Anna. "Didn't finding out about Helen's affair with Parley put a strain on your relationship with her?"

"I didn't learn about Mr. Tanner until that last time I saw her."

"You mean that last night you saw her alive? Friday?"

"Uh-huh."

I nodded. "How did the subject of her affair with Parley come up?"

"Helen was on her way out the door. I was worried because she was so drunk, and I asked her where she was going. She said she had to talk to Mrs. Tanner. Helen said she needed to get some things off her chest before she left for California. I asked what things. That's when Helen told me about this secret past of hers. The affair with Mr. Tanner. Telling Elizabeth to see Wooley. Getting pregnant with Mr. Tanner's baby. Or what she thought was his baby. Helen wanted to confess all of these things to Mrs. Tanner. She said she needed Mrs. Tanner to forgive her before she could leave."

I shut my eyes. Miriam Tanner's appearance had been seared into my consciousness, as indelible as a red-hot brand. Her gray curls, narrow face, and Mona Lisa smile; her small figure hidden under layers of ritzy clothing. Even when I first met her, without knowing a thing about her, I sensed tragedy only slightly below the surface. If what Anna was saying was true, Miriam might have been one of the last people to see Helen Pfalzgraf alive—*and not just see her alive.* Helen was visiting Miriam to beg her forgiveness for three devastating transgressions, any one of which could drive the most decent person over the precipice into a murderous rage.

"I tried to talk her out of it," said Anna, "but she wouldn't listen. She walked out of the house, and I never saw her again."

The entire room shook for a second, and I looked up at rattling chandelier crystals. Dr. Pfalzgraf rose and went over and parted the curtains at the very moment a bolt of lightning webbed across the skies above the mansion. The thunderclap sounded much louder this time. He stood at the window, watching clouds cast shadows in what was shaping up to be a tumultuous early spring storm. I knew where I had to go next, but I did not relish the confrontation ahead of me. I put on my Stetson and collected the love letters that C. W. Alexander had likely used to extract a decent sum of money from Parley Tanner.

"Sorry if I made you miss your train."

"All things considered, it may be wise for us to postpone this trip," said Anna.

"I agree," said her father. He returned to his open wall safe, fished something out, and brought it over and placed it on to the coffee table in front of me. "You should know, Mr. Oveson, that I never gave Sheriff Cannon a campaign donation. I would never donate a cent to that useless man."

I read the name on the label of the film canister sitting in front of me on the table, but it didn't mean anything to me. MAE CALKINS. 3/22/29.

I ran my fingertips along the cold metal, wondering who she was.

"Mae did not see me alone," he said. "Once in a while, a man will accompany the patient. The man who came in with Mae was Fred Cannon. He had to sign a consent form, because she was only seventeen. I thought he was her father, but I later found out that they knew each other through church, and he . . ."

Pfalzgraf paused for the right words. "He had his way with her. In the film, she expresses reluctance to have the surgery, so he asks me to leave the office. He says he wants privacy so he can—in his words—'talk sense into her.' I did as he asked. It may not have been a wise idea. Once I left the room, the film shows him striking her in the back of the head with the palm of his hand, calling her a fool, telling her she will ruin his marriage if she has the baby. He reduces her to tears. Then he summons me back in the office and tells me that Mae wants the surgery. I ask her if this is true. She says yes, signs on the dotted line, and goes through with it."

He blinked at the film. "At the time, I didn't know what happened when I was out of the room. I didn't watch the film until much later. I was shocked by what I saw. After Helen was murdered, I used the film to keep Cannon away from me. Not that I had anything to hide, mind you, but in my encounters with Cannon, I found him belligerent and vulgar. I suppose you could say I took a page out of Alexander's book."

He watched me looking at the canister. "Go on and take it," he said. "It's yours."

At first, I had a hard time finding the words to form a reply, because I was so shocked, but I snatched the canister off the table and stuffed it in my coat pocket. The canister was a little wide for my pocket, and I had to push it hard to get it in there. It formed a round imprint on the outside of my coat. "Why are you giving it to me?"

"I have a feeling you'll put it to better use than I will."

On my way out of the Pfalzgraf mansion, the doctor stopped and shook my hand. He squeezed it tightly before he released it and flashed an uncertain smile at me. By the time I left, it was raining—a harder and more violent rain than we're accustomed to in Salt Lake City, where we're doing well when a few drops fall on our valley.

Twenty-seven

On a sunny day, it would have seemed absurd to drive the short distance from Dr. Pfalzgraf's mansion on South Temple to the Tanners' house in Federal Heights, only a few blocks away, but today's downpour had flooded the gutters and roads. In Federal Heights, I steered onto the quiet, tree-lined street and drove slowly past the city's grandest dwellings. I parked at the curb, shut off the engine, and straightened my Stetson in the rearview mirror. My arm brushed up against the film canister in my pocket. I pulled it out and glanced down at the label, as if to assure myself it was not a dream. The name was still there. MAE CALKINS. 3/22/29. My gut told me I'd need this bargaining chip. I tucked it under my seat, in a safe crevice that seemed to be made to store movie reels this size. Next, I placed Parley's letters inside the glove compartment and locked it with a little silver key. Before leaping out into the storm, I made sure all of the car windows were rolled up tightly.

The Tanners' house loomed large at the top of that long flight of stairs, with lights glowing in its windows. I ran through the rain, my feet plunging into a street torrent that went halfway up my shoes. I reached the porch—dry ground—and leaned against an Adirondack chair to catch my breath. Lightning brightened the sky, and the tree branches overhead formed gnarled silhouettes against the flash. A Plymouth coupe chugged down the road, spraying a tidal wave onto the sidewalk and lawns. For a second, I thought about getting in my car, driving down to the Public Safety Building on State Street, and sharing everything I knew with Buddy Hawkins. His words from the night before—telling me he'd be waiting for me in his office today—echoed in my mind. I could turn the responsibility for this miserable deed over to him. What harm could he do? I knew Buddy was honest. He'd see to it personally that everybody received fair treatment and justice prevailed. And who knows? If I told him everything I knew, maybe it would put me in good stead for a job on the police force. Being out of work left me feeling weak and demoralized. I needed an income. I had a family to support, bills that needed paying. Clara's salary as an English teacher couldn't support all of us indefinitely.

These were some of the thoughts that raced through my mind as I leaned on that chair, reevaluating my decision. I was on the verge of leaving when a knob clicked and the door of the Tanner house opened. Parley stood in the doorway, handsome as ever and dressed in a cardigan and corduroys. He smiled and arched his eyebrows, as if genuinely happy to see me, and he opened the screen door and stepped out onto the porch.

"Art! Come on in! You're going to catch your death out in this stuff."

He held the door open for me, and I thanked him quietly as I walked past him. I stepped in the entrance hall, with Parley following and gently closing the door. All of the beveled glass windows were freshly shined, every picture on the wall hung perfectly straight, there wasn't a cobweb in sight in the vaulted ceilings, and fresh pine scent filled the air. Hands in my pockets, looking around, I could not help but wonder how much such a fancy house would set someone back. Nearing a staircase, I took off my Stetson, shook the rain droplets away, and glanced down at my soaking shoes.

"I can take off my shoes . . ."

"Oh, please, Art, don't bother," he said. "Come right this way. I'll get you something to drink."

"No thank you."

"I insist," he said, with his handsome grin revealing polished white teeth. "Miriam squeezed some fresh lemonade before she went to her sister Muriel's. You should try it."

"No. I'm not thirsty."

I followed him down a carpeted hall, turning right into a sitting room with high windows that looked out at the nearby foothills of the Wasatch Mountains. An ebony grand piano reflected a gleam from outside, and beside it stood a tall harp. I noticed the Tanners owned one of those fancy combination phonograph radios, with a pair of doors opening up to ebony knobs and a glowing dial. Parley gestured to a chair and a davenport. I went for the chair, unzipping and pulling off my coat before I planted my behind on the cushion.

"So what brings you out here on this rainiest of days, Art?" asked Parley, sitting on a chair facing me.

I noticed a framed picture of the Mormon temple in Manti sitting on a little round table next to me. I picked it up, and my focus shifted from the gleaming white towers to my smiling reflection in the glass.

"Manti," he said, smiling. "It's where I grew up."

I returned the picture to its place. "It's a lovely temple."

"We were married there, Miriam and I," he said. "It was the second-happiest day of my life. Right behind my daughter being born."

His words left me pained. He had lost so much. A daughter. A parent's worst nightmare is outliving his or her child. *It's not too late to turn around and go,* I thought.

"I just had a few . . ." A thought crossed my mind. What was Parley Tanner doing home on a Wednesday? One of the city's busiest lawyers in one of the state's biggest law firms, home on a Wednesday. It struck me as odd, but not odd enough to make me comment. I didn't want to make him feel uneasy. "I was wondering if you could help me."

His face went long and he blinked at me quizzically. "Help you with what?"

"I had a few more questions about the Helen Pfalzgraf case I wanted—"

"Wait. I thought Sheriff Cannon fired you from your job as deputy."

"Yeah. That's right. He did. I still . . ."

"So are you working for the police now?"

Parley's intense stare began to make me nervous, so I looked out the window, at the rain tapping the pane. "To tell you the truth, I'm self-employed at the moment."

"Well, then, I'd say you have no business working on this case. Wouldn't you?"

"I found out new information since we last spoke," I said. "Information I'm sure will clear C. W. Alexander's name."

"Oh? What sort of information?"

"According to reports from the police and county sheriff's office, and the testimony of the Pfalzgraf inquest, the last person Helen saw before she was murdered was C. W. Alexander on the night of Friday, February twenty-first." I cleared my throat, propped my right ankle on my left knee, and forced myself to make eye contact with Parley. "However, I found a Dictaphone interview of Alexander, conducted by journalist Seymour Considine, in which Alexander swears he dropped Helen off at the Pfalzgraf mansion the night of the twenty-first. I confirmed this information with Anna Pfalzgraf, who claims Helen came home drunk and said she was going to come over here to ask for Mrs. Tanner's forgiveness."

"Forgiveness? Forgiveness for what?"

I braced myself with a deep breath. "Helen wanted Miriam's forgiveness for the affair she had with you, which began when she was a stenographer in your office. She wanted forgiveness for telling your daughter, Elizabeth, that she should go see Dr. Wooley for an abortion. Oh, and Helen was pregnant. She told Anna she was pregnant with your baby. She planned to keep the baby and raise it alone. She wanted Miriam to forgive her for that, too. That's a lot to ask forgiveness for."

Parley laughed, a little too uproariously for my comfort, and slapped his knee for good measure. "Do you actually believe all of these fairy tales of Helen's?"

"Maybe. Maybe not," I said, shrugging. "Although I have to say, your love letters to Helen tend to uphold this version of events."

That grin disappeared, but fast. "L-love letters? What do you mean?"

"The ones I got from C. W. Alexander. The ones you apparently missed when you paid a visit to his cabin in Park City."

"Mr. Oveson, that is a vile accusation, and a completely false one. I had nothing whatsoever to do with Alexander's death, if that's what you're driving at. I'd like you to leave my house. Now."

"Before I go, I want you to tell me what happened the night Helen Pfalzgraf was murdered. She came over here. I want to know exactly what she did, what she said."

"Why are you doing this, Art? Why won't you let go? You know something? I liked you. I really liked you. I thought you were a fine young man, with a good head on your shoulders, destined to do good things in the world. Now it turns out you're a dog with a bone.

You seize onto something and you won't let up. What business is this of yours? Why do you pursue it so relentlessly?"

A metallic click behind my head—the familiar sound of a revolver hammer being pulled back. I felt the cold sting of steel against the back of my neck. A mirror on the other side of the room let me know the man with the gun was Floyd Samuelson. The thought of lunging for him and wresting the gun from his hand crossed my mind, but it wouldn't have worked. He stood at an angle that gave him the perfect opportunity to blow my brains out if I made a move. He knew it and I knew it. So I kept still.

"Get up, Art, with your arms raised where I can see them."

I did as Floyd ordered, rising slowly, arms up, turning around to get a look at him. He kept his gun trained on me with nary a tremble, glowering at me the entire time. I glimpsed fresh gauze wrapped around his left hand, where he'd been shot. In my peripheral vision, I noticed what at first appeared to be a giant glass hornet with a long metal stinger. Parley plunged the syringe into my neck, and I involuntarily yelped. Whatever had been inside of it now surged into me, right below my ear, and I was immediately struck by waves of dizziness.

The room started spinning; the ceiling ended up below me, the floor above me, and I thought the Wasatch Mountains outside would fall off the earth, along with everything else. I plunged to the floor, and my Stetson fell off my head and found a spot on the carpet next to me. I moved into the fetal position and threw up all over the rug. Parley squatted near me, his head tilted sideways, as if he had come to hear my last words.

"If anything happens to me," I whispered, wiping vomit off my chin. "The letters . . ."

"My, my, you're looking a little peaked, Art," said Parley. "Aren't you feeling well?"

"What was in . . . Did you . . . Poison?"

"No," said Parley. "It's an extrastrong version of choral hydrate. It's a sedative. You'll be out for a while. I injected quite a bit of it."

By now, I was paralyzed and flat on my stomach. My face was pressed against a Persian rug, and my Stetson sat a few inches away, its brim covered with vomit. How I hated the thought of having to buy a new one. I closed my eyes because I couldn't take all the spinning and nausea. I'd never been this miserable in my life. Part of me wanted to die right now, get it all over with. Someone had moved up close to me, I could sense that much. I opened my eyes enough to see a blurry Floyd. The cold steel from his gun pressed against my face gave me the chills, and I found it impossible to suppress a shudder.

"Dang shame," he said, his voice ringing, as though he were speaking into a metal garbage can. "Every time you came poking around, Art, it twisted me up a little inside."

That's when the burlap bag came over my head, pulled down in abrupt and rough jerks. The coarse fabric rubbed my face and neck and irritated my skin. A clinking buckle was my only warning of a belt being looped around my neck. The leather tightened to the point where I struggled to breathe, and that's when I blacked out.

Twenty-eight

I died once before, during the Great Influenza Epidemic of 1918.

I still have memories of the day I died.

I lay unconscious in bed, buried under levels of linen and wool covers. I couldn't see anything in the blackness, but I could hear people's voices and sense their presences.

Mom wept. Her sobbing funneled into my ears. Voices filled the room.

"I'm sorry, Mrs. Oveson. Your son is dead."

Footsteps surrounded me. When did the others arrive? Maybe an hour later. Maybe a day later. I couldn't be sure. Why can't I open my eyes? Why can't I leap out of bed and tell them I'm still alive?

"My Art, my dear, sweet Art," Mom said, between breaths. "My angel is gone."

"Let's lift him," said a man's voice, which I think belonged to Old Man Loftus, who ran Loftus Mortuary. "You get the ankles, I'll get the shoulder."

I felt my shoulders and ankles being lifted, but my buttocks refused to rise with them. "Someone help us. Lift his lower back."

I was no longer in bed. Three men were moving me. Their hands carried me from my soft bed to a much harder resting place.

"He fits in the casket."

"It's nice. Not too expensive, either."

"We can all chip in for it."

"It's good for Art, Mom. Heck, he almost looks comfy in there."

My eyes opened suddenly. The coarse fabric still covered my head, but I could see through the fibers it was dark around me.

"Don't go all the way to the road we use to get to the cabin," said Parley Tanner's voice. "Turn on one of these dirt roads coming up. Try this next one."

Handcuffs dug into my wrists, so much so that my fingers tingled with numbness. Rope bound my ankles and knees together. The only thing I could be certain of was that my captors had placed me in the backseat of a car. I squirmed and wiggled with a faint hope of breaking free, but my plan went nowhere. They had done a good job of securing me.

I lost all sense of time during the journey. How long had we been on the road? An hour? Two hours? Three? Thoughts swirled like a kaleidoscope, mostly filled with dread. Would I ever see my children again? Or feel Clara's arms around me? Or set foot in my home once more? Intense fear—nausea, trembling, thoughts of death—almost got the best of me.

Eventually, the car slowed, accompanied by brakes whining. The driver let the car idle in park, got out, and slammed the door. A moment later, the door to my left was flung open, and a pair of hands dragged me out of my seat by my arms. The air outside was extremely cold, and I felt the chill of it on my throat. I wormed upright, but a pair of hands shoved my back, toppling me to the earth. I landed in snow, and the next thing I felt was the rope loosening on my legs, then the handcuffs were unlocked. Within a minute I was untied, and the blood rushed to my hands and feet again.

"Off with the bag, Art," said Floyd.

I removed the burlap from my head and tossed it into the snow. Liberating as it seemed at first, I soon discovered I didn't feel much better with it off. The night sky swirled with clouds, and the automobile's headlamps illuminated snowy mountain woods, dense with pine trees. A freezing wind blew, agitating shrubs and branches. Floyd, aiming a gun at me, handed me an old digging shovel with a splintery handle and rusty blade.

"Go to work," he said. "Over there, in the light. Where I can see you."

He shoved me down an embankment with his free hand, and I hit a snowbank, slamming my face against the shovel blade. I licked blood off my lip and stood in the car's headlamp beams. I faced Floyd, shielding my eyes from the brightness, and when my sight adjusted, I detected his silhouette in the snowing darkness, next to the car.

"Start digging!"

"What am I digging exactly?"

"Your burial spot," he said. "I hope you like it out here."

"Where's here?"

A muzzle flash burst, then a piercing pop rang in my ears. The bullet clipped a rock near me. I started digging. I dug and dug, sending clumps of snow to a growing mound. Another man's silhouette appeared next to Floyd's, and I recognized the shoes as Parley's. The lights aimed at my eyes prevented me from seeing their faces.

"How's he doing?" asked Parley.

"He's digging."

"Hurry, Art. We don't wish to stay out here all night."

I spent several minutes scooping snow until I reached soil.

Then I went to work pushing the shovel blade into hard ground—still frozen in parts—and scooping heavy piles of earth into the snow.

"I can help you," I said. "I know people in—"

Floyd snapped, "Shut up and keep digging!"

I thrust the shovel into the ground, pressing it deeper with the heel of my shoe. "You know, Floyd, I get why you killed Wooley," I said, pouring my shovelful of dirt to the side. "He's responsible for Elizabeth's death."

"Pay him no mind," said Parley.

"All you wanted was to protect your aunt and uncle," I said, ramming shovel into soil. "They loved you like you were their own son. They saved you from your father—"

He leaped into the shallow trench, shoved me into the dirt, and aimed his pistol at my head. I closed my eyes. I thought I was a dead man. "I ought to shoot you now, you dirty dog!"

"Come back, son," said Parley, leaning forward and hooking his hand around Floyd's elbow. "Let him finish what he's doing. Don't let him get to you."

I opened my eyes to see the gun in my face and the rage in Floyd's eyes. He exhaled steam through clenched teeth, and his chest rose and fell rapidly. I swear I noticed his index finger twitch on the trigger.

"I can understand why you killed Wooley," I said, still lying on the ground. "If he'd done that to my daughter or my sister, I'd have killed the man, too. Especially if I knew he was going to butcher other people's daughters and sisters."

The muzzle flash almost blinded me, and the crack of the pistol hurt my ears. The bullet popped a mud geyser a few inches away from my left hand. Floyd aimed the gun at my chest, and I had no doubt he was ready to use it.

"Get up and start digging, Art, or I won't let you finish."

Floyd stepped up to the surface, so he stood next to Parley again, and he kept his gun on me the entire time. I stood, picked up my shovel, and resumed digging. "I can't imagine how awful your Aunt Miriam would've felt if Helen had a chance to tell her all those things—"

Parley cut me off. "Floyd didn't kill Helen. It's true she came over to the house that Friday night. In fact, Floyd gave her a ride. Miriam happened to be gone. Staying with her sister. I had the house to myself. Imagine my surprise when Helen showed up, demanding that I give her the telephone number where Miriam could be reached. Helen raised a ruckus. I thought she was going to wake up the entire neighborhood. She said she needed to ask Miriam to forgive her. For her affair with me. For giving bad advice to Elizabeth. For being pregnant with my baby. That night she pushed me to the breaking point. I saw that piece of ore sticking out of her purse and I grabbed hold of it and I . . ."

His voice trailed off as he watched snow falling in the headlamp beams, and he seemed overwhelmed by his own emotions. "This is the first time I've said any of this out loud. If you'll excuse me, I'm going to sit inside the car for a moment. Floyd, you can take care of this."

I kept digging. Out the corner of my eye, I watched Parley climb inside the car. The door closed, and things were quiet for a while. Until I broke the silence. "So you didn't have anything to do with Helen—"

"Shut up and dig or the next bullet goes in your head, Art."

More digging. I said, "I don't have any hard feelings."

"That's big of you," he said. "Dig faster."

"The Tanners are like parents to you. I can see why—"

"Shut up!"

I stopped digging and looked up at him, shielding my eyes from the light. "I have a son like you do," I said. "He turns two in August."

"I said shut up!"

"He'll wonder why I'm not home. Imagine Bert sitting by the front door, waiting, wondering when—"

"It's not going to work, what you're doing—"

"You're not making it easier for your aunt and uncle," I said, pitching my shovel in the ground and resting my elbow on the handle. "Or yourself."

"Who told you could stop digging?"

The next shot he fired jolted me, but not as badly as the others. The sound echoed through the pine forest, boomeranging back to us in a more muted form.

"You crossed the line when you shot Lund," I said. "They'll hunt you down."

"They don't have the foggiest idea I had anything to do with it! I got pals in the force, and they say they don't know who did it."

"They never tip their hand," I said. "You won't know they're closing in on you until it's too late—"

"Stop it!"

"That night at Grand Central, Roscoe didn't see your license plates, but he shot you in the hand, and you've got a bullet hole in your car door."

"I'll get it fixed!"

"I can help you, Floyd."

"I don't need your help! Keep digging or I'll shoot you now and dig the hole for you!"

I spent a while digging in silence. While I did, I watched Floyd's movements. It was hard to see him with the car's lights blinding me, but every now and then he would aim his gun at the sky while he blew warm air at his cold hands. He was shivering and would rub his free hand up and down on the opposite arm to warm himself. He started to relax, repeatedly shifting his attention away from me: pacing, shivering, coughing. During one of these moments when he had his back turned to me, I lifted my shovel and swung it as hard as I could against his calves. The loud thud of steel on his legs sent him sideways into the car's grille, yelling with pain.

I bolted.

I sprinted as fast as my legs would carry me, past the car and down the snowy road, in the direction of what I hoped would be a highway or, at the very least, a paved road. I could hear Floyd shouting behind me, although the only word I could make out was "Oveson." Three gunshots cracked through the forest, but I didn't look back. Running faster, I felt myself getting out of breath and became woozy, possibly from those drugs I'd ingested earlier. The white landscape formed a silent backdrop, with rolling snow hills shimmering under the moonlight. It was quiet—3:00 A.M. Christmas morning quiet; where the only sounds I could hear were snow falling, heavy breathing, and my feet crunching snow. Moving as fast as possible in the direction of the main road made the most sense to me. I could have run deeper into the woods, but I didn't know exactly where I was or where that would take me. What if I reached a cliff and I couldn't go any farther? What then?

A revving engine sent my heart racing. I wheeled and spotted headlamps winding around the trees, heading in my direction. I turned and ran. A gunshot rang out, exploding snow near my feet. Another shot nailed a nearby tree, and pieces of bark hit me as I ran. The car had almost caught up with me—the headlamps bathed the whole area in light—and I leaped off the road to avoid being hit. The car was about fifteen feet to my left now, and there was no missing that left arm emerging from the window, pointing a pistol at me. The flash and crack prompted me to jump behind a tree, and the bullet hit one of its branches. I couldn't take much more running. I was out of breath, exhausted, my legs ached, and my lungs were beginning to hurt from all the panting and the frigid air.

The highway was in sight. *Only a little bit more. You can do it, Art.* My legs were about to give out. Floyd maneuvered the speeding car and positioned his gun for another shot. I sprinted out of the woods, nearly stumbling on the black-ice pavement that reflected the moon and clouds. The main road dipped downward at a steep grade. On either side of it was dense forest with towering pines everywhere. I didn't have long to rest. The car roared out of that dirt road and skidded to a stop before reaching the gravelly shoulder. I started running again. Where was I going? Why was I running? Did I really think I could outrun an auto?

The car backed up several feet, turned and began coming at me full speed. I ran as fast I could, but I didn't have much left. My thoughts drifted back to that time I almost died during the influenza epidemic, when I was seventeen. That old adage about people seeing their lives flash before their very eyes prior to dying did not apply to me. The only thing that flashed before my eyes was a question: *How badly is this going to hurt?*

A gunshot went off, and a bullet grazed my left bicep. At that moment, I slipped on the icy surface and landed on my stomach. The car's engine roared with acceleration, and it must have been coming at me at fifty to sixty miles per hour. I craned my neck to see the headlamps closing in on me, and I knew if I stayed where I was, I'd suffer the same fate as Helen Pfalzgraf.

I closed my eyes and, with what strength I could muster, thrust my arms against the road and rolled hard to my right, in the direction of the gravel shoulder. I felt the heat from the car as it roared past, and I opened my eyes and watched red taillights streak away from me. Floyd slammed on the brakes, which sent the car spinning out of control and plunging down a snowy embankment. It rolled a hundred feet and crashed into a huge tree, sending Parley

Tanner facefirst through the windshield like a rag doll. I closed my eyes and turned away, but I still heard a gory burst when he hit the hood.

I hurried to the wreckage to survey the damage. The front of the car was accordion-crushed and belching steam clouds into the cold night. An ancient Ponderosa pine had managed to rip halfway into the passenger compartment, sandwiching Floyd Samuelson's mangled body between the dashboard and his seat back, which was now fused with the backseat. I waded through thigh-deep snow until I reached the bent running board and peered through the shattered window. Floyd wasn't moving. I thought he was dead. I made my way over to the passenger side. The moonlight allowed me to get as much of a glimpse of Parley Tanner's lifeless body as I wanted. I circled back to see if there was any way I could pull Floyd out of the car. When I reached the window to get a better look at him, he opened his eyes, startling me.

"Wh-where is P-P-Parley?" he whispered.

I thought it best to lie under the circumstances. "He went off to look for help."

"Oh." Floyd smiled as blood dripped from his hair. "Good. Good idea. Maybe he'll . . ." He swallowed and groaned in pain. "Maybe he'll find someone who can h-h-help us."

"Tell you what," I said. "I'll go with him. We'll get an ambulance up here and we'll get you guys to a hospital—"

Floyd grew panicky. He shook his head, reached his bandaged left hand out the window, and gripped my coat sleeve. "Don't go. Please. I don't want to die alone. Stay with me. Please."

He began to weep gently, his lower lip quivering, tears streaming. "I made a real mess of things. Everything is worse because of me."

"It's going to be OK," I said. "We'll get you to a hospital, and I'll help you. I'll testify on your behalf. I'll make some telephone calls and talk to people—"

He cut me off. "I'm gonna die, Art. I know it. It hurts. It hurts worse than anything I've ever felt in my life. God, it hurts."

He squeezed my forearm, and I moved closer to him and watched his blood mix with his tears. "Do me a favor, Art."

"Sure. Anything, Floyd."

"Make sure Bert doesn't find out about any of this. He's gonna wonder why I'm not home. He's used to me coming home and playing with him. He drew me a picture the other day. You shoulda seen it, Art. He drew it with crayons. Me and him fishing." Floyd's eyes widened, and he trembled in that steel and glass cocoon. "I don't want him knowing that I murdered all them people, Art."

"I understand. But I need you to level with me, Floyd, and tell me the names of the people you murdered. I'll make it easy for you. I'll say the names, and you just nod or shake your head."

"O-OK."

"Alright. Everett Wooley."

He nodded. "I'd do it again, if I had it to," he said. "He killed my sister. He didn't just murder her. She died slow, Art. Real slow. Cryin' out in pain. I'd do it all over again," he repeated. "If I had to."

I nodded. "Helen Pfalzgraf."

"That was Uncle Parley," he said. "She came over that night and made a scene. He hauled off and hit her on the head with the piece of ore, like he said. We took her out to the old Pole Line Road, to dump her body. As we was driving away, she . . ." He coughed up blood and gasped. "Sorry. I'm tired. I feel like going to sleep."

"I need more help," I said, "and then you can go to sleep. So you took Helen down to the Pole Line Road, but she was still alive. Right?"

He nodded. "I couldn't do it. Couldn't bring myself to run over a woman. He pushed me out of the car. Said, 'Here, I'll do it.' He took out all his anger on her, running over her, over and over again. I was shocked. I couldn't understand it. I can't remember how many times he hit her." He began to weep. "P-please don't tell Uncle Parley I told you. I don't want him to know I told you."

"I promise I won't," I said. "What about C. W. Alexander? Did you kill him?"

He dried his eyes with shaking fingers. "I set the whole thing up to look like a suicide. I went up to Alexander's place in Park City, plugged the sonofabitch and looked for Uncle Parley's let-letters. Uncle Parley told me they were legal documents. Didn't say nothing about no love letters."

"I see. Seymour Considine."

"Drove on down to his room at the motor court on, uh, State. Same day he called Uncle Parley, asking a bunch of questions. Uncle Parley told me Considine was asking about Everett Wooley. I went down there and confronted him and I brung a knife and I . . ." He coughed more blood and closed his eyes. "I put his body in the tr-trunk of his car and drove him to the Salt Lake and threw him in. Ditched his car near the water and used a pay phone at Saltair to call Uncle Parley to come and pick me up."

His eyes still closed, his head flopped down, as if he'd just died.

"Floyd? Floyd, you with me? It's not time yet. I need more help, so I can make it so Bert doesn't find out."

He slowly opened his eyes and looked at me.

I nodded. "One last one. Roscoe Lund. Was that you?"

He nodded. "Lund came out to Uncle Parley and Aunt Helen's on Saturday morning. Somehow, he got wind that Helen used to work at Uncle Parley's firm. When Roscoe came, only Aunt Miriam was home. He asked her a lot of questions about Helen. Quizzed her a good half hour. Before he left, he said he was coming back again and bringing you with him. Aunt Miriam got suspicious and confronted Uncle Parley. She asked him why Roscoe was asking all these questions. Uncle Parley waited till Aunt Miriam left. Called me. Told me what happened. So I drove that night over to Public Safety and waited. Little before midnight, Roscoe came out of the building, got in his car, and headed over to the market. I followed him. Watched him go inside. When he came out . . ."

He turned his head away from me and spit up something. I couldn't tell if it was blood or vomit, or maybe a mix of the two. I looked away, at the flattened snow on the white embankment where the car had driven off the road, and it amazed me that Floyd had survived this long.

Floyd watched me with tragic eyes and a bloody, crooked grin. "Sorry I was gonna kill you, Art. I woulda, too, if I had the chance. But it woulda eaten away at me, same as the others. I ain't a killer at heart. 'Sides, you're the most decent man I know. I'm glad you're alive."

I smiled. "I am, too."

His lower lip quivered, as if he were about to start crying. "If Aunt Miriam finds out about any of this, it'll destroy her. Lady's lost everything. Think about it."

"I'll do my best to make sure she doesn't," I said.

"P-promise?"

I nodded. There was no more color left in his face. He swallowed again, and when he ran his tongue along his lips, I could tell his mouth was dry. "I'd give anything for a drink of water."

I leaned down and picked up a snow clump, straightened, and reached over the pointed metal and broken glass to put it in his mouth. "Try some of this. It'll help hydrate . . ."

He stared into space, mouth agape, with no more life left in his eyes. Somehow, I knew he was gone. I didn't have to check for a pulse. Floyd Samuelson had found peace.

I lost track of how much time I spent sitting on the demolished running board, crying in a way that I've never cried in my adult life. My wailing echoed through the canyon.

At some point in the night, a truck stopped on the road at the top of the embankment, and the driver got out and came down to inspect the wreck. I told him what happened, and he offered me a ride to the nearest town so we could telephone the sheriff's office. I accepted, and on the way I found out I was in Summit County, northeast of Salt Lake City. That placed us in the forests of the Uinta Mountains. The driver kept eyeing my blood-saturated shirt-sleeve and asking if I was OK. I reassured him I was fine, even though I felt woozy and my neck still ached from being punctured with that hypodermic needle.

We reached a roadside café around dawn, and inside I found a mahogany and glass telephone booth to make two calls. The first went out to the Summit County Sheriff's Office to report the car crash I'd witnessed. The second was to Buddy Hawkins, at home. I apologized for waking him, and he said he was already up and eating a grapefruit. Good thing I had a pocketful of change and there wasn't a line of people waiting to use the telephone, because our conversation lasted a good hour.

An hour and a half after we said our good-byes, a Salt Lake police squad car picked me up from the café and drove me back to the city. I dozed off on the way home, but I slept fitfully and woke up for the final leg of the drive. Snaking through a craggy mountain canyon, the highway eventually plugged into the Salt Lake Valley, which glimmered in the morning sun. The patrolman behind the wheel delivered me to LDS Hospital for a set of stitches in my arm wound. Before leaving, I asked to see Roscoe, but a nurse on duty informed me it wasn't visiting hours. Buddy arrived to pick me up, and he waited while I telephoned Clara from the lobby. She raced to the hospital, taking our children to her sister's house on the way. We sat side by side on a waiting room bench, and I gave her as brief an explanation as I could about what had transpired in the past twenty-four hours. Before long, I'd have to tell the story all over again to the police. I was weary. I desperately wanted to go home, take a hot bath, and spend time with my family. Alas, it wasn't over. Not quite yet.

Twenty-nine

I sat alone at a long table, surrounded by chairs on all sides. Above me, a line of dangling light globes buzzed brightly, filling the room with a stark white light that hurt my eyes. The table in front of me was marred from years of use, and I didn't care much for the hard wooden chair under my behind. I looked around, hoping in vain to find a softer, upholstered chair, but they were all the same. A cork bulletin board to my right played home to a host of WANTED posters, and I scanned the grainy photostats of some of the grimmest-looking plug-uglies I've ever laid eyes on. In the center of the table, three pitchers of water stood next to a row of spotless glasses turned upside down on doilies.

They kept me waiting a long time, the police. They'd put me in this room almost two hours earlier, according to the ticking wall clock. I squirmed in my seat. What did they have in store for me? I couldn't even begin to venture a guess. I felt too exhausted to be nervous. I'd spent so many years being afraid, worried about what others might say or think, but seeing Floyd die in that jagged scrap heap changed me. It was as if something had snapped inside of me.

For whatever reason, I wasn't scared anymore. It felt liberating. I glanced at my jacket pocket and took solace in the imprint of the film canister I'd brought with me. I pulled it partway out of the wide pocket opening and read the label: MAE CALKINS. 3/22/29.

My bargaining chip with Sheriff Fred Cannon.

The door opened, and five men filed into the room: Detectives Wit Dunaway and Buddy Hawkins, Police Chief Otis Ballard, District Attorney Walter Rasmussen, and Sheriff Fred Cannon. Cannon closed the door behind him, and the five men pulled out chairs on the opposite side of the table from me and took their seats almost in unison. Ballard's long and dignified face, with lines etched deeply in places, provided a nice counterweight to Cannon's round, bulldoggish features. This was one of the few times I'd seen Wit Dunaway not sneering. He actually smiled slightly when I made eye contact with him. DA Rasmussen, a prim, three-piece-suit bureaucrat with slicked-back brown hair and wire-rimmed spectacles, harbored gubernatorial aspirations, or so I'd heard. He opened a leather-bound notebook to a blank lined page and removed a fountain pen and glass inkwell from his briefcase and set them on the table, with all the precision of a surgeon. A moment later, a knock sounded at the door, and in walked a woman in a floral dress, her brunette hair pulled back tightly in a bun. She sat at the end of the table and prepared to take shorthand notes.

"Mr. Oveson, we've a lot of ground to cover," said Chief Ballard, in a resonant voice that commanded everyone's attention. "I suppose you had better start from the beginning."

For the next two hours or so, I walked everybody in the room through the case, starting with the day Roscoe and I found Helen's body out at the Pole Line Road. I told them all about the investigation—finding C. W. Alexander murdered in his cabin in Park City, my connection to Seymour Considine, my decision to keep pursuing leads even after finding Alexander's body and his

suicide note, and my questioning of the different suspects—and all
of the men at the table watched me intently while the stenographer
took rapid notes, flipping pages every few minutes, starting on a
new notebook. I even backtracked through Wooley's story and
his violent death at the hands of Floyd Samuelson. My voice grew
raspy. Chief Ballard poured me a glass of water; I gulped it down
fast, and he refilled it. At times when I spoke about the night in the
mountains with Parley and Floyd, I choked up and had to pause.
Near the end of my account, my throat ached from talking so much,
and Fred Cannon's stare had turned fierce, complete with frown
and quivering eyebrows.

"That's quite a story," said Chief Ballard. "Are you prepared,
Arthur, to go on the record with all of this information?"

"No. None of this is going to be made public."

The men looked at each other, then looked at me, and the stenographer stopped taking shorthand and blinked in my direction.

"Come again?" asked Chief Ballard.

"None of this is going to be made public," I repeated. "The police are going to declare Helen Pfalzgraf's murder unsolved. That
means C. W. Alexander's name will be cleared, and the police will
publicly absolve him of any involvement in the crime. The public
will *not* learn of Parley Tanner's alleged involvement in Helen's
murder, just as they won't find out about their affair or her getting
pregnant by him. Same goes for Floyd Samuelson's involvement in
the slayings of Wooley and Considine, and his attempt on Roscoe
Lund."

"But Art," said Buddy, "there's no way under the sun we can
possibly—"

I cut him off. "You can tell the press that Parley and Floyd were
going up to the Tanners' cabin to open it up for the spring, and they
lost control of their automobile on a slick mountain road. You
wouldn't be lying about the second part."

Cannon said, "What makes you think you're in any position to give us orders?"

"Gentlemen," I said, "I have in my possession a box of eighty reels from Dr. Pfalzgraf's extensive collection of movies. Pfalzgraf spent years using hidden cameras to film his clients when they visited his office to request his illegal surgeries. I think you know precisely what type of surgeries I'm talking about. It turns out that many of these women are the wives of influential men. If any of this ever goes public, I'll see to it that the movies get turned over to the press and the feds. Believe me, gentlemen, a lot of important careers will be destroyed."

"Whose careers are we talking about?" asked Rasmussen, showing his first signs of nervousness.

"You know me. I never tip my hand."

Buddy smirked.

"Why are you doing this, Art?" asked Ballard.

"To protect someone."

"Miriam Tanner?" asked Buddy.

I didn't reply. He knew the answer.

An uneasy silence fell over the room. Rasmussen closed his notebook and returned it, along with his pen and capped inkwell, to his briefcase, and then he studied me while he scratched his chin. He broke the silence. "Releasing those films to the public has the potential to be very destructive, Mr. Oveson. You could ruin a lot of lives. Are you prepared to do this in order to protect the feelings of one individual?"

"I am."

Rasmussen nodded and arched his eyebrows. "Well, I suppose if a thorough police investigation confirms Mr. Oveson's assertions, my office is prepared to accept his conditions. I'm sure a less heavy-handed approach on Mr. Oveson's part would've won me over, but that's neither here nor there at this point. The important thing is *we* know who bears responsibility for this recent string of homicides. The public need not know of our findings."

Ballard turned toward Buddy. "How say you?"

Buddy, with his arms folded, watched me. He switched his gaze to the table and thought it over. "We'd have to keep a tight lid on this one. If it ever got out to the public that we withheld information about a series of high-profile crimes committed in our community, there'll be hell to pay." He paused, without taking his eyes off the table. "Then again, if Miriam Tanner were to find out what we all heard in this room today, she'd be crushed, in a far worse way than she is now. She's already devastated. Revealing the details of this case to the public would only add to her anguish. Which is why Art here is doing what he's doing."

"I can't believe what I'm hearing," said Cannon. "It astonishes me that men of your stature would allow yourselves to be pushed around by a sidewinder like Oveson. Well, gentlemen, I'm not playing ball here. I'm sure as heck not going to participate in any cover-up. The good people of this county have the right to find out all of the details of this case."

The time had come. I pulled the metal film canister out of my coat pocket, placed it on the table, and slid it over to Cannon like a hockey puck. It stopped at the edge of the table, in front of him. He read the label, and his eyes widened with recognition. He looked at the others at the table as he laid the canister on his lap.

"That's mine," he said quietly. "Been looking for it."

He cleared his throat and regained his composure. "Like I was saying. The people have the right to know. That's why, come tomorrow morning, I'm gonna call a press conference and tell the world exactly who murdered Helen Pfalzgraf."

"Why?" I asked. "So you can get reelected?"

"Dang straight," he said, with an exaggerated nod. "The men and women of this county deserve to have a sheriff who looks after their interests. Not like that bastard Blackham, and not a bunch of police who kowtow to a little desperado like you, Oveson!"

I smiled. "You don't think I'd actually leave the film in that can, do you?"

Another look of horror, rivaling his expression when he saw the canister, spread over his face. "You . . . mean . . ."

I nodded. "It's empty."

He pried the can open like a metallic clam and turned pale when he found nothing inside of it.

"Where is it? Tell me right now!"

"You know, Cannon," I said, "the people of this county would be a whole lot better off if you'd get in your car and drive as far away from here as possible and never come back."

"Why, you little son of a—"

Like a whale leaping out of the ocean, he lunged across the table, knocking over two of the upside-down glasses and one of the pitchers of ice water on his way. It happened in a blurry flash, that big, beefy body flying at me, those hands reaching for my throat. The sheer weight of him sent me backward, and he knocked the wind out of me with a punch to my gut. I heard the other men moving—getting out of their chairs, running around the table—but Cannon was smothering me and I couldn't see much. Men's voices overlapped, and in the confusion I couldn't tell whose was whose.

Cannon's weight eased off me as multiple fingers grasped his arms and shoulders and chest and lifted him. He got in one last punch—his hard, leathery knuckles connecting with my mouth and nose—before they peeled him off. A pair of uniformed police officers pulled him out of the room flailing and shouting and pointing at me. Spit flew out of his mouth as he shouted, "I'll dog you, Oveson! I swear to God, I'll dog you, boy! You ain't heard the last'a me! Goddamn backstabbing rattlesnake!"

The door closed, but he could still be heard in the hallway, raving like a lunatic. "Let me at him! I'll break his dang neck! I swear, I'll dog that kid . . ." Eventually, his voice faded into the distance. I remained flat on my back in a puddle of ice water until Buddy offered me his hand and helped me to my feet. Wit, Rasmussen, and Ballard straightened chairs, and Buddy lifted mine upright. We returned to our seats, momentarily too shaken to speak, catching our breaths and letting our pulses slow. Buddy broke the silence by bursting into laughter, and a few seconds later Wit joined him. Rasmussen bit into his lower lip in a vain attempt to keep a straight face, but restraint lost out. Before long, everybody in the room except Ballard was laughing, and even he had a slight a grin on his face.

"Alright, enough's enough," said the chief, shaking his head. "I'd like a little time alone with Arthur. Gentlemen, would you please excuse us?"

Chair legs scraped the floor, and the men stood and, one by one, left the room. Wit Dunaway closed the door behind him.

Chief Ballard kept his hands pressed together and covering his mouth, as if praying, and stared at me a long time with those squinting, dignified eyes of his. For a few seconds, I felt as if he were looking into my very soul, and for all I know, he may have been doing exactly that. He radiated an ancient wisdom, in an old Abraham Lincoln sort of way, and his firm yet taciturn style reminded me of my father.

"Are you OK?" asked Ballard.

"Yes, sir," I said, running my palm over my sore face. "I'm fine, thank you."

He leaned forward, rested his elbows on the table, and kept his eyes on me. "He hasn't changed one iota since he used to work here, Cannon. I share your sentiments about him. That doesn't justify your actions, though, Arthur. Extortion. Blackmail. Hindering a police investigation. Conducting a homicide investigation without being properly qualified to do so. I could sit here and list half a dozen other laws you've broken that I know of. I could easily send you to Sugar House Prison for the next decade."

He turned two glasses resting in the center of the table right side up, raised the pitcher, and filled them. He nudged a glass of water to me, and I reluctantly took a drink. I needed it. His withering stare left me parched. I could hear each gulp as he downed his, and he returned the glass to the table. "I wonder what your father would think if he'd lived to see this. Willard Oveson was my first partner, before you were even born. He didn't teach me *everything* I know about being a policeman, but he taught me all of the most important things. I'm certain Will would be as shocked as I am by your methods."

He didn't speak for a while; then he scooted his chair back and stood to leave. On his way out the door, he faced me. "Come back Monday. There'll be a job waiting for you, if you want it."

I reared my head back in surprise. "But I thought you said . . ."

"We need a new dispatcher."

My shoulders slumped. "Dispatcher?"

He must have heard the disappointment in my voice, because he looked me up and down. "You've got to start somewhere, Arthur."

Familiar words.

Chief Ballard left the door open when he walked out. I took that to mean I was free to go.

In the waiting room by the information desk, Clara was asleep on a chair. I nudged her gently, and she woke up, stood, and wrapped her arms around me. "I love you."

"I love you, too."

"Let's go home." Outside, my sensitive ears picked up every late-afternoon sound, from a distant locomotive whistle to a dog barking. My bandaged arm ached, my head throbbed, my neck was sore, and yet I'd never felt as happy to be alive as I did walking out of the Public Safety Building, holding hands with Clara. We faced bustling State Street, congested with streetcars, autos, and trucks, polluting the air with exhaust and yet brimming with life.

Thirty

Pioneer Day—July 24, 1930—fell on a Thursday.

Anyone who has been in Utah on Pioneer Day can attest that it is a bigger holiday in this state than July 4, and that is saying something because Utahns are a patriotic bunch. Pioneer Day celebrates the families who came to Utah in 1847 to build a city in an arid landscape at a time when the conventional wisdom of the day held that this land could not be settled. We had proved the naysayers wrong. Some of the more zealous celebrants even donned pioneer clothing—calico and homespun—and rode across the valley in the very same wagons their forebears arrived in eight decades ago.

Festivities commenced in the morning. A colossal, flapping banner over Main Street announced, PIONEER DAYS PARADE, JULY 24, 1930. Sun baked the pavement and sidewalks. People stood under trees and opened all of the windows in their houses and prayed for a breeze. The radio announced that a record fifteen thousand flocked to the beaches of Saltair that day. Streetcars ran double operations, depositing throngs at downtown stops to watch the parade. Crowds packed both sides of Main Street, waiting for the 9:00 A.M. parade to begin, eager to watch floats and marching bands and touring cars loaded with local celebrities and dignitaries.

Later that day, at Liberty Park, thousands of people—mostly families—filled the grounds to be part of the annual picnic. Hot dogs and hamburgers sizzled on the grill; kids ran from booth to booth, paying a nickel to play carnival games and toss balls at a dunk-tank target; colored biplanes buzzed overhead. Finding a parking spot within a mile of the park was nearly impossible, and city enforcers were working overtime, ticketing cars parked on lawns and sidewalks.

At night, people gathered in the park to watch one of the biggest fireworks exhibitions in the western United States. Roscoe and I arrived before starting our regular shift on the Dawn Patrol—midnight to 8:00 A.M.—a move upward from dispatch, yet still far from ideal. It's like Chief Ballard said, though: *You have to start somewhere.* My stiff black police uniform made my neck and arms itch, and my cap was too big for me, but Clara and Sarah Jane and Hyrum didn't seem to notice. They found us in the park, and Sarah Jane ran up to me and threw her arms around my neck. Clara held hands with Hyrum, and he toddled up to me and hugged my leg. I led them to the new patrol car, a 1930 Chevrolet with white stars on both front doors, each emblazoned with the gold words SALT LAKE CITY POLICE DEPARTMENT. A siren had been fitted below the right headlamp, and a blinking red light was fastened to the grille. It boasted vulcanized whitewalls and gleaming black metal spokes, and the interior smelled of fresh leather. My family huddled together on the running board, and Roscoe—by now a regular guest at our house for Sunday evening dinners—leaned against the hood of the car.

Colorful explosions of light filled the skies over Liberty Park with shimmering greens and violets, oranges and yellows, reds and silvers. Sitting on my lap, Hyrum saw the fireworks reflected in my chest badge, and he touched it and smiled at me. The more elaborate skyrockets prompted *oohs* and *ahhs* and clapping and finger pointing from the thousands of spectators sitting on the lawns, in the backs of flatbed trucks, on benches, in the seats of convertible autos. Somewhere in the distance, a phonograph or radio played patriotic band music that went along beautifully with the pyrotechnics over our heads.

The previous months had been eventful. I went to work for the Salt Lake City Police Department at the beginning of April, assigned to operate their radio station, KGPW. Inside a windowless room, I read alerts into a microphone plugged into a radio console with lots of dials. An operator would pass me messages written on slips of paper, which I'd announce with the squeeze of the mike key, and my voice went out to patrol cars across the valley. Boredom reigned most of the time on the job, although I'd have the occasional lively day, packed with alerts.

Roscoe spent weeks convalescing, eventually walking out of LDS Hospital with the help of a wooden cane. I picked him up the day of his release, and we passed under the shade of fragrant trees in the Avenues. When he entered his apartment, Barney—who'd been under my daily care while Roscoe was in the hospital—came running to his old friend and leaped into his arms, and the two experienced a joyful reunion full of petting and purring. I left, closing the door to let them enjoy their time together in peace. Two months later, Chief Ballard promoted me to Dawn Patrol, partnering me up with Roscoe. The two of us spent long nights breaking up quarrels, shutting down nocturnal gambling operations, destroying distilleries, arresting prowlers and perverts, helping ambulance drivers and morgue wagon boys retrieve car-wreck victims, and responding to false alarms and needless calls. Paired together every night, we grew closer, yet we hid our fondness for each other under a layer of joking and back patting.

Around the time I went to work for the Salt Lake City Police Department, Sheriff Fred Cannon announced he was resigning. Cannon told a press conference he was stepping down for "health reasons" and Assistant Sheriff Albert M. Sykes would be taking over as sheriff of Salt Lake County. Last I heard, Cannon loaded all of his worldly belongings into a touring car, along with his wife, Ida, and drove out of the city to points unknown. Upon assuming the duties of sheriff, Sykes promptly announced his decision not to run for the office in November, leaving Lorenzo Blackham's candidacy uncontested.

A big funeral was held for Parley Tanner at the Salt Lake City Cemetery in the Avenues. It was a sunny day, warm for late March, and I watched the whole thing from my car, parked on a dirt road overlooking the cemetery and the valley beyond it. A few days later, Floyd Samuelson's kin held a smaller funeral at Mount Olivet Cemetery on 500 South, burying him in the shade of a tall weeping birch tree. I showed up at Floyd's service, too, and—as at Parley Tanner's ceremony—kept my distance. I leaned against a stone wall, watching his widow dressed in black, held up by loved ones as she wept. Floyd's young son, Bert, gently placed a flower on the casket and kissed the wood before it was lowered into the ground.

By June, the police had declared Helen Pfalzgraf's murder unsolved, telling the public they had no suspects or leads. The trail had grown cold, Chief Ballard said, and the police simply had no explanation as to who killed Helen or why. Coincidentally, Sheriff Sykes changed the status of C. W. Alexander's death from a suicide to a homicide and issued a statement that there was no evidence linking the slain mining speculator to the Pfalzgraf homicide. Alexander's suicide note had been a hoax, said Sykes, planted at the crime scene by the murderer in an effort to throw off the police. He told a *Salt Lake Examiner* reporter there were no suspects in the Alexander homicide.

The investigation into the killing of Seymour Considine took a strange turn in the spring. Police in Asbury Park, New Jersey—Considine's hometown—got wind of his plans to write an exposé about Al Capone's brutal strong-arm tactics in Chicago and the power that Mr. Scarface wielded over the city's political establishment. Considine had interviewed about a dozen Chicagoans for the story before he was murdered. The Asbury Park investigators pinned Considine's murder on Capone's men. They figured Capone's enforcer, Frank Nitti, must've dispatched two torpedoes to Salt Lake City to finish off the true crime writer. "It will be hard, if not impossible, to prove," an unnamed police source told the *Asbury Park Tribune*, "but for now, all signs point to a Capone hit."

So Miriam Tanner remained shielded from the ugly truth—for now, at least.

On a breezy, overcast morning in May, I parked beside a curb in Federal Heights, a few houses down from the Tanner place. I opened a brown bag of taffy, ripped wax paper off of a piece, and chewed the candy—lemon—as I watched movers carefully load the Tanners' furniture into a long moving van. Miriam Tanner, in a wide-brimmed hat and willowy green dress, watched from the lawn with a stoic expression. Behind her stood Hans and Anna Pfalzgraf, and they'd occasionally talk to her or offer her a supportive rub on the shoulder while the movers did their work. It began to sprinkle lightly as the men in overalls carried the last of the furniture into the truck, closed the twin rear doors, and sealed them with a sliding bar. Miriam Tanner embraced Anna, then Dr. Pfalzgraf, and then climbed into a maroon Nash, started the engine, and drove away. Later, I found out she moved into a modest bungalow in Provo, to be closer to her sisters.

Dr. Pfalzgraf contacted me a few days later. He asked if we could meet in a secluded spot, far from the city. We agreed to the Bonneville Salt Flats, about as remote a location as you could get. We set up the meeting for a Saturday, so I wouldn't have to ask for a night off. It was a hot day in the West Desert, and I parked my car about fifteen miles from the foothills of the Silver Island Mountains. Here, in this vast salt pan, the horizon where sky and earth touch create the illusion of blue meeting white. This flat, uninhabitable land was once part of a mighty saltwater lake that would've given the Great Lakes a run for their money. Thousands of years later, the Great Salt Lake to the north was the only water that was left of that lake. Down here, these salt flats were all that remained, named after Benjamin Bonneville, a French-born U.S. Army officer and fur trapper who explored the Great Basin in 1833.

I popped open my timepiece and took a glance: 9:02 A.M. He was two minutes late. *Not like him to show up late for an appointment,* I thought, *especially one as important as this.* Ten minutes passed before a black speck appeared on the horizon, stirring a dust cloud behind it. As the car drew closer, I stepped out onto the crystal earth and walked a ways, my shoes scraping salty ground with each step.

The fancy car, a two-toned black and tan Pierce-Arrow, came to a halt about a hundred feet away. Dr. Pfalzgraf's security guard got out of the car, dressed in the same type of outfit once worn by Floyd Samuelson, and opened the back driver's side door. Pfalzgraf stepped onto the running board, wearing a burgundy homburg on his head, a navy blue suit, and a tie almost as white as his shirt, which was almost as white as the bleached earth below our feet. Sunlight bounced off his spectacles, making it difficult to see his beady eyes. His white mustache had the softness of a shaving brush, and it was long enough that you couldn't tell whether he was smiling or frowning. There was no missing the sadness imprinted on his face. It could be found in his sagging jowls, the bags under his eyes, and his perpetual frown. Here was a man who had lost so much and, unlike Miriam Tanner, had not been shielded from the bitter realities of betrayal. I had a hard time imagining the anguish he must've been feeling as he walked toward me, carrying a briefcase, and stopped a few feet away.

Before saying a single word, he unbuckled the briefcase and showed me the contents. Stacks of money, held together by paper bands. He'd said he'd give me the money—a hundred thousand dollars—in exchange for his films that C. W. Alexander stole from him. I stepped up and lifted a stack and flipped through twenties with my thumb. *Tempting offer.* I formed a catalog in my mind of all the things I could buy with that money: New house. New car. Start a college fund for the kids. Tickets for a South Seas cruise for the whole family . . .

I tossed the stack back into the briefcase and said no thanks. Those films were my security, I told him, and I'd return them to him when I felt safe again. I figured there were better ways, more honest ways, of making money than giving Dr. Pfalzgraf something that already belonged to him, and taking a hundred thousand in exchange for it. I assured him the films would be safe in my hands, that I'd never in a million years use them the way C. W. Alexander did. He believed me, buckled his briefcase closed, and climbed back into his car. For a long while, I watched Pfalzgraf's speeding car heading north toward the highway, sending clouds of dust blowing across the flats.

The July 24 fireworks ended around half past ten with an unforgettable grand finale that set off a multicolored fire in the skies above Salt Lake City and rattled windows and shook fence posts for miles. Once it was all over, people hurried to their cars and created traffic jams in all directions. The congestion reached a virtual standstill on nearby 700 East, with endless lines of headlamps and taillights going north and south. We stayed put as the park emptied, and Sarah Jane gave me a "July 24 present" in an oval-shaped white box, topped with a red bow. I removed the lid, tore aside the tissue paper, and lifted a brand-new white Stetson out of the box. It was a joyous moment, full of laughter and smiles, and even Roscoe was chuckling and telling me not to lose this one. I removed that loose-fitting police cap and tossed it in the backseat of the squad car. Wearing my new Stetson tipped far back, I wrapped an arm around my children and pulled them close to me and told them I loved them. Before we parted ways, I kissed Clara good night, and she whispered in my ear, "Be safe. I'll see you in the morning."

The night crept slowly. We spent our entire shift warning drunken revelers to calm down and issuing noise ordinance tickets. Right before dawn, we took a break from it all, and I drove up steep L Street to the top of the high hill on the northern end of the valley, parking on a dry, weed-choked plateau that real estate developers hadn't reached yet. From here, you could see the entire Salt Lake Valley, with tiny lights twinkling like stars. A warm wind from the west fanned grasses around me and dried sweat beads on my forehead. I closed my eyes and tried to imagine this place back before the temple and the tall buildings were built, before autos and streetcars filled asphalt streets, before people owned telephones and radios and washing machines. Back when there weren't any houses standing, and pioneers had to clear the land and build crude dwellings out of whatever they could find around here.

I wondered what those pioneers would think if they arrived at this place, in this day and age, with its electricity and modern con-veniences. Would they think we men and women of today had got-ten too soft? Or that we've lost our pioneer spirit? Would they feel sorrow when they saw what had become of *their* City of Saints, *their* Zion in the Desert? Salt Lake City had turned into just another modern metropolis, filled with as much crime and corruption as any other American city. What would those vanguard settlers of 1847 say if they found out about Helen Pfalzgraf and C. W. Alexander, Seymour Considine, Parley Tanner, and Floyd Samuelson? Would they forgive us for what we'd done to the haven they created, the place where they could escape mob violence and persecution in the Midwest?

"Let's get the fuck outta here," said Roscoe, dropping his cigarette butt on the ground and grinding it under his heel. "Not like we're getting any radio alerts."

Over breakfast at the Liberty Luncheonette on Third South, Roscoe lifted my spirits by joking about the unsavory characters we'd encountered in the middle of the night. Roscoe was that rare kind of friend who could cheer me up with a few well-timed quips. When I laughed, he laughed, and we kept feeding into each other, until we were both red-faced and barely able to finish what was left on our breakfast plates. In that booth in the back of the Liberty, I forgot all about the pioneers and the trials they faced in their times, and I turned my attention to the here and now, to the good things in life, the simple moments, when a laugh between friends made all the difference in the world.

At the end of my shift, I noticed the small parcel sitting in my locker, wrapped in brown paper, tied closed with twine. It had been in there for weeks, on the upper shelf, collecting dust. I pulled it out. It was addressed to "Mrs. Vera Higginbotham, 722 2nd Ave N., Twin Falls, Idaho." Helen Pfalzgraf's mother, that wispy phantom of a woman I saw when I visited Twin Falls. Despite our briefest of encounters, her face had been branded into my mind, and I knew I'd remember her until the day I die. *Maybe it's time to mail this,* I thought, as I read my own writing on the package.

I left the Public Safety Building about quarter past eight and walked two blocks south to the post office, parcel in hand. I entered a building with cathedral ceilings. My footsteps echoed against marble floors, and I was pleased to see there weren't any lines that early in the morning. I wound through the velvet-rope maze, approached the counter, and slipped my parcel underneath the wrought-iron bars. The postman put it on a scale and told me I owed twenty cents to send it first class.

I fished coins out of my pocket and dropped a pair of dimes in front of him. He slipped a receipt across the counter. I watched him take the package and walk it over to a bin at the end of a long table and drop it in.

It was out of my hands now.

The parcel contained the First National Pictures audition film that Helen Pfalzgraf appeared in before her death. It was accompanied by a slip of paper with my writing on it: *Your Helen.* That canister of footage was one of the few remnants to show that Helen Pfalzgraf had once lived and breathed and walked on this earth.

And dreamed.

Maybe Mrs. Higginbotham would be at home to receive the package when the postman delivered it in a few days. Maybe there'd come a time when she could figure out a way to smuggle the film out of the house while her brute of a husband was off at work or out like a light.

Maybe she could find a projectionist willing to show her the movie. Then she'd see what I saw: *Helen had talent.* The woman could act. She might've gone places, if only she'd been allowed to live.

Maybe, for a few short, bittersweet minutes, Mrs. Higginbotham would feel like she was being reunited with her daughter one last time, like being in a dream one never wants to end.

Maybe she would find some peace then.

Maybe.

A Note on the History
Behind the Novel

The explanatory note that follows contains spoilers about this novel and should only be read after you are finished with the book. That is why I have placed it at the end. *City of Saints* is a heavily fictionalized version of an actual unsolved homicide case in Utah, the murder of socialite Dorothy Dexter Moormeister on February 21, 1930. The Moormeister homicide was one of the most famous cases of the day and generated a mountain of publicity. For a good two years after it happened, newspapers across the country—especially the local press—reported extensively on developments in the investigation. Interestingly, the case is now largely forgotten, even in Utah.

I lived in Salt Lake City from the time I moved there with my family at age ten in 1978 until I took a position teaching history at the University of Waterloo in 1997 (I was also away for one year at graduate school in Wisconsin). During that period, and in all the times I went back to the state to visit my family, I had never once heard of this case. It had been consigned to an obscure spot in the annals of Utah history. I stumbled across it quite by accident a few years ago while going through some digitized old newspapers. I became obsessed with the case and continued to dig up everything I could find. In more recent years, a handful of articles on the Moormeister affair have appeared in local Utah publications— most notably, the *Salt Lake Tribune,* the *Deseret News,* and *Salt Lake* magazine—but these proved to be little more than fleeting footnotes to an otherwise forgotten case. This is puzzling, because the Moormeister story is packed with drama and twists.

Before writing *City of Saints,* I researched the Moormeister case and even considered writing a "true crime" history of the murder. Unfortunately, court documents and extensive press coverage are all that remains of the affair, and writing a solid history demands more than that. Any historian will tell you that a variety of sources are needed to reconstruct a vivid panorama of the past. These include memoirs, diaries, correspondence, personal papers, police files, and, ideally, oral histories. Regrettably, much of this type of information is unavailable. All of the participants in the case are dead, and they did not leave behind any useful accounts about it. So I opted for a fictionalized version of these events, with a satisfactory resolution to the murder at the end of the novel—a basic requirement of all mysteries.

If you have read *City of Saints,* you will notice right away that certain fragments of the real history have been preserved, such as the date of Helen Kent Pfalzgraf's murder, which falls on February 21, 1930—the same date Dorothy Dexter Moormeister was killed (her body was found the next day). Like Helen, Dorothy was murdered in a rural and largely isolated part of Salt Lake Valley called the Pole Line Road, now in Granger. Today, Granger has been absorbed into West Valley City, and those once uninhabited parts of the valley have now been filled up with suburbs, big-box stores, strip malls, restaurants, and convenience marts.

There are other similarities between the novel and actual events. Dr. Frank Moormeister, Dorothy's husband and the inspiration behind Dr. Hans Pfalzgraf, was a respected physician who inherited a substantial sum of money from a deceased German uncle and lived a double life as an abortionist. By all accounts, he was a safe and high-priced practitioner and sometimes traveled across the country to ply his trade. Dr. Moormeister was so dismayed by the inept official investigation of his wife's murder that he hired a high-priced sleuth, University of California professor and pioneering criminologist Dr. E. O. Heinrich, to come to Salt Lake City to find the murderer. Heinrich failed at the task, but he was still paid handsomely. The investigation of the Moormeister homicide, conducted largely by the Salt Lake County Sheriff's Office with some participation by the Salt Lake City Police Department, was heavily criticized at the time as a textbook bumbling effort. To make matters worse, the Moormeister murder came at the heels of a string of unsolved homicides in Salt Lake City, including the murder of twelve-year-old June Nelson (the inspiration for Hazel Hamilton) on either December 31, 1928, or January 1, 1929. These unsolved cases ultimately undermined Sheriff Clifford Patten, who was blasted over and over again in the press for his alleged mishandling of the investigation. Voters booted him out of office in the fall of 1930.

Like Helen in *City of Saints,* Dorothy was on the verge of leaving her relatively brief marriage, and had she lived, she most likely would have lit out for Los Angeles. She befriended actor Walter Pidgeon, frequently went back and forth between Salt Lake City and L.A., and had a circle of acquaintances in the City of Angels. At the time of her murder, the press hinted heavily that she was having an affair with Pidgeon. Dorothy appears to have been a serial adulteress, carrying on affairs with various men at once, including so-called "mining man" Charles Peter (the inspiration for C. W. Alexander) and Prince Farid XI of Persia, whom she met in Europe. Her relationship with Farid is shrouded in mystery. We know more about her involvement with Peter, who called himself a "mining engineer" but was actually a sketchy promoter of sorts. In the mid-1920s, he tried to con Dr. Moormeister out of a substantial sum of money, and, not surprisingly, he became a prime suspect in Dorothy's murder. He swore he had nothing to do with killing her, although it came out in the coroner's inquest that he and Dorothy were having a stormy affair. The sheriff's office eventually scratched Peter off the list of suspects, due to a lack of evidence.

In another parallel between the book and real life, Dr. Moormeister had a daughter, Peggy, by his previous marriage to a woman killed in an auto accident in 1917. Peggy, the inspiration for Anna in *City of Saints,* was quite close to Dorothy. The two were more like sisters than stepmother and stepdaughter, and Dorothy's death left Peggy devastated.

In an age that predated television, DVDs, and the Internet, the Moormeister affair (as it was then known) became a soap opera of sorts. New developments kept the investigation in the newspapers for a couple of years. There were several men who took credit for the murder, most of them mentally unstable convicts doing time in prisons for lesser crimes. These wannabes had too much time on their hands, overactive imaginations, and access to newspapers, crime magazines, and gossip rags. Committing a brutal murder such as this would enhance their credibility among their fellow inmates. Thus, the bogus confessions kept the headlines coming.

Adding another layer to the mystery was a series of break-ins at Dr. Moormeister's Salt Lake office, in which files and other odds and ends were stolen. These culminated with a bizarre event that happened on February 5, 1931. Someone telephoned Moormeister to set up a nighttime appointment. The doctor showed up at the agreed-upon time, only to have a harrowing encounter with a masked gunman, whom Moormeister managed to force out into the hallway. The assailant threatened to shoot the doctor, but Moormeister said he would summon the police. The gunman fled. Moormeister told the police he had no idea what the gunman wanted.

Another queer turn involved Frank Snyder, a thirty-eight-year-old Salt Lake City department store employee and widower who knew Dorothy Moormeister. Snyder, subject of an investigation by sheriff's deputies for his involvement in the case, took part in a night of heavy drinking with several friends at taverns and in his hotel room on the night of May 4, 1931, and into the wee hours of May 5. An unknown individual—or individuals—lured him to a secluded stretch of highway out near the airport and the Great Salt Lake and shot him to death. Eyewitnesses spoke of seeing Synder with a blond woman, and police found numerous empty liquor bottles in a hotel room where Snyder and some friends were partying. Sheriff's deputies remained vague about Snyder's involvement in the Moormeister slaying, although it came out in the press that he allegedly knew someone who had information about jewels stolen from Dorothy's body at the time of her murder. The Snyder killing, like the Moormeister homicide, was never solved.

Other unusual events transpired, too many to list here.

By 1932, the case had gone as cold as the snow where Dorothy's broken corpse was found. The Lindbergh kidnapping bumped it out of the newspapers. Salt Lakers moved on. The public forgot. Every now and then, an article would appear stating the obvious: We still don't know who killed Dorothy Dexter Moormeister. At the time Dr. Moormeister died of a heart attack at age sixty-two on January 13, 1941, police still listed his wife's murder as unsolved.

The nationwide media frenzy suddenly reignited in August 1964. Another confessor, William E. Sadler, a partially deaf sixty-one-year-old inmate in the Frio County jail in Pearsall, Texas, insisted he murdered Dorothy Moormeister thirty-four years earlier. The soft-spoken, white-haired Sadler provided the Frio County sheriff with a detailed account of his involvement in the Moormeister homicide. He said it was a "paid job," and he took a lie detector test that, according to Dewey Fillis, detective chief of the Salt Lake City Police Department, "indicates conclusively that Sadler was telling the truth." Authorities in Utah were astonished by the detail of Sadler's confession, right down to the precise position of the body at the murder site. "Where did he get that information if he was not there?" asked District Attorney Jay Banks. Sadler's tale proved so convincing that he was extradited to Utah to stand trial for the murder of Dorothy Dexter Moormeister.

Once his case went to court, however, he reversed his story and denied involvement in the murder. He said he confessed to the crime in order to escape the "intolerable and barbaric conditions" in the Frio County jail. In the end, a district court jury of twelve men took less than two hours to deliberate and found Sadler innocent of the murder. Sadler walked out of the courtroom vowing to remain in Salt Lake City "the rest of my days." He told reporters, "My name will never again be on a police blotter, not even for a traffic ticket." As soon as he left the courtroom, he disappeared for good.

Sadler's confession and subsequent trial turned out to be the Moormeister affair's last hurrah. By the time of his acquittal, most of the participants in the original investigation were either dead or gone or getting along in years. Like Los Angeles's gruesome 1947 Black Dahlia case, in which twenty-two-year-old Elizabeth Short was found mutilated and severed in two, the Moormeister murder was never solved. Yet Dorothy Moormeister would not assume the same mythic and legendary status as Elizabeth Short.

Finally, I would like to tip my Stetson to the authors whose books helped me re-create the Salt Lake City of 1930 and its inhabitants. These are *The Gathering Place: An Illustrated History of Salt Lake City* by my friend John McCormick; *Salt Lake City Then and*

Now by Kirk Huffaker; *Salt Lake City: 1890–1930 (Images of America)* by Gary Topping; *Wallace Stegner's Salt Lake City* by Robert C. Steensma; *Ogden (Images of America)* by my friend John Sillito; *Visions of Antelope Island and Great Salt Lake* by Marlin Stum; *The Big Rock Candy Mountain* and *Recapitulation* by Wallace Stegner; *This Is the Place: Utah* by Maurine Whipple; *Utah in the Twentieth Century* by Bryan Q. Cannon; *Mormonism in Transition: A History of the Latter-day Saints, 1890–1930,* by Thomas G. Alexander; and *Utah: A People's History,* by my mentor and friend, the late, great Dean L. May.